P9-BBU-547

What awaits us is miraculous.

Year's
Best
SF
14

Praise for previous volumes

"An impressive roster of authors."
Locus

"The finest modern science fiction writing."
Pittsburgh Tribune

Edited by David G. Hartwell

Edited by David G. Hartwell
& Kathryn Cramer

YEAR'S BEST SF 14

EDITED BY
DAVID G. HARTWELL
and KATHRYN CRAMER

An Imprint of HarperCollinsPublishers

This book is a collection of fiction. Names, characters, places, and incidents are products of the authors' imagination or are used fictitiously and are not to be construed as real. Any resemblance to actual events, locales, organizations, or persons, living or dead, is entirely coincidental.

Additional copyright information appears on pages 497–498.

EOS
An Imprint of HarperCollins*Publishers*
10 East 53rd Street
New York, New York 10022-5299

Copyright © 2009 by David G. Hartwell and Kathryn Cramer
Cover art by Bob Warner
ISBN 978-0-06-172174-8
www.eosbooks.com

First Eos paperback printing: June 2009

HarperCollins® and Eos® are registered trademarks of Harper-Collins Publishers.

Printed in the U.S.A.

10 9 8 7 6 5 4 3 2 1

This year we dedicate this volume to Gordon Van Gelder, a stubborn and heroic figure in contemporary SF, who not only kept *The Magazine of Fantasy & Science Fiction* going for another year by dint of enormous effort, but made it, in our opinion, the best of the venues for science fiction in 2008.

Acknowledgments

This year a number of anthologists were of particular help to us, including Jonathan Strahan, Ellen Datlow, Gardner R. Dozois, Lou Anders, Ian Whates, and Mike Allen. And together they led in making it a great year for short fiction.

Contents

Introduction

The year 2008 was the latest in a changing environment for SF. By the end of the year, one major publisher, formerly the largest in paperbacks, Bantam Books, had lost one of its SF editors and become merely an imprint of Ballantine Books, who shortly thereafter let one of their SF editors go; *The Magazine of Fantasy & Science Fiction* had announced a change to bi-monthly publication, and *Realms of Fantasy* announced it would cease publication with the April 2009 issue; *Analog* and *Asimov's* had reduced their page counts and changed format slightly; online magazine Helix had ceased publication and took its stories offline. And Tor.com had become the highest paying market for fiction for the present—technically Baen's Universe may pay a higher rate, but does so rarely. There were not a lot of ambitious new online SF ventures. And in the related genres, the venerable Datlow-Grant-Link *Year's Best Fantasy & Horror* ceased publication with the volume covering 2007.

There was an economic collapse worldwide that continues into 2009 as we write, and a major change in the political life of the United States surrounding the 2008 presidential election and the coming change in administration with the election of Barack Obama. For people under age forty, this is probably the worst economic environment of their lives. Those of us who are older than that know how much worse it was on occasion in the twentieth century, and that it could get in the next few years, and hope it will not.

Basically, SF book publishing is being forced into a contraction by rising costs without rising sales, and it is likely that fewer books will be published in the genre by trade publishers, at least for a while—especially fewer in mass market paperback, which has lost most of its distribution system to a few concentrated giants that scorn all but the best-selling prospects. There is a collapse in advertising expenditures, that affects the internet as seriously as it affects print media, and is driving some mainstream print media to the brink of bankruptcy.

We will be interested to see what creative solutions internet enterpreneurs come up with to generate income in the coming years. A lot of what has grown up in the last decade on the internet depends on the free time of employed people, or the free time generated by a person with a job in the household, and maybe even some of the household discretionary spending. Some of that free time and money has just evaporated, along with trillions of dollars from the national economies of the developed countries. So we look forward to creativity on a shoestring and more coffee all around.

All that said, it was a fine year for the SF short story, a fine year for quality in the fiction magazines, and an especially excellent year for original anthologies. We are still enjoying a short fiction boom in science fiction and the associated genres of the fantastic, and there were few signs of a halt in 2008. Not an economic boom—no one is getting paid much—but certainly an increase in numbers, and it has been building for several years, and perhaps even growing the audience for short fiction, it appears, though an audience that might more readily purchase an anthology than a magazine subscription. The highest concentrations of excellence were still in the professional publications regardless of their financial decline, the anthologies from the large and small presses, and the highest paying online markets, though the small press zines and little magazines were significant contributors as well. We had immense riches to choose from for this book. We wish it could be twice as long this year, particularly.

There was a notable bunch of really good anthologies of original fiction in the U.S. and UK. U.S. entries include *The Starry Rift, Eclipse 2, Fast Forward 2, Clockwork Phoenix*, and nearly a dozen primarily fantasy anthologies that contained some SF. Australia and Canada each produced high spots (Jack Dann's *Dreaming Again* and Claude Lalumière's *Tesseracts 12*). High points include Daryl Gregory's first novel, *Pandemonium*, and Paolo Bacigalupi's first collection, *Pump Six and Other Stories*, possibly the two most important first books in our field in 2008. We should probably single out Subterranean and PS as particularly distinguished small presses this year, with Night Shade and Small Beer of equal quality to them, though with fewer titles. The ambitious UK publication, *Postscripts*, announced its evolution from a magazine into an anthology series. Three cool original anthologies from the UK you might otherwise miss are *Celebrations, Myth-Understandings,* and *Subterfuge*, all edited by Ian Whates under the Newcon imprint, and all containing interesting selections of fantasy and SF. Among the magazines, *Fantasy & Science Fiction* had a particularly good year, *Interzone* got darker but had some real high spots, *Asimov's* and *Analog* got smaller (fewer pages per issue by the end of the year), and *Postscripts* bigger, morphing into an anthology series.

In the aether (online), Subterranean switched from print to electronic, Orson Scott Card's Intergalactic Medicine Show, Strange Horizons, and Jim Baen's Universe persisted, and Lone Star Fiction, Aeon, and Flurb continued and improved, in our opinion.

The stories that follow show, and the story notes point out, the strengths of the evolving genre in the year 2008 and the dominant recurring themes and ideas. We like to point out interesting comparisons. This book is full of science fiction—every story in this book is clearly that and not something else. We have a high regard for horror, fantasy, speculative fiction, and slipstream, and postmodern literature. We (Kathryn Cramer and David G. Hartwell) edit the *Year's Best Fantasy* as well, a companion volume to this one—look for it if you enjoy short fantasy fiction, too. But here, we choose science fiction. It is our opinion that it is a good thing to have genre boundaries. If we didn't, young writers would have to find something else, perhaps less interesting, to transgress or attack to draw attention to themselves.

We try in each volume of this series to represent the varieties of tones and voices and attitudes that keep the genre vigorous and responsive to the changing realities out of which it emerges, in science and daily life. It is supposed to be fun to read, a special kind of fun you cannot find elsewhere. This is a book about what's going on now in SF. So we repeat, for readers new to this series, our usual disclaimer: This selection of science fiction stories represents the best that was published in the genre during the year 2008. And we believe that representing the best from year to year, while it is not physically possible to encompass it all in one even very large book, implies presenting a substantial variety of excellence, and we left some worthy stories and talented writers out in order to include others in this limited space.

We make a lot of additional comments about the writers and the stories, and what's happening in SF, in the individual introductions accompanying the stories in this book. Welcome to the *Year's Best SF* in 2008. Read on.

David G. Hartwell & Kathryn Cramer
Pleasantville, NY

Arkfall

CAROLYN IVES GILMAN

Carolyn Ives Gilman lives in St. Louis, Missouri and is an internationally recognized historian specializing in North American history, particularly frontier and Native history. Her most recent nonfiction book, Lewis and Clark: Across the Divide, *published in 2003 by Smithsonian Books, was featured by the History Book Club and Book of the Month Club. She is a curator of the museum of the Missouri Historical Society and is currently writing a history of the American Revolution west of the Appalachians. She has published seventeen or more SF stories since 1986, and one novel,* Halfway Human (1998), *in the tradition of groundbreaking SF books that deal with gender. She can reasonably be considered as a writer to be among the descendents of Ursula K. Le Guin. Her most recent book,* Aliens of the Heart (2007), *is a collection of short fiction from Aqueduct Press, and her novella* Candle in a Bottle *also appeared from Aqueduct Press in 2006.*

"Arkfall" appeared in Fantasy & Science Fiction, *which published a particularly notable batch of science fiction in 2008. The ark Cormorin is a bio-ship, a partly biological sub-marine habitat for humans, in the dark seas of a very alien planet being colonized. The humans on it have a communal life, with a detailed and plausible culture upon which their survival depends. And when an undersea volcano erupts disastrously, the rules and habits come into question in their quest to survive.*

1. Golconda Station

Normally, the liquid sky over Golconda was oblivion black: no motion, no beacons to clock the passage of time. But at Arkfall the abyss kindled briefly with drifting lights. From a distance, they looked like a rain of photisms, those false lights that swim in darkened eyes. First a mere smudge of light, then a globe, and finally a pockmarked little world floating toward the seafloor station.

The arks were coming home.

From the luminous surface of the ark *Cormorin*, Osaji felt the opacity that had oppressed her for months lifting. All around her, arks floated like wayward thoughts piercing the deep unconsciousness of the sea. The sight was worth having put on the wetsuit and squeezed out to see. She was oblivious to the pressure of the deep water, having been born and bred to it. Even the chill, only a few degrees above freezing, seemed mild to her, warmed by the volcanic exhalations of the Cleft of Golconda on the seafloor below.

After months of drifting through the Saltese Sea, the ark-swarm had come for respite to the station of Golconda, the place where their rounds began and ended. Osaji's light-starved eyes, accustomed to seeing only the glowing surface of her own ark and any others that happened to be drifting nearby, savored the sense of space and scale that the glowing domes and refinery lights below her created. There was palpable distance here, an actual landscape.

It would have looked hellish enough to other eyes. A chain of seafloor vents snaked along the valley floor, glowing in places with reddish rock-heat. Downstream, black smokers belched out a filthy brew loaded with minerals from deep under the planet's gravity-tortured crust. Tall chimneys encased the older vents. Everywhere the seafloor was covered with thick, mucky vegetation feeding on the dissolved nutrients: fields of tubeworms, blind white crabs, brine shrimp, clams, eels, seagrass, tiny translucent fish. The carefully nurtured ecosystem had been transported from faraway Earth to this watery planet of Ben. To Osaji, the slimy brown jungle looked like the richest crop, the most fertile field, a welcoming abundance of life. Patient generations had created it.

Beside her, a pore in the lipid membrane of the ark released a jet of bubbles, making the vessel sink slowly toward the floodlit harbor where a dozen other arks already clustered, docked to flexible tube chutes that radiated from the domes like glowing starfish arms. It was time for Osaji to go inside, but still she lingered. All her problems lay inside *Cormorin*'s membrane, neatly packaged. Once she went inside, they would immerse her again.

A voice sputtered over her ear radio, "Will she be coming in soon?" It was the Bennite idiom: tentative, nonconfrontational. But no less coercive for that. Osaji sighed, making her breather mask balloon out, and answered, "She will be pleased to."

Pushing off, she dived downward past the equator of the ark's globe, gliding over its silvery surface. The top portion of the ark was filled with bladders of gas that controlled buoyancy and atmosphere, along with the tanks of bacteria and algae that processed seawater into usable components. Only at the bottom did the humans live, like little mitochondria in their massive host.

On the ark's underbelly Osaji found a pore, tickled its edges till it expanded, then thrust her arms and head in, pulling herself through the soft, clinging lips of the opening. Inside, she shook the water off her short black hair and removed her facemask and fins. She was in a soft-walled, gently glowing tube leading upward to the living quarters.

As she walked, her feet bounded back from the rubbery floor.

The quarters seemed brightly lit by the snaking vapor-tubes on the ceiling. As soon as Osaji entered the bustling corridor, Dori's two children crowded around her, asking questions. Their mother peered out the aperture of her room and called to them, "Is it polite to bother her when she has so much packing to do?" The comment was really aimed at Osaji. Dori's family had left her in no doubt that she and her baggage would be leaving the ark at Golconda.

Osaji ran her finger along the sensitive lip of the aperture into her own small rooms, and the membrane retracted to let her through. The first cavity inside, where Osaji had lived for the last round, was stripped bare, all her belongings packed into sacks and duffels. She paused at the aperture to the adjoining vacuole and called out, "Mota?"

"Saji?" came a thin voice from within. Osaji coaxed the membrane open and had to suppress a groan of dismay. Inside, a frail, white-haired woman sat amid a disorganized heap of belongings. She had not packed a thing since Osaji had left her. If anything, she had emptied out some of the duffels already packed.

The old woman's mild face lit up. "Thank goodness you're back! I was getting worried. Where did you go?"

"Outside. I told you I was going outside."

"Did you." She was not contradicting, just commenting. No argument or reproach ever came from Mota. She was the sweetest-tempered aged on the planet. It sometimes drove her granddaughter to distraction.

"Time is short now," Osaji said, seizing a sack and starting to shove clothes in it. "*Cormorin* docks at Golconda in a few minutes."

"I remember Golconda," Mota said reflectively.

"I know you do. You must have been there sixty times."

"Your mother, Manuko, got off there one round and tried going barnacle. She could never get used to it. But your sister—she actually married a barnacle." She said it as if Osaji had never heard the news.

"Yes, we're going to see her in a few minutes."

"Oh, good," Mota said. "That will be nice."

Osaji didn't say: And you are going to stay with her from now on, and set me free.

The gentle jostle of docking came before Osaji was ready. Dori poked her head in the aperture to say, "We've arrived. Everyone can leave now."

Seething inside, Osaji said pleasantly, "In a moment."

Cormorin had not been a happy ark this round. When joining, Osaji had mistaken Dori's conventional expressions of respect for real tolerance of the aged. Once under way, Dori had voiced one sweetly phrased complaint after another, and it had become obvious that she resented Mota's presence. The old lady should not walk the corridors alone, because she might fall. She shouldn't be allowed in the kitchen, because she might put on a burner and forget it. She shouldn't help with the cleaning, because her eyes were too poor to see dirt. Once, Dori had said to Osaji, "Caring for an aged is so much responsibility. I already have as much as I can bear." So she had taken no responsibility at all for Mota. Everything had landed on Osaji, making Dori hint with false sympathy that she wasn't pulling her weight around the ark. Mota had ended the round a virtual prisoner in her room, because just seeing her seemed to give Dori a fresh case of martyrdom.

The corridors of Golconda station were a shock to anyone fresh from floatabout. A floater's world was a yielding womb of liquid where there was never a raised voice, never a command given; floaters all went their lone ways, within the elaborate choreography of their shared mission. The barnacles' world was a gray, industrial place of hard floors, angles, crowds, and noise. Barnacles had to move in coordinated lockstep—cooperative obedience, they called it. They were packed in too close to survive any other way. The two ways of life were the yin and yang of Ben: each needed the other, but neither partook of the other's nature.

A line of porters stood by with electric carts in the hallway, so Osaji approached one, trying to conceal her diffidence. Codes of courtesy were abrupt here, because barnacles always thought time for interaction was short. The porter named an outrageous price. When she attempted to tell her story, he said the Authority set the amount, and there was nothing he could do about it. She gave in, feeling diminished.

Mota's baggage filled the cart, so Osaji gave the porter the address, saw the old lady safely seated beside him, and hefted her own bags to walk, more to avoid dealing with another driver than to save the money. Soon she was feeling jostled and invaded-upon. The corridor was half blocked off by some noisy construction, and the moving crowd was compressed into a narrow chute made dingy with too many passing feet and too much human exhalation. When she emerged into one of the domes, she looked for a spot out of traffic to gaze at the wonder of wide space. The brightly lit geodesic framework spanned a parklike area of greenery ringed with company shops and Authority offices. A grove of trees soared a breathtaking twenty feet over her head. They lifted her heart on their branches: she, too, had the potential to grow lofty. If only she could worm past this stricture in her life, she would be able to reach up again.

And yet, above the trees, the weight of a frigid planetary ocean pressed down. It was a Quixotic gesture of the builders, really, to have nurtured a form of life so unsuited to the environment. Perhaps the human genome was coded for this urge to put things where they didn't belong. Osaji knew floaters who spoke of the trees with hauteur, for they were symbols of inadaptibility. The floaters were the ones who had pioneered a truly Bennite way of life, not this transplanted impossibility of a habitat. Osaji caught her breath in wonder as a bright bird winged overhead.

The impulse to act on her long-laid plans grew strong in her. Why not now, before she saw her family, so it would be an accomplished fact? She knew the proper place to go, for she had sought it out last round, but without enough resolve. This time would be different.

The Immigration Authority was a neatly aligned place. The agents sat behind a row of plain desks, and the clients sat in three straight lines of chairs facing them, waiting for their numbers to be called. No one looked at anyone else. The agents' soft voices filled the room with a background of sibilant word-sounds that made no words.

When Osaji's turn came to face an agent, she dropped her bags in an untidy heap on the floor around her chair. She had barely sat down before she blurted out, "Your client wishes to leave the planet."

The agent was a young woman about Osaji's age, but much prettier, wearing a blue uniform with a crisp white collar. Calm and competent, she said, "Why would that be?"

Osaji had not come prepared to answer this question. She swam in a sea of reasons, drowning in them. She was afraid to open her mouth for fear she would choke on them. At last she chose one that seemed least dangerous. "To see new places."

"So it is a tourism desire?" the young woman asked politely. Her hands were folded on the desktop.

"No." Osaji realized that she had made it sound trivial and self-indulgent. "It is necessary for opportunity. To broaden one's self."

"Education, then?"

Knowing the next question would be which offworld academy had admitted her, Osaji said, "No. It is better to work one's way."

"Financial enrichment?"

"No!" That was antisocial selfishness. "A person needs to learn the ways of the great worlds, to experience different cultures. How else can a person's mind expand? Ben is small and stifling."

Though she had spoken the last words very softly, the agent caught them. Outwardly, the woman did not react, but her questions changed.

"Has the Great Work ceased to inspire?"

"No." Osaji shifted nervously. She still felt the Great Work of creating a habitable planet from this cratered ball of ice was a noble one, and she honored the dedication of the generations who had gotten this far. But it was slow, centuries-slow, and she would not live to see it done. If she did not leave, she would never even see what a habitable planet looked like. "It is just. . . . We *are* free to leave? They always say so."

The agent smiled, making her even more formidably pretty. "Of course. It is just that clients often think they wish to leave when what they really need is to solve some personal problem. It would be very selfish to ask us to spend the resources to send a person off-planet just because someone cannot face an obligation."

The shame Osaji felt then was like nausea, a sickness rising from her stomach. The woman had seen right through her. Osaji had tried to cloak her cowardice in brave fantasies to make it look less ugly. The truth was, leaving Ben meant abandoning her own grandmother, that sweet and helpless aged who had raised her and who now chained her with responsibility she didn't want. It was so low, Osaji sat staring at her hands folded in her lap, unable to raise her eyes. And yet, losing her hope of escape felt so painful she couldn't move from the chair, couldn't let some other more deserving person take her place.

The agent said gently, "Very few people who leave Ben like it on other worlds. We are not suited for that sort of life. Besides, it is nobler to face things here than to flee."

Osaji made no sound, but prickly tears began to brim over and drip on her clasped hands. She tried to think as a noble person ought to, about bravely facing her problems, but instead she felt a black resentment. Mota would live for many years yet. Her body did not make her old; her straying mind was the problem. The disease had come upon her early—so early that Osaji, the last grandchild, did not yet have a life of her own, and so became the family solution. The true tragedy was Mota's. But being her caretaker, there was nothing to aim for—no goal, only monotonous endurance until the end. And then what? All Osaji's chances would be gone by then.

At that lowest point, when her prison seemed impenetrable, she was distracted in the most irritating way, by a raised voice at the desk next to her. A wiry, weatherbeaten foreigner was berating his agent.

"Are you going to get your prigging rear in gear, or do I have to raise hell?"

The man's agent, a timid young woman who looked acutely embarrassed by the attention he was drawing, tried to calm him in a low tone.

"Don't you whisper at me, you simpering little bureaucrat," he said even louder. "You are going to give me a visa and a ticket on the first shuttle out of this clam steamer, or you are going to hear some real decibels."

"Please, sir," she pleaded. "Shouting at your agent will not solve your problem."

"You don't know what a problem is, sister. At this rate, you're going to know pretty soon."

Osaji's agent went to the rescue of her traumatized colleague. "What seems to be the issue?"

The unkempt offworlder turned on her. He was only half-shaved, and wore mercenary coveralls. "The *issue*, my dear, is this whole lickspittle planet—on which vertebrate life does not yet exist. The entire goddamned culture is based on passive aggression. Don't you all know this is a *frontier*? Where's your initiative, your self-reliance? Where are your new horizons? I've never seen such an insular, myopic, conformist, small-minded bunch of people in my life. This planet is a small town preserved in formaldehyde. Get me *out* of here!"

Osaji had often thought the same things about Ben, but hearing them expressed so coarsely made her bristle. The intensity of the emotions she had been feeling reversed polarity, turning outward at the hateful offworlder beside her. He had had chances she would never get, and what had he done with them?

A manager came out from one of the back offices and tried to draw the man into a private room to pacify him. The offworlder, perhaps sensing he would lose his audience, stood up to defend his ground. He was short and his spindly legs were a little bowed, but he had a ferocious demeanor.

"Do you know who you're talking to, son?" he said. "Ever hear of Scrappin' Jack Halliday, who captured Plamona Outpost in the War of the Wrist?" When no one around him showed the slightest recognition, he gave an oath. "Of course not. You bottom-dwellers don't care about anything unless it happens ten feet in front of your noses."

The manager tried to be conciliatory, but Osaji could see it would have no effect. Her anger had been burning like a slow fuse all last round, and now it reached the end. She stood up and shouted, "Did you come here just to make us listen to your profanity and your complaints? If you can't make it on Ben, that's too bad—but stop whining!"

Scrappin' Jack looked like he had been ambushed from the direction he least expected. Rattled, he stared at Osaji as if hearing phantom sniper fire, and all he said was, "What the—?"

A little appalled at what she had done, Osaji sat down again facing her agent. At last the manager was able to lead the intemperate offworlder away. The office slowly resumed its normal functioning.

"That's what they're all like on the other worlds," Osaji's agent said in a low voice. "An emigrant has to cope with that, day in and day out. Are you sure—?"

"No," Osaji said. "I think the lifestream put him there to show me something. I am not supposed to leave Ben."

The agent smiled encouragingly.

"I am grateful for your good work." Outwardly composed again, Osaji gathered up her bags and left, feeling wrung out but relieved.

2. Barnacles and Floaters

Osaji's sister Kitani lived with her family in a dome that was divided up into pie-shaped Domestic Units surrounding a central dining and recreation area. Kitti's DU was on the second floor, meaning it was smaller, though the family had been on the waiting list for an upgrade for two rounds. It was one of the compromises people made to live barnacle. Brother-in-law Juko answered the door with a red-faced, howling baby in his arms. He was a gangling man with a perpetual, slightly goofy smile—and it was just as well, for the hubbub he ushered her into would have induced hypertension in anyone less tuned out. The DU had only two rooms—a sleeproom and an everything-else room—and their older daughter was having a tantrum in the sleeproom. The main room was simply crammed with furniture, cookware, baby strollers, clothes, and diaper bins. Mota's baggage formed an obstacle in the middle of the floor. "Tell your Aunt Saji it is good to see her," Juko shouted to the baby in his arms. As an in-law, it wasn't polite for him to speak to Osaji directly.

Osaji dumped her bags on the floor—there was nowhere else to put them—and tried to give Juko a greeting just as the baby threw up all down his front. He smiled as if his face didn't know what else to do, and disappeared into the sleeproom.

Osaji's grandmother sat in an armchair, looking slightly dazed. Kitti came out of the sleeproom and gave Osaji a frazzled hug. Looking at the mound of baggage, she said, "Is it that you're changing arks?"

"Yes," Osaji said. "It wasn't a good fit, with *Cormorin*." Propriety forbade her to come any closer to speaking ill of others.

"That's too bad," Kitti said with a remote, distracted sympathy, as if it didn't concern her. Osaji wanted to pull her aside right then and make her plea, but it didn't seem like the right moment.

The right moment didn't come that evening, either—a crowded, chaotic succession of rearrangements, feedings, and infant outbursts. Not until the next morning did Osaji and Kitti get some time alone together, when they took the children to the playground in an adjoining dome. They sat on a bench and watched barnacle children frolic under the overhanging sea.

Kitti was first to bring up the subject. "Mota's really deteriorated," she said. The bald declaration—not tentative, not a question—showed how shocked she had been. It made Osaji uncomfortable.

"You think so?" she said, though it was exactly what she had wanted to talk about.

"Don't you? She's much more weak and unsteady on her feet. You ought to get her more exercise. You know, ageds can still build up muscle tone if they work at it."

"Ah," Osaji said.

"And her mind seems to be wandering. She repeats herself, and loses track of what people are saying. You need to stimulate her more, challenge her mentally, get her involved."

"Isn't it just that she is old?" Osaji said.

Kitti mistook it for a real question. "Age doesn't have to mean deterioration. There are plenty of ageds who are still intelligent and active."

"But Mota's not."

"No, she needs to be encouraged to improve herself."

Osaji felt an upwelling of desperation. "I've been wondering whether an ark is the best setting for her. Perhaps she would be better off elsewhere."

"Where?" Kitti said. "The domes for the aged are overcrowded, and you can't get anyone in without a medical permit. She's not that badly off."

"Still, it's really hard in an ark. There's no room for unproductives in an ark. And it's not just her; she makes me an unproductive too, because I have to look after her. It's two wasted berths, not just one." And two wasted lives.

Abruptly, Kitti changed the subject. "What about you? Have you met anyone?"

Osaji thought back on the slow torture of the last round: every day regimented by the need to look after Mota punctually. Not once had she broken free from that elastic band of obligation. Not for one moment had Mota been completely out of her mind. There had been no space left for anything else.

"You could register, you know," Kitti said. "The computers do a good job matching people."

Most Bennites found mates this way. In a place where everyone lived in isolated pockets scattered about the seafloor, it was the most practical way to meet someone compatible. Osaji had resisted it for years, out of a waning hope that she would meet someone the old, magical way, guided by the fateful currents of the lifestream. At the thought of her naivete, she felt a sharp ache of disappointment. "Who would take a mate with an aged attached?" she said, and the bitterness sounded in her voice.

Kitti finally heard it. "You can't let her ruin your life," she said.

Though Kitti had not meant to sound accusatory, Osaji felt it that way. She burst out, "Kitti, if you would only take her for a round. . . ."

"Me?" Kitti said in astonishment. "I have the young ones. You've seen our DU."

"I know." But the young ones, the DU—they were all Kitti's choices. Osaji had had no choices of her own. Kitti's had foreclosed all of hers.

The feeling of constriction returned. The thought of another round like the last was unendurable.

"I'm afraid," Osaji said in a low voice, "that I'm going to start to hate her."

Warmly, Kitti put an arm around Osaji's shoulder and hugged her tight. "Oh, you would never do that. You're a good and loving granddaughter. What you do for her is really admirable." She looked in Osaji's bleak face and said coaxingly, "Come on, smile. I know you love her, and that's what counts."

Kitti had gotten so used to dealing with children that she couldn't interact any other way. All problems seemed like childhood problems to her, all solutions reduced to lollipops and lullabies. Osaji stood abruptly, wanting to do something evil, wanting to do anything but what a good and loving granddaughter would do.

That evening, after dinner, she rose and said, "It is necessary to go on an errand." Luckily, Kitti and Juko were busy with the children, and no one offered to go with her.

The docks were still crowded with delivery carts, baggage handlers, and floaters coming and going. She walked down the harshly lit aisle, pausing at each tubular port where arkmates had posted their crew needs. She hurried past *Cormorin*'s port, noting resentfully that they were advertising two berths.

While she was reading a posting for a hydroponics technician, wondering if she could pass, a too-familiar voice made her whirl around and look. There he was—the outworlder, Scrappin' Jack, trying to impress a circle of young longshoremen. She could hardly believe the authorities had not gotten rid of him. As her eyes fell on him, he looked up and saw her. "Holy crap," he said, "it's the shrew."

Quickly she looked away to avoid any further contact, but he was not so easily discouraged. Pushing through the traffic, he came to her side. He was barely taller than she, a compressed packet of offensiveness. "Listen," he said, "about yesterday, in that office—you've got to understand, I was tripped out on cocaine."

As if that were an excuse. She scowled. "Why would an outworld mercenary come here?"

He gave a dry, rasping laugh. "Sister, you're not the first to ask. They asked me all through those godawful treatments for high-pressure adaptation. But rumor was, there were empty spaces here, unexplored territory, room to spread out. All true—it's just under tons of water, and the habitations are a bit too togetherly for me."

An idea occurred to her, brilliant in its spitefulness. "Has he considered going on floatabout? That is the way to explore Ben." To spend months trapped in a bubble drifting through opaque blackness, that was the real Ben. It would drive the man mad.

"You think so?" he said.

"Yes," she said encouragingly. "There is an ark looking for new crew. It's named *Cormorin*, just down the hall there. An applicant should ask for Dori."

He looked like he was actually considering it. "Why not?" he said. "It couldn't get worse. Thanks, kiddo."

As he was turning to go, the floor shifted slightly underfoot, and the hanging lamps swayed. He stumbled. "Whoa," he said, "I thought I was sober." Osaji didn't bother to tell him it had been a ground tremor, all too common here along the cleft. She turned to escape the other way.

Across the hall, at the mouth to the next port, a tall, lean woman with a patch over one eye was watching, cross-armed. As Osaji passed, she said, "Is someone looking for an opening?"

Osaji stopped. The woman's shaggy hair was gray-streaked, but she looked fit, with a composed, cool look of self-sufficience about her. The eye patch seemed like an affectation, a declaration of nonconformity, and Osaji suddenly decided she liked it.

"Lura of *Divernon*," the woman introduced herself.

"Osaji of . . . nowhere, right now."

"*Divernon* needs a hand to help out at odd jobs, particularly wet ones."

Osaji looked down. "Your applicant enjoys wet." She could not say she was good at it—that would seem unhumble—but she was. "Her profile is listed in the registry."

"I don't need to see her profile," Lura said. "I just saw her handle that offworld jerk."

Osaji looked up, astonished that anyone would commit to a crewmate without studying their compatibility profile. Lura's one eye was disconcertingly alert, but laughing. From her face, it looked like she often laughed.

"Does the young adventurer come with anyone else?" she asked.

Osaji blushed, feeling a pang, but said, "No."

"It would not matter if they were less than married." Lura had mistaken the cause of the blush.

"How many does *Divernon* hold?" Osaji asked, to change the subject.

"Myself, Mikita—and you. We were hoping to get a couple to join us, but we can't wait any longer. The Authority wants us to vacate this port tonight."

"Just three?" It was a skeleton crew. They would work hard, but enjoy a lot of privacy.

"*Divernon*'s last crew got married and left us," Lura said wryly. "Maybe a single will be safer."

That sounded like a happy ark, if a little lonely. But just now, lonely seemed good. "The ark leaves tonight?" she said.

"Can Osaji of nowhere be ready?"

"Yes. She needs to fetch her baggage."

"Fetch away," Lura said.

As Osaji hailed an electric cart, she could scarcely believe what she was doing. Joining an ark on impulse, without studying the others' profiles, without even meeting one of the two she would spend the next round with. It was an act of lunacy, or desperation.

When she got back to Kitti's DU, she had the cart driver wait out of sight while she went in, hoping to find the others preparing for bed so she could slip out unseen. Juko was in the sleeproom putting the children to bed, but Kitti was still in the front with Mota. She had opened up Mota's baggage and was sorting through it. One wastebasket was already overflowing with items she had decided to discard.

"What are you doing?" Osaji said.

"Getting rid of some of the useless junk she is hauling around," Kitti said with efficient cheerfulness. "Really, Saji, haven't you looked through these bags? Some of this stuff must be fifty years old." She held up a battered wooden flute, missing its reed. "What's this for?"

It was the flute Great-uncle Yamada had played on the day they married the two arks, *Steptoe* and *Elderon*, when Mota was young. Osaji had heard the story so many times she had often thought she would scream before hearing it again. She looked to Mota, expecting her to start the tale, but the old lady was withdrawn and silent.

"Do you play it?" Kitti asked pointedly. Mota shook her head. "Then what use is it? Why carry it around?"

"Do whatever you want with it," Mota said, looking away. "I don't mind."

Kitti stuffed it in the trash bin.

Osaji looked at the discards. There was the dirty plush toy their grandfather had given Mota when she first got pregnant, the rock Yamada had brought from the surface, the little shell pendant for luck. Osaji knew all the stories. "Kitti, these things are hers. You can't just throw them out."

"I'm asking her," Kitti said. "She agrees."

Osaji could see it now: Mota was going to become an improvement project for Kitti. And Mota would just acquiesce, as she always had done. She had spent so many years trying to please others, she didn't even remember what it was like to want something for herself. A tweak of compassion made Osaji say, "Can I talk to her, Kitti?"

Kitti climbed to her feet. "I've got to go check on the little ones."

Osaji sat down next to Mota. The old woman took her hand and squeezed it, but said nothing.

"Mota, I need to know something," Osaji said softly. "Do you want to come with me for another round on an ark, or would you rather stay here?"

Mota said nothing. Osaji waited, then said, "You have to decide. I'm leaving tonight."

"I want whatever you want," Mota said. "Whatever makes you happy."

Even though she had half known that would be the answer, Osaji still felt a familiar burn of frustration. Her grandmother's passivity was a kind of manipulation: a way to put all the responsibility onto others, an abdication of adulthood. Mota had always been like this, and there was absolutely no way to fight it. It made everyone around her into petty dictators. Osaji hated the role, and she hated Mota for forcing her into it.

It should have been a decision made in love, but instead it was grim duty in Osaji's heart when she said, "All right. You're coming with me."

She emptied out the wastebasket and stuffed all the things back into the bag they had come from, then hefted as many duffels as she could carry and took them down to the waiting cart. The baggage took three trips, and on the fourth she helped Mota to the door. It crossed her mind to leave without saying anything, but at the last moment she stuck her head in the sleeproom door. "Kitti, we're going now. Our ark is leaving."

"Now?" Kitti sounded startled, but not unhappy at the news. She got up to hug them both, wish them a happy round, and to press some food on them, which Osaji declined.

All the way to the docks Osaji rehearsed what to say to her new arkmates. But when they got to *Divernon*, there was no sign of Lura, or anyone else. She helped Mota through the flexible tube into the ark, calling out "Hello? *Divernons?*" There was no answer.

Finding the spare quarters was easy, so she left Mota inside and went back to ferry in the baggage. It occurred to her that it would be easy to hide Mota's presence till they had embarked, and then it would be too late for anyone to object.

She had just hooked the last bag over her shoulder and paid the driver when a shout from down the hall made her freeze. "Hey, shrike!"

It was Scrappin' Jack, coming down the hall like a torpedo locked on her coordinates. She would have ducked inside the ark, but feared he would just follow her.

From twenty feet away he bellowed, "What's the idea, sending me to that shrink-wrapped prig?"

Everyone in earshot was staring, and Osaji could feel her ears glow. "A man should be quiet," she pleaded.

"You thought you could pull a fast one on Scrappin' Jack, did you? Well, news flash: it takes more balls than you've got to screw me over." He waved a hand as if to clear away invisible gnats. "That didn't come out right."

"Go away!" Osaji commanded. Down the hall, Lura was approaching with another woman at her side. Keenly aware of first impressions, Osaji tried to pretend that the raging eruption in front of her did not exist. She waved at them cheerfully.

With a deafening crash, the floor jerked sideways, flinging everyone to the ground. Carts overturned, their contents scattered, and broken glass rained down. Again the floor bucked, sending Osaji skidding across tile into a wall with bruising force. For a moment there was silence, except for the groan of stressed girders and the ominous sound of falling water. A stream of it was running down the floor. Then a third jolt came. Osaji scrabbled for a handhold.

"Quick, into the ark!" said a voice, and Lura's strong hand was pulling her up. Osaji was lying across the entry, blocking the way into the ark. Not trusting her balance, she scrambled on hands and knees up the chute. When she got into the ark, it was bobbing around in the turbulent water like a balloon on a string. Barely able to keep upright, she turned to help Lura through—and found it was not Lura behind her after all. It was the spacer, Jack.

"What is the awful man doing here?" Osaji cried.

He looked as buffeted as she. "Some pirate dyke shoved me in the umbilical and told me to climb. I climbed."

"Where is she?"

At that moment the room turned sideways and they were thrown in a heap onto the yielding wall. The aperture connecting them to the mooring tube contracted and disappeared. That meant they had broken free of the tube; but still the ark wasn't rising. Instead of floating in the smooth motion of the sea, *Divernon* was jerking like a leashed animal.

"There's still a mooring line attached," Osaji said. She snatched up the breather and face mask that had been knocked from their pocket on the wall. "I'm going to find Lura. You, stay here."

There was no time to put on a suit, so she just stripped to her underwear, strapped on the mask, and thrust head-first through the lips of the orifice. Only a few bubbles of air escaped with her.

The first shock was the temperature of the water—bathtub warm. The second was the noise—a mere growl inside, here it was like the roar of a thousand engines. The water was nearly opaque, full of roiled-up sediment. The harbor lights were still on, turning everything into a golden brown fog. Feeling her way along the surface of the ark, she searched blindly for the line that was tying them down, for it would lead to the station.

It was taut when she found it; the ark was tugging on it like a creature mad to escape. By feel, she traced it down to a clip attached to a U-bolt on the dock. Now she realized what must have happened; the other two lines had broken, detaching the ark from the landing tube before Lura and her companion could get in. Now Osaji only had to find the tube in this blinding muck.

Before she could move, she felt the metal under her foot bowing out. The last U-bolt was giving way. She clutched the line tight as if she could pull the ark down, and keep it tethered.

There was a metallic pop and the bolt came loose. With Osaji still clinging to the line, the ark rose swiftly into the upwelling water. Instinctively she hung on as water raced past her ears.

They quickly cleared the turbid layer, and Osaji saw what lay below. The Cleft of Golconda was erupting. A raging glow of blood-red lava snaked along the seafloor, obscured by hellish clouds of steam. As she looked down on the station, another tremor passed through it, and a panel on the largest dome collapsed. In seconds, the adjacent panels were caving inward, the dome crumpling. A huge bubble of air escaped, and all the lights went out except the livid lava.

The ark was caught in a steam-propelled plume of hot water, flying upward. Darkness closed in. Osaji could no longer see the cleft below, nor the line above; the only light in the world was the dim bioluminescent globe of *Divernon*. Her hands were turning numb. She forced them to clamp down on the line. If she let go, she was lost.

Her ears began to pop. They were rising too fast; the pressure was dropping dangerously. She needed to get inside quickly. Setting her teeth, she tried to climb the line, hand over hand; but she was pulling against the rushing water, and didn't have the strength.

Then she felt a tug on the line, and her spirits revived. She kicked to draw closer. Pain shot through her legs. *Get me in!* she prayed.

· The skin of *Divernon* was stretched taut, she saw as she came closer to it. If the ark kept on rising, it would pop like an overfilled balloon, unless someone inside vented gas. Slowly, too slowly, the distance between her and the ark's skin lessened. At last she could reach up and grasp the edge of the hole where the line disappeared inside. But when it began to open to admit her, the pressurized gas inside came shooting out in a jet, sending the ark spinning and wrapping the line around it. Osaji's body thumped against the surface hard enough to knock the breath out of her. But it was just what she needed. She let go of the line and it snaked away

into darkness while she clung to the tacky surface of the ark.
It felt reassuringly familiar. Slowly, muscles cramping, she
crept along till she got to the orifice, and dived inside.

Someone was swearing. It sounded like, "Bull banging
damn!"

The ark was still spinning; Osaji was thrown forward on
top of Scrappin' Jack as the wall turned into the floor, then
into a wall again. As the rotation slowed, they came to rest a
few feet apart, staring at each other.

"What the gutting hell are you doing alive?" he said, holding up the empty end of the line. When she had let go, he must
have thought her lost.

"Such concern is touching," she said sourly. Ignoring the
shooting pains in her arms, she started barefoot up the rubbery organic tube toward the control pod. Jack followed
close on her heels.

The control pod of *Divernon* was more elaborately equipped
than any she had seen. Arrayed around a curving console, four
screens lit the darkened room in eerie colors. Things tumbled
about in the spin still littered the floor.

Osaji had been in control pods many times, but had never
navigated. Gingerly, she sat down in the swiveling seat, staring at the screens to figure out the ark's status. Jack peered
over her shoulder, muttering.

"Sonar, temperatures . . . what the hell is that?" he pointed
at a screen with an animated 3-D diagram.

Osaji was looking at that one, too. "Currents," she said,
then pointed to a tiny red point. "That is us."

It showed their true peril. All around them, angry pillars
of heated water rose, a forest of deadly plumes, dwarfing
them.

Osaji looked for the pressure ratio, and exclaimed, "May the
lifestream preserve us!" The pressure inside was enough to
burst the ark. "We've got to vent gas, now, or we'll explode."

But her hand hung motionless over the control, for the
choice of where to vent was critical. The jet of released air
would propel them in the opposite direction, and if they
floated into one of those hot plumes, that would be the end.
She searched desperately for a safe choice. There was none.

"What are you waiting for?" Jack said.

"I can't decide. . . ."

"Just do it! Do you want to die?"

Still she hesitated, searching for a solution.

With an oath, Jack reached over her shoulder and slammed his palm down on the control himself.

"You evil, reckless man!" Osaji cried out. "You have killed us."

"You're the one who'll kill us, with your anal dithering," Jack yelled back.

The pressure dropped into a safer range, but just as Osaji had feared, they were slowly floating toward one of the hot upwellings.

Desperately she vented more air to stop their motion. But the plumes on the screen were shifting, converging, leaving *Divernon* no space. Again she vented as a plume seemed to reach out toward them. But it only sent them into the arms of another.

She sat back resignedly. "It is our fate."

"What is?" Jack demanded. He had no idea what was going on.

She didn't answer. She could feel *Divernon* shudder, then rock, as the swift current took it. They were rising again, like a bubble in boiling water, little bumps and shifts betraying their speed. Osaji wanted to look away, but couldn't take her eyes from the screen. Even as she watched, the heat was probably killing the bioengineered outer surface of the craft, the membrane on which their lives depended. It did not matter; they would die anyway, in the terrible heights where no human or habitation was meant to be.

3. Through the Gap

The sonar screen was showing something strange. To their west was a solid return, something gigantic. Osaji increased the range, and felt a flutter of terror in her belly. It was a wall, a sheer cliff towering over them. There was only one thing it could be: the underwater mountain range that rimmed the ancient basin where life had taken such a precarious hold. Improbably, it seemed to curve outward over them like a mouth about to bite down. Osaji stared at the screen for several seconds before she realized what it showed. "Save us!" she exclaimed.

"What?" Jack asked.

"It is showing the bottom of the ice."

All her life it had been a rumor—the unseen cap on the sky, the lightless place where the world turned solid and all life stopped. She could feel it now, hanging above her, miles thick, heavy enough to crush them. She swallowed to quell a claustrophobic flutter in her chest. "The light shuns what is not meant to be looked on," she quoted a saying of the paracletes. Legend said that the underside of the ice was studded with the frozen corpses of people who had died without proper burial, and had floated up.

"I don't understand your problem," Jack said. He pointed to the screen. "The upwellings aren't as bad along the mountain range. Can't you just steer over there?"

Osaji closed her eyes and shook her head at his ignorance. "Our visitor thinks like a spacer," she said.

"So?"

"Arks are not ships. We have no propulsion system."

Jack looked thunderstruck. "You mean you can't control this thing?"

"We can rise and fall. In an emergency, we can vent air from the sides. But we go where the currents take us."

"What if there's no current that happens to be going where you want?"

"Now the visitor understands our problem."

As they rose toward the cap on the world, the screen showing the currents above them changed. Where the upwellings hit the bottom of the ice, there was a region of turbulent eddies and horizontal flows.

Jack was fidgeting nervously. "What happens when we hit that?"

"We will go where the lifestream takes us."

"If the lifestream means to feed me to the crabs, I'm swimming against the current."

"On Ben, feeding crabs is a noble calling," Osaji answered. One was supposed to feel serene about it. "It is all part of the Great Work of seeding the ocean with life."

"No offense to Ben," said Jack darkly, "but a body donation wasn't in my plans."

How little anyone's plans counted now! Osaji stood up, saying, "I have to go check on something."

"You're leaving?" he said incredulously. "Now?"

"I need to see if my grandmother is all right."

"You've got an old lady in the ship?"

"Yes. She is not in good health. It would be good for someone to watch the screens while I am gone."

She sprinted down the springy corridor to the quarters where she had left Mota. The room was tumbled and chaotic from the ark's gymnastics. Mota was sitting on the bed, unharmed but confused and disoriented. "Saji, where am I?" she asked.

"Don't worry, Mota," Osaji said. She was about to explain the situation—the eruption, the heat plumes, their danger—when she saw that what Mota really wanted was much simpler. "We're in an ark called *Divernon*. This is your room. Don't unpack yet. I'll come back as soon as I can."

"This is my room?" Mota said, looking around fearfully.

"Yes. Think about how you want to fix it up."

"What ark are we in?"

With a shrinking feeling Osaji repeated, *"Divernon."*

"Aren't we going to Golconda?"

"We just came from Golconda. It—" The last sight of the station flashed vividly before her, cutting off her voice. She didn't want to say what she feared; she didn't even want to think it. Kitti and Juko, the trees, the playground where they had talked—all dark, all cold, all drowned. . . . She forced it out of her mind. If she thought about it, it might come true.

"Your sister lives there," Mota said. "I don't know how people can live that way, so crowded."

"Well, you don't have to worry about it," Osaji said. She caught Mota's hand and pressed it between hers, longing for the days when she was the child and Mota the one who took care of things. "Mota, I love you," she said. "I wish I could keep you safe."

She left wondering which would have been the more terrible error: dragging Mota along, or leaving her behind.

When she got back to the control pod, the displays had changed. While she had been gone, *Divernon* had hit the turbulent zone, and now a horizontal current was sweeping them swiftly westward, toward the rock wall. It looked like they were going to smash into it. Osaji stood next to the chair Jack was occupying, to indicate she wanted to sit down in it, but he was mesmerized by the screens and didn't notice her body language. She cleared her throat. "I might be able to keep us alive a little longer," she said.

"How?" he said.

Courtesy was wasted on him, so she said, "If you would allow me to sit. . . ."

At last he got the message and let her have the chair.

The cliff was approaching at an alarming rate. Osaji vented air on their forward side to brake their speed, but they still felt the jar when *Divernon* hit, even inside all the cushioning internal organs. Osaji winced for the poor tortured membrane.

They caromed off the cliff and back into the current, spinning like a top. Now the sonar showed cliffs on every side of them. It took Osaji several seconds to realize they had been swept into a narrow cleft in the rim rock. For several minutes she kept busy sending out strategic jets of air to keep them from crashing into the rocks again.

"Is it safe to be venting so much air?" Jack asked.

It was his spacer instincts talking again. Preoccupied, Osaji said, "Oxygen is a waste product of the membrane cells' metabolism. We are constantly having to get rid of it."

At last the turbulence eased and the cliffs drew back, but the current was still swift. Osaji glanced at the compass to see where they were headed. Then she looked again, for what it showed was impossible.

"That can't be," she said.

"What?"

"We're still going west. But the mountains are behind us."

Ahead, the sonar showed a rugged plain sloping downward. Every moment the current was carrying them farther into it. "We have been swept through a gap in the mountains," Osaji said. Her lips felt numb around the words.

"Is that bad?" Jack said.

"There is only one inhabited region on Ben. The Saltese Sea, behind us, beyond the mountains. We are going into the uninhabited waste."

There was a short silence as Jack absorbed this information. "What's in the uninhabited waste?" he said at last.

"Rocks, water, darkness. No life." No seafloor stations, no other arks, no human voices. For the next round, perhaps for every round after that, until their ark died.

"Send out a distress call," Jack said.

Osaji reached for the low-frequency radio, and spoke into it. "This is the ark *Divernon*. Can anybody hear me?" They waited. Only the hiss of an empty channel came back. Osaji spoke again. "This is *Divernon*. We have been swept through the mountains on the edge of the Saltese Sea. If you can hear us, please answer."

Only silence.

The empty hiss grew oppressive; Osaji switched it off.

"There's got to be something we can do," Jack said.

Trying to sound calm, Osaji said, "If the ark is not too badly damaged, it should recover. It is a self-sustaining system; it can live for many rounds."

"You're telling me this is it," he said. "I'm trapped till I die. In a goddamned underwater balloon along with an invalid and a harpy."

Osaji gave the grimmest smile in the world. "The outworlder is the lucky one," she said. "We are the ones trapped with him."

4. The Wasteland

Three days later, Jack was still rebelling against their situation. He was a bundle of restless energy. While Osaji unpacked and arranged her quarters comfortably for herself and Mota, he prowled the ark, reading the manuals, trying to find a solution. At first she ignored him; but soon the time came to talk about dividing up the essential tasks of keeping an ark running. Osaji drew up a task wheel and brought it into the kitchen to negotiate the division of labor. It was a familiar routine to her, usually done on the third day of round.

But the daunting list of jobs made not a dimple in his monomania. All he wanted to talk about was another of his endless schemes.

"It's not like you don't have engine fuel," Jack said. "You've got a bagful of waste hydrogen up there."

"The hydrogen's not waste," Osaji said. "It is for our fuel cells, to make electricity."

"Then why not rig an electric motor to some propellers?"

"Does someone here know how to make an engine and propellers?"

He gave off a flare of indignation. "I'm not a bleeding mechanic. But damn it, I'd *try*. It's better than rolling over and taking whatever the lifestream sends you."

"It is antisocial to make one's personal problems into everyone's problems," Osaji said.

"Thank you, Miss Priss," Jack said acidly. He paced up and down before the kitchen table, two steps one way, two steps back. He was constantly in motion like that. It was like having a trapped animal in your home. "What possessed you Bennites to invent a vehicle without any controls?"

"An ark isn't a way of getting someplace," Osaji explained. "It is a place in itself."

He looked ready to ignite, a small two-legged bag of hydrogen himself. "Thanks, but *I* want to steer the place I'm in. This 'wherever you go, there you are' crap is why you've spent two centuries in the Saltese Sea without ever once having poked your noses out to see the rest of Ben. Wasn't anyone curious? No, you're content in your little bubbles. You've got an entire culture of agoraphobes."

Irritated at his refusal to focus on the practical demands of their situation, Osaji set a pair of flippers and breather down on the table in front of him. "Here. Anyone who doesn't wish to be here can swim back."

"Go to hell."

Osaji had had enough of him. She took back the swim gear, and said, "All right, I am going out."

"Out? What do you mean?" He followed her into the corridor.

"Someone has to check the membrane. I should have done it before."

"Isn't that dangerous?"

"Yes." She stopped and turned to him. "It will be a shame if you are left without someone to abuse. Now let me go."

Above the living quarters, the enormous bladders for air, fuel, and ballast water were swollen, shadowy shapes in the dim glow of the outer membrane. Taking a handful of the tough, fibrous white roots that grew on the inside of the globe surface, Osaji hoisted herself up the outer wall. The roots were wet, and soon her hands and feet were glowing white, covered with luminescent bacteria. The smell was fresh and invigorating, for the air here was rich with oxygen. When she had been a child, it had been a favorite game to climb the globe wall and then throw herself down onto the pillowy bladders below. Then, she had not appreciated the consequences of accidentally puncturing one of the membranes.

She had come this way because, despite her bravado in front of Jack, she was afraid to go out. The main orifice to the outside was at the bottom of the ark, and normally she would have used it. But there were emergency entry pores scattered throughout, and one of them was close to the part of the membrane she most needed to inspect.

It was odd; she had never been afraid of the outside before. In fact, she had relished escaping from the close confines of the ark, and always volunteered for wet work. But back home in the Saltese Sea, she had known exactly what lay outside. All the landmarks were mapped, the waters familiar. Here, her rational mind knew from the sensors that nothing was different, but the animal-instinct part of her brain didn't care.

She squeezed out the aperture like a slippery melon seed, into the embrace of cold and silence. At first she clung with her back to the tacky surface of the ark, peering into the water. The dark had a different quality here. In the Saltese Sea, you always knew that light and life hovered just beyond the edge of sight. Here, the dark was absolute ruler. Their ark was a mote in an emptiness the size of continents.

She unhooked the battery-powered searchlight from her belt. For a moment before turning it on, she had to steel herself, not quite knowing what she feared. When at last she shone it out into the water, it revealed nothing. Or, rather, only one thing: the water was extraordinarily clear. No suspended sediments lit the beam, since this was lifeless water. She aimed it up next, out of irrational fear that ice would be hanging over them, but again the beam disappeared. At last she shone it down. Nothing was visible. A hundred meters below them lay the rugged seafloor terrain of pillow lavas and tumbled boulders, but the beam did not reach so far.

Relieved, she pushed away from the ark to scan its surface. It was easy to see where *Divernon* had collided with the cliff, since a patch had been scraped clean of the luminous bacteria that made the rest of the craft glow white. She swam in close to run her hand across the surface, smoothing new bacteria onto the injured spot so it would heal. Then she slowly skimmed the circumference of the sphere, checking for scorches and barren spots, till she came to rest on the top, looking out on her world.

In its way, *Divernon* was alive, like a giant cell: a lipid membrane full of organelles designed to feed on the dissolved salts and carbon dioxide of the sea, and process them into amino acids and hydrocarbons to release again. It was part of the metabolic chain that would slowly, over the centuries, turn Ben's sea into a living ocean. The ark was a giant fertilizer, a life-creator, an indispensable part of the Great Work. But out here there was no Great Work. Isolated from its fellows, *Divernon* was a lost soul.

Why *had* no ark ever ventured out here before? Now that her irritation had washed away, the thought flowed into her that Jack was right. For so many generations Bennites had been content to pursue their rounds, following the currents in an ever-renewing cycle. They had never pushed beyond the boundaries of the familiar, out into the places without names.

Suddenly, Osaji ached with homesickness for the familiar floatabout cycle. If they had left Golconda as usual, just now they would be coming to the Swirl, a spot where the great current eddied, bringing many arks together. It was always a festive time; people visited from ark to ark, exchanging gifts and sometimes moving to find more compatible crewmates. The arks were gaily decorated, full of music, and there was lighthearted romance and water dancing.

The cold began to seep into her joints, so she kicked off to view the ark from below. As she dove down along the flank of the great globe, the feeling of something looming in the blackness behind her grew, so when she reached bottom she abandoned her inspection and wormed into the aperture as quickly as she could.

She brought a bulb of warm soup for Mota's lunch. When she entered Mota's vacuole, she noticed the stuffy, rank smell of age. She increased the ventilation. The rhythmic expansion and contraction of the air vessels made it sound like the room was breathing.

"Lunch, Mota!" she said in a cheerful tone.

Mota had taken all the clothes from one of the wall pockets, and was busy refolding everything and putting it back. She had done it at least ten times before, and with every repetition the clothes got a little more disordered. She looked up from her work and said anxiously, "Saji, where *were* you? I waited and waited. I thought something had happened to you!"

"I've only been gone an hour," Osaji said, her spirits falling. These reproaches were all she had gotten recently. She knew it would not stop unless she spent every hour of the day in the room. "Come eat your soup." She set it down on the little table they used to take their meals.

Mota looked in agitation at the clothing strewn all over the bed. She picked up a sweater she had just folded, shook it out, then put it down again. "Everything is all out of order," she said.

It was not the clothes that were out of order; it was something inside of Mota's mind. The behavior was simultaneously so unlike her grandmother and so very like her that Osaji felt trapped between laughter, dread, and impatience. Mota had always had a passion for tidiness; cleaning up after other people had been half her life, a way of expressing the love she couldn't put in words. Now it seemed like the trait was betraying her.

"I'll help you after lunch," Osaji said, but suspected that doing the task rather than completing it was what Mota needed.

A little reluctantly, the old woman came to the table and sat sipping her soup from the bulb. Her features looked stiff, her lips a little apart, stained with soup. Osaji tried to talk about the ark, but it was hard to keep it up alone. She kept fishing for responses and receiving none.

Suddenly Mota roused and got up restlessly. She started wandering around the room, looking for something in the wall pockets, underneath the bedclothes, in the washvac. After watching a while Osaji said, "What are you looking for?"

Mota paused as if having to search her mind for an answer. "My hand cream," she said at last.

"It's in the washvac, where it always is."

"Yes, of course." Mota went in the washvac, saw where it was, but did not pick it up. She came back out and settled in her chair.

The feeling in Osaji's stomach was much like the homesickness she felt for the Saltese Sea. It was a gnawing feeling that things were wrong, a yearning for a normality that was never coming back. And beneath it all lay buried anger at Mota for letting this confused stranger take over her body. An unworthy feeling.

"Would you like to go for a walk?" Osaji asked.

"No thank you, sweetheart."

"Should I read to you?"

"If you want to," Mota said neutrally.

"I'm asking if *you* want me to." Osaji was unable to keep the desperate impatience from her voice. Mota fell silent. Feeling guilty, Osaji said, "Or would you like to take a nap?"

"Yes, that would be nice."

Mota had only agreed because it would be the least trouble. Nevertheless, Osaji seized upon it. She was feeling claustrophobic in this room, as if the smell was going to hang onto her forever. When she got up, Mota said anxiously, "Are you leaving?"

"Yes, I'm going to let you sleep." She came over and kissed the old woman's hair. Mota took her hand and said, "You're a good girl, Saji."

Controlling her inner rebellion, Osaji said, "Have a good rest, Mota."

When she was outside in the corridor, Osaji punched the wall with her fist, but it only yielded pliantly. "I am *not* a good girl," she said fiercely under her breath. How could Mota look at her—selfish and angry as she was—and say such a thing? It denied the reality of her resentment, and that diminished her. Her own grandmother, who ought to know her better than anyone in the world, saw not the individual Osaji but that generic thing, a "good girl." It made her feel like a mannikin, her personality negated.

They drifted steadily westward, across a rocky plain that seemed to have no end. There was no navigation to do. The automated systems kept the ark at a steady depth and scanned for underwater obstacles, but there were none. Osaji made sure the machines were recording *Divernon*'s speed and direction; after that there was no need to visit the control pod more than once a day, to make sure nothing had changed. Nothing ever did.

An ark was supposed to work like a symphony, each person playing an indispensable part in the harmonic whole. But Jack made that impossible. He was unpredictable: one day torpid and morose, the next roaming the ark in a restless rage, throwing off sparks. All Osaji's attempts to suggest a useful role for him met a kind of egotistical nihilism.

"What's the point?" he said. "It only puts off the inevitable. We're going to die out here."

"We're going to die no matter where we are," Osaji said.

"Spare me the philosophy. Come on: how long before we run out of food and fuel?"

Puzzled by the question, she said, "Never."

"We can't restock out here."

"We don't need to, except for luxuries. The ark is self-sustaining."

"That's impossible. You would have invented a perpetual motion machine if that were so."

"The ark is not a machine," she protested. "It is not a closed system at all; it's an open one, based on autopoiesis. It's in a state of dynamic equilibrium with the sea. It exchanges chemicals in a chain, a process, that builds up complex molecules from simple ones."

"That's not possible. Not without fuel. The laws of thermodynamics are against it."

"Life violates thermodynamics all the time."

"Until it dies."

Back to that again. "All right, the ark will eventually die," Osaji admitted. "But not until after we do. Unless we don't maintain it. We are part of the system."

Even that failed to rouse any sense of responsibility in him. There was no alternative: Osaji had to try to do it all herself. And so her days became a numbing rush from one task to the next, never pausing to rest, always dragging her aching body on.

One day, she went to the clinic to get some sleeping medicine for Mota and found the drug supply ransacked. At first she stood staring at the pilfered wall pockets, unable to believe what she saw. Then her outrage boiled over.

She found Jack in the exercise vac, where he often spent time uselessly lifting weights. He was working the bench press with an aggressive intensity when she came in. She stood over him till he put the weights on their rack and sat up. "If it isn't the Guppy Girl," he said.

"It is impossible not to notice that the drugs are missing," she said.

"Oh yeah?"

She waited for him to look guilty, or excuse himself. He did neither. "Such egotism is . . ." she searched for a truly damning word, "antisocial. How can a man put his own temporary pleasure over the legitimate needs of others? What if one of us gets injured, or ill? You have robbed us of lifesaving cures that—"

"Oh, put a cork in it," Jack said.

Osaji's indignation exceeded her eloquence then. "You are an animal!" she cried. "You have stolen from my grandmother!"

Slowly, he stood up. He had no shirt on, and though he was short and wiry, his muscles were hard like knotted ropes. She took a step backward, for the first time realizing that he could easily overpower her. Fear urged her to flee, but anger made her stand her ground. "You see that tube there?" She pointed to the corridor outside. "On this side of it is yours, on the other side is mine. Don't cross it. If I catch you on my side, I swear I'll do you harm."

She turned and fled then. Stopping in the kitchen, she found a sharp knife. Feeling a little safer, she went to Mota's vac and found the old lady dozing peacefully. Osaji settled down, knife in hand, guarding the aperture.

Never had she faced such a situation. There were always personality conflicts in arks, but the social pressure kept them hidden. But here, for the first time in her life, Osaji was not part of a larger community. She was an independent being who needed to protect herself and her grandmother as best she could. Fingering the knife hilt, she hated Jack for making her into that most contemptible of all things, an egotist.

She saw little of Jack in the time that followed. At first, she longed for him to overdose and drop dead, so she could push his body out into the sea and live the rest of her life in peace. But gradually, she began to realize that he had at least been a kind of twisted distraction.

Her days came to revolve around Mota's constant needs for feeding, cleaning, and protection, and her other duties suffered. Immersed in age and infirmity day after day, Osaji herself began to feel dead and shriveled. She slept more than ever before, and woke with aching joints. When she hobbled to the mirror in the morning, she half expected to see white hair.

There was no one day when Mota took a turn for the worse, just a long series of imperceptible declines. It was not so much her hearing and sight failing as her will to hear or see. With her other senses went something Osaji could only describe as her sense of pleasure. No food tasted appealing to Mota, no sensation brought comfort, no activity brought content. Osaji could work until she was exhausted trying to satisfy her, all in vain. Mota's capacity for enjoyment was gone.

Osaji's only refuge was in the hydroponic nursery. Looking after the plants was a chore she actually liked. It took very little effort, but she lavished time on it anyway, because in the nursery she could pretend she wasn't on *Divernon*, or even on Ben.

One day she came as usual to tend the plants. The protective gear was still in the sac by the orifice, meaning no one was inside. She put on the hat, gloves, and dark glasses to shield her from the full-spectrum light, and entered.

Even with the goggles on, she squinted against the brilliance inside. The nursery was a sausage-shaped vesicle with long trays of greenery lining each wall, and a tank down the middle. An adjoining sac held the deep, lightless pool where underwater species grew in a chemical broth that mimicked their natural sea-vent habitat.

She started down the row of greenery, pinching off dead leaves and spraying the plants with nutrient-water. As she parted one thicket of foliage, she noticed something peculiar. On the counter behind the screen of plants stood a row of glass jars full of cloudy liquid. They had not been there when she last tended the plants, she was sure. As she reached out to pick one up, a voice behind her grated, "Don't touch that."

Jolted, she whirled around. Jack was sitting on the floor behind her, hidden by a tank.

He raised his hands and said, "Lower your weapon. I surrender."

She realized she was holding the plant sprayer in front of her like a gun, as if to spritz him with water. Ridiculous as it was, she didn't lower it. "What do you want?" she demanded.

Stiffly, he got up. "I want a joint and a ticket out of here, for all the good it does me."

He wasn't wearing any protective gear. She said, "A man should be wearing glasses."

With a harried look he said, "Don't you ever let up?"

"But the radiation is dangerous in here!"

"Don't worry, this is the only room that doesn't seem dim as a dungeon to me."

He took a step forward. She pointed the sprayer at him, and he stopped. "Okay, okay," he said. "Look, we can't go on like this. We're the only two damned people in this ship. We've got to call a cease fire."

Suspicious of this new ploy, she said, "So someone can go on raiding our drugs?"

"I apologize for that." He didn't look apologetic, more like desperately irritated at himself. "The thing is—I'm going bugfuddled crazy. I haven't been clean and sober at the same time in about ten years. It doesn't improve me. That's why—" He nodded at the jars behind her plants.

"What are they?" she said.

"I'm making wine."

Osaji said, "You shouldn't keep them here."

Bitterly sarcastic, he said, "Sorry for polluting your sanctum."

"No, I mean, they won't ferment properly in the light. They should be somewhere dark and cool."

He paused. "I knew that." He came over and gathered the jars off the counter. It seemed like he was about to leave, but he stopped. Then, eyes fixed on something beyond her, he began to talk in a rush, as if he were bleeding words.

"During the war, I was on a ship called *Viper*. It was a godless piece of junk, really. We used to joke about it, called it the *Vindow Viper*. One day they sent us in to take over a communication station owned by an asteroid-mining company. Only it turned out to be a secret military installation. They blew our piece-of-shit cruiser to bits before we had time to wet our pants. Eleven of us managed to escape in space suits, with only a marker buoy to hang to. We waited there for rescue. You know what it's like in space? It's dark, and your body has no weight. There's nothing to smell, or see, or feel. If you kick, nothing happens. It's just yourself all alone, thinking till your brain echoes like the whole universe.

"We had a big argument while we were waiting for rescue. Some of them thought the oxygen would last longer if we linked our tanks together. I was against it, me and two others. The rest decided to do it, and eventually persuaded everyone but me. It was four days before a ship picked us up. Their oxygen ran out at three and a half. If I'd helped them, I would have died too. I used to think I was the smart one, the lucky one."

Osaji was so taken aback she forgot to point the sprayer at him.

"Look," he said, "I came to this godforsaken planet to shed my self like an old dirty T-shirt into the laundry. I was hunting for a clean break. I wanted to be a new person, but the old person sticks to me like a bad smell. My past is something I stepped in long ago and can't get off my shoe."

This only made Osaji's own self-pity well up to match his. "You are not the only one trapped here unwillingly. Do you think I do all this work for pleasure? Do you think I want to maintain this ark and wash and dress and feed someone as if I were some kind of appliance? No one would choose this. It is degrading."

Finally he seemed to focus on her. "Then for God's sake, give me something to do! If I have to sit around thinking any more, I'm going to start chewing my leg off."

Suspicious at this change, she said, "What can a spacer do?"

"I don't know. Teach me, while I still have a few brain cells left alive."

It came to her then: the job she most wanted rid of. "I can teach the spacer to go outside."

To her surprise, he blanched. "No, you don't want me out there. I'd just be a drag on you."

"Our breathers are easier to use than yours. You don't have to carry oxygen; the breather extracts it from the water. And it's not like space. When you kick, something happens."

"Listen," he said, "I've got to tell you something. Truth is, I was a complete screwup as a spacer. You see, I couldn't turn off my mind. I couldn't stop thinking of consequences, and caring about them. I couldn't stop seeing the danger, and the stupidity, and the venality, and the faces. . . ."

He had wandered off again, into some haunted territory of his mind. To pull him back, she said, "There are no faces in the sea. No venality either."

With a hoarse laugh he said, "Well, that leaves danger and stupidity."

"Only if you bring them."

"Shit! Shit! Shit!" he said.

5. *Through Shadow Valley*

The aperture to the outside was located in the floor at the very bottom of the globe. The trick to getting through it was, once suited up, to take a little leap and plunge in feet first, as if jumping into a pool. Osaji had never thought of it as a skill till she watched Jack trying to follow her out. He got stuck halfway, struggling ineptly and letting air escape in big bubbles that rolled up the ark's side. Trying not to laugh, Osaji grasped one flailing ankle and gave a sharp tug, ignoring the curses emanating from her radio earpiece.

He was awkward and jerky in the water, and she had to make him swim to and fro a while to get the hang of the flippers. Then she took him on a tour of the ark's exterior, showing him the emergency entry pores and the scars of their encounter with the heat plumes and the mountain.

With Jack beside her, the darkness no longer seemed so

oppressive. It gave her the courage to do something she had not contemplated in a long time: gather water samples. They had to be taken at some distance, to avoid contamination from the cloud of organic molecules the ark gave off.

As soon as they left the sheltering bulge of the ark, they were enveloped in a dark so inky that all direction disappeared. Osaji stripped the covers from the phosphor patches on her suit so Jack could see where she was. She turned back to show him how to do the same, but he had already figured it out.

Though they swam slowly, the ark soon dwindled to a dim ball behind. It was icy cold. Jack switched on the searchlamp, but the beam just disappeared into water in every direction. They seemed suspended in nothingness.

Jack muttered, "A dark illimitable ocean without bound, where length, breadth, time and place are lost."

"What does that mean?" Osaji asked.

"It's poetry, kid. Damn spooky, that's what it means."

Osaji took the sampling bottle from the pack at her belt and held it out at arm's length as she swam, releasing the cap. As she was covering it again, something touched her face.

She gave a startled exclamation, and was suddenly blinded by the light as Jack turned it on her. "What is it?" he said.

"Turn that off!"

He did, but light still danced before her dazzled eyes. For a terrifying moment, she couldn't even tell up from down. She blinked until the dim glow of Jack's phosphor patches swam into view. "Can you see the ark?" she said.

"Right there," he said, presumably pointing with an invisible arm.

She saw it then as well, dimly, farther off than it should be. But as she started for it, Jack said, "Hey, where are you going?"

The photism she had been following vanished, and as she turned, the real *Divernon* swam into view. If he had not been there to stop her, she might have wandered off, chasing a mirage.

"Let's go back," she said, rattled.

They raced back as fast as they could swim. When they were inside again, he said, "What the hell happened out there?"

"This swimmer thought she felt a heat tendril."

"What's that?"

"A current of warmer water. No one else felt it?"

"Warm! You've got to be kidding."

"It must have been an illusion, then."

Still, she went to check the ark's temperature records. They were disappointingly flat. She had to tamp down the tiny updraft of hope that it had been a hint of geothermal activity. Another rift zone would mean a site for colonization—an energy source for life.

She couldn't entirely suppress the thought. The currents here were robust. They had to be driven by something. Just the possibility was like an infusion of energy. She felt buoyant and excited as she went to check on Mota, like the little girl she had once been, running to tell her grandmother of some discovery.

Mota roused from an open-eyed doze and smiled sweetly when Osaji told her what had just happened. "That's nice, dear," she said. Stiffly, she rose from her chair, and Osaji saw that the back of her dress was soaked.

"Mota, you've wet yourself," she said, shocked.

"No, I haven't," Mota said, turning so Osaji couldn't see it.

"Here, I'll help you change." Osaji tried to make her voice neutral.

"No, no," Mota said, "don't worry. I can do it myself." She stood looking around uncertainly, as if she had never seen the room before. Silently, Osaji went to the wall pocket and found some dry clothes. She felt irrationally humiliated by this new infirmity. It was so unlike Mota.

Mota took a long time changing clothes in the washvac. Osaji sat at the table, all at once too enervated to move. Her bubble of high spirits was leaking air, and she was sinking into stagnant water again.

The trip outside revived Jack's fund of hare-brained schemes. "What if we were to rig a really big antenna?" he said.

"Maybe we could generate a low-frequency signal that could penetrate all this water and ice."

Osaji was skeptical that any length of antenna would help them, but it did no harm to try. So she helped him string floats on a braided carbon-steel mooring line and paid it out into the water. Before long *Divernon* was trailing a long tail of wire.

It did not improve their communications. The radio still hissed white noise. But the antenna did succeed in an unexpected way.

As the current carried them inexorably westward, the seafloor landscape became more rugged. The sonar showed the hunched shoulders of hills below them, concealed by inky water. Then one day the bottom dropped out of the world.

On a routine check of the control pod, Osaji was startled to see no sonar reading at all. Going back to check the record, she found that the soundings had stopped only two hours before. When a diagnostic turned up no problem with the equipment, she came to the only plausible conclusion: they had been swept over the edge of an underwater chasm. The ark was caught in a gentle eddy, and as it floated backward her conjecture was confirmed, for the sonar picked up the edge of fluted organ-pipe cliffs dropping away into darkness so deep the signal could not reach the bottom.

By then, she and Jack were both watching the screen, mesmerized. "What should we do?" Osaji asked. It was the first navigation decision they had had to make.

"What are the options?" Jack said.

"We could go down, or stay at our present depth. If we stay, we'll probably pick up the westward current again. If we drop down. . . ."

"Yes?" he prompted when she failed to continue.

"Well, there is no telling. There might be no current down there. Then we would just come up again. There might be a current that would sweep us some place we don't want to be."

"As opposed to now?" Jack said ironically.

"That is a point."

Often, decisions like this took hours, because everyone

was afraid to be first to voice an opinion, and they talked until a consensus emerged without anyone having to say it aloud. But Jack suffered no inhibitions about expressing himself. "I say go for it. Take the plunge," he said. "What good are we doing out here if we don't take time to see the sights?"

She smiled at him, because she agreed.

He stared at her open-mouthed till she said, "Is something wrong?"

"I don't think I've ever seen you smile before," he said.

That made her feel self-conscious, so she turned to the controls and input the sequence of commands that would take them downward.

As soon as they dropped below the edge of the cliff, they lost their current. They were close enough to the cliff that the side-sounding sonar could show an image of the stately columns of basalt plunging into unknowable depths below. Osaji pushed back her chair and rose.

"Where are you going?" Jack said.

"It will take a long time to sink," she said. "We have to adjust to the pressure as we go down. It could be hours."

He couldn't tear himself from the screens, so she left him there, watching.

In the end, it took three days. As they descended, the water temperature slowly rose one degree, and Osaji's hopes rose with it. When the sonar finally picked up the bottom, they both sat watching the screen intently while the detail improved scan by scan. What it showed was only another tumbled slope of boulders leading down to a rumpled seafloor. "Look at the edges of the rocks," Osaji said, pointing at the screen. "They are sharp, not eroded. That means this area could be geologically active."

But they saw nothing else in any way remarkable.

They did pick up a new current, sweeping them slowly north along the line of the cliffs. The next day, the side sonar picked up another trace opposite them—the other side of the canyon, closing in fast. As the gorge became narrower, the current sped up, and Osaji began to fear that the gap would become too narrow for them to pass.

"What should we do?" she said.

"Ride it out, I guess," Jack said, his eyes glued to the monitors. "Like whitewater ballooning. Yee-ha."

Soon the giant cliffs were marching by, close on either side. For a moment the sonars showed nothing but rock in every direction—they were being swept around a curve. A gap appeared ahead. They were heading toward it.

Then all motion seemed to stop. The cliffs were behind them. They had entered onto the floor of a dark, hidden valley.

At first it seemed that they had just exchanged one lightless wasteland for another. Day by day they traveled northwest, their rocky surroundings unchanged. But there was a difference: as if they had passed a wall severing them forever from home.

Even Mota seemed to be drifting into another world Osaji could not enter, or imagine. As her memory failed, the old woman lost her ability to detect a sequence of events, to tell the *before* from the *after*; and with sequence gone, time itself disappeared. At first her own confusion frightened her, and she asked constantly what time it was, as if to force her experiences into order. But as she grew accustomed to it, she learned to exist in a bath of time where all the past was present simultaneously. She began to confuse Osaji with long-dead people from her childhood. Whenever it happened, Osaji corrected her more sharply than she should have; but she couldn't help it. The reaction came from deep down, like the reflex to breathe, or defend her life—except it was her individuality she was defending. As Mota's failing senses saw her less and less distinctly, Osaji felt like she was disappearing, turning invisible as water.

She was in Mota's vac when a shudder and a jerk went through the ark. "Did you feel that?" she said.

"What, dear?"

Osaji was very attuned to *Divernon*'s motions by now, and knew something was amiss. There was a faint rushing sound that seemed to come from everywhere at once. She sprinted up to the control pod, arriving only moments before Jack did. "*You* felt it," she said, forgetting to be polite.

"Damn straight I did."

Osaji's biggest fear, that they had collided with something, turned out not to be true. *Divernon* had come to a sudden halt in mid-stream. The sound she heard was water flowing past the membrane.

"The antenna!" Jack said.

Osaji had forgotten all about it. She saw now what he meant: one or more of the floats must have come loose and allowed the line to sink. They had been dragging a line along the seafloor, and now it was caught on something.

"We should have brought it in long ago," Osaji said, reproaching herself for irresponsibility. "Now we will lose a good mooring cable. We will have to cut it away."

"Well, maybe we can salvage part of it," Jack said.

"Do you think someone would be willing to go out there to cut it?"

"Not by myself," Jack said. "I'd go with you."

They planned it out carefully this time, since there would be more risk than their last job had entailed. The combination of tether and current had brought *Divernon* down closer to the bottom than it ought to be, and as soon as it was freed it would float up. They needed to be sure not to lose it.

The water was noticeably warmer to Osaji. It was, of course, just as black. Lit by their headlamps, the mooring cable stretched taut, a straight line leading diagonally downward, punctuated by floats every few yards. They set out, swimming along it. The farther they went before cutting it, the more of it they would be able to salvage.

The ark disappeared into the darkness behind them. Osaji noticed that she could now see the narrow beam of light from her headlamp; there was something dissolved in the water. For some reason, she did not want to get close to the bottom. The thought of monstrous rock shapes below her, hidden since the beginning of eternity, filled her with dread. She was about to suggest that they had come far enough and should cut the cable when Jack said, "What's that?"

"What?" she said, drawing in her feet out of fear that they would touch something.

"Turn on the searchlight," he said.

When she did, she gasped.

They were surrounded by glass towers. Not solid glass, but intricate meshworks of spun filaments that glinted silver and azure in the beam of Osaji's light. As the searchlight touched the nearest ones, they seemed to ignite in a cascade, as if conducting the light from one glass strand to the next, till the entire landscape around them glowed. Latticework turrets towered over them, gazebos and arcades of glistering mesh lay below. In the distance, some were broken and toppled, but the ones nearby looked perfectly preserved. It was like a city of hoarfrost, magnified to the size of monuments.

As her light played over the intricate structures, Osaji could not help the impression that it was a sort of architecture, created by design. But what strange intelligence would have built a monument down here, in a lightless gulf where no one would ever see it?

Even Jack at her side, after an initial exhalation of astonishment, was awed into silence. He slowly swam forward, and Osaji followed, drawn to touch, to be *in* the tracery sculpture, to see it from every angle.

They glided through arches that dwarfed them, down a tube woven of glowing geometric webs, and looked up from inside an open spiral that towered into the black water sky. They swam along lacework corridors, into honeycomb spheres of overlapping glass threads. Nowhere was there any sign of life. Not a thing moved but themselves.

In a glowing, cathedral-like space they found three hexagonal glass pillars, of uneven heights, whose surfaces were inscribed with patterns like worm tracks. Jack swam around the cluster of stelae, then said what Osaji was thinking: "Do you suppose it's writing?"

"I don't know. We ought to record it."

All thought of cutting the mooring line was gone now. It had been a stroke of the most astonishing luck that it had caught just here. They swam back toward it, chilled and eager to fetch some recording devices.

When they emerged into the womb of the ark and stripped off their diving gear, the awe that had held them in silence broke, and Jack let out a whoop of exhilaration. "Holy crap, that was the most amazing thing I've ever seen. Who do you think they were?"

He was leaping to the assumption that Osaji had tried cautiously to suppress. "It did not look natural," she admitted. "But it might have been a coral or something similar."

"Great big humping underwater spiders," Jack speculated. "But spiders that could read and write. Where's the camera?"

Osaji was rubbing her feet, which were the color and temperature of oysters. "We ought to warm up before going back. If one of us could heat some soup, the other will find the camera."

They were about to split up when the ark gave a shudder and moved. The cable was slipping. "No!" Jack shouted at it. "Don't give way!"

It was too late. There was a jerk, then suddenly the ark was rising, floating free again.

Jack let out a stream of profanity more heartfelt than any Osaji had heard from him. "Can't we drop an anchor?" he said. Osaji leaped to draw in the line, but long before they managed to attach an anchor to it, they both knew their chance was gone. The ark had floated on, and they were left with nothing but their memory of what they had seen.

That evening Osaji came down from the control pod, where she had been studying the sonar readings to see if they had recorded evidence of the glass city, to find Jack and Mota together in the kitchen.

"Mota!" she exclaimed. "What are you doing here?"

"Hello, dear," Mota said brightly. "Do you remember Yamada?"

Osaji felt embarrassed that Jack had seen Mota so confused, and was about to usher her back to her vac when he stopped her. "We've been having an interesting conversation. How come you've been hiding away this charming lady?"

Mota giggled like a girl.

Osaji stared at Jack, suspicious that he was mocking both Mota and her.

"She's been telling me about one round when a man named Sabo transferred from her ark to another one," Jack said, then turned to Mota. "So what happened next?"

She looked confused. "Oh, nothing in particular."

It was like most of Mota's stories these days; they trailed off into pointlessness. Osaji stirred restlessly, wanting to get Mota away.

"I see," Jack said. "Well, more power to Sabo. I say that's how a man ought to act."

Mota beamed at him fondly. He leaned over and whispered to Osaji, "Who the hell is Yamada?"

"Her brother. My great-uncle," Osaji said.

"Bit of a scapegrace, I take it?"

Osaji nodded. "He was her favorite sibling."

"I'm honored to be him," he said, and rose to fetch a bottle from a cupboard. "In view of the occasion, I think we ought to have some wine."

"It's too soon," Osaji warned him. "It will taste awful."

"Then it should suit me nicely," he said, and broke the seal. She watched him pour some into a glass. He smelled it and winced, then took a mouthful and downed it. He grimaced, then glared at the glass resentfully.

"It is vile, true?" Osaji said.

"On the contrary," he said. "It's a belligerent little vintage with a sarcastic attitude. I like it very much." He took another swig.

Osaji took down a glass and held it out. Jack poured her a glassful, and she took a sip. It was vinegary and revolting.

"Care for some?" Jack asked Mota.

"Oh, don't give it to her," Osaji said.

"She wants some. An adventurous spirit, I see," he said, and poured her a tiny amount. She sipped, and made a sour face. Jack laughed. "You're never going to trust me again now, are you?"

"You're always playing jokes on me," Mota said with mock severity.

"Come on, Mota, this man is a bad influence," Osaji said, rising.

"Bring her back soon. I'll turn her into a lush yet."

"Not with that wine," Osaji said.

When she had gotten Mota safely back to her vac, Osaji returned to the kitchen. Jack was studying the sonar print-outs she had brought down from the control pod. They showed next to nothing. The glass structures had been too fragile and airy to give a clear return.

"I'd think I had imagined the whole thing, if you hadn't seen it too," Jack said.

"Even if we ever get back, no one will believe us."

They continued drinking the wine in silence.

Osaji felt as if a vast weight of sadness were hanging above her, pressing inward, making it hard to breathe. "Jack," she said, "we ought to make an effort to remember. Think of those people, or whatever they were, who built the city. They created all that, and now they are forgotten, so forgotten it's as if they never existed. And now we don't even have any proof we saw the city they made. We owe it to them to re-member, to make them real. It's the least we can do."

He gave a slight, bitter smile. "As if we mattered our-selves."

She saw what he meant. They were next to forgotten as well. The farther they traveled from home, the less they would be remembered. No doubt they were already given up for lost; soon they would drift farther and farther into the night, until all trace of their existence disappeared. Nothing would remain in the end.

"If everyone has forgotten us, do you suppose we'll still exist?" Osaji said.

He stirred restlessly. "You don't have enough to forget. Try living a life like mine. You'll know then, memory's a disease."

He was silent a while, and she thought he was going to say no more, but he went on, "If those city builders thought they'd be remembered, they were crazy. Forgetting is what nature does best. The universe is a huge forgetting machine. It erases information no matter how hard we try to hang onto it. How could it be any different? What if the memory of everything that ever happened still existed? The universe would be clogged with information, so packed with it we couldn't move. We'd be paralyzed, because every moment we ever lived would still be with us. It would be hell."

Osaji thought of Mota, in whom memory was the most evanescent thing of all. Already Osaji existed only fleetingly for Mota, and Jack was not even a separate person, only the shadow of the long-dead Yamada. And soon Mota, then all of them, would arrive at the ultimate forgetting toward which they were traveling. They were all swimming temporarily in a sea of darkness, and then they would be gone.

The sadness pressed in, crushing her. Her eyes were tightly closed, but seawater was leaking from them anyway. It was for the lost city, for poor *Divernon*, for Mota, and for herself, the most futile of them all.

Jack reached across the table and took her hand. "Don't listen to me, kid. I don't think I'm going to forget you. Not a chance."

She clutched his hand as if he were the only thing that made her real.

6. Garden of the Deep

It was impossible for Osaji to keep Mota and Jack apart in the weeks that followed. Whenever Osaji's back was turned, Mota would creep out looking for him, and when she found him he teased her, told her inappropriate jokes, and fed her the sweet treats that were the only food she really craved. She would sit in the kitchen playing hostess to him, so polite that only Osaji could tell it was play-acting, like a little girl pretending to be an adult. Gradually, Osaji learned to stop resenting it.

As they traveled, she reduced the ark's cruising depth and pored over the sensor readings in hopes of finding another underwater city. Though they now kept an anchor ready to drop on a moment's notice, she saw no hint of anything but barren rock and rumpled lava on the seafloor.

Then one day the water temperature shot up. When she discovered it, Osaji consulted the sonar, but the images were fuzzy and hard to interpret. She went to find Jack. "I think a man should check to see what's outside," she said.

"Why a man?" he said, to be irritating.

"Because someone else needs to be inside ready to throw the anchor out."

They both went down to the hatch pod. Only seconds after he disappeared through the aperture, her radio earpiece started emitting ear-blistering vulgarities.

"What is it?" she asked.

There was no answer for several seconds. Then, "There's *light* out here."

The thought that there might be erupting lava made her hopeful. Then the more likely explanation occurred to her. "You mean the ark?"

"Well, yes, it's glowing like gangbusters. But I meant the trees."

"Trees?"

"There's a prigging forest out here!"

"Should one drop the anchor?"

"Yes! Then get your ass out here. No offense."

When she emerged from the ark, the sight struck her dumb. The ark hovered over an undulating landscape of dimly glowing lifeforms that covered the seafloor thickly in every direction, till they disappeared on the dark horizon. When she trained the searchlamp on them, the greenish phosphor glow disappeared and the biotic canopy proved to be made up of pinkish fronds gently undulating in the current, attached to tall stalks that looked in every way like tree trunks, except that they were larger than any tree she had seen.

Osaji and Jack swam down till they were hovering over the fronds, and could see their scale. The central rib of each branch was twenty to thirty feet long, and the splayed-out fern covered an area as wide as *Divernon*'s diameter. Jack reached out to touch the nearest one, and with a violent jerk the whole thing retracted into its tube, leaving behind a cloud of disturbed water. Several adjacent brushtops retracted as well.

"They are tubeworms!" Osaji said in astonishment. But tubeworms of a size she had never dreamed of.

"What do they eat?" Jack said, still rattled by the violent reaction he had stimulated.

"Not us. They are filter feeders. But it would be easy to get pulled down into the tube and crushed."

"You're telling me."

They swam down into the space thus cleared. Below the palmlike tops, the tubes were ribbed and hard, and so wide around that Osaji and Jack could not span them with their arms, even by linking hands. The trunks were crusted with orange and yellow growths that looked for all the world like fungus—except when touched, they moved.

Osaji felt something brush her face, but could see nothing. "Turn off your light a moment," she said. When Jack complied, they found themselves in a wholly different world. The water under the tubeworm canopy was alive with glowing filaments that outlined segmented bodies, hourglass-shaped bags, lacy things like floating doilies, others like paintbrushes or fringed croissants. It was as if the trees were strung with optic fiber ornaments, or fireflies in formation. When Osaji switched her light on again, they all disappeared. "Jellies!" she said. "The light goes right through them."

Lower down, there was a dense undergrowth that showed a riot of colors in their lights. There were frilly orchidlike things, huge bushes of feathers, clusters of translucent orange bottles, in one place a fan lazily waving to and fro, stirring the still water. "Look, your spiders!" Osaji called out, training her light on a china-white creature with six spindly legs, picking its way over a thing that looked like a brain.

When they turned around at last, Jack swam ahead, with Osaji lighting the way. She barely saw the thing that came arrowing out of the darkness at him. It hit him in the chest and drove him backward through the water so fast that Osaji lost him for a moment. With panic pounding in her ears, she swept her light around and saw him, seemingly impaled on a tubeworm trunk with a thrashing, snakelike body attached to his chest. She churned through the water toward him, and with no weapon but her light, she gave the creature a blow. It did not let go or cease whipping its paddle-shaped tail. Jack now had ahold of it and was trying to pull it away, a maneuver that would almost surely tear his suit. She grasped the paddletail near the front and squeezed with all her strength. It took what seemed like minutes, but the creature finally went limp and let go. She shone her light on it. It had no head, just a giant sucker where a mouth should be. With an exclamation of revulsion, she threw it away and it floated downward into the blackness.

"Is your suit all right?" she said, inspecting the place where the paddletail had attached. To make sure, she took some repair goo from her utility belt and smeared it on.

"Never mind the suit. What about *me*?" Jack said irritably.

"Are you all right?"

"Some wear and tear, thanks for asking."

"Let's get back."

They could see the ark through the branches above, like a bright full moon. Its bioluminescent bacteria were thriving in this nutrient-rich water. When they were inside, she inspected the bruise on Jack's chest but determined that no ribs were broken. "We need to be more careful," she said.

"You have a way with understatement," he answered.

They spent three days documenting the new world they had discovered before floating on. At first they stayed outside a great deal as they floated, anxious not to miss anything; then Jack figured out how to rig a camera on the outside of the ark so they could watch from the comfort of the control pod. Osaji marveled that she had never thought of such a thing—but then, in the Saltese Sea there was nothing to see outside and no light to see it by anyway. Everything there was focused inward.

The underwater woodland of tubeworms slowly gave way to a wide plain of sea grass. They sat atop the ark and watched the glowing prairie undulate in the currents, while their light beams picked out raylike creatures circling in the updrafts above. One day there was a shower of mineral particles. Pebble-sized bits pattered around them like raindrops, and soon a mist of smaller ash descended. It was what was fertilizing this oasis of life.

Eventually the land began to rise and they saw the first of the smoker chimneys belching out thick clouds of steam and dissolved minerals from deep within the planet's crust. Here, a spiny red growth dominated the ecosystem, like a branched bottle brush the size of a tower. In the sediment below the spine trees grew blooming fields of small tubeworms like chrysanthemums and daisies, and enigmatic things shaped like mesh stockings. They saw many more of the whiplike paddletails, always swimming upstream in the direction opposite to the one the ark was floating. Occasionally, some of the brainless things would attach to the downstream side of the ark, their tails still paddling frantically as if to push the ark against the current. Then Osaji and Jack would have to go outside and weed the ark.

What they never saw, though they looked all the time, was any evidence of the species that had built the glass city.

"I don't get this," Jack said. "We find a city with no life, and life with no city."

Osaji wanted to be outside all the time now. The ark's interior seemed drab and claustrophobic, and she rushed through her duties there to get into the water again.

They were moored on the edge of a mazy badlands of extinct smokers, their sides streaked like candles with brightly colored deposits of copper, sulphur, and iron, when the accident happened. Osaji was preparing to go outside when she bustled into Mota's vac and found the old lady lying on the floor, conscious but unable to speak. Panicky, Osaji knelt beside her. "Mota, what happened?"

Mota only looked up with round, watery eyes. Her mouth worked; nothing came out but a thin line of saliva. It filled Osaji with horror to see her grandmother so robbed of humanity. She jumped up and raced out to find Jack.

When they tried to move Mota to the bed, she groaned in pain, her eyes wild and staring. "She's probably broken something," Jack said.

"What can we do?" Osaji said.

"Not a lot," Jack said grimly. "Make her comfortable. Wait here, I'll be right back."

He disappeared. Osaji sat on the floor holding Mota's hand. Mota gripped back, hanging on as if a strong current were sweeping her from the world. "We'll try to do something for you, Mota," Osaji said. "Just relax, don't worry."

Jack came back with a little sack of pills. "Here, see if she can swallow this," he said.

"What is it?" Osaji frowned at the pill he handed her.

"Codeine," he said.

So he hadn't consumed all of them. She glanced at him, but he had turned away.

She managed to get Mota to swallow the pill and wash it down from a cup with a straw. Almost at once, far quicker than the drug could have taken effect, Mota closed her eyes and relaxed. They waited till they were sure she was asleep, then moved her onto the bed.

When they had done all they could, Jack said, "You want me to leave or stay?"

At first Osaji was unsure of what she wanted. Then at last she said, "Stay."

So began a long ordeal of waiting. From time to time Mota would rouse and reach out for one of them; it didn't seem to matter which one. As Osaji sat looking at Mota's face, she was forced to think: I longed to be free of her, yet now I don't want her to die.

More than anyone Osaji knew, Mota had forsaken her own wants in order to live for others. Selflessness. It was a virtue; everyone said so. And yet, it was as if her individuality had slowly withered away from neglect over the years. She had spent a lifetime making herself transparent, till she had no substance of her own, and all you saw was the substance of others seen through her.

As Osaji studied Mota's face, it seemed impossible that those mild and vacant features had ever known obsession, rage, or remorse. Had Mota ever believed deeply in something, or taken risks? She had never spoken of herself—never even known herself, perhaps. Now she never would.

"She doesn't deserve this," Osaji said softly.

After a few seconds, Jack said, "No one does. But we all get it, in the end."

"I mean, to die out here, so far from everyone else. She lived for other people. Without them, there's nothing left of her."

There was a long silence. At last Jack said, "Just to warn you, this takes a long time. It's messy and hard. People fight it. Even her."

He was right. She struggled painfully against the ebbing of her life. Osaji and Jack took turns sitting with her and giving her medicine when she roused. They were soon worn out, but still she hung on. At the very end she looked up at Osaji, and seemed to recognize her. "Why is it so dark?" she said.

"Don't worry about it, Mota. We're right here with you."

Her hand contracted around Osaji's, and she said, "I wish. . . ."

Osaji never found out what she wished.

Osaji dressed Mota's body in her favorite clothes and they wrapped her in one of the weighted nets used for burial in the Saltese Sea. At home, they would have laid her among barren rocks to nourish the microorganisms, so she could become mother to all the life that followed. Here, they laid her in a spot that was already like a garden: a cushiony bed of tubeworm flowers. Then they raised the anchor and floated on.

It was the next day before the grief came. Osaji had gone to Mota's vac to clean up, and found in one of the wall pockets a sweater that Mota had worn till it was the shape of her. When Osaji held it up, it seemed so empty, and yet still full of her. She hugged it tight, and it gave off the smell of love.

All at once, Osaji missed Mota so intensely her throat squeezed tight around her breath, and around her heart, and tears pried their way out between her eyelids. She knew then she had lost the only person who would ever love her just for being herself. It was the only *inadvertent* love she would ever know—love as deep as the genes that knit them together. There would never be anyone else who simply *had* to love her.

They had come to a place where, far away through the water, they could see the flickering light of eruptions from a line of undersea volcanoes. They went outside to sit on top of the ark and watch.

"Do you believe in an afterlife?" Osaji said.

Jack paused, as if considering whether to lie. At last he said, "No."

"So when we die, that's the end?"

"We can only hope." After a few seconds he added, "Sorry. I ought to give you comforting platitudes, I suppose."

"No. I hope death is the end, too. Because if Mota knew we'd left her so far from everything familiar, she'd feel lost and scared forever."

A paddletail shot past them, swimming upstream. "Where do you suppose they're going?" Osaji said.

"Nowhere. They're just crazy. Always swimming against the current, as if—" Suddenly, he stopped.

"What?" she said.

"I've got an idea."

It was as crazy as all his other ideas. But at least it didn't require technology they didn't have, or skills they couldn't acquire. It wasn't a spacer idea, it was a Bennish idea.

They set about gathering paddletails. They used sheets of plastic scavenged from inside the ark—vat covers, tarpaulins, anything that could be spared. They spread them wide to catch the creatures speeding past. Once affixed to a surface, the paddletails held on tenaciously, still whipping their tails against the current. As their numbers increased, Osaji and Jack repositioned some to the upstream side of the ark, where they strained against the lines holding them as if they were in harness. Others went to the downstream side to push against the ark like so many flailing motors.

The moment when *Divernon* started moving slowly against the current, Osaji and Jack slapped each other's hands in triumph, then swam to catch up with the ark.

For many days they experimented and refined the rigging before they were satisfied with the way their herd of snakes was deployed. It looked absurd, as if their washing were spread out in a tattered array all around the ark. But it pulled them slowly, inexorably, backward the way they had come.

They still couldn't steer, of course. The paddletails would go only one direction, upstream. But if they kept going long enough, they would take *Divernon* home.

Back they went, over the seagrass plains, past the tubeworm jungle. Every day Osaji went to the control pod to search for the best current—strong enough to keep the paddletails going, weak enough not to overpower them. Every day she and Jack went outside to catch more, fearful their present herd would die. In a few weeks they began to discover eggs embedded in the rough outer membrane of the ark, the spawn of their captives. Uncertain of the paddletail life cycle, they gathered some to raise in one of their tanks and left the rest to hatch outside, in hopes that the creatures' instincts would bring them back to spawn in the place where they were born.

They must have passed the glass city, but they did not see it and could not stop to search. They rose up over the edge of the rift valley and into the primeval waste with some misgiving. The current was much gentler here, so they made better headway; but the paddletails did not thrive. Carefully they nursed along their second generation, experimenting to see what they ate. One day, having tried everything else, Jack poured some of his home-brewed rotgut into their tank, and they went into a frenzy trying to drink it.

"Kindred souls!" he whooped. "They need to be plastered to stay alive!"

After that, Osaji and Jack devoted as much biomass as they could spare to the production of alcohol. Across the dark plain, *Divernon* became like a floating distillery. "At least *something* around here is lit," Jack observed.

Despite their best efforts, their creatures were much depleted by the time the sonar began to show the outline of mountains ahead. Remembering the strength of the current that had swept them through the gap, Osaji worried that their paddletail propulsion system wouldn't have the power to get them through. She and Jack were both in the control pod when they made the first attempt. The paddletails pulled them unerringly toward the pass where the current flowed strongest; but as the water velocity increased, the ark slowed. Barely a hundred yards from the gap, they came to a complete stop. The paddletails, pushing as hard as they could, could not draw them through.

"We've got to drop down out of the current," Osaji said. "They can't do it. We're going to wear them out."

"Wait," Jack said, looking at the screen. "What's that above us?"

"The ice," Osaji said, dread in her heart. Here, at the mountain pass, it was perilously close.

"Go up," he said.

She shook her head. "We could get trapped." People had warned of it all her life.

"It's our only choice," he said.

So, quelling her fear, she input the command that would dump ballast water from the tank and send them slowly upward.

As they rose, she watched the image of the ice's underside grow clearer on the screen. It was not smooth, but carved into channels, with knifelike ridges projecting down like the keels of enormous, frozen boats. The water temperature was falling. The cold made the paddletails sluggish; soon they would cease to pull. "This isn't going to work," Osaji said softly.

"Hang on," Jack said.

They were almost close enough to touch the ice when they felt the stirring of a countercurrent flowing east. The paddletails, paralyzed with cold, did not respond. *Divernon* started floating toward the mountains again, this time swept on the breath of the sea.

Ahead, the sonar showed that the ice and the mountain peaks converged. "Get into one of those channels in the ice," Jack suggested.

"But what if—"

"Just try it, for chrissake! What have we got to lose?"

They entered a deep cleft with ice walls on either side. As

the mountains rose to block their way, a floor formed beneath them, cutting them off from below. Now, there was no longer an option of dropping back down. They were in a tunnel of ice and rock. Ahead, the walls closed in. They felt a gentle jostle, then heard the sound of water rushing past the membrane.

Divernon had come to a stop in the stream. The passage was too narrow, and they were stuck.

They sat motionless for a few moments. Then Jack said, "Sorry."

"No!" Osaji said. "We can't give up now. I'm going to vent air. Maybe it will push us past this narrow spot."

The first jet of air had no effect. "Keep going," Jack said. "Less air, smaller balloon. Maybe it'll shrink us down to size."

They had vented an alarming amount when *Divernon* stirred, slipped, and then floated on down the tunnel. Two hundred yards beyond, the floor fell out from beneath them again. Eager to escape the entrapping ice, Osaji commanded the ark to begin a descent. A valley opened up before them, and the navigational station that had gone dead months before suddenly came to life. "It's recognized where we are!" Osaji cried out. "We're back in the Saltese Sea!"

The map on the screen showed that they had returned over the mountain range barely twenty miles from the place where they had left it, close to the Cleft of Golconda. No longer were there any boiling plumes; far below them, the familiar currents had resumed. There was even a scattering of dots for the beacons of an arkswarm. Osaji seized the radio and put out a call.

"Any ark, this is *Divernon*. Please respond."

There was silence. She repeated the call.

A crackly, faraway voice came from the speaker. "Which ark is that? Please repeat your call."

"It's *Divernon*!" Osaji nearly shouted.

"*Divernon*?" There was a pause. "Where are you?"

"Above you, just under the ice. We've just come back over the mountains. We were swept across when Golconda erupted, but we made it back."

There were some staticky sounds from the radio that might have been exclamations of surprise, or a conversation on the other end, or merely interference.

"*Divernon*, did you say mountains?" the radio finally said. "We can't have heard you right. Please repeat."

7. Breaking Free

They repeated their story many times in the hours, and finally days, that followed, as they sank back into the inhabited depths and the radio communication improved. They learned that the seafloor station at Golconda had not been utterly destroyed. Though the main dome had collapsed in the earthquake, and the port facilities had been severely damaged, the auxiliary domes had survived, and now the main one was being rebuilt. Through a friend of a friend, Osaji even learned that Kitti and her family were all right.

"She will be very surprised to see her sister again," the woman said over the radio. "The name of Osaji was listed among the casualties."

The paddletails revived as they sank into warmer water, and started towing them upstream again. Since this would take the ark by the fastest route to Golconda, they let them continue. Osaji relished the idea of arriving pulled by a snakeherd in their makeshift harnesses.

As they neared the station, Osaji dutifully started to pack and clean in order to vacate their purloined vessel. She had not entered Mota's vacuole since they had started the journey home. It was just as she had left it. Hardening herself against the memories, Osaji started to fill a recycling bin with the possessions of Mota's lifetime. She was standing with Uncle Yamada's flute in her hand when Jack peered in.

"Do you suppose anyone would value Yamada's flute?" she said.

He came in and took the flute, but gave it back. "Not like you would," he said.

"I can't keep it," she said. "Someone else will use this vac next round. One must clear everything away so the next round can begin." She stuffed the flute in the trash.

"I'll take it, then," Jack said, and fished it out.

"Does it play?" she asked.

He blew over the airhole and it let out a protesting squawk. "I guess I'll have to learn how," he said. "Or Yamada will haunt me."

He looked around the small bubble. "She was a nice lady. Not at all like you." Realizing what he'd said, he winced. "That's not what I meant."

Osaji knew what he'd meant, and didn't mind. She didn't want to be like Mota. At least one person on Ben knew that about her.

"So what's next for you?" he said. "You going to settle down and have a normal life now?"

Osaji felt as if the room were listening for her answer. Claustrophobia suddenly oppressed her. "Let's go outside," she said. "Maybe we can see Golconda now."

All was blackness outside, except the glowing ark itself. They swam around and sat atop it, silent with their crowded thoughts. At last Osaji said, "Do spacers always go back to space?"

"No, I think I'll give Ben another try," he said.

"Good," Osaji answered.

He turned to look at her. Through his facemask, his expression was indistinguishable. "You never answered my question."

Osaji still couldn't answer right away. Even out here, she felt the pull of community and family and duty, tugging at her to become the woman she ought to be.

Then, defying it all, she said, "I want to go over the mountains again."

"Really?" he said.

"Yes. I want to find what else is out there. I want to explore the glass city, and know what happened to its builders."

"Yeah," he said.

"Will Jack go back?"

"I think I may. I've decided you Bennites have something here, with these arks, this autopoiesis thing."

"It's not a new idea," Osaji said. It was, in fact, as old as life.

"No, but it's a better idea than you realize. Permeable membranes, that's the key: a constant exchange between outside and in. You've got to let the world leak in, and let yourself flow out into the nutrient bath around you. You've got to let in ideas, and observations, and . . . well, affection . . . or you become hard and dead inside. Life is all about having a permeable self—not so you're unclear who you are, but so you overlap a little with the others on the edges."

Osaji was too surprised to say anything. She could not imagine anyone less permeable than Jack. But as she thought about it, and herself, she said hesitantly, "Some people are too permeable. They spend their lives trying to flow out, and never take in nutrient for themselves. They end up thin and empty inside."

Just then, she saw a mote of light ahead. "Look!" she cried.

It was Golconda. Ahead waited joyous reunions, amazing tales, celebrations of a new future. Once they arrived with their news, the planet would never be the same.

"All the same," Jack said, "I think I'll take an outboard motor next time."

Orange

NEIL GAIMAN

Neil Gaiman (www.neilgaiman.com) lives near Minneapolis. He rose to prominence as a popular writer of intellectually and aesthetically satisfying comics, a writer whom champions of the form pointed to when challenged on whether comics could be really literate and good art. Since crossing over to writing novels and short stories, he has been greeted by similarly hospitable audiences who have showered him with awards and honors. Most recently, he won the Newbery Medal for his children's book, The Graveyard Book *(2008). He is the only fantasy writer today other than Stephen King whose works often get made into movies. The movie of his children's novel* Coraline *came out at the beginning of 2009, and an off-Broadway musical based on* Coraline *opened in New York City in June 2009. Nonetheless, he remains a public figure in the field, always wears black, and remains cool. He is Guest of Honor at Anticipation, the World Science Fiction Convention in Montreal in 2009.*

"Orange" was published in The Starry Rift, *an original anthology of SF for teenagers, edited by Jonathan Strahan and one of the best SF anthologies of a strong year. It is the story of how one teenaged girl handles the invasion of Earth by aliens, told in the form of her responses to an interviewer questioning her about her sister, who has been experimenting with something out of this world. It is insightful and witty.*

(Third Subject's Responses to Investigator's Written Questionnaire). *EYES ONLY.*

1. Jemima Glorfindel Petula Ramsey.

2. Seventeen on June the ninth.

3. The last five years. Before that we lived in Glasgow (Scotland). Before that, Cardiff (Wales).

4. I don't know. I think he's in magazine publishing now. He doesn't talk to us anymore. The divorce was pretty bad and Mum wound up paying him a lot of money. Which seems sort of wrong to me. But maybe it was worth it just to get shot of him.

5. An inventor and entrepreneur. She invented the Stuffed Muffin™, and started the Stuffed Muffin™ chain. I used to like them when I was a kid, but you can get kind of sick of Stuffed Muffins™ for every meal, especially because Mum used us as guinea pigs. The Complete Turkey Christmas Dinner Stuffed Muffin™ was the worst. But she sold out her interest in the Stuffed Muffin™ chain about five years ago, to start work on My Mum's Colored Bubbles (not actually TM yet).

6. Two. My sister Nerys, who was just fifteen, and my brother Pryderi, twelve.

7. Several times a day.

8. No.

9. Through the Internet. Probably on eBay.

10. She's been buying colors and dyes from all over the world ever since she decided that the world was crying out for brightly colored Day-Glo bubbles. The kind you can blow, with bubble mixture.

11. It's not really a laboratory. I mean, she calls it that, but really it's just the garage. Only she took some of the Stuffed Muffins™ money and converted it, so it has sinks and bathtubs and Bunsen burners and things, and tiles on the walls and the floor to make it easier to clean.

12. I don't know. Nerys used to be pretty normal. When she turned thirteen, she started reading these magazines and putting pictures of these strange bimbo women up on her wall, like Britney Spears and so on. Sorry if anyone reading this is a Britney fan; but I just don't get it. The whole orange thing didn't start until last year.

13. Artificial tanning creams. You couldn't go near her for hours after she put it on. And she'd never give it time to dry after she smeared it on her skin, so it would come off on her sheets and on the fridge door and in the shower, leaving smears of orange everywhere. Her friends would wear it too, but they never put it on like she did. I mean, she'd slather on the cream, with no attempt to look even human colored, and she thought she looked great. She did the tanning salon thing once, but I don't think she liked it, because she never went back.

14. Tangerine Girl. The Oompa-Loompa. Carrot-top. Go-Mango. Orangina.

15. Not very well. But she didn't seem to care, really. I mean, this is a girl who said that she couldn't see the point of science

or math because she was going to be a pole dancer as soon as she left school. I said, nobody's going to pay to see you in the altogether, and she said how do you know? and I told her that I saw the little Quicktime films she'd made of herself dancing nuddy and left in the camera and she screamed and said give me that, and I told her I'd wiped them. But honestly, I don't think she was ever going to be the next Bettie Page or whoever. She's a sort of squarish shape, for a start.

16. German measles, mumps, and I think Pryderi had chicken pox when he was staying in Melbourne with the grandparents.

17. In a small pot. It looked a bit like a jam jar, I suppose.

18. I don't think so. Nothing that looked like a warning label anyway. Yes, there was a return address. It came from abroad, and the return address was in some kind of foreign lettering.

19. You have to understand that Mum had been buying colors and dyes from all over the world for five years. The thing with the Day-Glo bubbles is not that someone can blow glowing colored bubbles, it's that they don't pop and leave splashes of dye all over everything. Mum says that would be a lawsuit waiting to happen. So, no.

20. There was some kind of shouting match between Nerys and Mum to begin with, because Mum had come back from the shops and not bought anything from Nerys's shopping list except the shampoo. Mum said she couldn't find the tanning cream at the supermarket, but I think she just forgot. So Nerys stormed off and slammed the door and went into her bedroom and played something that was probably Britney Spears really loudly. I was out the back, feeding the three cats, the chinchilla, and a guinea pig named Roland who looks like a hairy cushion, and I missed it all.

21. On the kitchen table.

22. When I found the empty jam jar in the back garden the next morning. It was underneath Nerys's window. It didn't take Sherlock Holmes to figure it out.

23. Honestly, I couldn't be bothered. I figured it would just be more yelling, you know? And Mum would work it out soon enough.

24. Yes, it was stupid. But it wasn't uniquely stupid, if you see what I mean. Which is to say, it was par-for-the-course-for-Nerys stupid.

25. That she was glowing.

26. A sort of pulsating orange.

27. When she started telling us that she was going to be worshipped like a god, as she was in the dawn times.

28. Pryderi said she was floating about an inch above the ground. But I didn't actually see this. I thought he was just playing along with her newfound weirdness.

29. She didn't answer to "Nerys" anymore. She described herself mostly as either My Immanence, or the Vehicle. ("It is time to feed the Vehicle.")

30. Dark chocolate. Which was weird because in the old days I was the only one in the house who even sort of liked it. But Pryderi had to go out and buy her bars and bars of it.

31. No. Mum and me just thought it was more Nerys. Just a bit more imaginatively weirdo Nerys than usual.

32. That night, when it started to get dark. You could see the orange pulsing under the door. Like a glowworm or something. Or a light show. The weirdest thing was that I could still see it with my eyes closed.

33. The next morning. All of us.

34. It was pretty obvious by this point. She didn't really even look like Nerys any longer. She looked sort of *smudged*. Like an after-image. I thought about it, and it's . . . Okay. Suppose you were staring at something really bright, that was a blue color. Then you close your eyes, and you'd see this glowing yellowy-orange afterimage in your eyes? That was what she looked like.

35. They didn't work either.

36. She let Pryderi leave to get her more chocolate. Mum and I weren't allowed to leave the house anymore.

37. Mostly I just sat in the back garden and read a book. There wasn't very much else I really could do. I started wearing dark glasses, so did Mum, because the orange light hurt our eyes. Other than that, nothing.

38. Only when we tried to leave or call anybody. There was food in the house, though. And Stuffed Muffins™ in the freezer.

39. "If you'd just stopped her wearing that stupid tanning cream a year ago, we wouldn't be in this mess!" But it was unfair, and I apologized afterward.

40. When Pryderi came back with the dark chocolate bars. He said he'd gone up to a traffic warden and told him that his sister had turned into a giant orange glow and was controlling our minds. He said the man was extremely rude to him.

41. I don't have a boyfriend. I did, but we broke up after he went to a Rolling Stones concert with the evil bottle-blond former friend whose name I do not mention. Also, I mean, the Rolling Stones? These little old goat-men hopping around the stage, pretending to be all rock and roll? Please. So, no.

42. I'd quite like to be a vet. But then I think about having to put animals down, and I don't know. I want to travel for a bit before I make any decisions.

43. The garden hose. We turned it on full, while she was eating her chocolate bars, and distracted, and we sprayed it at her.

44. Just orange steam, really. Mum said that she had solvents and things in the laboratory, if we could get in there, but by now Her Immanence was hissing mad (literally) and she sort of fixed us to the floor. I can't explain it. I mean, I wasn't stuck, but I couldn't leave or move my legs. I was just where she left me.

45. About half a meter above the carpet. She'd sink down a bit to go through doors so she didn't bump her head. And after the hose incident she didn't go back to her room, just stayed in the main room and floated about grumpily, the color of a luminous carrot.

46. Complete world domination.

47. I wrote it down on a piece of paper and gave it to Pryderi.

48. He had to carry it back. I don't think Her Immanence really understood money.

49. I don't know. It was Mum's idea more than mine. I think she hoped that the solvent might remove the orange. And at that point, it couldn't hurt. Nothing could have made things worse.

50. It didn't even upset her, like the hose-water did. I'm pretty sure she liked it. I think I saw her dipping her chocolate bars into it before she ate them, although I had to sort of squint up my eyes to see anything where she was. It was all a sort of great orange glow.

51. That we were all going to die. Mum told Pryderi that if the Great Oompa-Loompa let him out to buy chocolate again, he just shouldn't bother coming back. And I was getting really upset about the animals—I hadn't fed the chinchilla or Roland the guinea pig for two days, because I couldn't go into the back garden. I couldn't go anywhere. Except the loo, and then I had to ask.

52. I suppose because they thought the house was on fire. All the orange light. I mean, it was a natural mistake.

53. We were glad she hadn't done that to us. Mum said it proved that Nerys was still in there somewhere, because if she had the power to turn us into goo, like she did the fire-fighters, she would have done. I said that maybe she just wasn't powerful enough to turn us into goo at the beginning and now she couldn't be bothered.

54. You couldn't even see a person in there anymore. It was a bright orange pulsing light, and sometimes it talked straight into your head.

55. When the spaceship landed.

56. I don't know. I mean, it was bigger than the whole block, but it didn't crush anything. It sort of materialized around us, so that our whole house was inside it. And the whole street was inside it too.

57. No. But what else could it have been?

58. A sort of pale blue. They didn't pulse either. They twinkled.

59. More than six, less than twenty. It's not that easy to tell if this is the same intelligent blue light you were just speaking to five minutes ago.

60. Three things. First of all, a promise that Nerys wouldn't

be hurt or harmed. Second, that if they were ever able to return her to the way she was, they'd let us know, and bring her back. Thirdly, a recipe for fluorescent bubble mixture. (I can only assume they were reading Mum's mind, because she didn't say anything. It's possible that Her Immanence told them, though. She definitely had access to some of "the Vehicle's" memories.) Also, they gave Pryderi a thing like a glass skateboard.

61. A sort of a liquid sound. Then everything became transparent. I was crying, and so was Mum. And Pryderi said, "Cool beans," and I started to giggle while crying, and then it was just our house again.

62. We went out into the back garden and looked up. There was something blinking blue and orange, very high, getting smaller and smaller, and we watched it until it was out of sight.

63. Because I didn't want to.

64. I fed the remaining animals. Roland was in a state. The cats just seemed happy that someone was feeding them again. I don't know how the chinchilla got out.

65. Sometimes. I mean, you have to bear in mind that she was the single most irritating person on the planet, even before the whole Her Immanence thing. But yes, I guess so. If I'm honest.

66. Sitting outside at night, staring up at the sky, wondering what she's doing now.

67. He wants his glass skateboard back. He says that it's his, and the government has no right to keep it. (You are the government, aren't you?) Mum seems happy to share the patent for the colored bubble recipe with the government though. The man said that it might be the basis of a whole new branch of molecular something or other. Nobody gave me anything, so I don't have to worry.

68. Once, in the back garden, looking up at the night sky. I think it was only an orangeyish star, actually. It could have been Mars; I know they call it the red planet. Although once in a while I think that maybe she's back to herself again, and dancing, up there, wherever she is, and all the aliens love her pole dancing because they just don't know any better, and they think it's a whole new art form, and they don't even mind that she's sort of square.

69. I don't know. Sitting in the back garden talking to the cats, maybe. Or blowing silly-colored bubbles.

70. Until the day that I die.

I attest that this is a true statement of events.

Signed:

Date:

Memory Dog

KATHLEEN ANN GOONAN

Kathleen Ann Goonan (www.goonan.com) lives in Tavernier, Florida, and in the mountains of Tennessee. She drew the attention of the SF field in the mid 1990s with Queen City Jazz *(1995), which became the first of four volumes to date in her Nanotech Chronicles, an ambitious postmodern blend of literary appropriation and hard SF. She has published a number of short stories that often show a fascination with history and popular culture. Her latest novel,* In War Times, *based on the true experiences of her father in World War II, with SF added, was published in 2007 and won awards. Her forthcoming novel,* This Shared Dream, *is an independent sequel.*

"Memory Dog" was published in Asimov's, *which continued to be a leading SF magazine in a declining market. It is an excellent story in a dystopian setting very much like the year 2008 in some regards, about advances in memory technologies. The protagonist is a man who has chosen to have his personality and memories irrevocably transferred into the body of a dog, knowing that his life is shortened. This he does in penance for the death of his young daughter, for which his ex-wife will never forgive him. Then he returns home in doggy disguise.*

She is always busy and today the temperature is dropping. So she splits wood and I lie next to her, paws outstretched, belly on cold ground, panting breath outflowing, white. Memory huge and bleeding, not keeping to one track, mammalian but skipping, skipping.

She is ferocious with energy. She is mad. The chips fly everywhere and so do the split logs. Splinter, splinter, splinter: kindling. The insides of trees smell sweet; sharp.

Arnold Wentworth watches from his wheelchair at the window. She is not angry at him. We brought him here. It was an arduous journey. But my kind likes journeys. Their imperativeness pulls us, gives us purpose. We know we will find you, eventually. Take us for a ride, throw us out of the car and drive off. We will think you made a big mistake and make it home again.

Split and long crunch of log-fiber. She does not know me, but I know her. She used to be different, and I was too. I am her memory-device, but she has lost the key. This happened before our memories were beamed down to us; among us. Our thoughts, our feelings, re-edited and re-cut events—some true, some false, but all completely manipulative—emanate from the Allover Station in a constant flood. Some of us knew it was coming, or at least suspected, and took steps. The three of us in our strange symbiosis are immune, but we have to live out here, alone. People would notice. And there are those who want to find us.

A pale flare curves against gathering storm clouds. It

comes from Evan's Ridge, which used to be a tourist town but which is now a rebel stronghold. They have a missile launcher hidden in a bread delivery truck—at least that's what Jake says. I even hear the small pop when the missile hits the floater, but she cannot; her senses are dimmer than mine.

I would not have guessed how many people just wanted, needed, an excuse to use weapons. Everything went to hell fast—overnight, it seemed, and everywhere. Individuals joyously got out their guns, knives, bombs, and missiles. Nations happily suspended diplomatic relations and declared war. We are safe here, at least today. Elizabeth still believes she can change people, that Arthur's smacks can do that.

The worst memories, the deepest, most searing, and most universal, are inside a small, protective bubble. The bubble is inside of me.

She has no idea.

Perhaps I am loving this too much, watching her, being with her. Putting off what needs to be done. But I am in heaven.

I hear it before her, the low sound of the truck engine, the hiccup of the driver shifting gears, and jump up, stiff, growling. Alerted, she lowers her ax and stands waiting, wondering: is this the time? She picks up the pistol she left on the rock next to the chopping block. "Who is it, girl? Get him, Daisy!"

By now, I've recognized the sound of Jake's truck, relax, and run down the steep hidden road wagging my tail. Jake, a local farmer that Elizabeth has known since she was a teenager, brings us supplies. Food, gasoline for the generator so we can save the propane in the big buried tank, and local news. Not regularly. The dead-end tree-hidden dirt road below us also goes to property he owns, so it is far more likely that the smoke from our woodstove would give us away than Jake's visits. But this has been a vacation hideaway for years, so we could be anyone. Jake understands the need for not revealing who we are.

I was cast off, taken for a ride, thrown out of the car, but I came back. I will always come back. I am a dog.

*   *   *

Rain strikes the leaves, making them shiver. Fall is almost over and they are few. By tomorrow, according to the weathernews that is so submerged in my brain that I no longer have to access it deliberately, the trees will be cloaked in ice.

Jake gone, Elizabeth continues to split wood, glancing at the sky nervously. Weather is just about the only kind of uncorrupted television information she can get now. The rest of television, a million stations, with no exaggeration, is sheer entertainment, even what they call the news. I call it the Allover Station because every station and all of the news is the same, essentially. The weight of Allover draws everyone in, together, the same way a hearth fire would. It is almost impossible to resist. It is so full of death and murder and pain that we take it for granted that this is the way of the world and nothing can be done.

They are wrong.

Truth comes in the form of newspods, released into the air, drawn hither and yon by the magnetic call of those who swallowed the black-market pill that gives them access to a million independent podders. They call these newspods smacks: you get smacked with the truth, every once in a while; the pod, an electromagnetic bundle of information, smacks your face—really, just a light caress—and then true news—if you believe the source—unfolds within you.

Arnold Wentworth was a smacker, one of the most well-known and respected. The smacks were in the air, tangible things, like seeds adrift in the wind, after we all knew that it was truthuseless on the airwaves. He composed and sent smacks, and they were not the right smacks because they too often told the truth. He was Elizabeth's mentor, and her fury and her wit brought him here. Many people believed Arnold Wentworth—so many that he was considered to be a threat to the government and tortured. Millions of people worldwide took the Arnold Wentworth Pill, disseminated on the black market. All based on the deepest trust, and Arnold, over the years, had earned that trust.

Now only Elizabeth has Arnold's smack code. Only she can release his smacks.

I am a forbidden creature—or at least I would be in All-over. My brain is my entire body, every bit of it pressed into many functions at once, for I am a memory dog, the only one of my kind. I am adrift in places and thoughts that are not really here. *Here* is quickly baring branches, lake marsh behind with ice creeping across its surface, low gray sky and gray geese flying, honking, saying simply go, go, go, their amazing brains taken up by getting there, by magnetism. *Here* is the pile of supplies Jake deposited on the porch before driving away. *Here* is the strict chop of her ax, her low muttered "Fuck them all!" which issues as rhythmically as the downblow of the blade and its thunk into the block beneath the split log, fuck them all, thunk, fuck them all, thunk, fuck them all. The pile of split wood grows. The man watches from the window and I am thankful that I do not have his memories too, for they are hideous.

Here is free from feeling my own memories. Mostly.

I still know them, though. Knowing is a form of enormous selfishness.

I revel, for now, in knowing: Wendy. Jolly. Elizabeth.

And me: Mike. Sometimes I remember. My name is Mike.

Arnold may heal eventually. He cannot talk, not yet, but is beginning to. He had a stroke—a specially administered stroke. Tears well constantly and creep down his face and he cannot or does not bother to wipe them away.

I nudge his resting hands with my long nose from time to time and his hand sometimes stirs and rests on my head. I get little from him, but whatever I get is becoming stronger. Perhaps he is recovering. From her, I get electric anger, stabbing fury, the energy that still cannot be words. She moves quickly, bringing in armfuls of split wood and clonking them onto the pile next to the hot stove. It is too hot in here, but maybe it is good for Arnold. She hauls in the supplies, too, piling them up on the kitchen table, getting them in out of the rain.

She was not always so angry. She was in love with Arnold. She podded lyrically to him, and the pods, I know, unfolded within him, potent flowers of information, sharp and intense as her, and he could not help answering. After a year of this, he left his wife, and his wife reported him, out of jealousy and sadness, and the government came because of the truth of his pods and now we are left with what-once-was-Arnold.

I am memory. And memory is pain. But I was made strong enough to bear it. For I made myself. I—the self that knows myself—cannot get out of the bargain, the deep-being of my cells. Oh, I could be killed; I could die if injured. I cannot, though, knowingly cause injury to myself. I am like a robot in this regard. I did this because I so often contemplated suicide, so often thought of the tree speeding toward me as I drove, or the wrists in the bathtub, or the gun in the drawer. This dance around oblivion tired me tremendously, but with a long-regarded plan, and then in an instant of strength and resolve, I did away with it.

Rain turns to snow outside. Elizabeth plays jazz on the radio, even as the Allover Station, behind her, fills the screen with silent written opinion-molding headlines and alerts. Right now we hear an Oscar Peterson piece. It is a special talent of mine, one I was pleased to retain: a jazz encyclopedia. I can tell who plays, instantly, who sings. The sounds are horizontal planes that slide across one another. Mostly they stay distinct, but sometimes, precisely, they intersect. With a dog's fine ears, augmented by songbird genes, I find my pleasure. It is not the only reason I stick with her, but it is a plus: jazz. The wood in the stove snaps and pops. We are a joyous popping rhythm laced with the anger that is always there, that makes her movements quick and impatient, that erodes her heart with anger-generated substances.

She wheels Arnold to the shower room and I pad along behind. I hope it's warm enough now, she says, and unbuttons his shirt, unbuckles his belt, slides off his clothes, tests the temperature of the water, and rolls him under it, wheelchair and all. Water draws his gray-black curly hair straight down his face, over his eyes. Her long, blonde, pulled-back hair holds beads of water in the fine tendrils around her face.

"Juh," he says. "Juh."

"Uh, huh," she says. "Good." But her face does not say good. I think he is trying to say the name of his first wife, Jane. He is saying more consonants now. "Guh." And then, his eyes shift and he looks right at me. "Muh."

Elizabeth twists off the taps and grabs a towel from a pile on a nearby chair. She rubs Arnold's hair. She lifts his chin and looks into his eyes, kisses him swiftly, sighs, and gets his shoulders. "Grab hold," she says and he obediently grasps the bar in front of him and pulls himself up, shaking, his pale skin sagging from his ribs, his chest hair white although he is only fifty. They made him old. She briskly dries his back, his buttocks, the backs of his legs, and plops a dry towel onto the wheelchair seat. "Okay." He gasps and falls back into his chair. She's dried his face, so the wet tracks are new tears. She is gentle; her anger abates when she touches him. I am glad for her; I am sad for her; I am simply a wraith of emotion, rising around her. I nudge her elbow; she pats my head absently.

After she dries and dresses him, he sits on the couch. He can sit up without falling over. Every day she makes him exercise, moves his limbs, tries to make him reach, or grip, or try to repeat sounds or words after her.

"Kuh," he says, slowly, drawing out the sound. "Kuuuuuh."

I lie on my side by the stove into which she has shoved her split logs. The television is on, tuned low. She thinks it helps Arnold. All that is on it is stuff, stuff, stuff. Lies that they call news, celebrities, murders, gossip. A low, growling sigh escapes me as I relax into the warmth.

I think of Arnold's first face, when they were colleagues, not lovers, and I was Elizabeth's husband. Are these my memories? Hers? Jolly's? I no longer know.

That is what is so wonderful.

It is getting too hot in the cabin. I scratch the door, she lets me out, and I lie on the porch, on guard.

Mist flows in and obscures some of the details. Everything is still there, behind the mist, like brilliant red and yellow maples on a far ridge. You know they are there, you just can't see them. Think of the cloud, with its wind-driven fringes, as beautiful. Think of your mind as weather. Think of your brain as a storm. Arnold is stuck in a storm, locked, unable to move.

Being a dog is a joyful thing.

First, way back when it was a new, it was a memory pill. Yes, say it, memory *drug*. I worked on a lot of the original research. Initially for those who were terribly impaired, it was such a boon that its quick spread to the rest of the population could not be stopped. It was to help people with memory deficits, which is to say most people. And it was to help with useful memories: where did I put the car keys, what the hell is his name? However, it of course did not distinguish between users who were terrifically impaired and the rest of us. And, most importantly, it did not sort memories as to importance. It bypassed mechanisms that do such things. It turned up all the signals. So it became the drug of choice for anyone who could lay hands on it. The possible dangers were trumpeted by the press, but if you could enhance your doctoral, legal, or high-school pop-quiz performance, why not? It raised the bar for everyone. Real and counterfeit pills, injections, and patches were for sale in the third world and in the school parking lot.

The world was awash in memories.

They were all imperative. People wrote memoirs, previously the domain of those obsessed with the past, just to take the pressure off. The intense numinosity of memories caused constant reruns of one's life; memory overload became a common plea in traffic accidents. The memory of a grievous wrong sharpened and would not let the wronged one rest until it was avenged. One way or another, when we are stretched out of our previous shape, we jostle the status quo in ways we could not have predicted. So here we all went, our memories stretched and teeming with visual, audible replays, as if we were all schizophrenics, into a well-to-be-remembered future.

For some—writers, painters, musicians, those who dealt in emotions—the memory drug was a boon. It produced a heightening of affect. The present always led to the past; the past was therefore always present, layered and linked and resonate with longing, love, and resolution—or hate, revenge, plots laid and hatched and brought to fruition and the results lived with. And lived with. Inescapably. Christian churches, with their confession and absolution, experienced a resurgence. We were all evil, deeply evil, and could not forget it; we could only hand over the guilt to an almighty being. Or we remembered joyous, pagan interconnectedness with nature, danced in circles, and our minds floated into a golden ether of faeries, dwarves, witches, tree-gods, and druids. Whatever. I'm telling you, the whole thing was a godawful mess.

It was not all bad. Some learned to control their memories. The visual used pictures or objects to set off links of associations.

Meditation, emptying one's mind, became big. Our minds and memories tortured us. Forgetting was a blessing.

Many people had permanent memory-release modules implanted in their bodies, and some, like myself, were genetically engineered to produce the necessary enhancing chemicals.

I will never forget the whole of Elizabeth's being after Wendy, our three-year-old, died.

That, and my own grief, and Jolly's, is the key that I hold.

It really was my fault.

Because, Elizabeth screamed, after we came home from the hospital, gently ejected from the E.R. and then the chapel and then the lobby after Wendy was pronounced dead, I had taken too many memory drugs, too much of them, and could no longer pay attention to the simplest thing.

"Mike! You didn't even know she was out in the street!"

It was true.

I can see the various angles of Elizabeth's fury-stretched face, her anger-stunned eyes, her chest heaving as she gasps for breath, hear the hoarseness of her voice as it devolves into small shreds of sound. Her face is mottled red, like some pale, mineral-dappled stone, and her straight blonde hair is pasted onto her cheeks by tears. Her smell is of sweat too, sharp, one she has never had before. It tastes sour and unpleasant.

This grief is memory, and it is Jolly's memory, for our collie rushed out the front door after Wendy, tried to keep her from the road, the neighbor who was also running toward her at the time told us. When we got back from the hospital, Jolly ran to Elizabeth, emitting hoarse barks, licking the back of her hand, pawing at her leg, and then jumping up, planting her paws square on Elizabeth's chest, barking like fury right in her face until Elizabeth drew Jolly tightly to her and they both collapsed backwards onto a chair, Elizabeth crying, Jolly licking her face as she was never, never allowed to do, while I stood dumb and stunned and empty.

The next day, Jolly disappeared. We knew she was looking for Wendy, trying to find her and bring her back. As Elizabeth made funeral arrangements I walked the neighborhood, and later that night while Elizabeth sobbed I called "Jolly!" out the car window, driving slowly down nearby roads. I put up signs. The next morning, while I was walking into the dog pound, Elizabeth called my cell phone. "A man just found Jolly in a ditch next to Bartello Street. Down where it curves." Her voice was flat. She thought Jolly's death was my fault too. She was probably right. I was supposed to fix the fence. I hadn't.

I went and lifted Jolly from the ditch. He was stiff. I took him down the road to our vet's and asked that he be flash-frozen. They do this all the time at the vet's; people don't always have time to deal with their dead pets immediately. "Step back," he said, as he lifted Jolly's shrink-wrapped body into the open freezer, but I didn't and tears froze on my face.

I was not fit to be a person. I wasn't fit to be alive at all. Not any more. I shared Elizabeth's opinion in this matter.

After everything was done with, after we buried Wendy, after I realized that Elizabeth would never speak to me again and with good reason, I watched her take up with Ar-

nold who was a good man, an exemplary man, a man dedicated to the good of humankind and not addicted to memory
pills. You would never find him standing in a daze in his
kitchen being perhaps his grandmother cutting carrots in a
another high-ceilinged marble-tabled kitchen while his toddler wandered out the door. He was definitely not me.

I decided to become a dog.

I would doggedly survive. Perhaps at some point I could
be of use to Elizabeth.

Oh, of course, the form and deep being of many creatures
were inviting to me, as I contemplated. The long life and
intelligence of elephants, of parrots. The interior brilliance
of panthers, snow leopards, tigers. Yet I could have them all,
in this form: the dog.

No mammal save the human kills itself. But there was no
room for big cats, or elephants, where I was going to live: in
this world of humans. Was it penance, of a sort? I cannot say
I do not remember, for that is about all I do. But there are
rooms I do not go into. I do not go into the room of Wendy.
There is no understanding that room.

I admire Elizabeth. She lives in the room of Wendy. Still.
That is her anger. I cannot get in the door, because I am
Dog. Wendy, the true real room of Wendy, is in the smack I
so carefully composed, encased in its protective bubble. I
have locked myself out. If I went in the door I would kill
myself. And that is something I cannot do. Understanding is
in the hands of God and God does not exist. There are many
logical conundrums on the threshold of Wendy's door, and
as a dog, I am free to not examine them.

It was not really much of a decision. I remember those
days as great swaths of scent, of grief-smelling spring wind
that Wendy would never again smell, the green rich sea-
smell, fresh and mineral-damp when I lifted a handful of wet
sand to my eyes to see what she had seen, translucent prisms
of obsidian green, pure true brown, golden sharp-planed bits
that dried and blew away before I could move, so perhaps I
was already inclined to dog, thinking in dog-memories of
overwhelming smell. I guess that somewhat distantly I was
considering my options and I can see so much more clearly

now what I was thinking, as I have said: the elephant; the cat. Animal seemed the only option: to change shape; to give misery a different vessel, a different shape in which to bounce its energy about, as if emotion were the straight geometry of billiards. On this day, I saw a dog running down the beach between a man and a woman. Their child ran with the dog and grabbed his long black tail. The dog twisted free, frolicked and leapt, and he seemed happy.

I craved the relief of what looked like simple happiness.

That afternoon I drove back from the beach, went to the big-mart, and loaded up on dog food. Ellie Wills was in the next line; we all shop at the big-mart now, even for a gallon of milk.

"I thought your dog died." Then she looked aghast and embarrassed for an instant, remembering my greater loss.

I pretended not to see the look. "I'm thinking about getting another one."

"What kind?"

Huh. What kind. A dog-like dog. Wag, bark, happy.

"Another collie."

"Collies are stupid."

I'd never much liked Ellie Wills, but for an instant I purely loathed her. "No they're not," I said, bristling in advance for my future self, and for dear Jolly.

It was the right choice for various reasons. I wouldn't want to be a menace; collies are kind, not inclined to viciousness, and filled with love like me, bursting with love, with infinite flavors of regret.

I wiped my eyes. "I've got a cold."

"I know," she said. "I'm so sorry about Wendy. It's not your fault."

I reeled with memories not just of Wendy but of everything, everything, echoing into forever, and reached for the seventy-five-pound bag and hauled it onto the belt.

"Any coupons?" asked the check-out clerk.

Love has no pride.

I needed Elizabeth. She did not need me. She despised

and hated me. She wished me dead. So when I left the note saying that I was leaving and that she should not try to find me I am sure she did not grieve. She was probably relieved.

There was penance, too, in my decision to become a dog. I had enough reason to feel guilty, certainly; enough for several men for several lifetimes, even without the weight of Wendy. Because of what we did to the snails, the mice. We transferred memories from one mouse to the other. Memories of how to run the maze. Then we killed them, casually, by the thousands. It was the job of a grad student, his or her choice about how to do it. But that was long before the drug, long before my addictive hypermnesia, the opposite of amnesia: remembering everything; having, even, mental events that you think are memories but which are not.

Dr. Lorenzo, at first horrified, finally agreed after hearing my whole story, after knowing who I was and what I had done and why it was so necessary to me. I had read of her work for years in journals; we had spoken at the same international meetings. I offered myself as an experiment. There was no paper trail, none at all—so both of us knew that actually it was too subjective to be any kind of an experiment. It was a favor to me. For all she knew, she was murdering me, but I easily convinced her that otherwise I would kill myself anyway, because it was true.

It took me several months in the lab to distill the essence I was after. Almost all of us are able to feel grief and loss. But it is so painful and overwhelming that we soon become numb, in various degrees. Some of us can kill others without feeling any remorse. We can justify it. Others of us are capable of causing pain on a large scale. We command armies and call it necessary and civilized.

What might change this?

Arnold Wentworth had his ideas.

I had mine.

Becoming a dog: I cohabited gently, slowly. The initial work took weeks. It was a matter of the cells remembering; deep memories, cross-species, the work of a brilliant memory-master, experimental and forbidden. And: remember: we could do specific. So from Jolly, frozen since her death, I got Jolly's Wendy, and Jolly's extreme grief. We could also do long-term change. We could fix an emotion, a vision, a scene, in long-term memory by precisely implanting specific molecules of one brain into the other.

In the early days of memory work, we learned how to change the neurostructure of mice in various ways. We took out genes or inserted them. We traced protein encoding; we traced the precise mechanisms by which long-term memories survive in the brain. By then, we were able to transfer exact memories—how to run the maze; what color symbolized an exit; what sound meant food—from one mouse to another. Behavior was then replicated without the experience needed by the first mouse to form the memory.

That was the dawn, years ago. There were many more steps to go, much more to learn, before we reached the final, complex product: me. The puppy had preparatory genetic work done; the infusion of identity structures—mine—distilled from a myriad of information Dr. Lorenzo retrieved from my human body. I am, perhaps, a precursor. Perhaps not. My reasons for becoming a dog are unique, and neither the process, as it stands now, nor the product, would be approved by any government.

The puppy, so new, welcomed me, not surprised, and our neurons intertwined quickly, for she was growing like all new things, swiftly, her brain branching and branching. I thought I could keep out of her way; I had no real wish to use her body in any way other than to be near Elizabeth. But it was inevitable that we become one.

It was just my way of driving into a tree.

I am happy with the results. I am always happy, now. I am a dog.

I had to learn to be a dog. At first it was awkward to have four legs, but then it was liberating. I surprisingly remembered what it was like to be human and a toddler, like Wendy, so low to the ground. As I tumbled along on four short legs, I remembered my own two short ones, the sense of growth and maturity I'd felt when finally I could balance on one leg, take the next step, then balance on that leg, and take the next step, instead of putting both feet on each step at the same time. In six months I had grown to be an almost-full-sized female collie, tricolored.

I was cast off, taken for a ride, thrown out of the car, for the wrong I did, for my deep negligence as a human, but I came back. But it was my own ride, and I will always come back, now. I am a dog.

One of Dr. Lorenzo's grad students released me near my old house, as agreed, though she hadn't a clue about anything. The student loved me. She'd walked and fed me for weeks. She scratched behind my ears, patted my side heartily, called Dr. Lorenzo three times to make sure. "I can't just leave her here." Doglike, I loved the student so much that I wouldn't have minded staying with her, but she obeyed my previous instructions, sternly relayed by Dr. Lorenzo, and put me out eventually.

As you see, this was no remedy for my problem, as I had hoped. Already the minutiae of memory crowded round. But it was intimate memory, the memory of learning how to control one's own body, the second sensory explosion my own consciousness, my own identity, had experienced. My love of the world returned, and my guilt receded. For a time.

First, I walked doubtfully down the sidewalk. Next, I trotted, and then galloped, liquid memory, a mere outline of a dog, through which flowed images, smells, imperative, striking me fully in the brain, loudly, immediately, like a live symphony orchestra. The spring earth was thawing, rich and damp. I scrambled beneath the fence, using the same hole Jolly used to escape, which I ought to have boarded up but, assailed with too much memory, paradoxically forgot to do. I ran to the basement crawl space door, pushed away its rotted door, and bellied inside. I ripped through the industrial-strength plastic bag I'd wrapped the dog food in and crunched down on the brown, intensely delicious nuggets. Upstairs I heard Lester Young on the stereo, and Arnold. "What's for dinner," he said.

What's for dinner? The bastard didn't even cook for her. I barked.

"What's that?" she said and her voice thrilled me. A million instants like stars shot through me in the underhouse darkness: her.

I barked again, and ran around to the front door, squealing and jumping up onto the door. She opened it and laughed. "Look, Arnold. A collie!"

"I see."

She opened the door and let me in.

I ran to every corner, sniffing joyfully, whining and emitting small barks, smelling her and smelling Elizabeth and Wendy and Jolly and our whole lives. I smelled this that and the other thing. I was bursting with the joy and sadness of the past. I ran into every room—her office; mine; the kitchen, faster than fast, at four-legged dog-speed, scrabbling and twisting as if bringing a gazelle to ground. Elizabeth laughed hard, with great joy. I shook myself into a frenzy, wheeling and barking until Elizabeth grabbed me and said Hey, HEY. She looked into my eyes and for an instant I thought she knew.

But how could she.

"Someone's lost him," said Arnold. "We need to call the dog pound."

"Her. She doesn't have a collar."

"Someone will be looking for her. Dogs like this don't grow on trees."

No, we grow in labs.

I licked her face. I swallowed her memories.

A rumble arose in my chest and I transmuted it into a sharp bark. Elizabeth reached down, ruffled my head-fur, and I happily danced, all dog, threw in a few leaps. Elizabeth said, "She stays."

Arnold's scent was slightly sour. He smiled. "Whatever you want, honey." His eyes, when he looked at me, were irritated. I didn't care. He was not the boss.

She was.

Memory is anatomical change. Period. Neuronal change. Synaptic change.

Aplysia, a giant marine snail, has few brain cells, compared to mammals, and they are comparatively large. It was a good subject for early memory studies. It is a beautiful marine animal, its head arching up and around, topped by what looks like fronds of a stubby palm. However, it is usually ensconced in its shell, so you can't see all of that. It is a hermaphrodite.

Training creates actual anatomical changes.

Memory is physical.

I wanted to remember love. I wanted to remember Elizabeth and Wendy. I wanted to remember the extraordinary web of being in which I had lived, and because I did not know whether or not the experiences that you or I might call "bad"—the disappointments, the setbacks—might have contributed to the overall flavor of that being, like a wash of one pigment over another gives a watercolor depth or a pinch of spice gives a dish an indefinable flavor and because, let's face it, I was a memory addict, I wanted it all. All of it in the skull of a dog.

The heads of true collies are not pinched, and they are herding dogs, so their memories have to do with the big picture, and being bossy, and with speed, direction, and following complex signals. Their long, flowing coats are beautiful. I chose to be a female because I did not want to be reflexively aggressive.

Because I wanted to be like Jolly.

Lying at Elizabeth's feet, I knew I had made the right choice.

After they were in bed, that first night, I padded to the door of Wendy's room.

This was not the room of Wendy that is inside me, the room I made, the room I can't go into, the room full of pain. This was her real, lovely, physical room, frilly purple and green like she wanted. Moonlight stretched across the bed, washed the pillows. Rumble, her beloved teddy bear, lay there, stub arms outstretched, his black bead eyes facing the window.

I whined. I stretched out on my belly, put my chin on the floor.

I howled, and was surprised. I did not know I could howl. It was a truly mournful sound, a soul-releasing "O*wooooo*!"

"Goddammit!" Arnold's voice.

"Shhh. It's okay. Get back in bed."

I still had teeth; I could bite if I decided to do so. My growl was low, but sufficiently ferocious. When I heard Elizabeth's moans through the doorway (they did not bother to close the door) I could have shot through that doorway, leapt onto the bed, and torn out Arnold's throat. Rapid pictures filled my mind. Elizabeth's naked legs, parted for me.

I padded to the kitchen, tipped over the garbage can. "What's that?" I heard Elizabeth say, and then whatever Arnold did made her shriek with delight. I teased a trail of chicken bones and rotted vegetables across the kitchen floor and cracked the delicious bones between my teeth. Bacon grease drooled onto the rug beneath the dining room table.

Deeply satisfied, I trotted back to Wendy's room. Without pausing, I leapt onto her bed, curled up, took Rumble in my mouth, and fell asleep, my mind a train wreck, a bonfire, an amusement park, of memories. A slide show. I saw it all going one way, each snapshot: Elizabeth's slow joy at realizing our love, a lazy morning in a sunstruck St. Paul hotel room, her smile across the table at the diner the day she found out she was pregnant. Fast, flash, flash, flash.

Now I was going away. Seeing it all from the other side.

"We have to take her to the pound!" Arnold's voice was reedy when it rose. "She's ruined the rug. It's a very good rug, isn't it?" He sounded hopeful.

I was sitting rather far away, in the living room, half-behind a chair, trying to be small. Elizabeth was on her knees with some cleaner and paper towels. It was her grandmother's Oriental rug. "It's all right."

"I don't think so."

She looked up at him and said sharply, "It's my rug, Arnold, and it's all right."

A thrill shot through me.

* * *

I have two brains. My human brain is evenly distributed throughout my dog body, intertwined with everything else. It makes what we call thinking slow, since distances to be traveled are greater. This was a decision I made. I wanted to be able to control my body easily, and therefore the dog brain needed to be where it has been for hundreds of thousands of years. The dog brain is on tap. It is ready.

But where was *I*? *What* was I?

I was a religious experience. I was, and am, Awe of Elizabeth. I was able to lie next to her on the bed, feel her hand absently play with my fur as she read, which is something that my human self would never have felt again. I was, I *am*, the future I never would have had, I am life beyond death.

After a weak, "I don't want that dog in the bed," Arnold succumbed. "You don't want the dog in the bed, but I do," she replied, calmly, firmly, and leaving him with no doubt about his choices.

We are in that heaven that all the saints so longed for and predicted, pens scritching across rough vellum in damp towers, heads bent beneath sputtering candles. Heat, ample light, plenty, near-infinite knowing. But man is still enemy to himself, and man still must find god within himself to go beyond the oppression; the killing. And first, he must find killing wrong. That seems to be a sticking point in some parts. What if, suddenly, we all simply could not kill. If it was impossible. Memory drugs might do this.

I left my grad students with a particular prototype. If everyone had it, if it became active all at once, all wars, all firing, all missiles, would stop. Men in bars, poised to cut during the Saturday Night Knife and Gun Club boys' night out would drop their knives. Women in the Air Force with a load of cluster bombs would overfly without pressing the button. Any death would be accidental, not intentional. No revenge.

How would we pass our time? How would we spend our money?

Oh, there were a million problems with this drug, no probability that it would be brought to production in my lifetime. It was just a dream, and there was just one dose, one infinitely expandable dose, which had never been tested. I distilled it into pure smack-quality intensity and kept it, then handed the information over to Juanita, the brightest and best, the most committed, the most feisty, the one who could muster the most money. The most likely to succeed.

I *did* have a plan . . . what was it?

The memory key. Yes. That's it. My dog self sometimes forgets.

When I remember Juanita, I feel hopeful. Glad.

But I am a dog. Gladness is my nature.

I found that I could read.

At first, it was slow going. Elizabeth had left the newspaper on the floor, open to the Sunday funnies. I tried lying down on top of the paper and looking at it between my paws, but I had to back up, and finally I stood and looked down at it. This was especially painful. I imagine that stroke patients might feel this way—the loss of an especially treasured skill.

But then, it came together! A sharp bark! I danced! It was just the brain-slowness, the long journey of the information—

"Look," said Arnold. "You'd think that silly dog could read."

Elizabeth glanced over and looked at me very thoughtfully. I reached down with my head, grasped the edge of the dry newspaper in my teeth, held the page down with my paw, and tore it in half. I am just a silly dog. What is printed on the paper means nothing to me.

"No!" she said, jumping up and grabbing the newspaper.

But she continued to look at me thoughtfully just the same.

Well, I no longer had to worry about such things. I was a dog.

Wendy, still, was everywhere in the house. I ran through it every morning as if a spell struck me; I sniffed frantically, disconsolate, while Arnold worked, composing his dangerous, seditious smacks, which said that the government had been subverted by evil men and that we must all take action. His smacks were, and are, full of specificity; his research was superb. I know; I was quite aware of him before Wendy died; he was Elizabeth's colleague. Her smacks were quieter, but smoothly ferocious, with sharp, sudden legal barbs, like those of sea creatures, emerging to puncture arguments and positions. They really were two of a kind.

Occasionally he said lie down and be quiet, but didn't move from his chair, or even move his eyes from his screen.

That particular morning, Elizabeth was out, teaching. The house, with pale winter sunlight striping the dark wood floor, seemed empty; Arnold was invisible to me. I sensed that things were no longer all that good between Arnold and Elizabeth, but I didn't care. I was deeply happy just to be near her.

In the afternoon, I jumped up on Wendy's bed, took Rumble gently in my jaws, and stretched out, aching. Arnold came to the doorway and looked at me.

"You shit," he said. "You think I don't know what's possible? I'm working on it." As he walked away, shaking his head, he muttered, "But sometimes a dog is just a dog. Right? Right? Of course."

I'm a dog, I barked. I'm a dog, dog, dog.

"Shut up," he yelled, and went back into his office.

A few hours later, I heard him shout "God damn it!" He staggered from his office and leaned against the doorframe of Wendy's room. I rolled my eyes to look at him. He let loose with a sob, dropped his head into his hands, reeled, and walked away.

I ran to his side, curious, a dog, overwhelmed by his scent. His pure, political goodness engulfed me. How did this smell? Oddly, like the ocean. Several kinds of sea. An openness. This apparently did not translate into personal openness—he was jealous of a dog, and that stunk—but he was famous for this sea-goodness, and for the sheer efficaciousness of his sea-wrath, a pounding ceaseless wave of good sense he released daily from relayed locations, helping to keep people open-minded. In a world where we could choose to become dogs, we could quite easily be made into dogs without choosing. Right?

Right. And that was just a small taste of the nasty possibilities. So he was quite necessary.

He also emanated the scent of something-bad-has-happened: worry, defeat, fear.

I returned to the bed, jumped onto it, and bit down tightly on Rumble.

Elizabeth came home flushed and angry. "You wouldn't believe what they've done!" She slammed the door behind her.

I dashed to her, danced around—carefully, so carefully, not jumping up. She crouched down, hugged me. She was crying. "They let me go! Fired me! I have tenure, but . . . Oh, hell!"

Then Arnold was there pulling her away, up, giving her a long, tall hug, saying, "I know, honey, I know. Look, we have to get out of here. I've been packing. It's my fault. It's me."

After I crawled onto Wendy's bed, I rested my head on Rumble, who was very damp.

It was not Elizabeth's fault. It was not Arnold's fault. Every bad thing in the world was my fault. My memory fault. My memory addiction fault.

But I would fix it.

Outside, the sky was raining hate. Small pictures of Arnold descended and popped, and neighborhood kids led the police to our house and they dragged him away. I realized that he had been in hiding. There would have been better places.

Elizabeth was magnificent, promising many specific forms of legal action, even when they threatened her too.

They did not take Elizabeth, which, I think, made her more angry. They only took Arnold, said that he was a traitor and that they did not need any further legal justification for taking him. They shoved him in a truck that had a government insignia on it and that was that.

We stood on the wintry stoop. The gray sky backgrounded darker gray trees, and the mundane houses of the neighborhoods, their yards yellow and brown, seemed the saddest place in the world.

My dogness kept back the surging memory of seeing Wendy lying on the street on a similar day. I was that strong, that much dog, my humanness, my Mikeness, firmly tamped into my paws, the tip of my tail, my entrails. And I knew what she was thinking: Loss. Nothing but loss.

She collapsed onto the stoop, put her head in her hands, and cried. I pressed next to her, licked her salty tears. She put her arm around me.

I was sad for her. I was glad of the moment; deeply satisfied, and some yearning was settled, for just that tipping instant. Finally, I could be of some use to her, if only as furry animal into which she could press her face, and sob, and hug me so tightly that my entire being rejoiced.

They were watching Elizabeth, of course, her information paths, with their computers, but she knew the triggers as she had defended clients against their prying. Besides, they have so many people to watch. She knew the back alleys to the back alleys, all the ways to make her searches innocuous, all the ways to subvert their attempts. And she found out where they took Arnold.

She talked to me, of course, all the time, told me everything she did and everything she planned to do. She forgot to eat, and became very thin, and ran twice a day, with me at her side, and got strong.

By that time, I knew that Arnold would never die, not for her. "He left an entire library of smacks," she said. "These people are so predictable. He said that tyrants always are. I'll only have to modify each one a bit to make it perfectly up-to-date when I release it."

They will know you are doing it, I barked. I barked straight at her, standing up, as if I were talking to her. I heard each word in my head as I barked. I thought of plans. I could tear out tiny newspaper words and assemble them for her. I could talk to her if I really wanted to.

No. *Mike* could talk to her. I knew quite well that she would throw Mike out of the house, onto the street. She would never let Mike back in. She really could not suspect who I was. She was already puzzled at times.

She leaned back in her computer chair, tired and anxious. "They'll know it's me, of course. If they take me, I'll be of no use. But if I do nothing, I'm of goddamn little use either. Hell."

For three days, then, she packed. She went into the garage and got out all of our old camping and backpacking gear, our emergency flee-the-government food about which we laughed, but nervously, when we assembled it years ago. The smells of it all threw me into ecstasies of a million hikes. One year, we hiked the entire Appalachian Trail. When we started in Georgia, in the spring, red trilliums dotted the slopes of the mountains. Our tent smelled of Gore-Tex, a few steps removed from plastic, and as she unrolled it and set it up in the garage to see if it was still good I went inside, breathed deeply, and, if I could have, I would have cried. I curled up there on the sleeping bags she tossed into the door, enveloped in a deeply scented panacea of the past. The good times. Us.

"I know where he is," she said. "And the government is going down. It will be chaos. He won't be at all useful; he'll be killed. Here's the plan. Listening? Good dog. I've got an aunt with a cabin in the north Georgia mountains. Her name is Cecile. She's very old, hasn't gone there for years. But first, we have to get him."

Why? I thought. We don't need him. My traitor tail, though, thumped in agreement, ringing against a Coleman stove she'd shoved inside.

I wanted all of her, everything, just like I had when we'd met. I wanted that still, her first wagon ride, the day she'd fallen from the monkey bars and broken her arm, the feeling she'd had when she launched from Cove Mountain, into the wind, her arms in the hang gliding loops, moving the bar. When we met, we'd talked and talked, trying to get to that place where we would be one, the same person.

* * *

Where does memory reside? We do not know. It is a system, a process, a constant recreation. What accounts, then, for its specificity? I'd transfused blood from one white mouse to another, after giving them the memory drug. I watched the new mouse run the maze, which it had never before run, perfectly. Strange but true. All that information, so compact, just needing the medium into which to expand.

I was that medium, now. I was like water. Elizabeth and Jolly and Wendy were the folded Japanese paper flower that would unfold inside me.

She packed the truck, tied down everything beneath a tarp. The back seat of the truck was full of electrical equipment which might soon be useless. Cecile had a generator, and a huge buried propane tank, and when that was gone, that would be it.

Elizabeth took all the money she had in the bank, all the jewelry, odd things she thought might be useful for barter. One night she went next door and traded Mr. Monroe's license plates for ours. "He'll never notice," she said, bolting them onto the truck. She was ready to go get Arnold and head for the hills.

Inside the hollow garage, sounds were magnified. I heard the car come up the street and jumped to my feet. It was three in the morning.

"What is it girl?" and then she froze too. "Shhhh." She held me tightly, and then held my mouth shut, too.

Footsteps, coming up the walk. A thump.

The car sounds receded down the street.

She hurried through the dark house, opened the front door.

It was Arnold, tossed like a package onto the doorstep. He was naked, bloody, bruised, curled up, moaning.

"Oh, no!" She tried to pick him up, but he was too heavy. She pulled him onto the hall rug, slammed the door. "Arnold! Arnold!"

He opened his eyes. They were empty. Except for the tears.

* * *

She had her mother's wheelchair and walker and all kinds of old folk equipment in the attic. She worked quickly, fury in every motion. From taking care of her mother, she knew how to position him, how to hoist him into the truck. When she was finished, his clothes were packed, he was wearing a diaper, wheelchair and walker were in the back of the truck. He stared straight ahead.

The last thing she put in the truck was Rumble. Slowly, sadly, almost as if she wanted to leave Rumble, leave Wendy, behind. She sighed and locked the house door. She said, "Come on, girl." I jumped into the truck, between her and Arnold, and sat up so I could see where we were going.

Everything seemed in order outside. The fast food chains were doing a brisk business; the parking lots at grocery stores were crowded, like before a blizzard, but there was no hysteria. Perhaps no one really understood how long this might last. It was a government coup—them against us. It was spreading, as if a virus had engulfed the entire world. Maybe it had, spread by Allover.

After we had driven for most of the day, she pulled off a narrow country road and lifted a portable podcaster from the back seat, tucked it beneath her arm. She thrashed through the woods for a few minutes, found a flat rock, set it up, and turned it on.

It is a magnetic thing, the podding; the smacks. It is a precise frequency, except that it is constantly changing in order to elude the government, and you swallow it, and it disseminates into your cells and stays there for a while. That's all. You are an antenna, constantly conducting a blisteringly fast search, and you get Arnold's new smack. Or whoever's. Arnold's, as I said, was by far the pill most swallowed. Internationally. He was the most true, most courageous. Most energetic.

The most dangerous.

This setup would just help disguise the source.

She stood up straight and dusted off her hands. "There. They'll find it pretty soon—maybe. If they have time. It's kind of like a chain of bubbles though. One will release several, and those will release several. Time-delayed. Some for years. Mike and I went to Czechoslovakia right after it was returned to independence, in 1989. There was a museum exhibit there of all of the lost years, the years during which they'd been allowed no news. It was called Lest We Forget. Well, this is my Lest We Forget."

My laugh, and my tears, were just a bark.

A slight snow spits outside the cabin. Elizabeth has made it cozy and warm for Arnold. It is too hot for me, but I would rather stay in here with people than go outside and be comfortable. I am a dog.

I lie on the couch so I can look over Elizabeth's shoulder while she works. She is in touch with a hacker.

"I think he's in the Netherlands," she says to Arnold. "His name is The Great and Powerful U. You, get it? All of us; one of us. But maybe U is a woman." She takes a sip of coffee and resumes her work.

All the hackers want to figure out a universal hack that will leave us bare to one strong message, one big smack. But what will that message be? Most hackers don't really care. They just want to open everything up. For them, it's a game, a challenge. For most people, it's the ultimate fear: mind control.

But U seems to be addicted to Arnold's smacks. She believes in him, in his messages of the importance of truth and transparency. Every day, U posts, somewhere, about the latest smack that Elizabeth has brought up-to-date and released.

What is the truth? I know what the truth is. Truth is loss, death, grief, and pain, and knowing the preciousness of each individual. Truth is living always on that edge. Truth is trying to prevent all that from happening. Humans have a special way of forgetting truth, of not thinking about what others might feel. Have I said it? Memory is physical.

Knowing can be changed.

I slowly lick the white top of my paw, straighten the curly fur into smooth lines, feel with my tongue the smack-bump inside. It is just a tiny bump, but it is powerful. It contains the essence of what I distilled in the lab.

My brain is storm.

Much later, when it is dark and Elizabeth is making dinner, I lie on the floor, still licking the smack-bump. It itches. In front of me is the local newspaper which Jake brought and which Elizabeth tossed onto the floor. There is news of local militias, an ad for hen-fresh eggs on Angle Ridge Road, obituaries. I move my head so I can see the next page.

"Mi," says Arnold. "Kuh."

I start, as if I've had an electric shock. My tongue pauses. My ears swivel. I turn my head to look at him. I can't help it.

I know that the weird expression on his face is a smile.

How would he have known? I told you, his research network was astounding. He could find out anything he wanted to. He worked on many edges. Maybe he had a pod about what I'd done waiting in his library. He might even have tracked down Dr. Lorenzo, held her feet to the coals, forced her to talk.

It doesn't matter now.

I am asleep on the couch, but her sudden snort wakes me around one in the morning.

"Ha," she breathes. Her computer screen glows, the little keys are lit from within. The only other light is from the stove, where the fire flickers with soothing snaps. Arnold snores on the bed.

"U did it," she breathes. "She made the hack." Elizabeth starts the download. "Now, we've got them. Every fucking person in the world, no matter what kind of smack they usually get, no matter whose pill they've swallowed. And we've got to get to them first." She watches the screen, sighs. "Damn, this computer is slow."

It is dawn. I am on the porch. Elizabeth is inside, frantically modifying pods, as she does this time of day. Usually, we go for a long hike and put them in the relay in the woods. It is stupid and dangerous but she says that if she doesn't do this she might as well not be alive anyway.

Today is different, though. Today she has the hack.

Something—*something*—has me on my feet and drives my memories down to the tips of my paws, crushes them flat with the pure and absolute present.

My barks thunder and I am like an arrow running to the approaching vehicle. I meet it as it rounds the sharp bend at the top of the hill that keeps us hidden and leap to one side.

The soldier is alone in the jeep and surprised by me. There is no door on his jeep and I leap onto him, going for his throat.

He is yelling and I smell the cold metal of his pistol. I am a whirlwind but his other hand reaches the gun and draws. I bite his hand as the pistol goes off.

Elizabeth is on the porch, her shotgun raised. "Get away!" she yells and I know she means me but I cannot, I am a pure and total dog, with only a wisp of human somewhere.

She fires the rifle. He puts the jeep in reverse and flees.

And I know it's time.

"Are you all right?" She runs to me, hugs me. I ignore her. I am chewing, licking, gnawing. "Is it a bullet?"

No; the bullet went somewhere else, and it does not matter. It only makes a small sting, an ache.

She reaches into the bloody hole I gnawed and pulls out the blood-smeared bubble, a standard smack-storing bubble.

"A . . . *smack*?" She is stunned.

YES, I bark.

She stares at me, hard. "What are you?" She kicks me. "Some kind of spy?"

I run to the cabin, up the stairs; she follows. "They'll be coming soon. Arnold! Arnold! We have to leave! And Daisy . . ."

At the door, she whirls on me, still holding the rifle.

Arnold makes a grunting sound. Moves his arms. Makes a horrified face. I *bark! Bark! Bark!*

She looks back and forth between us. Arnold begins keening "hmmm hmmm hmmm hmmm . . ."

He can still kind of carry a tune. This is easy. The alphabet tune.

"All right then," she snaps. "Just one try. A? B? C? D? Oh, this is ridiculous!"

"Hmmmm," hums Arnold. As always, tears creep down his face. I smell his ocean-openness, coming back. And then, with great difficulty, he roars, "Mi. Mi. MIKE."

I bark, I dance.

Yes, I say yes with all my dog-tools. I grab Rumble, toss him in the air. It takes a surprising amount of energy.

"MIKE?"

I brace for another kick, but she hugs me and begins to sob. "Mike? Mike! Oh my God." She steps back, looks at Arnold. "How is this possible? How do you know?" I can see her thinking then, thinking about all the things I'd done as a memory scientist.

I nudge her pocket. The smack.

She pulls out the bloody, protective bubble. Then she grabs a knife, sets the bubble on the table, and carefully slits it open.

Out it falls, the smack that I so carefully, lovingly made.

I cringe back, whine.

"What is it?"

It is something I cannot do, because I am a dog.

But I must. Again, I pick up Rumble, and this time just hold him in my jaws. Then I put him down and lick his face.

"Okay," she says heavily. "Okay. Something to do with Wendy." Her shoulders sag. "I'll do it." Her smile is wan and she is crying. "First. Wendy goes first."

She puts the smack I made into the sequence that she has prepared. The sequence is prefaced by U's hack. After a minute, the smack is ready. All she has to do is press a key to send it.

On the Allover Station, firing seems to have gotten heavier this morning. I am not sure why the local soldiers haven't come back. Perhaps there is too much disarray. The television says so. The long, grinding, universal violence is creeping upward, always upward.

A deep, low growl shakes the ground. I hear loud cracking sounds. Out the window, I see the tips of trees topple.

"Must be a tank," says Elizabeth. "The bastards."

"Tuh," says Arnold. "Tuh. Gu. Nnnn." He gestures toward the rifle. He is healing. The smack, I think, might hurry things along. I bark, loudly. Go! Go! Go!

She does it. She makes the smack, biological information now converted into electrical signals, rush down the wires at the speed of light and just as quickly is in the air, relaying, disseminating, *smacking*.

The tank slowly comes round the bend, ponderously slow, and stops fifty yards from the cabin. A gun on top rotates, adjusts straight at us.

"Fu!" yells Arnold.

And then—

The top opens and three men climb out. They hug each other, they are crying.

The same thing is happening on the Allover Station. A reporter is in some war-torn downtown where suddenly everyone looks around, bewildered. Two men fling down their rifles. The same look, of awful grief, comes over their faces. Tears flow. They grab one another, reel around.

The television reporter is weeping too. "What is going on?" she cries out in a parody of the reporter's false concern. "What is going *on*? Sir?" She shoves her microphone in someone's face. "Sir? How do you feel?"

"I," he gasps. "I—oh, my god." He falls to his knees.

Elizabeth grabs me, hard. "Wendy," she whispers. "It's Wendy. Oh, God, I remember, oh, my sweet baby."

All that grief and longing. Now everyone feels it. Everyone feels the loss of just one child.

Just one precious person.

But there is no revenge. No anger. Because this is not just our grief, not just Elizabeth's and mine distilled and refined and full of blame. It is Jolly's: pure, whole love and longing.

That smack, and its heavy burden, and the chemicals it was secreting, are gone. Gone from my blood. Mike is leaving too, ebbing away. It is good. It is as I planned.

I did not plan the bullet. But it doesn't matter. I am, of course, happy.

"My god!" Elizabeth gasps. She just stares at me, then falls and hugs me, hugs me, hugs me. "You GENIUS!" I glimpse for a brief instant a look of horror on her face as she draws back her hand, sticky with blood, before I close my eyes, deeply satisfied.

This exquisite grief, this unwillingness to kill, this respect for all others, may last for years, universally, making loss impossible, removing the numbness that most people live with and leaving them raw and open and kind, unable to hurt another human. Or someone like The Wonderful Wizard of U might hack it quickly, just for fun, and make everything as it was.

I no longer care.

I am a brilliance, like when the sun is on the water and you can't see into it. I am the brilliance of Elizabeth and of Wendy, and then I am golden grains of glad, glad sand, blowing in the wind, free of almost all memory.

All that is left is one little girl, who stands there on the beach.

"Jolly!" she calls, and claps her hands. "Jolly!"

I run to her.

Pump Six

PAOLO BACIGALUPI

Paolo Bacigalupi (www.windupstories.com) *lives in Paonia, Colorado, where he has worked as a writer and online editor for* High Country News. *He said in a* Locus *interview, "we can have all the technology in the world and still make some really, really bad decisions. We can create a hell where nothing is left alive except for us, but where we can be very comfortable, because we'll accept whatever we have to in order to meet our immediate desires." His first story was "Pocketful of Dharma" (1999). He says, "Harlan Ellison called me up soon after . . . told me not to get stuck in the science fiction genre . . . and to get out while I could. . . . I ended up writing three novels, and none of them were sci-fi. One historical fiction piece. One contemporary "literary" (whatever) book. And one mystery. And then . . . decided that I actually liked writing science fiction quite a lot and went back to it." His short SF is collected in* Pump Six and Other Stories *(Night Shade, 2008). His first novel,* The Windup Girl, *is forthcoming from Night Shade.*

"Pump Six" was published in Fantasy & Science Fiction, *and as the title story in his 2008 collection. It is centrally in the tradition of Kornbluth's "The Marching Morons." In this bleak and darkly humorous view of the not very distant future, human selfishness and the pursuit of immediate pleasure have triumphed over intelligence and advanced technology. Pump Six is a sewage pump. And the literal shit is about to overflow civilization. Maybe you'll feel better if you take a pill.*

The first thing I saw Thursday morning when I walked into the kitchen was Maggie's ass sticking up in the air. Not a bad way to wake up, really. She's got a good figure, keeps herself in shape, so a morning eyeful of her pretty bottom pressed against a black mesh nightie is generally a positive way to start the day.

Except that she had her head in the oven. And the whole kitchen smelled like gas. And she had a lighter with a blue flame six inches high that she was waving around inside the oven like it was a Tickle Monkey revival concert.

"Jesus Christ, Maggie! What the hell are you doing?"

I dove across the kitchen, grabbed a handful of nightie and yanked hard. Her head banged as she came out of the oven. Frying pans rattled on the stovetop and she dropped her lighter. It skittered across the tuffscuff, ending up in a corner. "Owwwwww!" She grabbed her head. "Oooowwww!"

She spun around and slapped me. "What the fuck did you do that for?" She raked her nails across my cheek, then went for my eyes. I shoved her away. She slammed into the wall and spun, ready to come back again. "What's the matter with you?" she yelled. "You pissed off you couldn't get it up last night? Now you want to knock me around instead?" She grabbed the cast-iron skillet off the stovetop, dumping Nifty-Freeze bacon all over the burners. "You want to try again, trogwad? Huh? You want to?" She waved the pan, threatening, and started for me. "Come on then!"

I jumped back, rubbing my cheek where she'd gouged me. "You're crazy! I keep you from getting yourself blown up and you want to beat my head in?"

"I was making your damn breakfast!" She ran her fingers through her black tangled hair and showed me blood. "You broke my damn head!"

"I saved your dumb ass is what I did." I turned and started shoving the kitchen windows open, letting the gas escape. A couple of the windows were just cardboard curtains that were easy to pull free, but one of the remaining whole windows was really stuck.

"You sonofabitch!"

I turned just in time to dodge the skillet. I yanked it out of her hands and shoved her away, hard, then went back to opening windows. She came back, trying to get around in front of me as I pushed the windows open. Her nails were all over my face, scratching and scraping. I pushed her away again and waved the skillet when she tried to come back. "You want me to use this?"

She backed off, eyes on the pan. She circled. "That's all you got to say to me? 'I saved your dumb ass'?" Her face was red with anger. "How about 'Thanks for trying to fix the stove, Maggie,' or 'Thanks for giving a damn about whether I get a decent breakfast before work, Maggie.'" She hawked snot and spat, missing me and hitting the wall, then gave me the finger. "Make your own damn breakfast. See if I try to help you again."

I stared at her. "You're dumber than a sack of trogs, you know that?" I waved the skillet toward the stove. "Checking a gas leak with a lighter? Do you even have a brain in there? Hello? Hello?"

"Don't talk to me like that! You're the trogwad—" She choked off mid sentence and sat, suddenly, like she'd been hit in the head with a chunk of concrete rain. Just plopped on the yellow tuffscuff. Completely stunned.

"Oh." She looked up at me, wide-eyed. "I'm sorry, Trav. I didn't even think of that." She stared at her lighter where it lay in the corner. "Oh, shit. Wow." She put her head in her hands. "Oh . . . Wow."

She started to hiccup, then to cry. When she looked up at me again, her big brown eyes were full of tears. "I'm so sorry. I'm really really sorry." The tears started rolling, pouring off her cheeks. "I had no idea. I just didn't think. I. . . ."

I was still ready to fight, but seeing her sitting on the floor, all forlorn and lost and apologetic took it out of me.

"Forget it." I dropped the pan on the stove and went back to jamming open the windows. A breeze started moving through, and the gas stink faded. When we had some decent air circulation, I pulled the stove out from the wall. Bacon was scattered all over the burners, limp and thawed now that it was out of its NiftyFreeze cellophane, strips of pork lying everywhere, marbled and glistening with fat. Maggie's idea of a home-made breakfast. My granddad would have loved her. He was a big believer in breakfasts. Except for the NiftyFreeze. He hated those wrappers.

Maggie saw me staring at the bacon. "Can you fix the stove?"

"Not right now. I've got to get to work."

She wiped her eyes with the palm of her hand. "Waste of bacon," she said. "Sorry."

"No big deal."

"I had to go to six different stores to find it. That was the last package, and they didn't know when they were going to get more."

I didn't have anything to say to that. I found the gas shut-off and closed it. Sniffed. Then sniffed all around the stove and the rest of kitchen.

The gas smell was almost gone.

For the first time, I noticed my hands were shaking. I tried to get a coffee packet out of the cabinet and dropped it. It hit the counter with a water balloon plop. I set my twitching hands flat on the counter and leaned on them, hard, trying to make them go still. My elbows started shaking instead. It's not every morning you almost get yourself blown up.

It was kind of funny, though, when I thought about it. Half the time, the gas didn't even work. And on the one day it did, Maggie decided to play repairman. I had to suppress a giggle.

Maggie was still in the middle of the floor, snuffling. "I'm really sorry," she said again.

"It's okay. Forget it." I took my hands off the counter. They weren't flapping around anymore. That was something. I ripped open the coffee packet and chugged its liquid cold. After the rest of the morning, the caffeine was calming.

"No, I'm really sorry. I could have got us both killed."

I wanted to say something nasty but there wasn't any point. It just would have been cruel. "Well, you didn't. So it's okay." I pulled out a chair and sat down and looked out the open windows. The city's sky was turning from yellow dawn smog to a gray-blue morning smog. Down below, people were just starting their day. Their noises filtered up: Kids shouting on their way to school. Hand carts clattering on their way to deliveries. The grind of some truck's engine, clanking and squealing and sending up black clouds of exhaust that wafted in through the window along with summer heat. I fumbled for my inhaler and took a hit, then made myself smile at Maggie. "It's like that time you tried to clean the electric outlet with a fork. You just got to remember not to look for gas leaks with a fire. It's not a good idea."

Wrong thing to say, I guess. Or wrong tone of voice.

Maggie's waterworks started again: not just the snuffling and the tears, but the whole bawling squalling release thing, water pouring down her face, her nose getting all runny and her saying, "I'm sorry, I'm sorry, I'm sorry," over and over again, like a Ya Lu aud sample, but without the subsonic thump that would have made it fun to listen to.

I stared at the wall for a while, trying to wait it out, and thought about getting my earbug and listening to some real Ya Lu, but I didn't want to wear out the battery because it took a while to find good ones, and anyway, it didn't seem right to duck out while she was bawling. So I sat there while she kept crying, and then I finally sucked it up and got down on the floor next to her and held her while she wore herself out.

Finally she stopped crying and started wiping her eyes. "I'm sorry. I'll remember."

She must have seen my expression because she got more

insistent. "Really. I will." She used the shoulder of her nightie on her runny nose. "I must look awful."

She looked puffy and red-eyed and snotty. I said, "You look fine. Great. You look great."

"Liar." She smiled, then shook her head. "I didn't mean to melt down like that. And the frying pan. . . ." She shook her head again. "I must be PMS-ing."

"You take a Gynoloft?"

"I don't want to mess with my hormones. You know, just in case. . . ." She shook her head again. "I keep thinking maybe this time, but. . . ." She shrugged. "Never mind. I'm a mess." She leaned against me again and went quiet for a little bit. I could feel her breathing. "I just keep hoping," she said finally.

I stroked her hair. "If it's meant to happen, it will. We've just got to stay optimistic."

"Sure. That's up to God. I know that. I just keep hoping."

"It took Miku and Gabe three years. We've been trying, what, six months?"

"A year, month after next." She was quiet, then said, "Lizzi and Pearl only had miscarriages."

"We've got a ways to go before we start worrying about miscarriages." I disentangled and went hunting for another coffee packet in the cabinets. This one I actually took the time to shake. It heated itself and I tore it open and sipped. Not as good as the little brewer I found for Maggie at the flea market so she could make coffee on the stove, but it was a damn sight better than being blown to bits.

Maggie was getting herself arranged, getting up off the floor and starting to bustle around. Even all puffy faced, she still looked good in that mesh nightie: lots of skin, lots of interesting shadows.

She caught me watching her. "What are you smiling at?"

I shrugged. "You look nice in that nightie."

"I got it from that lady's estate sale, downstairs. It's hardly even used."

I leered. "I like it."

She laughed. "Now? You couldn't last night or the night before, but now you want to do it?"

I shrugged.

"You're going to be late as it is." She turned and started rustling in the cabinets herself. "You want a brekkie bar? I found a whole bunch of them when I was shopping for the bacon. I guess their factory is working again." She tossed one before I could answer. I caught it and tore off the smiling foil wrapper and read the ingredients while I ate. Fig and Nut, and then a whole bunch of nutrients like dextro-forma-albuterolhyde. Not as neat as the chemicals that thaw NiftyFreeze packets, but what the hell, it's all nutritional, right?

Maggie turned and studied the stove where I'd marooned it. With hot morning air blowing in from the windows, the bacon was getting limper and greasier by the second. I thought about taking it downstairs and frying it on the sidewalk. If nothing else, I could feed it to the trogs. Maggie was pinching her lip. I expected her to say something about the stove or wasting bacon, but instead she said, "We're going out for drinks with Nora tonight. She wants to go to Wicky."

"Pus girl?"

"That's not funny."

I jammed the rest of the brekkie bar into my mouth. "It is to me. I warned both of you. That water's not safe for anything."

She made a face. "Well nothing happened to me, smarty pants. We all looked at it and it wasn't yellow or sludgy or anything—"

"So you jumped right in and went swimming. And now she's got all those funny zits on her. How mysterious." I finished the second coffee packet and tossed it and the brekkie bar wrapper down the disposal and ran some water to wash them down. In another half hour, they'd be whirling and dissolving in the belly of Pump Two. "You can't go thinking something's clean, just because it looks clear. You got lucky." I wiped my hands and went over to her. I ran my fingers up her hips.

"Yep. Lucky. Still no reaction."

She slapped my hands away. "What, you're a doctor, now?"

"Specializing in skin creams. . . ."

"Don't be gross. I told Nora to meet us at eight. Can we go to Wicky?"

I shrugged. "I doubt it. It's pretty exclusive."

"But Max owes you—" she broke off as she caught me leering at her again. "Oh. Right."

"What do you say?"

She shook her head and grinned. "I should be glad, after the last couple nights."

"Exactly." I leaned down and kissed her.

When she finally pulled back, she looked up at me with those big brown eyes of hers and the whole bad morning just melted away. "You're going to be late," she said.

But her body was up against mine, and she wasn't slapping my hands away anymore.

Summer in New York is one of my least favorite times. The heat sits down between the buildings, choking everything, and the air just . . . stops. You smell everything. Plastics melting into hot concrete, garbage burning, old urine that effervesces into the air when someone throws water into the gutter; just the plain smell of so many people living all packed together. Like all the skyscrapers are sweating alcoholics after a binge, standing there exhausted and oozing with the evidence of everything they've been up to. It drives my asthma nuts. Some days, I take three hits off the inhaler just to get to work.

About the only good thing about summer is that it isn't spring so at least you don't have freeze-thaw dropping concrete rain down on your head.

I cut across the park just to give my lungs a break from the ooze and stink, but it wasn't much of an improvement. Even with the morning heat still building up, the trees looked dusty and tired, all their leaves drooping, and there were big brown patches on the grass where the green had just given up for the summer, like bald spots on an old dog.

The trogs were out in force, lying in the grass, lolling around in the dust and sun, enjoying another summer day with nothing to do. The weather was bringing them out. I stopped to watch them frolicking—all hairy and horny without any concerns at all.

A while back someone started a petition to get rid of them, or at least to get them spayed, but the mayor came out and said that they had some rights, too. After all, they were somebody's kids, even if no one was admitting it. He even got the police to stop beating them up so much, which made the tabloids go crazy. They all said he had a trog love child hidden in Connecticut. But after a few years, people got used to having them around. And the tabloids went out of business, so the mayor didn't care what they said about his love children anymore.

These days, the trogs are just part of the background, a whole parkful of mash-faced monkey people shambling around with bright yellow eyes and big pink tongues and not nearly enough fur to survive in the wild. When winter hits, they either freeze in piles or migrate down to warmer places. But every summer there's more of them.

When Maggie and I first started trying to have a baby, I had a nightmare that Maggie had a trog. She was holding it and smiling, right after the delivery, all sweaty and puffy and saying, "Isn't it beautiful? Isn't it beautiful?" and then she handed the sucker to me. And the scary thing wasn't that it was a trog; the scary thing was trying to figure out how I was going to explain to everyone at work that we were keeping it. Because I loved that little squash-faced critter. I guess that's what being a parent is all about.

That dream scared me limp for a month. Maggie put me on perkies because of it.

A trog sidled up. It—or he or she, or whatever you call a hermaphrodite critter with boobs and a big sausage—made kissy faces at me. I just smiled and shook my head and decided that it was a him because of his hairy back, and because he actually had that sausage, instead of just a little pencil like some of them have. The trog took the rejection pretty well. He just smiled and shrugged. That's one nice thing about them: they may be dumber than hamsters, but they're pleasant-natured. Nicer than most of the people I work with, really. Way nicer than some people you meet in the subway.

The trog wandered off, touching himself and grunting, and I kept going across the park. On the other side, I walked down a couple blocks to Freedom Street and then down the stairs into the command substation.

Chee was waiting for me when I unlocked the gates to let myself in.

"Alvarez! You're late, man."

Chee's a nervous skinny little guy with suspenders and red hair slicked straight back over a bald spot. He always has this acrid smell around him because of this steroid formula he uses on the bald spot, which makes his hair grow all right for a while, but then he starts picking at it compulsively and it all falls out and he has to start all over with the steroids, and in the meantime, he smells like the Hudson. And whatever the gel is, it makes his skull shine like a polished bowling ball. We used to tell him to stop using the stuff, but he'd go all rabid and try to bite you if you kept it up for long.

"You're late," he said again. He was scratching his head like an epileptic monkey trying to groom himself.

"Yeah? So?" I got my work jacket out of my locker and pulled it on. The fluorescents were all dim and flickery, but climate control was running, so the interior was actually pretty bearable, for once.

"Pump Six is broken."

"Broken how?"

Chee shrugged. "I don't know. It's stopped."

"Is it making a noise? Is it stopped all the way? Is it going slowly? Is it flooding? Come on, help me out."

Chee looked at me blankly. Even his head-picking stopped, for a second.

"You try looking at the troubleshooting indexes?" I asked.

Chee shrugged. "Didn't think of it."

"How many times have I told you, that's the first thing you do? How long has it been out?"

"Since midnight?" He screwed up his face, thinking. "No, since ten."

"You switch the flows over?"

He hit his forehead with the palm of his hand. "Forgot."

I started to run. "The entire Upper West Side doesn't have sewage processing since LAST NIGHT? Why didn't you call me?"

Chee jogged after me, dogging my heels as we ran through the plant's labyrinth to the control rooms. "You were off duty."

"So you just let it sit there?"

It's hard to shrug while you're running full-out, but Chee managed it. "Stuff's broken all the time. I didn't figure it was that bad. You know, there was that bulb out in tunnel three, and then there was that leak from the toilets. And then the drinking fountain went out again. You always let things slide. I figured I'd let you sleep."

I didn't bother trying to explain the difference. "If it happens again, just remember, if the pumps, any of them, die, you call me. It doesn't matter where I am, I won't be mad. You just call me. If we let these pumps go down, there's no telling how many people could get sick. There's bad stuff in that water, and we've got to stay on top of it, otherwise it bubbles up into the sewers and then it gets out in the air, and people get sick. You got it?"

I shoved open the doors to the control room, and stopped.

The floor was covered with toilet paper, rolls of it, all unstrung and dangled around the control room. Like some kind of mummy striptease had gone wrong. There must have been a hundred rolls unraveled all over the floor. "What the hell is this?"

"This?" He looked around, scratching his head.

"The paper, Chee."

"Oh. Right. We had a toilet paper fight last night. For some reason they triple delivered. We didn't have enough space in the storage closet. I mean, we haven't had ass wipes for two months, and then we had piles and piles of it—"

"So you had a toilet paper fight while Pump Six was down?"

Something in my voice must have finally gotten through. He cringed. "Hey, don't look at me that way. I'll get it picked up. No worries. Jeez. You're worse than Mercati. And anyway, it wasn't my fault. I was just getting ready to reload the dispensers and then Suze and Zoo came down and we got into this fight." He shrugged. "It was just something to do, that's all. And Suze started it, anyway."

I gave him another dirty look and kicked my way through the tangle of t.p. to the control consoles.

Chee called after me, "Hey, how am I going to wind it back up if you kick it around?"

I started throwing switches on the console, running diagnostics. I tried booting up the troubleshooting database, but got a connection error. Big surprise. I looked on the shelves for the hard copies of the operation and maintenance manuals, but they were missing. I looked at Chee. "Do you know where the manuals are?"

"The what?"

I pointed at the empty shelves.

"Oh. They're in the bathroom."

I looked at him. He looked back at me. I couldn't make myself ask. I just turned back to the consoles. "Go get them, I need to figure out what these flashers mean." There was a whole panel of them winking away at me, all for Pump Six.

Chee scuttled out of the room, dragging t.p. behind him. Overhead, I heard the Observation Room door open: Suze, coming down the stairs. More trouble. She rustled through the t.p. streamers and came up close behind me, crowding. I could feel her breathing on my neck.

"The pump's been down for almost twelve hours," she said. "I could write you up." She thumped me in the back, hard. "I could write you up, buddy." She did it again, harder. *Bam.*

I thought about hitting her back, but I wasn't going to give her another excuse to dock pay. Besides, she's bigger than me. And she's got more muscles than an orangutan. About as hairy, too. Instead, I said, "It would have helped if somebody had called."

"You talking back to me?" She gave me another shove and leaned around to get in my face, looking at me all squinty-eyed. "Twelve hours down-time," she said again. "That's grounds for a write-up. It's in the manual. I can do it."

"No kidding? You read that? All by yourself?"

"You're not the only one who can read, Alvarez." She turned and stomped back up the stairs to her office.

Chee came back lugging the maintenance manuals. "I don't know how you do this," he puffed as he handed them over. "These manuals make no sense at all."

"It's a talent."

I took the plastirene volumes and glanced up at Suze's office. She was just standing there, looking down at me through the observation glass, looking like she was going to come down and beat my head in. A dimwit promo who got lucky when the old boss went into retirement.

She has no idea what a boss does, so mostly she spends her time scowling at us, filling out paperwork that she can't remember how to route, and molesting her secretary. Employment guarantees are great for people like me, but I can see why you might want to fire someone; the only way Suze was ever going to leave was if she fell down the Observation Room stairs and broke her neck.

She scowled harder at me, trying to make me look away. I let her win. She'd either write me up, or she wouldn't. And even if she did, she might still get distracted and forget to file it. At any rate, she couldn't fire me. We were stuck together like a couple of cats tied in a sack.

I started thumbing through the manuals' plastic pages, going back and forth through the indexes as I cross-referenced all the flashers. I looked up again at the console. There were a lot of them. Maybe more than I'd ever seen.

Chee squatted down beside me, watching. He started picking his head again. I think it's a comfort thing for him. But it makes your skin crawl until you get used to it. Makes you think of lice.

"You do that fast," he said. "How come you didn't go to college?"

"You kidding?"

"No way, man. You're the smartest guy I ever met. You totally could have gone to college."

I glanced over at him, trying to tell if he was screwing with me. He looked back at me, completely sincere, like a dog waiting for a treat. I went back to the manual. "No ambition, I guess."

The truth was that I never made it through high school. I dropped out of P.S. 105 and never looked back. Or forward, I guess. I remember sitting in freshman algebra and watching the teacher's lips flap and not understanding a word he was saying. I turned in worksheets and got Ds every time, even after I redid them. None of the other kids were complaining, though. They just laughed at me when I kept asking him to explain the difference between squaring and doubling variables. You don't have to be Einstein to figure out where you don't belong.

I started piecing my way through the troubleshooting diagrams. No clogs indicated. Go to Mechanics Diagnostics, Volume Three. I picked up the next binder of pages and started flipping. "Anyway, you've got a bad frame of reference. We aren't exactly a bunch of Nobel Prize winners here." I glanced up at Suze's office. "Smart people don't work in dumps like this." Suze was scowling down at me again. I gave her the universal salute. "You see?"

Chee shrugged. "I dunno. I tried reading that manual about twenty times on the john, and it still doesn't make any sense to me. If you weren't around, half the city would be swimming in shit right now."

Another flasher winked on the console: amber, amber, red. . . . It stayed red.

"In a couple minutes they're going to be swimming in a lot worse than that. Believe me, buddy, there's lots worse things than shit. Mercati showed me a list once, before he retired. All the things that run through here that the pumps are supposed to clean: polychlorinated biphenyls, bisphenyl-A, estrogen, phlalates, PCBs, heptachlor. . . ."

"I got a Super Clean sticker for all that stuff." He lifted his shirt and showed me the one he had stuck to his skin, right below his rib cage. A yellow smiley face sticker a little like the kind I used to get from my grandpa when he was feeling generous. It said SUPER CLEAN on the smiley's forehead.

"You buy those?"

"Sure. Seven bucks for seven. I get 'em every week. I can drink the water straight, now. I'd even drink out of the Hudson." He started scratching his skull again.

I watched him scratch for a second, remembering how zit girl Nora had tried to sell some to Maria before they went swimming. "Well, I'm glad it's working for you." I turned and started keying restart sequences for the pumps. "Now let's see if we can get this sucker started up, and keep all the neighbors who don't buy stickers from having a pack of trogs. Get ready to pull a reboot on my say-so."

Chee went over to clear the data lines and put his hands on the restart levers. "I don't know what difference it makes. I went through the park the other day and you know what I saw? A mama trog and five little baby trogs. What good does it do to keep trogs from getting born to good folks, when you got those ones down in the park making whole litters?"

I looked over at Chee to say something back, but he kind of had a point. The reboot sequences completed and Pump Six's indicators showed primed. "Three . . . two . . . one. . . . Primed full," I said. "Go. Go. Go."

Chee threw his levers and the consoles cleared green and somewhere deep down below us, sewage started pumping again.

We climbed the skin of the Kusovic Center, climbing for heaven, climbing for Wicky. Maggie and Nora and Wu and me, worming our way up through stairwell turns, scrambling over rubble, kicking past condom wrappers and scattering Effy packets like autumn leaves. Wicky's synthesized xylophones and Japanese kettle drums thrummed, urging us higher. Trogs and sadsack partiers who didn't have my connections watched jealously as we climbed. Watched and whispered as we passed them by, all of them knowing that Max owed me favors and favors and favors and that I went to the front of the line because I kept the toilets running on time.

The club was perched at the very top of the Kusovic, a bunch of old stock broker offices. Max had torn down the

glass cubicles and the old digital wallscreens that used to
track the NYSE and had really opened the space up. Unfortunately, the club wasn't much good in the winter anymore
because we'd all gotten rowdy one night and shoved out the
windows. But even if it was too damn breezy half the year,
watching those windows falling had been a major high point
at the club. A couple years later people were still talking
about it, and I could still remember the slow way they came
out of their frames and tumbled and sailed through the air.
And when they hit bottom, they splashed across the streets
like giant buckets of water.

At any rate, the open-air thing worked really good in the
summer, with all the rolling brownouts that were always
knocking out the A/C.

I got a shot of Effy as we went in the door, and the club
rode in on a wave of primal flesh, a tribal gathering of sweaty
jumping monkeys in half-torn business suits, all of us going
crazy and eyeball wide until our faces were as pale and big
as fish wallowing in the bottom of the ocean.

Maggie was smiling at me as we danced and our whole
oven fight was completely behind us. I was glad about that,
because after our fork-in-the-outlet fight, she acted like it
was my fault for a week, even after she said she forgave me.
But now, in the dance throb of Wicky, I was her white knight
again, and I was glad to be with her, even if it meant dragging Nora along.

All the way up the stairs, I'd tried to not stare at Nora's
zit-pocked skin or make fun of her swollen-up face but she
knew what I was thinking because she kept giving me dirty
looks whenever I warned her to step around places where
the stairway was crumbling. Talk about stupid, though.
She's about as sharp as a marble. I won't drink or swim in
any of the water around here. It comes from working with
sewage all the time. You know way too much about everything that goes in and out of the system. People like Nora
put a Kali-Mary pendant between their tits or stick a Super
Clean smiley to their ass cheek and hope for the best. I drink
bottled water and only shower with a filter head. And sometimes I still get creeped out. No pus rashes, though.

The kettle drums throbbed inside my eyeballs. Across the club, Nora was dancing with Wu and now that my Effy was kicking into overdrive, I could see her positive qualities: she danced fast and furious . . . her hair was long and black . . . her zits were the size of breasts.

They looked succulent.

I sidled up to her and tried to apologize for not appreciating her before, but between the noise and my slobbering on her skin, I guess I failed to communicate effectively. She ran away before I could make it up to her and I ended up bouncing alone in Wicky's kettle drum womb while the crowds rode in and out around me and the Effy built up in ocean throbs that ran from my eyeballs to my crotch and back again, bouncing me higher and higher and higher. . . .

A girl in torn knee socks and a nun's habit was mewling in the bathroom when Maggie found us and pulled us apart and took me on the floor with people walking around us and trying to use the stainless steel piss troughs, but then Max grabbed me and I couldn't tell if we'd been doing it on the bar and if that was the problem or if I was just taking a leak in the wrong place but Max kept complaining about bubbles in his gin and a riot a riot a RIOT that he was going to have on his hands if these Effy freaks didn't get their liquor and he shoved me down under the bar where tubes come out of vats of gin and tonic and it was like floating inside the guts of an octopus with the waves of the kettle drums booming away above me.

I wanted to sleep down there, maybe hunt for the nun's red panties except that Max kept coming back to me with more Effy and saying we had to find the problem, the bubbly problem the bubbly problem, take some of this it will clear your damn head, find where the bubbles come from, where they fill the gin. No no no! The tonic the tonic the tonic! No bubbles in the tonic. Find the tonic. Stop the RIOT, make it all okay before the gag-gas trucks come and shut us down and dammit what are you sniffing down under there?

Swimming under the bar. . . . Swimming long and low . . . eyeballs wide . . . prehistoric fishy amongst giant mossy root-laced eggs, buried under the mist of the swamp, down with the bar rags and the lost spoons and the sticky slime of bar sugar, and these huge dead silver eggs lying under the roots, growing moss and mildew but nothing else, no yolky tonic coming out of these suckers, been sucked dry, sucked full dry by too many thirsty dinosaurs and of course that's the problem. No tonic. None. None at all.

More eggs! More eggs! We need more eggs! More big silver tonic dispensing eggs need to rumble in on handtrucks and roll in on whitejacketed bow-tie bartender backs. More eggs need to take the prod from the long root green sucking tubes and then we can suck the tonic of their yolk out, and Max can keep on making g-and-t's and I'm a hero hey hey hey a hero a goddamn superstar because I know a lot about silver eggs and how to stick in the right tubes and isn't that why Maggie's always pissed at me because my tube is never ready to stick into her eggs, or maybe she's got no eggs to stick and we sure as hell aren't going to the doctor to find out she's got no eggs and no replacements either, not a single one coming in on a handtruck and isn't that why she's out in the crowd bouncing in a black corset with a guy licking her feet and giving me the finger?

And isn't that why we're going to have a RIOT now when I beat that trogwad's head in with this chunk of bar that I'm going to get Max to loan me . . . except I'm too far underwater to beat up boot licker. And little smoking piles of Effy keep blooming on the floor, and we're all lapping them up because I'm a goddamn hero a hero a hero, the fixit man of all fixit men, and everyone bows and scrapes and passes me Effy because there isn't going to be a RIOT and we won't get shut down with gag-gas, and we won't do the vomit crawl down the stairwells to the streets.

And then Max shoves me back onto the dance floor with more shots of Effy for Maggie, a big old tray of forgiveness, and forgiveness comes easy when we're all walking on the ceiling of the biggest oldest skyscraper in the sky.

Blue kettle drums and eyeball nuns. Zits and dinner dates. Down the stairs and into the streets.

By the time we stumbled out of Wicky I was finally coming out of the Effy folds but Maggie was still flying, running her hands all over me, touching me, telling me what she was going to do to me when we got home. Nora and Wu were supposed to be with us, but somehow we'd gotten separated. Maggie wasn't interested in waiting around so we headed uptown, stumbling between the big old city towers, winding around sidewalk stink ads for Diabolo and Possession, and dodging fishdog stands with after-bar octopi on a stick.

The night was finally cool, in the sweet spot between end of midnight swelter and beginning of morning smother. There was a blanket of humidity, wet on us, and seductive after the club. Without rain or freezes, I barely had to watch for concrete rain at all.

Maggie ran her hands up and down my arm as we walked, occasionally leaning in close to kiss my cheek and nibble on my ear. "Max says you're amazing. You saved the day."

I shrugged. "It wasn't a big deal."

The whole bar thing was pretty hazy, bubbled-out by all the Effy I'd done. My skin was still singing from it. Mostly what I had was a warm glow right in my crotch and a stuttery view of the dark streets and the long rows of candles in the windows of the towers, but Maggie's hand felt good, and she looked good, and I had some plans of my own for when we got back to the apartment, so I knew I was coming down nice and slow, like falling into a warm featherbed full of helium and tongues.

"Anyone could have figured out his tonic was empty, if we hadn't all been so damn high." I stopped in front of a bank of autovendors. Three of them were sold out, and one was broken open, but there were still a couple drinks in the last one. I dropped my money in and chose a bottle of Blue Vitality for her, and a Sweatshine for me. It was a pleasant surprise when the machine kicked out the bottles.

"Wow!" Maggie beamed at me.

I grinned and fished out her bottle. "Lucky night, I guess: first the bar, now this."

"I don't think the bar thing was luck. I wouldn't have thought of it." She downed her Blue Vitality in two long swallows, and giggled. "And you did it when your eyes were as big as a fish. You were doing handstands on the bar."

I didn't remember that. Bar sugar and red lace bras, I remembered. But not handstands. "I don't see how Max keeps that place going when he can't even remember to restock."

Maggie rubbed up against me. "Wicky's a lot better than most clubs. And anyway, that's why he's got you. A real live hero." She giggled again. "I'm glad we didn't have to fight our way out of another riot. I hate that."

In an alley, some trogs were making it. Clustered bodies, hermaphroditic, climbing on each other and humping, their mouths open, smiling and panting. I glanced at them and kept going, but Maggie grabbed my arm and tugged me back.

The trogs were really going at it, all in a flounder, three of them piled, their skins gleaming with sweat slick and saliva. They looked back at us with yellow eyes and not a bit of shame. They just smiled and got into a heavy groaning rhythm.

"I can't believe how much they *do* it," Maggie whispered. She gripped my arm, pressing against me. "They're like dogs."

"That's about how smart they are."

They changed positions, one crouching as though Maggie's words had inspired them. The others piled on top of him . . . or her. Maggie's hand slid to the front of my pants, fumbled with the zipper and reached inside. "They're so. . . . Oh, God." She pulled me close and started working on my belt, almost tearing at it.

"What the hell?" I tried to push her off, but she was all over me, her hands reaching inside my pants, touching me, making me hard. The Effy was still working, that was for sure.

"Let's do it, too. Here. I want you."

"Are you crazy?"

"They don't care. Come on. Maybe this time it'll take. Knock me up." She touched me, her eyes widening at my sudden size. "You're never like this." She touched me again. "Oh God. Please." She pressed herself against me, looking over at the trogs. "Like that. Just like that." She pulled off her shimmersilk blouse, exposing her black corset and the pale skin of her breasts.

I stared at her skin and curves. That beautiful body she'd teased me with all night long. Suddenly I didn't care about the trogs or the few people walking by on the street. We both yanked at my belt. My pants fell down around my ankles. We slammed up against the alley wall, pressing against old concrete and staring into each other's eyes and then she pulled me into her and her lips were on my ear, biting and panting and whispering as we moved against each other.

The trogs just grinned and grinned and watched us with their big yellow eyes as we all shared the alley, and all watched each other.

At five in the morning, Chee called again, his voice coming straight into my head through my earbug. In all the excitement and Effy, I'd forgotten to take it out. Pump Six was down again. "You said I was supposed to call you," he whined.

I groaned and dragged myself out of bed. "Yeah. Yeah. I did. Don't worry about it. You did good. I'll be there."

Maggie rolled over. "Where you going?"

I pulled on my pants and gave her a quick kiss. "Got to go save the world."

"They work you too hard. I don't think you should go."

"And let Chee sort it out? You've got to be kidding. We'd be up to our necks in sludge by dinner time."

"My hero." She smiled sleepily. "See if you can find me some donuts when you come back. I feel pregnant."

She looked so happy and warm and fuzzy I almost climbed back into bed with her, but I fought off the urge and just gave her another kiss. "Will do."

Outside, light was just starting to break in the sky, a slow yellowing of the smog. The streets were almost silent at the early hour. It was hard not to be bitter about being up at this ungodly hungover time, but it was better than having to deal with the sewage backup if Chee hadn't called. I headed downtown and bought a bagel from a girly-faced guy who didn't know how to make change.

The bagel was wrapped in some kind of plastic film that dissolved when I put it in my mouth. It wasn't bad, but it ticked me off that bagel boy got confused with the change and needed me to go into his cash pouch and count out my own money.

It seems like I always end up bailing everyone out. Even dumb bagel guys. Maggie says I'm as compulsive as Chee. She would have just stood there and waited until bagel boy sorted it out, even if it took all day. But I have a damn hard time watching some trogwad drop dollars all over the sidewalk. Sometimes it's just easier to climb out of the oatmeal and do things yourself.

Chee was waiting for me when I got in, practically bouncing up and down. Five pumps down, now.

"It started with just one when I called you, but now there's five. They keep shutting off."

I went into the control room. The troubleshooting database was still down so I grabbed the hardcopy manuals again. Weird how the pumps were all going off-line like that. The control room, normally alive with the hum of the machines, was quieter with half of them down. Around the city, sewage lines were backing up as we failed to cycle waste into the treatment facilities and pump the treated water out into the river.

I thought about Nora with her rash, thanks to swimming in that gunk. It could really make you nervous. Looks clean, makes you rash. And we're at the bottom of the river. It's not just our crap in it. Everyone upstream, too. Our treatment plants pump water up from underground or pipe it in and treat it from lakes upstate. At least that's the theory. I don't really buy it; I've seen the amount of water we move through here and there's no way it's all coming from the lakes. In reality, we've got twenty-million-odd people all sucking water that we don't know where it's coming from or what's in it. Like I said, I drink bottled water even if I have to hike all over the city to find it. Or soda water. Or . . . tonic, even.

I closed my eyes, trying to piece the evening back together. All those empty canisters of tonic under the bar. Travis Alvarez saves the world while flying to the moon on Effy, and two rounds of sex yesterday.

Hell, yeah.

Chee and I brought the PressureDynes up one by one. All of them came back online except Pump Six. It was stubborn. We reprimed it. Fired. Reprimed. Nothing.

Suze came down to backseat drive, dragging Zoo, her secretary, behind her. Suze was completely strung out. Her blouse was half-tucked in, and she had big old fishy Effy eyes that were almost as red as the flashers on the console. But her fishy eyes narrowed when she saw all the flashers. "How come all these pumps went down? It's your job to keep them working."

I just looked at her. Zoned out of her mind at six A.M., romping around with her secretary girlfriend while she tried to crack the whip on the rest of us. Now that's leadership. Suddenly I thought that maybe I needed to get a different job. Or needed to start licking big piles of Effy before I came to work. Anything to take the edge off Suze.

"If you want me to fix it, I'll need you to clear out so I can concentrate."

Suze looked at me like she was chewing on a lemon. "You better get it fixed." She poked my chest with a thick finger. "If you don't, I'm making Chee your boss." She glanced at Zoo. "It's your turn on the couch. Come on." They trooped off.

Chee watched them go. He started picking at his head. "They never do any work," he said.

Another flasher went amber on the console. I flipped through the manual, hunting for a reason. "Who does? A job like this, where nobody gets fired?"

"Yeah, but there ought to be a way to get rid of her, at least. She moved all her home furniture into the office, the other day. She never goes home now. Says she likes the A/C here."

"You shouldn't complain. You're the guy who was throwing t.p. around yesterday."

He looked at me, puzzled. "So?"

I shrugged. "Never mind. Don't worry about Suze. We're the bottom of the pile, Chee. Get used to it. Let's try the reboot again."

It didn't work.

I went back to the manual. Sludge was probably coming up a hundred thousand toilets in the city by now. Weird how all the pumps shut down like that: one, two, three, four. I closed my eyes, thinking. Something about my Effy spree kept tickling the back of my head. Effy flashbacks, for sure. But they kept coming: big old eggs, big old silver eggs, all of them sucked dry by egg-slurping dinosaurs. Wow. That was some kind of weird spree. Nuns and stainless steel eggs. The urinals and Maggie . . . I blinked. Everything clicked. Pieces of the puzzle coming together. Cosmic Effy convergence: Emptied silver eggs. Max forgetting to restock his bar.

I looked up at Chee, then down at the manuals, then back up at Chee. "How long have we been running these pumps?"

"What do you mean?"

"When did they get installed?"

Chee stared at the ceiling, picked his head thoughtfully. "Hell if I know. Before I came on, that's for sure."

"Me too. I've been here nine years. Have we got a computer that would tell us that? A receipt? Something?" I flipped to the front of the manual in my hands. "Pressure-Dyne: Hi-Capacity, Self-Purging, Multi-Platform Pumping Engine. Model 13-44474-888." I frowned. "This manual was printed in 2020."

Chee whistled and leaned over to finger the plasticized pages. "That's pretty damn old."

"Built to last, right? People built things to last, back then."

"More than a hundred years?" He shrugged. "I had a car like that, once. Real solid. Engine hardly had any rust on it at all. And it had both headlights. But too damn old." He picked something out of his scalp and examined it for a second before flicking it onto the floor. "No one works on cars anymore. I can't remember the last time I saw a taxi running."

I looked at him, trying to decide if I wanted to say anything about flicking scalp on the floor, then just gave it up. I flipped through the manual some more until I found the part I wanted: "Individual Reporting Modules: Remote Access, Connectivity Features, and Data Collection." Following the manual's instructions, I opened a new set of diagnostic windows that bypassed the PressureDynes' generalized reports for pump station managers and instead connected directly with the pumps' raw log data. What I got was: "Host source data not found."

Big surprise.

The rest of the error text advised me to check the remote reporting module extension connectors, whatever those were. I closed the manual and tucked it under my arm. "Come on. I think I know what's wrong." I led Chee out of the control room and down into the bowels of the tunnels and plant system. The elevator was busted so we had to take the access stairs.

As we went deeper and deeper, darkness closed in. Grit and dust were everywhere. Rats skittered away from us. Isolated LEDs kept the stairwell visible, but barely. Dust and shadows and moving rats were all you could see in the dim amber. Eventually even the LEDs gave out. Chee found an emergency lantern in a wall socket, blanketed with gray fluffy dust, but it still had a charge. My asthma started to tickle and close in, sitting on my chest from all the crud in the air. I took a hit off my inhaler, and we kept going down. Finally, we hit bottom.

Light from Chee's lantern wavered and disappeared in the cavern's darkness. The metal of the PressureDynes glinted dimly. Chee sneezed. The motion sent his lantern rocking. Shadows shifted crazily until he used a hand to stop it. "You can't see shit down here," he muttered.

"Shut up. I'm thinking."

"I've never been down here."

"I came down, once. When I first came on. When Mercati was still alive."

"No wonder you act like him. He trained you?"

"Sure." I hunted around for the emergency lighting.

Mercati had shown the switches to me when he brought me down, nearly a decade before, and told me about the pumps. He'd been old then, but still working, and I liked the guy. He had a way of paying attention to things. Focused. Not like most people who can barely say hello to you before they start looking at their watch, or planning their party schedule, or complaining about their skin rashes. He used to say my teachers didn't know shit about algebra and that I should have stayed in school. Even knowing that he was just comparing me to Suze, I thought it was a pretty nice thing for him to say.

No one knew the pump systems as well as he did, so even after he got sick and I took over his job, I'd still sneak out to the hospital to ask him questions. He was my secret weapon until the cancer finally took out his guts.

I found the emergency lighting and pulled the switches. Fluorescent lights flickered, and came alive, buzzing. Some bulbs didn't come on, but there were enough.

Chee gasped. "They're huge."

A cathedral of engineering. Overhead, pipes arched through cavern dimness, shimmering under the muted light of the fluorescents, an interconnecting web of iron and shadows that centered in complex rosettes around the ranked loom of the pumps.

They towered over us, gleaming dully, three stories tall, steel dinosaurs. Dust mantled them. Rust blossoms patterned their hides in complex overlays that made them look like they'd been draped in oriental rugs. Pentagonal bolts as big as my hands studded their armored plating and stitched together the vast sectioned pipes that spanned the darkness and shot down black tunnels in every compass direction, reaching for every neighborhood in the city. Moisture jewels gleamed and dripped from ancient joints. The pumps thrummed on. Perfectly designed. Forgotten by everyone in the city above. Beasts working without complaint, loyal despite abandonment.

Except that one of them had now gone silent.

I stifled an urge to get down on my knees and apologize for neglecting them, for betraying these loyal machines that had run for more than a century.

I went over to Pump Six's control panel, and stroked the dinosaur's vast belly where it loomed over me. The control panel was all covered with dust, but it glowed when I ran my hand over it. Amber signals and lime text glowing authoritatively, telling me just what was wrong, telling me and telling me, and never complaining that I hadn't been listening.

Raw data had stopped piping up to the control room at some point, and had instead sat in the dark, waiting for someone to come down and notice it. And the raw data was the answer to all my questions. At the top of the list: Model 13-44474-888, Requires Scheduled Maintenance. 946,080,000 cycles completed.

I ran through the pump diagnostics:

Valve Ring Part# 12-33939, Scheduled for Replacement.

Piston Parts# 232-2, 222-5, 222-6, 222-4-1, Scheduled for Replacement.

Displacement Catch Reservoir, Part# 37-37-375-77, Damaged, Replace.

Emergency Release Trigger Bearing, Part# 810-9, Damaged, Replace.

Valve Kit, Part# 437834-13, Damaged, Replace.

Master Drive Regulator, Part# 39-23-9834959-5, Damaged, Replace.

Priority Maintenance:

Compression Sensors, Part# 49-4, Part# 7777-302, Part# 403-74698

Primary Train, Part# 010303-0

Gurney Belt Valve, Part# 9-0-2 . . .

The list went on. I keyed into the maintenance history. The list opened up, running well into Mercati's tenure and even before, dozens of maintenance triggers and scheduled work requests, all of them blinking down here in the darkness, and ignored. Twenty-five years of neglect.

"Hey!" Chee called. "Check this out! They left magazines down here!"

I glanced over. He'd found a pile of trash someone had stuffed under one of the pumps. He was down on his hands and knees, reaching underneath, rooting things out: magazines, what looked like old food wrappers. I started to tell him to quit messing with stuff, but then I let it go. At least he wasn't breaking anything. I rubbed my eyes and went back to the pump diagnostics.

For the six years I'd been in charge, there were over a dozen errors displayed, but the PressureDynes had just kept going, chugging away as bits and pieces of them rattled away, and now, suddenly this one had given way completely, coming apart at the seams, loyally chugging until it just couldn't go on anymore and the maintenance backlog finally took the sucker down. I went over and started looking at the logs for the nine other pumps.

Every one of them was riddled with neglect: warning dumps, data logs full of error corrections, alarm triggers.

I went back to Pump Six and looked at its logs again. The men who'd built the machines had built them to last, but enough tiny little knives can still kill a big old dinosaur, and this one was beyond dead.

"We'll need to call PressureDyne," I said. "This thing is going to need more help than we can give it."

Chee looked up from a found magazine with a bright yellow car on the cover. "Do they even exist anymore?"

"They better." I grabbed the manual and looked up their customer support number.

It wasn't even in the same format as our numbers. Not a single letter of the alphabet in the whole damn thing.

Not only did PressureDyne not exist, they'd gone bankrupt more than forty years ago, victims of their overly well-designed pump products. They'd killed their own market. The only bright spot was that their technology had slouched into the public domain, and the net was up for once, so I could download schematics of the PressureDynes. There was a ton of information, except I didn't know anyone who could understand any of it. I sure couldn't.

I leaned back in my desk chair, staring at all that information I couldn't use. Like looking at Egyptian hiero-glyphs. Something was there, but it sure beat me what I was supposed to do with it. I'd shifted the flows for Pump Six over to the rest of the pumps, and they were handling the new load, but it made me nervous thinking about all those maintenance warnings glowing down there in the dark: Mercury Extender Seal, Part# 5974-30, Damaged, Replace . . . whatever the hell that meant. I downloaded everything about the PressureDynes onto my phone bug, not sure who I'd take it to, but damn sure no one here was going to be able to help.

"What are you doing with that?"

I jumped and looked around. Suze had snuck up on me.

I shrugged. "Dunno. See if I can find someone to help, I guess."

"That's proprietary. You can't take those schematics out of here. Wipe it."

"You're crazy. It's public domain." I got up and popped my phone bug back into my ear. She made a swipe at it, but I dodged and headed for the doors.

She chased after me, a mean mountain of muscle. "I could fire you, you know!"

"Not if I quit first." I yanked open the control room door and ducked out.

"Hey! Get back here! I'm your boss." Her voice followed me down the corridor, getting fainter. "I'm in charge here, dammit. I can fire you! It's in the manual! I found it! You're not the only one who can read! I found it! I can fire you! I will!" Like a little kid, having a fit. She was still yelling when the control room doors finally shut her off.

Outside, in the sunshine, I ended up wandering in the park, watching the trogs, and wondering what I did to piss off God that he stuck me with a nutjob like Suze. I thought about calling Maggie to meet me, but I didn't feel like telling her about work—half the time when I tried to explain stuff to her, she just came up with bad ideas to fix it, or didn't think the things I was talking about were such a big deal—and if I called up halfway through the day she'd definitely wonder why I'd left so early, and what was going on, and then when I didn't take her advice about Suze she'd just get annoyed.

I kept passing trogs humping away and smiling. They waved at me to come over and play. I just waved back. One of them must have been a real girl, because she was distendedly obviously pregnant, bouncing away with a couple of her friends, and I was glad again that Maggie wasn't with me. She had enough pregnancy hang-ups without seeing the trogs breeding.

I wouldn't have minded throwing Suze to the trogs, though. She was about as dumb as one. Christ, I was surrounded by dummies. I needed a new job. Someplace that attracted better talent than sewage work did. I wondered how serious Suze had been about trying to fire me. If there really was something in the manuals that we'd all missed about hiring and firing. And then I wondered how serious I was about quitting. I sure hated Suze. But how did you get a better job when you hadn't finished high school, let alone college?

I stopped short. Sudden enlightenment: College. Columbia. They could help. They'd have some sharpie who could understand all the PressureDyne information. An engineering department, or something. They were even dependent on Pump Six. Talk about leverage.

I headed uptown on the subway with a whole pack of snarly pissed-off commuters, everyone scowling at each other and acting like you were stealing their territory if you sat down next to them. I ended up hanging from a strap and watching two old guys hiss at each other across the car until we broke down at 86th and we all ended up walking.

I kept passing clumps of trogs, lounging around on the sidewalks. A few of the really smart ones were panhandling, but most of them were just humping away. I would have been annoyed at having to shove through the orgy, if I wasn't actually feeling jealous. I kept wondering why the hell was I out here in the sweaty summer smog taking hits off my inhaler while Suze and Chee and Zoo were all hanging around in air-con comfort and basically doing nothing.

What was wrong with me? Why was I the one who always tried to fix things? Mercati had been like that, always taking stuff on and then just getting worked harder and harder until the cancer ate him from the inside out. He was working so hard at the end I think he might have been glad to go, just for the rest.

Maggie always said they worked me too hard, and as I dragged my ass up Broadway, I started thinking she was right. Then again, if I left things to Chee and Suze, I'd be swimming up the Broadway River in a stew of crap and chemicals instead of walking up a street. Maggie would have said that was someone else's problem, but she just thought so because when she flushed the toilet, it still worked. At the end of the day, it seemed like some people just got stuck dealing with the shit, and some people figured out how to have a good time.

A half-hour later, covered with sweat and street grime and holding a half-empty squirt bottle of rehydrating Sweatshine that I'd stolen from an unwary trog, I rolled through Columbia's gates and into the main quad, where I immediately ran into problems.

I kept following signs for the engineering building, but they kept sending me around in circles. I would have asked for directions—I'm not one of those guys who can't—but it's pretty damn embarrassing when you can't even follow a simple sign, so I held off.

And really, who was I going to ask? There were lots of kids out in the quad, all sprawled out and wearing basically nothing and looking like they were starting a trog colony of their own, but I didn't feel like talking to them. I'm not a prude, but you've got to draw the line somewhere.

I ended up wandering around lost, going from one building to the next, stumbling through a jumble of big old Roman- and Ben Franklin-style buildings: lots of columns and brick and patchy green quads—everything looking like it was about to start raining concrete any second—trying to figure out why I couldn't understand any of the signs.

Finally, I sucked it up and asked a couple half-naked kids for directions.

The thing that ticks me off about academic types is that they always act like they're smarter than you. Rich-kid, free-ride, prep-school ones are the worst. I kept asking the best and brightest for directions, trying to get them to take me to the engineering department, or the engineering building, or whatever the hell it was, and they all just looked me up and down and gibbered at me like monkeys, or else laughed through their Effy highs and kept on going. A couple of them gave me a shrug and a "dunno," but that was the best I got.

I gave up on directions, and just kept roaming. I don't know how long I wandered. Eventually I found a big old building off one of the quads, a big square thing with pillars like the Parthenon. A few kids were sprawled out on the steps, soaking up the sun, but it was one of the quietest parts of the campus I'd seen.

The first set of doors I tried was chained, and so was the second, but then I found a set where the chain had been left undone, two heavy lengths of it, dangling with an old open padlock on the end. The kids on the steps were ignoring me, so I yanked open the doors.

Inside, everything was silence and dust. Big old chandeliers hung down from the ceiling, sparkling with orangey light that filtered in through the dirt on the windows. The light made it feel like it was the end of day with the sun starting to set, even though it was only a little past noon. A heavy blanket of dust covered everything; floors and reading tables and chairs and computers all had a thick gray film over them.

"Hello?"

No one answered. My voice echoed and died, like the building had just swallowed up the sound. I started wandering, picking doorways at random: reading rooms, study carrels, more dead computers, but most of all, books. Aisles and aisles with racks full of them. Room after room stuffed with books, all of them covered with thick layers of dust.

A library. A whole damn library in the middle of a university, and not a single person in it. There were tracks on the floor, and a litter of Effy packets, condom wrappers, and liquor bottles where people had come and gone at some point, but even the trash had its own fine layer of dust.

In some rooms, all the books had been yanked off the

shelves like a tornado had ripped through. In one, someone had made a bonfire out of them. They lay in a huge heap, completely torched, a pile of ash and pages and backings, a jumble of black ash fossils that crumbled to nothing when I crouched down and touched them. I stood quickly, wiping my hands on my pants. It was like fingering someone's bones.

I kept wandering, running my fingers along shelves and watching the dust cascade like miniature falls of concrete rain. I pulled down a book at random. More dust poured off and puffed up in my face. I coughed. My chest seized and I took a hit off my inhaler. In the dimness, I could barely make out the title: "Post-Liberation America. A Modern Perspective." When I opened it, its spine cracked.

"What are you doing here?"

I jumped back and dropped the book. Dust puffed around me. An old lady, hunched and witchy, was standing at the end of the aisle. She limped forward. Her voice was sharp as she repeated herself. "What are you doing here?"

"I got lost. I'm trying to find the engineering department."

She was an ugly old dame: Liver spots and lines all over her face. Her skin hung off her bones in loose flaps. She looked a thousand years old, and not in a smart wise way, just in a wrecked moth-eaten way. She had something flat and silvery in her hand. A pistol.

I took another step back.

She raised the gun. "Not that way. Out the way you came." She motioned with the pistol. "Off you go."

I hesitated.

She smiled slightly, showing stumps of missing teeth. "I won't shoot if you don't give me a reason." She waved the gun again. "Go on. You aren't supposed to be here." She herded me back through the library to the main doors with a brisk authority. She pulled them open and waved her pistol at me. "Go on. Get."

"Wait. Please. Can't you at least tell me where the engineering department is?"

"Closed down years ago. Now get out."

"There's got to be one!"

"Not anymore. Go on. Get." She brandished the pistol again. "Get."

I held onto the door. "But you must know someone who can help me." I was talking fast, trying to get all my words out before she used the gun. "I work on the city's sewage pumps. They're breaking, and I don't know how to fix them. I need someone who has engineering experience."

She was shaking her head and starting to wave the gun. I tried again. "Please! You've got to help. No one will talk to me, and you're going to be swimming in crap if I don't find help. Pump Six serves the university and *I don't know how to fix it!*"

She paused. She cocked her head first one way, then the other. "Go on."

I briefly outlined the problems with the PressureDynes. When I finished, she shook her head and turned away. "You've wasted your time. We haven't had an engineering department in over twenty years." She went over to a reading table and took a couple swipes at its dust. Pulled out a chair and did the same with it. She sat, placing her pistol on the table, and motioned me to join her.

Warily, I brushed off my own seat. She laughed at the way my eyes kept going to her pistol. She picked it up and tucked it into a pocket of her moth-eaten sweater. "Don't worry. I won't shoot you now. I just keep it around in case the kids get belligerent. They don't very often, anymore, but you never know. . . ." Her voice trailed off, as she looked out at the quad.

"How can you not have an engineering department?"

Her eyes swung back to me. "Same reason I closed the library." She laughed. "We can't have the students running around in here, can we?" She considered me for a moment, thoughtful. "I'm surprised you got in. I'm must be getting old, forgetting to lock up like that."

"You always lock it? Aren't you librarians—"

"I'm not a librarian," she interrupted. "We haven't had a librarian since Herman Hsu died." She laughed. "I'm just an old faculty wife. My husband taught organic chemistry before he died."

"But you're the one who put the chains on the doors?"

"There wasn't anyone else to do it. I just saw the students partying in here and realized something had to be done before they burned the damn place down." She drummed her fingers on the table, raising little dust puffs with her boney digits as she considered me. Finally she said, "If I gave you the library keys, could you learn the things you need to know? About these pumps? Learn how they work? Fix them, maybe?"

"I doubt it. That's why I came here." I pulled out my earbug. "I've got the schematics right here. I just need someone to go over them for me."

"There's no one here who can help you." She smiled tightly. "My degree was in social psychology, not engineering. And really, there's no one else. Unless you count them." She waved at the students beyond the windows, humping in the quad. "Do you think that any of them could read your schematics?"

Through the smudged glass doors I could see the kids on the library steps, stripped down completely. They were humping away, grinning and having a good time. One of the girls saw me through the glass and waved at me to join her. When I shook my head, she shrugged and went back to her humping.

The old lady studied me like a vulture. "See what I mean?"

The girl got into her rhythm. She grinned at me watching, and motioned again for me to come out and play. All she needed were some big yellow eyes, and she would have made a perfect trog.

I closed my eyes and opened them again. Nothing changed. The girl was still there with all of her little play friends. All of them romping around and having a good time.

"The best and the brightest," the old lady murmured.

In the middle of the quad, more of the students were stripping down, none of them caring that they were doing it in the middle of broad daylight, none of them worried about who was watching, or what anyone might think. A couple hundred kids, and not a single one of them had a book, or a notebook, or pens, or paper, or a computer with them.

The old lady laughed. "Don't look so surprised. You can't say someone of your caliber never noticed." She paused, waiting, then peered at me, incredulous. "The trogs? The concrete rain? The reproductive disorders? You never wondered about any of it?" She shook her head. "You're stupider than I guessed."

"But. . . ." I cleared my throat. "How could it . . . I mean. . . ." I trailed off.

"Chemistry was my husband's field." She squinted at the kids humping on the steps and tangled out in the grass, then shook her head and shrugged. "There are plenty of books on the topic. For a while there were even magazine stories about it. 'Why breast might not be best.' Stuff like that." She waved a hand impatiently. "Rohit and I never really thought about any of it until his students started seeming stupider every year." She cackled briefly. "And then he tested them, and he was right."

"We can't all be turning into trogs." I held up my bottle of Sweatshine. "How could I buy this bottle, or my earbug, or bacon, or anything? Someone has to be making these things."

"You found bacon? Where?" She leaned forward, interested.

"My wife did. Last packet."

She settled back with a sigh. "It doesn't matter. I couldn't chew it anyway." She studied my Sweatshine bottle. "Who knows? Maybe you're right. Maybe it's not so bad. But this is the longest conversation that I've had since Rohit died; most people just don't seem to be able to pay attention to things like they used to." She eyed me. "Maybe your Sweatshine bottle just means there's a factory somewhere that's as good as your sewage pumps used to be. And as long as nothing too complex goes wrong, we all get to keep drinking it."

"It's not that bad."

"Maybe not." She shrugged. "It doesn't matter to me,

anymore. I'll kick off pretty soon. After that, it's your problem."

It was night by the time I came out of the university. I had a bag full of books, and no one to know that I'd taken them. The old lady hadn't cared if I checked them out or not, just waved at me to take as many as I liked, and then gave me the keys and told me to lock up when I left.

All of the books were thick with equations and diagrams. I'd picked through them one after another, reading each for a while, before giving up and starting on another. They were all pretty much gibberish. It was like trying to read before you knew your ABCs. Mercati had been right. I should have stayed in school. I probably wouldn't have done any worse than the Columbia kids.

Out on the street, half the buildings were dark. Some kind of brownout that ran all the way down Broadway. One side of the street had electricity, cheerful and bright. The other side had candles glimmering in all the apartment windows, ghost lights flickering in a pretty ambiance.

A crash of concrete rain echoed from a couple blocks away. I couldn't help shivering. Everything had turned creepy. It felt like the old lady was leaning over my shoulder and pointing out broken things everywhere. Empty autovendors. Cars that hadn't moved in years. Cracks in the sidewalk. Piss in the gutters.

What was normal supposed to look like?

I forced myself to look at good things. People were still out and about, walking to their dance clubs, going out to eat, wandering uptown or downtown to see their parents. Kids were on skateboards rolling past and trogs were humping in the alleys. A couple of vendor boxes were full of cellophane bagels, along with a big row of Sweatshine bottles all glowing green under their lights, still all stocked up and ready for sale. Lots of things were still working. Wicky was still a great club, even if Max needed a little help remembering to restock. And Miku and Gabe had their new baby, even if it took them three years to get it. I couldn't let myself wonder if that baby was going to turn out like the college kids in the quad. Not everything was broken.

As if to prove it, the subway ran all the way to my stop for a change. Somewhere on the line, they must have had a couple guys like me, people who could still read a schematic and remember how to show up for work and not throw toilet paper around the control rooms. I wondered who they were. And then I wondered if they ever noticed how hard it was to get anything done.

When I got home, Maggie was already in bed. I gave her a kiss and she woke up a little. She pushed her hair away from her face. "I left out a hotpack burrito for you. The stove's still broke."

"Sorry. I forgot. I'll fix it now."

"No worry." She turned away from me and pulled the sheets up around her neck. For a minute, I thought she'd dozed off, but then she said, "Trav?"

"Yeah?"

"I got my period."

I sat down beside her and started massaging her back. "How you doing with that?"

"S'okay. Maybe next time." She was already dropping back to sleep. "You just got to stay optimistic, right?"

"That's right, baby." I kept rubbing her back. "That's right."

When she was asleep, I went back to the kitchen. I found the hotpack burrito and shook it and tore it open, holding it with the tips of my fingers so I wouldn't burn myself. I took a bite, and decided the burritos were still working just fine. I dumped all the books onto the kitchen table and stared at them, trying to decide where to start.

Through the open kitchen windows, from the direction of the park, I heard another crash of concrete rain. I looked out toward the candleflicker darkness. Not far away, deep underground, nine pumps were chugging away; their little flashers winking in and out with errors, their maintenance logs scrolling repair requests, and all of them running a little harder now that Pump Six was down. But they were still running. The people who'd built them had done a good job. With luck, they'd keep running for a long time yet.

I chose a book at random and started reading.

BOOJUM

ELIZABETH BEAR AND SARAH MONETTE

Elizabeth Bear (www.elizabethbear.com) *lives in Hartford, Connecticut. She won the 2005 John W. Campbell Award for Best New Writer, and the 2008 Hugo Award for Best Short Story for "Tideline." Prolific as well as talented, she has published fourteen SF and fantasy novels since 2005, more than forty stories since 2003, and a collection,* The Chains That You Refuse *(2006). Her 2009 novel will be the Norse fantasy* By the Mountain Bound, *and she is currently gearing up to help start the second season of the virtual TV show,* Shadow Unit.

Sarah Monette (www.sarahmonette.com) *was born and raised in Oak Ridge, Tennessee, "one of the secret cities of the Manhattan Project." She studied English and Classics and has a Ph.D. in English Literature. Her novels are* Mélusine *(2005),* The Virtu *(2006),* The Mirador *(2007),* Corambis *(2009), and, in collaboration with Elizabeth Bear,* A Companion to Wolves *(2007). Her short stories have appeared in* Lady Churchill's Rosebud Wristlet, Alchemy, Weird Tales, *and* Strange Horizons, *and are collected in* The Bone Key *(2007).*

"Boojum" was published in the excellent original anthology of fantasy and SF pirate stories, Fast Ships, Black Sails, *edited by Jeff and Ann VanderMeer. It turns the premise of the anthology on its head. A tale of living spaceships that are brain-thieves, this story, in the tradition of Anne McCaffrey's* The Ship Sang, *is one of this year's most entertaining.*

The ship had no name of her own, so her human crew called her the *Lavinia Whateley*. As far as anyone could tell, she didn't mind. At least, her long grasping vanes curled—affectionately?—when the chief engineers patted her bulkheads and called her "Vinnie," and she ceremoniously tracked the footsteps of each crew member with her internal bioluminescence, giving them light to walk and work and live by.

The *Lavinia Whateley* was a Boojum, a deep-space swimmer, but her kind had evolved in the high tempestuous envelopes of gas giants, and their offspring still spent their infancies there, in cloud-nurseries over eternal storms. And so she was streamlined, something like a vast spiny lionfish to the earth-adapted eye. Her sides were lined with gasbags filled with hydrogen; her vanes and wings furled tight. Her color was a blue-green so dark it seemed a glossy black unless the light struck it; her hide was impregnated with symbiotic algae.

Where there was light, she could make oxygen. Where there was oxygen, she could make water.

She was an ecosystem unto herself, as the captain was a law unto herself. And down in the bowels of the engineering section, Black Alice Bradley, who was only human and no kind of law at all, loved her.

Black Alice had taken the oath back in '32, after the Venusian Riots. She hadn't hidden her reasons, and the captain had looked at her with cold, dark, amused eyes and said, "So long as you carry your weight, cherie, I don't care. Betray me, though, and you will be going back to Venus the cold way." But it was probably that—and the fact that Black Alice couldn't hit the broad side of a space freighter with a ray gun—that had gotten her assigned to Engineering, where ethics were less of a problem. It wasn't, after all, as if she was going anywhere.

Black Alice was on duty when the *Lavinia Whateley* spotted prey; she felt the shiver of anticipation that ran through the decks of the ship. It was an odd sensation, a tic Vinnie only exhibited in pursuit. And then they were under way, zooming down the slope of the gravity well toward Sol, and the screens all around Engineering—which Captain Song kept dark, most of the time, on the theory that swabs and deckhands and coal-shovelers didn't need to know where they were, or what they were doing—flickered bright and live.

Everybody looked up, and Demijack shouted, "There! There!" He was right: the blot that might only have been a smudge of oil on the screen moved as Vinnie banked, revealing itself to be a freighter, big and ungainly and hopelessly outclassed. Easy prey. Easy pickings.

We could use some of them, thought Black Alice. Contrary to the e-ballads and comm stories, a pirate's life was not all imported delicacies and fawning slaves. Especially not when three-quarters of any and all profits went directly back to the *Lavinia Whateley*, to keep her healthy and happy. Nobody ever argued. There were stories about the *Marie Curie*, too.

The captain's voice over fiberoptic cable—strung beside the *Lavinia Whateley*'s nerve bundles—was as clear and free of static as if she stood at Black Alice's elbow. "Battle stations," Captain Song said, and the crew leapt to obey. It had been two Solar since Captain Song keelhauled James Brady, but nobody who'd been with the ship then was ever likely to forget his ruptured eyes and frozen scream.

Black Alice manned her station, and stared at the screen. She saw the freighter's name—the *Josephine Baker*—gold on black across the stern, the Venusian flag for its port of registry wired stiff from a mast on its hull. It was a steelship, not a Boojum, and they had every advantage. For a moment she thought the freighter would run.

And then it turned, and brought its guns to bear.

No sense of movement, of acceleration, of disorientation. No pop, no whump of displaced air. The view on the screens just flickered to a different one, as Vinnie skipped—apported—to a new position just aft and above the *Josephine Baker*, crushing the flag mast with her hull.

Black Alice felt that, a grinding shiver. And had just time to grab her console before the *Lavinia Whateley* grappled the freighter, long vanes not curling in affection now.

Out of the corner of her eye, she saw Dogcollar, the closest thing the *Lavinia Whateley* had to a chaplain, cross himself, and she heard him mutter, like he always did, *Ave, Grandaevissimi, morituri vos salutant.* It was the best he'd be able to do until it was all over, and even then he wouldn't have the chance to do much. Captain Song didn't mind other people worrying about souls, so long as they didn't do it on her time.

The Captain's voice was calling orders, assigning people to boarding parties port and starboard. Down in Engineering, all they had to do was monitor the *Lavinia Whateley*'s hull and prepare to repel boarders, assuming the freighter's crew had the gumption to send any. Vinnie would take care of the rest—until the time came to persuade her not to eat her prey before they'd gotten all the valuables off it. That was a ticklish job, only entrusted to the chief engineers, but Black Alice watched and listened, and although she didn't expect she'd ever get the chance, she thought she could do it herself.

It was a small ambition, and one she never talked about. But it would be a hell of a thing, wouldn't it? To be somebody a Boojum would listen to?

She gave her attention to the dull screens in her sectors, and tried not to crane her neck to catch a glimpse of the ones with the actual fighting on them. Dogcollar was making the rounds with sidearms from the weapons locker, just in case. Once the *Josephine Baker* was subdued, it was the junior engineers and others who would board her to take inventory.

Sometimes there were crew members left in hiding on captured ships. Sometimes, unwary pirates got shot.

There was no way to judge the progress of the battle from Engineering. Wasabi put a stopwatch up on one of the secondary screens, as usual, and everybody glanced at it periodically. Fifteen minutes on-going meant the boarding parties hadn't hit any nasty surprises. Black Alice had met a man once who'd been on the *Margaret Mead* when she grappled a freighter that turned out to be carrying a division's-worth of Marines out to the Jovian moons. Thirty minutes on-going was normal. Forty-five minutes. Upward of an hour on-going, and people started double-checking their weapons. The longest battle Black Alice had ever personally been part of was six hours, forty-three minutes, and fifty-two seconds. That had been the last time the *Lavinia Whateley* worked with a partner, and the double-cross by the *Henry Ford* was the only reason any of Vinnie's crew needed. Captain Song still had Captain Edwards' head in a jar on the bridge, and Vinnie had an ugly ring of scars where the *Henry Ford* had bitten her.

This time, the clock stopped at fifty minutes, thirteen seconds. The *Josephine Baker* surrendered.

Dogcollar slapped Black Alice's arm. "With me," he said, and she didn't argue. He had only six weeks seniority over her, but he was as tough as he was devout, and not stupid either. She checked the Velcro on her holster and followed him up the ladder, reaching through the rungs once to scratch Vinnie's bulkhead as she passed. The ship paid her no notice. She wasn't the captain, and she wasn't one of the four chief engineers.

Quartermaster mostly respected crew's own partner choices, and as Black Alice and Dogcollar suited up—it wouldn't be the first time, if the *Josephine Baker*'s crew decided to blow her open to space rather than be taken captive—he came by and issued them both tag guns and x-ray pads, taking a retina scan in return. All sorts of valuable things got hidden inside of bulkheads, and once Vinnie was done with the steelship there wouldn't be much chance of coming back to look for what they'd missed.

Wet pirates used to scuttle their captures. The Boojums were more efficient.

Black Alice clipped everything to her belt and checked Dogcollar's seals.

And then they were swinging down lines from the *Lavinia Whateley*'s belly to the chewed-open airlock. A lot of crew didn't like to look at the ship's face, but Black Alice loved it. All those teeth, the diamond edges worn to a glitter, and a few of the ship's dozens of bright sapphire eyes blinking back at her.

She waved, unself-consciously, and flattered herself that the ripple of closing eyes was Vinnie winking in return.

She followed Dogcollar inside the prize.

They unsealed when they had checked atmosphere—no sense in wasting your own air when you might need it later—and the first thing she noticed was the smell.

The *Lavinia Whateley* had her own smell, ozone and nutmeg, and other ships never smelled as good, but this was . . . this was . . .

"What did they kill and why didn't they space it?" Dogcollar wheezed, and Black Alice swallowed hard against her gag reflex and said, "One will get you twenty we're the lucky bastards that find it."

"No takers," Dogcollar said.

They worked together to crank open the hatches they came to. Twice they found crew members, messily dead. Once they found crew members alive.

"Gillies," said Black Alice.

"Still don't explain the smell," said Dogcollar and, to the gillies: "Look, you can join our crew, or our ship can eat you. Makes no never mind to us."

The gillies blinked their big wet eyes and made finger-signs at each other, and then nodded. Hard.

Dogcollar slapped a tag on the bulkhead. "Someone will come get you. You go wandering, we'll assume you changed your mind."

The gillies shook their heads, hard, and folded down onto the deck to wait.

Dogcollar tagged searched holds—green for clean, purple for goods, red for anything Vinnie might like to eat that couldn't be fenced for a profit—and Black Alice mapped. The corridors in the steelship were winding, twisty, hard to track. She was glad she chalked the walls, because she didn't think her map was quite right, somehow, but she couldn't figure out where she'd gone wrong. Still, they had a beacon, and Vinnie could always chew them out if she had to.

Black Alice loved her ship.

She was thinking about that, how, okay, it wasn't so bad, the pirate game, and it sure beat working in the sunstone mines on Venus, when she found a locked cargo hold. "Hey, Dogcollar," she said to her comm, and while he was turning to cover her, she pulled her sidearm and blastered the lock.

The door peeled back, and Black Alice found herself staring at rank upon rank of silver cylinders, each less than a meter tall and perhaps half a meter wide, smooth and featureless except for what looked like an assortment of sockets and plugs on the surface of each. The smell was strongest here.

"Shit," she said.

Dogcollar, more practical, slapped the first safety orange tag of the expedition beside the door and said only, "Captain'll want to see this."

"Yeah," said Black Alice, cold chills chasing themselves up and down her spine. "C'mon, let's move."

But of course it turned out that she and Dogcollar were on the retrieval detail, too, and the captain wasn't leaving the canisters for Vinnie.

Which, okay, fair. Black Alice didn't want the *Lavinia Whateley* eating those things, either, but why did they have to bring them *back*?

She said as much to Dogcollar, under her breath, and had a horrifying thought: "She knows what they are, right?"

"She's the captain," said Dogcollar.

"Yeah, but—I ain't arguing, man, but if she doesn't know . . ." She lowered her voice even farther, so she could barely hear herself: "What if somebody *opens* one?"

Dogcollar gave her a pained look. "Nobody's going to go opening anything. But if you're really worried, go talk to the captain about it."

He was calling her bluff. Black Alice called his right back. "Come with me?"

He was stuck. He stared at her, and then he grunted and pulled his gloves off, the left and then the right. "Fuck," he said. "I guess we oughta."

For the crew members who had been in the boarding action, the party had already started. Dogcollar and Black Alice finally tracked the captain down in the rec room, where her marines were slurping stolen wine from broken-necked bottles. As much of it splashed on the gravity plates epoxied to the *Lavinia Whateley*'s flattest interior surface as went into the marines, but Black Alice imagined there was plenty more where that came from. And the faster the crew went through it, the less long they'd be drunk.

The captain herself was naked in a great extruded tub, up to her collarbones in steaming water dyed pink and heavily scented by the bath bombs sizzling here and there. Black Alice stared; she hadn't seen a tub bath in seven years. She still dreamed of them sometimes.

"Captain," she said, because Dogcollar wasn't going to say anything. "We think you should know we found some dangerous cargo on the prize."

Captain Song raised one eyebrow. "And you imagine I don't know already, cherie?"

Oh shit. But Black Alice stood her ground. "We thought we should be *sure*."

The captain raised one long leg out of the water to shove a pair of necking pirates off the rim of her tub. They rolled onto the floor, grappling and clawing, both fighting to be on top. But they didn't break the kiss. "You wish to be sure," said the captain. Her dark eyes had never left Black Alice's sweating face. "Very well. Tell me. And then you will know that I know, and you can be *sure*."

Dogcollar made a grumbling noise deep in his throat, easily interpreted: *I told you so.*

Just as she had when she took Captain Song's oath and slit her thumb with a razorblade and dripped her blood on the *Lavinia Whateley*'s decking so the ship might know her, Black Alice—metaphorically speaking—took a breath and jumped. "They're brains," she said. "Human brains. Stolen. Black-market. The Fungi—"

"Mi-Go," Dogcollar hissed, and the Captain grinned at him, showing extraordinarily white strong teeth. He ducked, submissively, but didn't step back, for which Black Alice felt a completely ridiculous gratitude.

"Mi-Go," Black Alice said. Mi-Go, Fungi, what did it matter? They came from the outer rim of the Solar System, the black cold hurtling rocks of the Öpik-Oort Cloud. Like the Boojums, they could swim between the stars. "They collect them. There's a black market. Nobody knows what they use them for. It's illegal, of course. But they're . . . alive in there. They go mad, supposedly."

And that was it. That was all Black Alice could manage. She stopped, and had to remind herself to shut her mouth.

"So I've heard," the captain said, dabbling at the steaming water. She stretched luxuriously in her tub. Someone thrust a glass of white wine at her, condensation dewing the outside. The captain did not drink from shattered plastic bottles. "The Mi-Go will pay for this cargo, won't they? They mine rare minerals all over the system. They're said to be very wealthy."

"Yes, captain," Dogcollar said, when it became obvious that Black Alice couldn't.

"Good," the captain said. Under Black Alice's feet, the decking shuddered, a grinding sound as Vinnie began to dine. Her rows of teeth would make short work of the *Josephine Baker*'s steel hide. Black Alice could see two of the gillies—the same two? she never could tell them apart unless they had scars—flinch and tug at their chains. "Then they might as well pay us as someone else, wouldn't you say?"

Black Alice knew she should stop thinking about the canisters. Captain's word was law. But she couldn't help it, like scratching at a scab. They were down there, in the third subhold, the one even sniffers couldn't find, cold and sweating and with that stench that was like a living thing.

And she kept wondering. Were they empty? Or were there brains in there, people's brains, going mad?

The idea was driving her crazy, and finally, her fourth off-shift after the capture of the *Josephine Baker*, she had to go look.

"This is stupid, Black Alice," she muttered to herself as she climbed down the companion way, the beads in her hair clicking against her earrings. "Stupid, stupid, stupid." Vinnie bioluminesced, a traveling spotlight, placidly unconcerned whether Black Alice was being an idiot or not.

Half-Hand Sally had pulled duty in the main hold. She nodded at Black Alice and Black Alice nodded back. Black Alice ran errands a lot, for Engineering and sometimes for other departments, because she didn't smoke hash and she didn't cheat at cards. She was reliable.

Down through the subholds, and she really didn't want to be doing this, but she was here and the smell of the third subhold was already making her sick, and maybe if she just knew one way or the other, she'd be able to quit thinking about it.

She opened the third subhold, and the stench rushed out.

The canisters were just metal, sealed, seemingly airtight. There shouldn't be any way for the aroma of the contents to escape. But it permeated the air nonetheless, bad enough that Black Alice wished she had brought a rebreather.

No, that would have been suspicious. So it was really best for everyone concerned that she hadn't, but oh, gods and little fishes the stench. Even breathing through her mouth was no help; she could taste it, like oil from a fryer, saturating the air, oozing up her sinuses, coating the interior spaces of her body.

As silently as possible, she stepped across the threshold and into the space beyond. The *Lavinia Whateley* obligingly lit the space as she entered, dazzling her at first as the over-head lights—not just bioluminescent, here, but LEDs chosen to approximate natural daylight, for when they shipped plants and animals—reflected off rank upon rank of canisters.

When Black Alice went among them, they did not reach her waist.

She was just going to walk through, she told herself. Hesitantly, she touched the closest cylinder. The air in this hold was so dry there was no condensation—the whole ship ran to lip-cracking, nosebleed dryness in the long weeks between prizes—but the cylinder was cold. It felt somehow grimy to the touch, gritty and oily like machine grease. She pulled her hand back.

It wouldn't do to open the closest one to the door—and she realized with that thought that she was planning on opening one. There must be a way to do it, a concealed catch or a code pad. She was an engineer, after all.

She stopped three ranks in, lightheaded with the smell, to examine the problem.

It was remarkably simple, once you looked for it. There were three depressions on either side of the rim, a little smaller than human fingertips but spaced appropriately. She laid the pads of her fingers over them and pressed hard, making the flesh deform into the catches.

The lid sprang up with a pressurized hiss. Black Alice was grateful that even open, it couldn't smell much worse. She leaned forward to peer within. There was a clear membrane over the surface, and gelatin or thick fluid underneath. Vinnie's lights illuminated it well.

It was not empty. And as the light struck the grayish surface of the lump of tissue floating within, Black Alice would have sworn she saw the pathetic unbodied thing flinch.

She scrambled to close the canister again, nearly pinching her fingertips when it clanked shut. "Sorry," she whispered, although dear sweet Jesus, surely the thing couldn't hear her. "Sorry, sorry." And then she turned and ran, catching her hip a bruising blow against the doorway, slapping the controls to make it fucking *close* already. And then she staggered sideways, lurching to her knees, and vomited until blackness was spinning in front of her eyes and she couldn't smell or taste anything but bile.

Vinnie would absorb the former contents of Black Alice's stomach, just as she absorbed, filtered, recycled, and excreted all her crew's wastes. Shaking, Black Alice braced herself back upright and began the long climb out of the holds.

In the first subhold, she had to stop, her shoulder against the smooth, velvet slickness of Vinnie's skin, her mouth hanging open while her lungs worked. And she knew Vinnie wasn't going to hear her, because she wasn't the captain or a chief engineer or anyone important, but she had to try anyway, croaking, "Vinnie, water, please."

And no one could have been more surprised than Black Alice Bradley when Vinnie extruded a basin and a thin cool trickle of water began to flow into it.

Well, now she knew. And there was still nothing she could do about it. She wasn't the captain, and if she said anything more than she already had, people were going to start looking at her funny. Mutiny kind of funny. And what Black Alice did *not* need was any more of Captain Song's attention and especially not for rumors like that. She kept her head down and did her job and didn't discuss her nightmares with anyone.

And she had nightmares, all right. Hot and cold running, enough, she fancied, that she could have filled up the captain's huge tub with them.

She could live with that. But over the next double dozen of shifts, she became aware of something else wrong, and this was worse, because it was something wrong with the *Lavinia Whateley.*

The first sign was the chief engineers frowning and going into huddles at odd moments. And then Black Alice began to feel it herself, the way Vinnie was . . . she didn't have a word for it because she'd never felt anything like it before. She would have said *balky*, but that couldn't be right. It couldn't. But she was more and more sure that Vinnie was less responsive somehow, that when she obeyed the captain's orders, it was with a delay. If she were human, Vinnie would have been dragging her feet.

You couldn't keelhaul a ship for not obeying fast enough. And then, because she was paying attention so hard she was making her own head hurt, Black Alice noticed something else. Captain Song had them cruising the gas giants' orbits—Jupiter, Saturn, Neptune—not going in as far as the asteroid belt, not going out as far as Uranus. Nobody Black Alice talked to knew why, exactly, but she and Dogcollar figured it was because the captain wanted to talk to the Mi-Go without actually getting near the nasty cold rock of their planet. And what Black Alice noticed was that Vinnie was less balky, less *unhappy*, when she was headed out, and more and more resistant the closer they got to the asteroid belt.

Vinnie, she remembered, had been born over Uranus.

"Do you want to go home, Vinnie?" Black Alice asked her one late-night shift when there was nobody around to care that she was talking to the ship. "Is that what's wrong?"

She put her hand flat on the wall, and although she was probably imagining it, she thought she felt a shiver ripple across Vinnie's vast side.

Black Alice knew how little she knew, and didn't even contemplate sharing her theory with the chief engineers. They probably knew exactly what was wrong and exactly what to do to keep the *Lavinia Whateley* from going core meltdown like the *Marie Curie* had. That was a whispered story, not the sort of thing anybody talked about except in their hammocks after lights out.

The *Marie Curie* had eaten her own crew.

So when Wasabi said, four shifts later, "Black Alice, I've got a job for you," Black Alice said, "Yessir," and hoped it would be something that would help the *Lavinia Whateley* be happy again.

It was a suit job, he said, replace and repair. Black Alice was going because she was reliable and smart and stayed quiet, and it was time she took on more responsibilities. The way he said it made her first fret because that meant the Captain might be reminded of her existence, and then fret because she realized the Captain already had been.

But she took the equipment he issued, and she listened to the instructions and read schematics and committed them both to memory and her implants. It was a ticklish job, a neural override repair. She'd done some fiber optic bundle splicing, but this was going to be a doozy. And she was going to have to do it in stiff, pressurized gloves.

Her heart hammered as she sealed her helmet, and not because she was worried about the EVA. This was a chance. An opportunity. A step closer to chief engineer.

Maybe she had impressed the captain with her discretion, after all.

She cycled the airlock, snapped her safety harness, and stepped out onto the *Lavinia Whateley*'s hide.

That deep blue-green, like azurite, like the teeming seas of Venus under their swampy eternal clouds, was invisible. They were too far from Sol—it was a yellow stylus-dot, and you had to know where to look for it. Vinnie's hide was just black under Black Alice's suit floods. As the airlock cycled shut, though, the Boojum's own bioluminescence shimmered up her vanes and along the ridges of her sides— crimson and electric green and acid blue. Vinnie must have noticed Black Alice picking her way carefully up her spine with barbed boots. They wouldn't *hurt* Vinnie—nothing short of a space rock could manage that—but they certainly stuck in there good.

The thing Black Alice was supposed to repair was at the principal nexus of Vinnie's central nervous system. The ship didn't have anything like what a human or a gilly would consider a brain; there were nodules spread all through her vast body. Too slow, otherwise. And Black Alice had heard Boojums weren't supposed to be all that smart—trainable, sure, maybe like an Earth monkey.

Which is what made it creepy as hell that, as she picked her way up Vinnie's flank—though *up* was a courtesy, under these circumstances—talking to her all the way, she would have sworn Vinnie was talking back. Not just tracking her with the lights, as she would always do, but bending some of her barbels and vanes around as if craning her neck to get a look at Black Alice.

Black Alice carefully circumnavigated an eye—she didn't

think her boots would hurt it, but it seemed discourteous to
stomp across somebody's field of vision—and wondered,
only half-idly, if she had been sent out on this task not because she was being considered for promotion, but because
she was expendable.

She was just rolling her eyes and dismissing that as bor-
rowing trouble when she came over a bump on Vinnie's
back, spotted her goal—and all the ship's lights went out.

She tongued on the comm. "Wasabi?"

"I got you, Blackie. You just keep doing what you're doing."

"Yessir."

But it seemed like her feet stayed stuck in Vinnie's hide a
little longer than was good. At least fifteen seconds before
she managed a couple of deep breaths—too deep for her
limited oxygen supply, so she went briefly dizzy—and continued up Vinnie's side.

Black Alice had no idea what inflammation looked like in
a Boojum, but she would guess this was it. All around the
interface she was meant to repair, Vinnie's flesh looked
scraped and puffy. Black Alice walked tenderly, wincing,
muttering apologies under her breath. And with every step,
the tendrils coiled a little closer.

Black Alice crouched beside the box, and began examining connections. The console was about three meters by
four, half a meter tall, and fixed firmly to Vinnie's hide. It
looked like the thing was still functional, but something—a
bit of space debris, maybe—had dented it pretty good.

Cautiously, Black Alice dropped a hand on it. She found
the access panel, and flipped it open: more red lights than
green. A tongue-click, and she began withdrawing her tethered tools from their holding pouches and arranging them
so that they would float conveniently around.

She didn't hear a thing, of course, but the hide under her
boots vibrated suddenly, sharply. She jerked her head
around, just in time to see one of Vinnie's feelers slap her
own side, five or ten meters away. And then the whole Boojum shuddered, contracting, curved into a hard crescent of
pain the same way she had when the *Henry Ford* had taken

that chunk out of her hide. And the lights in the access panel lit up all at once—red, red, yellow, red.

Black Alice tongued off the *send* function on her headset microphone, so Wasabi wouldn't hear her. She touched the bruised hull, and she touched the dented edge of the console. "Vinnie," she said, "does this *hurt*?"

Not that Vinnie could answer her. But it was obvious. She was in pain. And maybe that dent didn't have anything to do with space debris. Maybe—Black Alice straightened, looked around, and couldn't convince herself that it was an accident that this box was planted right where Vinnie couldn't . . . quite . . . reach it.

"So what does it *do*?" she muttered. "Why am I out here repairing something that fucking hurts?" She crouched down again and took another long look at the interface.

As an engineer, Black Alice was mostly self-taught; her implants were second-hand, black market, scavenged, the wet work done by a gilly on Providence Station. She'd learned the technical vocabulary from Gogglehead Kim before he bought it in a stupid little fight with a ship named the *V. I. Ulyanov*, but what she relied on were her instincts, the things she knew without being able to say. So she *looked* at that box wired into Vinnie's spine and all its red and yellow lights, and then she tongued the comm back on and said, "Wasabi, this thing don't look so good."

"Whaddya mean, don't look so good?" Wasabi sounded distracted, and that was just fine.

Black Alice made a noise, the auditory equivalent of a shrug. "I think the node's inflamed. Can we pull it and lock it in somewhere else?"

"No!" said Wasabi.

"It's looking pretty ugly out here."

"Look, Blackie, unless you want us to all go sailing out into the Big Empty, we are *not* pulling that governor. Just fix the fucking thing, would you?"

"Yessir," said Black Alice, thinking hard. The first thing was that Wasabi knew what was going on—knew what the box did and knew that the *Lavinia Whateley* didn't like it. That wasn't comforting. The second thing was that whatever was going on, it involved the Big Empty, the cold vastness between the stars. So it wasn't that Vinnie wanted to go home. She wanted to go *out*.

It made sense, from what Black Alice knew about Boojums. Their infants lived in the tumult of the gas giants' atmosphere, but as they aged, they pushed higher and higher, until they reached the edge of the envelope. And then— following instinct or maybe the calls of their fellows, nobody knew for sure—they learned to skip, throwing themselves out into the vacuum like Earth birds leaving the nest. And what if, for a Boojum, the solar system was just another nest?

Black Alice knew the *Lavinia Whateley* was old, for a Boojum. Captain Song was not her first captain, although you never mentioned Captain Smith if you knew what was good for you. So if there *was* another stage to her life cycle, she might be ready for it. And her crew wasn't letting her go.

Jesus and the cold fishy gods, Black Alice thought. Is this why the *Marie Curie* ate her crew? Because they wouldn't let her go?

She fumbled for her tools, tugging the cords to float them closer, and wound up walloping herself in the bicep with a splicer. And as she was wrestling with it, her headset spoke again. "Blackie, can you hurry it up out there? Captain says we're going to have company."

Company? She never got to say it. Because when she looked up, she saw the shapes, faintly limned in starlight, and a chill as cold as a suit leak crept up her neck.

There were dozens of them. Hundreds. They made her skin crawl and her nerves judder the way gillies and Boojums never had. They were man-sized, roughly, but they looked like the pseudoroaches of Venus, the ones Black Alice still had nightmares about, with too many legs, and horrible stiff wings. They had ovate, corrugated heads, but no faces, and where their mouths ought to be, sprouting writing tentacles.

And some of them carried silver shining cylinders, like the canisters in Vinnie's subhold.

Black Alice wasn't certain if they saw her, crouched on the Boojum's hide with only a thin laminate between her and the breathsucker, but she was certain of something else. If they did, they did not care.

They disappeared below the curve of the ship, toward the airlock Black Alice had exited before clawing her way along the ship's side. They could be a trade delegation, come to bargain for the salvaged cargo.

Black Alice didn't think even the Mi-Go came in the battalions to talk trade.

She meant to wait until the last of them had passed, but they just kept coming. Wasabi wasn't answering her hails; she was on her own and unarmed. She fumbled with her tools, stowing things in any handy pocket whether it was where the tool went or not. She couldn't see much; everything was misty. It took her several seconds to realize that her visor was fogged because she was crying.

Patch cables. Where were the fucking patch cables? She found a two-meter length of fiberoptic with the right plugs on the end. One end went into the monitor panel. The other snapped into her suit comm.

"Vinnie?" she whispered, when she thought she had a connection. "Vinnie, can you hear me?"

The bioluminescence under Black Alice's boots pulsed once.

Gods and little fishes, she thought. And then she drew out her laser cutting torch, and started slicing open the case on the console that Wasabi had called the *governor*. Wasabi was probably dead by now, or dying. Wasabi, and Dogcollar, and . . . well, not dead. If they were lucky, they were dead.

Because the opposite of lucky was those canisters the Mi-Go were carrying.

She hoped Dogcollar was lucky.

"You wanna go *out*, right?" she whispered to the *Lavinia Whateley*. "Out into the Big Empty."

She'd never been sure how much Vinnie understood of what people said, but the light pulsed again.

"And this thing won't let you." It wasn't a question. She had it open now, and she could see that was what it did. Ugly fucking thing. Vinnie shivered underneath her, and there was a sudden pulse of noise in her helmet speakers: screaming. People screaming.

"I know," Black Alice said. "They'll come get me in a minute, I guess." She swallowed hard against the sudden lurch of her stomach. "I'm gonna get this thing off you, though. And when they go, you can go, okay? And I'm sorry. I didn't know we were keeping you from . . ." She had to quit talking, or she really was going to puke. Grimly, she fumbled for the tools she needed to disentangle the abomination from Vinnie's nervous system.

Another pulse of sound, a voice, not a person: flat and buzzing and horrible. "We do not bargain with thieves." And the scream that time—she'd never heard Captain Song scream before. Black Alice flinched and started counting to slow her breathing. Puking in a suit was the number one badness, but hyperventilating in a suit was a really close second.

Her heads-up display was low-res, and slightly miscalibrated, so that everything had a faint shadow-double. But the thing that flashed up against her own view of her hands was unmistakable: a question mark.

<?>

"Vinnie?"

Another pulse of screaming, and the question mark again. <?>

"Holy shit, Vinnie! . . . Never mind, never mind. They, um, they collect people's brains. In canisters. Like the canisters in the third subhold."

The bioluminescence pulsed once. Black Alice kept working.

Her heads-up pinged again: <ALICE> A pause. <?>

"Um, yeah. I figure that's what they'll do with me, too. It looked like they had plenty of canisters to go around."

Vinnie pulsed, and there was a longer pause while Black Alice doggedly severed connections and loosened bolts.

<WANT> said the *Lavinia Whateley*. <?>

"Want? Do I *want* . . . ?" Her laughter sounded bad. "Um, no. No, I don't want to be a brain in a jar. But I'm not seeing a lot of choices here. Even if I went cometary, they could catch me. And it kind of sounds like they're mad enough to do it, too."

She'd cleared out all the moorings around the edge of the governor; the case lifted off with a shove and went sailing into the dark. Black Alice winced. But then the processor under the cover drifted away from Vinnie's hide, and there was just the monofilament tethers and the fat cluster of fiber optic and superconductors to go.

<HELP>

"I'm doing my best here, Vinnie," Black Alice said through her teeth.

That got her a fast double-pulse, and the *Lavinia Whateley* said, <HELP>

And then, <ALICE>

"You want to help *me*?" Black Alice squeaked.

A strong pulse, and the heads-up said, <HELP ALICE>

"That's really sweet of you, but I'm honestly not sure there's anything you can do. I mean, it doesn't look like the Mi-Go are mad at *you*, and I really want to keep it that way."

<EAT ALICE> said the *Lavinia Whateley*.

Black Alice came within a millimeter of taking her own fingers off with the cutting laser. "Um, Vinnie, that's um . . . well, I guess it's better than being a brain in a jar." Or suffocating to death in her suit if she went cometary and the Mi-Go *didn't* come after her.

The double-pulse again, but Black Alice didn't see what she could have missed. As communications went, *EAT ALICE* was pretty fucking unambiguous.

<HELP ALICE> the *Lavinia Whateley* insisted. Black Alice leaned in close, unsplicing the last of the governor's circuits from the Boojum's nervous system. <SAVE ALICE>

"By eating me? Look, I know what happens to things you eat, and it's not . . ." She bit her tongue. Because she *did* know what happened to things the *Lavinia Whateley* ate. Absorbed. Filtered. Recycled. "Vinnie . . . are you saying you can save me from the Mi-Go?"

A pulse of agreement.

"By eating me?" Black Alice pursued, needing to be sure she understood.

Another pulse of agreement.

Black Alice thought about the *Lavinia Whateley*'s teeth. "How much *me* are we talking about here?"

<ALICE> said the *Lavinia Whateley*, and then the last fiber-optic cable parted, and Black Alice, her hands shaking, detached her patch cable and flung the whole mess of it as hard as she could straight up. Maybe it would find a planet with atmosphere and be some little alien kid's shooting star.

And now she had to decide what to do.

She figured she had two choices, really. One, walk back down the *Lavinia Whateley* and find out if the Mi-Go believed in surrender. Two, walk around the *Lavinia Whateley* and into her toothy mouth.

Black Alice didn't think the Mi-Go believed in surrender.

She tilted her head back for one last clear look at the shining black infinity of space. Really, there wasn't any choice at all. Because even if she'd misunderstood what Vinnie seemed to be trying to tell her, the worst she'd end up was dead, and that was light-years better than what the Mi-Go had on offer.

Black Alice Bradley loved her ship.

She turned to her left and started walking, and the *Lavinia Whateley*'s bioluminescence followed her courteously all the way, vanes swaying out of her path. Black Alice skirted each of Vinnie's eyes as she came to them, and each of them blinked at her. And then she reached Vinnie's mouth and that magnificent panoply of teeth.

"Make it quick, Vinnie, okay?" said Black Alice, and walked into her leviathan's maw.

Picking her way delicately between razor-sharp teeth, Black Alice had plenty of time to consider the ridiculousness of worrying about a hole in her suit. Vinnie's mouth was more like a crystal cave, once you were inside it; there was no tongue, no palate. Just polished, macerating stones. Which did not close on Black Alice, to her surprise. If anything, she got the feeling the Vinnie was holding her . . . breath. Or what passed for it.

The Boojum was lit inside, as well—or was making herself lit, for Black Alice's benefit. And as Black Alice clambered inward, the teeth got smaller, and fewer, and the tunnel narrowed. Her throat, Alice thought. I'm inside her.

And the walls closed down, and she was swallowed.

Like a pill, enclosed in the tight sarcophagus of her space suit, she felt rippling pressure as peristalsis pushed her along. And then greater pressure, suffocating, savage. One sharp pain. The pop of her ribs as her lungs crushed.

Screaming inside a space suit was contraindicated, too. And with collapsed lungs, she couldn't even do it properly.

alice.

She floated. In warm darkness. A womb, a bath. She was comfortable. An itchy soreness between her shoulderblades felt like a very mild radiation burn.

alice.

A voice she thought she should know. She tried to speak; her mouth gnashed, her teeth ground.

alice. talk here.

She tried again. Not with her mouth, this time.

Talk . . . here?

The buoyant warmth flickered past her. She was . . . drifting. No, swimming. She could feel currents on her skin. Her vision was confused. She blinked and blinked, and things were shattered.

There was nothing to see anyway, but stars.

alice talk here.

Where am I?

eat alice.

Vinnie. Vinnie's voice, but not in the flatness of the heads-up display anymore. Vinnie's voice alive with emotion and nuance and the vastness of her self.

You ate me, she said, and understood abruptly that the numbness she felt was not shock. It was the boundaries of her body erased and redrawn.

!

Agreement. Relief.

I'm . . . in you, Vinnie?

=/=

Not a "no." More like, this thing is not the same, does not compare, to this other thing. Black Alice felt the warmth of space so near a generous star slipping by her. She felt the swift currents of its gravity, and the gravity of its satellites, and bent them, and tasted them, and surfed them faster and faster away.

I am you.

!

Ecstatic comprehension, which Black Alice echoed with passionate relief. Not dead. Not dead after all. Just, transformed. Accepted. Embraced by her ship, whom she embraced in return.

Vinnie. Where are we going?

out, Vinnie answered. And in her, Black Alice read the whole great naked wonder of space, approaching faster and faster as Vinnie accelerated, reaching for the first great skip that would hurl them into the interstellar darkness of the Big Empty. They were going somewhere.

Out, Black Alice agreed and told herself not to grieve. Not to go mad. This sure beat swampy Hell out of being a brain in a jar.

And it occurred to her, as Vinnie jumped, the brainless bodies of her crew already digesting inside her, that it wouldn't be long before the loss of the *Lavinia Whateley* was a tale told to frighten spacers, too.

Exhalation

TED CHIANG

Ted Chiang lives in Bellevue, Washington. He is a technical writer who occasionally writes distinctive and highly accomplished short SF that is widely admired, then usually nominated for, or the winner of, awards. His short fiction was collected in Stories of Your Life and Others *(2002), and his novella,* The Merchant and the Alchemist's Gate, *was published as a book in 2007. His short stories are among the best in the science fiction field. And since they are so infrequent, they are awaited with eager anticipation. China Mieville said in* The Guardian: *"In Chiang's hands, SF really is the "literature of ideas" it is often held to be, and the genre's traditional "sense of wonder" is paramount." Chiang says, "To the extent that a work of SF reflects science, it's hard SF. And reflecting science doesn't necessarily mean consistency with a certain set of facts; more essentially, it means consistency with a certain strategy for understanding the universe. Science seeks a type of explanation different from those sought by art or religion, an explanation where objective measurement takes precedence over subjective experience."*

"Exhalation" was published in Jonathan Strahan's anthology of SF & fantasy, Eclipse 2, *the second in this important annual series. The protagonist devises an unusual way to explore the nature of the universe. As Chiang says above, this is a work of hard SF.*

It has long been said that air (which others call argon) is the source of life. This is not in fact the case, and I engrave these words to describe how I came to understand the true source of life and, as a corollary, the means by which life will one day end.

For most of history, the proposition that we drew life from air was so obvious that there was no need to assert it. Every day we consume two lungs heavy with air; every day we remove the empty ones from our chest and replace them with full ones. If a person is careless and lets his air level run too low, he feels the heaviness of his limbs and the growing need for replenishment. It is exceedingly rare that a person is unable to get at least one replacement lung before his installed pair runs empty; on those unfortunate occasions where this has happened—when a person is trapped and unable to move, with no one nearby to assist him—he dies within seconds of his air running out.

But in the normal course of life, our need for air is far from our thoughts, and indeed many would say that satisfying that need is the least important part of going to the filling stations. For the filling stations are the primary venue for social conversation, the places from which we draw emotional sustenance as well as physical. We all keep spare sets of full lungs in our homes, but when one is alone, the act of opening one's chest and replacing one's lungs can seem little better than a chore. In the company of others, however, it becomes a communal activity, a shared pleasure.

If one is exceedingly busy, or feeling unsociable, one might simply pick up a pair of full lungs, install them, and leave one's emptied lungs on the other side of the room. If one has a few minutes to spare, it's simple courtesy to connect the empty lungs to an air dispenser and refill them for the next person. But by far the most common practice is to linger and enjoy the company of others, to discuss the news of the day with friends or acquaintances and, in passing, offer newly filled lungs to one's interlocutor. While this perhaps does not constitute air sharing in the strictest sense, there is camaraderie derived from the awareness that all our air comes from the same source, for the dispensers are but the exposed terminals of pipes extending from the reservoir of air deep underground, the great lung of the world, the source of all our nourishment.

Many lungs are returned to the same filling station the next day, but just as many circulate to other stations when people visit neighboring districts; the lungs are all identical in appearance, smooth cylinders of aluminum, so one cannot tell whether a given lung has always stayed close to home or whether it has traveled long distances. And just as lungs are passed between persons and districts, so are news and gossip. In this way one can receive news from remote districts, even those at the very edge of the world, without needing to leave home, although I myself enjoy traveling. I have journeyed all the way to the edge of the world, and seen the solid chromium wall that extends from the ground up into the infinite sky.

It was at one of the filling stations that I first heard the rumors that prompted my investigation and led to my eventual enlightenment. It began innocently enough, with a remark from our district's public crier. At noon of the first day of every year, it is traditional for the crier to recite a passage of verse, an ode composed long ago for this annual celebration, which takes exactly one hour to deliver. The crier mentioned that on his most recent performance, the turret clock struck the hour before he had finished, something that had never happened before. Another person remarked that this was a coincidence, because he had just returned from a nearby district where the public crier had complained of the same incongruity.

No one gave the matter much thought beyond the simple acknowledgement that seemed warranted. It was only some days later, when there arrived word of a similar deviation between the crier and the clock of a third district, that the suggestion was made that these discrepancies might be evidence of a defect in the mechanism common to all the turret clocks, albeit a curious one to cause the clocks to run faster rather than slower. Horologists investigated the turret clocks in question, but on inspection they could discern no imperfection. In fact, when compared against the timepieces normally employed for such calibration purposes, the turret clocks were all found to have resumed keeping perfect time.

I myself found the question somewhat intriguing, but I was too focused on my own studies to devote much thought to other matters. I was and am a student of anatomy, and to provide context for my subsequent actions, I now offer a brief account of my relationship with the field.

Death is uncommon, fortunately, because we are durable and fatal mishaps are rare, but it makes difficult the study of anatomy, especially since many of the accidents serious enough to cause death leave the deceased's remains too damaged for study. If lungs are ruptured when full, the explosive force can tear a body asunder, ripping the titanium as easily as if it were tin. In the past, anatomists focused their attention on the limbs, which were the most likely to survive intact. During the very first anatomy lecture I attended a century ago, the lecturer showed us a severed arm, the casing removed to reveal the dense column of rods and pistons within. I can vividly recall the way, after he had connected its arterial hoses to a wall-mounted lung he kept in the laboratory, he was able to manipulate the actuating rods that protruded from the arm's ragged base, and in response the hand would open and close fitfully.

In the intervening years, our field has advanced to the point where anatomists are able to repair damaged limbs and, on occasion, attach a severed limb. At the same time we have become capable of studying the physiology of the living; I have given a version of that first lecture I saw, during which I opened the casing of my own arm and directed my students' attention to the rods that contracted and extended when I wiggled my fingers.

Despite these advances, the field of anatomy still had a great unsolved mystery at its core: the question of memory. While we knew a little about the structure of the brain, its physiology is notoriously hard to study because of the brain's extreme delicacy. It is typically the case in fatal accidents that, when the skull is breached, the brain erupts in a cloud of gold, leaving little besides shredded filament and leaf from which nothing useful could be discerned. For decades the prevailing theory of memory was that all of a person's experiences were engraved on sheets of gold foil; it was these sheets, torn apart by the force of the blast, that was the source of the tiny flakes found after accidents. Anatomists would collect the bits of gold leaf—so thin that light passes greenly through them—and spend years trying to reconstruct the original sheets, with the hope of eventually deciphering the symbols in which the deceased's recent experiences were inscribed.

I did not subscribe to this theory, known as the inscription hypothesis, for the simple reason that if all our experiences are in fact recorded, why is it that our memories are incomplete? Advocates of the inscription hypothesis offered an explanation for forgetfulness—suggesting that over time the foil sheets become misaligned from the stylus which reads the memories, until the oldest sheets shift out of contact with it altogether—but I never found it convincing. The appeal of the theory was easy for me to appreciate, though; I too had devoted many an hour to examining flakes of gold through a microscope, and can imagine how gratifying it would be to turn the fine adjustment knob and see legible symbols come into focus.

More than that, how wonderful would it be to decipher the very oldest of a deceased person's memories, ones that he himself had forgotten? None of us can remember much more than a hundred years in the past, and written records—accounts that we ourselves inscribed but have scant memory of doing so—extend only a few hundred years before that. How many years did we live before the beginning of written history? Where did we come from? It is the promise of finding the answers within our own brains that makes the inscription hypothesis so seductive.

I was a proponent of the competing school of thought, which held that our memories were stored in some medium in which the process of erasure was no more difficult than recording: perhaps in the rotation of gears, or the positions of a series of switches. This theory implied that everything we had forgotten was indeed lost, and our brains contained no histories older than those found in our libraries. One advantage of this theory was that it better explained why, when lungs are installed in those who have died from lack of air, the revived have no memories and are all but mindless: somehow the shock of death had reset all the gears or switches. The inscriptionists claimed the shock had merely misaligned the foil sheets, but no one was willing to kill a living person, even an imbecile, in order to resolve the debate. I had envisioned an experiment which might allow me to determine the truth conclusively, but it was a risky one, and deserved careful consideration before it was undertaken. I remained undecided for the longest time, until I heard more news about the clock anomaly.

Word arrived from a more distant district that its public crier had likewise observed the turret clock striking the hour before he had finished his new year's recital. What made this notable was that his district's clock employed a different mechanism, one in which the hours were marked by the flow of mercury into a bowl. Here the discrepancy could not be explained by a common mechanical fault. Most people suspected fraud, a practical joke perpetrated by mischief makers. I had a different suspicion, a darker one that I dared not voice, but it decided my course of action; I would proceed with my experiment.

The first tool I constructed was the simplest: in my laboratory I fixed four prisms on mounting brackets and carefully aligned them so that their apexes formed the corners of a rectangle. When arranged thus, a beam of light directed at one of the lower prisms was reflected up, then backward, then down, and then forward again in a quadrilateral loop. Accordingly, when I sat with my eyes at the level of the first prism, I obtained a clear view of the back of my own head. This solipsistic periscope formed the basis of all that was to come.

A similarly rectangular arrangement of actuating rods allowed a displacement of action to accompany the displacement of vision afforded by the prisms. The bank of actuating rods was much larger than the periscope, but still relatively straightforward in design; by contrast, what was attached to the end of these respective mechanisms was far more intricate. To the periscope I added a binocular microscope mounted on an armature capable of swiveling side to side or up and down. To the actuating rods I added an array of precision manipulators, although that description hardly does justice to those pinnacles of the mechanician's art. Combining the ingenuity of anatomists and the inspiration provided by the bodily structures they studied, the manipulators enabled their operator to accomplish any task he might normally perform with his own hands, but on a much smaller scale.

Assembling all of this equipment took months, but I could not afford to be anything less than meticulous. Once the preparations were complete, I was able to place each of my hands on a nest of knobs and levers and control a pair of manipulators situated behind my head, and use the periscope to see what they worked on. I would then be able to dissect my own brain.

The very idea must sound like pure madness, I know, and had I told any of my colleagues, they would surely have tried to stop me. But I could not ask anyone else to risk themselves for the sake of anatomical inquiry, and because I wished to conduct the dissection myself, I would not be satisfied by merely being the passive subject of such an operation. Auto-dissection was the only option.

I brought in a dozen full lungs and connected them with a manifold. I mounted this assembly beneath the worktable that I would sit at, and positioned a dispenser to connect directly to the bronchial inlets within my chest. This would supply me with six days' worth of air. To provide for the possibility that I might not have completed my experiment within that period, I had scheduled a visit from a colleague at the end of that time. My presumption, however, was that the only way I would not have finished the operation in that period would be if I had caused my own death.

I began by removing the deeply curved plate that formed the back and top of my head; then the two, more shallowly curved plates that formed the sides. Only my faceplate remained, but it was locked into a restraining bracket, and I could not see its inner surface from the vantage point of my periscope; what I saw exposed was my own brain. It consisted of a dozen or more subassemblies, whose exteriors were covered by intricately molded shells; by positioning the periscope near the fissures that separated them, I gained a tantalizing glimpse at the fabulous mechanisms within their interiors. Even with what little I could see, I could tell it was the most beautifully complex engine I had ever beheld, so far beyond any device man had constructed that it was incontrovertibly of divine origin. The sight was both exhilarating and dizzying, and I savored it on a strictly aesthetic basis for several minutes before proceeding with my explorations.

It was generally hypothesized that the brain was divided into an engine located in the center of the head which performed the actual cognition, surrounded by an array of components in which memories were stored. What I observed was consistent with this theory, since the peripheral subassemblies seemed to resemble one another, while the subassembly in the center appeared to be different, more heterogenous and with more moving parts. However the components were packed too closely for me to see much of their operation; if I intended to learn anything more, I would require a more intimate vantage point.

Each subassembly had a local reservoir of air, fed by a hose extending from the regulator at the base of my brain. I focused my periscope on the rearmost subassembly and, using the remote manipulators, I quickly disconnected the outlet hose and installed a longer one in its place. I had practiced this maneuver countless times so that I could perform it in a matter of moments; even so, I was not certain I could complete the connection before the subassembly had depleted its local reservoir. Only after I was satisfied that the component's operation had not been interrupted did I continue; I rearranged the longer hose to gain a better view of what lay in the fissure behind it: other hoses that connected it to its neighboring components. Using the most slender pair of manipulators to reach into the narrow crevice, I replaced the hoses one by one with longer substitutes. Eventually, I had worked my way around the entire subassembly and replaced every connection it had to the rest of my brain. I was now able to unmount this subassembly from the frame that supported it, and pull the entire section outside of what was once the back of my head.

I knew it was possible I had impaired my capacity to think and was unable to recognize it, but performing some basic arithmetic tests suggested that I was uninjured. With one subassembly hanging from a scaffold above, I now had a better view of the cognition engine at the center of my brain, but there was not enough room to bring the microscope attachment itself in for a close inspection. In order for me to really examine the workings of my brain, I would have to displace at least half a dozen subassemblies.

Laboriously, painstakingly, I repeated the procedure of substituting hoses for other subassemblies, repositioning another one farther back, two more higher up, and two others out to the sides, suspending all six from the scaffold above my head. When I was done, my brain looked like an explosion frozen an infinitesimal fraction of a second after the detonation, and again I felt dizzy when I thought about it. But at last the cognition engine itself was exposed, supported on a pillar of hoses and actuating rods leading down into my torso. I now also had room to rotate my microscope around a full three hundred and sixty degrees, and pass my gaze across the inner faces of the subassemblies I had moved. What I saw was a microcosm of auric machinery, a landscape of tiny spinning rotors and miniature reciprocating cylinders.

As I contemplated this vista, I wondered, where was my body? The conduits which displaced my vision and action around the room were in principle no different from those which connected my original eyes and hands to my brain. For the duration of this experiment, were these manipulators not essentially my hands? Were the magnifying lenses at the end of my periscope not essentially my eyes? I was an everted person, with my tiny, fragmented body situated at the center of my own distended brain. It was in this unlikely configuration that I began to explore myself.

I turned my microscope to one of the memory subassemblies, and began examining its design. I had no expectation that I would be able to decipher my memories, only that I might divine the means by which they were recorded. As I had predicted, there were no reams of foil pages visible, but to my surprise neither did I see banks of gearwheels or switches. Instead, the subassembly seemed to consist almost entirely of a bank of air tubules. Through the interstices between the tubules I was able to glimpse ripples passing through the bank's interior.

With careful inspection and increasing magnification, I discerned that the tubules ramified into tiny air capillaries, which were interwoven with a dense latticework of wires on which gold leaves were hinged. Under the influence of air escaping from the capillaries, the leaves were held in a variety of positions. These were not switches in the conventional sense, for they did not retain their position without a current of air to support them, but I hypothesized that these were the switches I had sought, the medium in which my memories were recorded. The ripples I saw must have been acts of recall, as an arrangement of leaves was read and sent back to the cognition engine.

Armed with this new understanding, I then turned my microscope to the cognition engine. Here too I observed a latticework of wires, but they did not bear leaves suspended in position; instead the leaves flipped back and forth almost too rapidly to see. Indeed, almost the entire engine appeared to be in motion, consisting more of lattice than of air capillaries, and I wondered how air could reach all the gold leaves in a coherent manner. For many hours I scrutinized the leaves, until I realized that they themselves were playing the role of capillaries; the leaves formed temporary conduits and valves that existed just long enough to redirect air at other leaves in turn, and then disappeared as a result. This was an engine undergoing continuous transformation, indeed modifying itself as part of its operation. The lattice was not so much a machine as it was a page on which the machine was written, and on which the machine itself ceaselessly wrote.

My consciousness could be said to be encoded in the position of these tiny leaves, but it would be more accurate to say that it was encoded in the ever-shifting pattern of air driving these leaves. Watching the oscillations of these flakes of gold, I saw that air does not, as we had always assumed, simply provide power to the engine that realizes our thoughts. Air is in fact the very medium of our thoughts. All that we are is a pattern of air flow. My memories were inscribed, not as grooves on foil or even the position of switches, but as persistent currents of argon.

In the moments after I grasped the nature of this lattice mechanism, a cascade of insights penetrated my consciousness in rapid succession. The first and most trivial was understanding why gold, the most malleable and ductile of metals, was the only material out of which our brains could be made. Only the thinnest of foil leaves could move rapidly enough for such a mechanism, and only the most delicate of filaments could act as hinges for them. By comparison, the copper burr raised by my stylus as I engrave these words and brushed from the sheet when I finish each page is as coarse and heavy as scrap. This truly was a medium where erasing and recording could be performed rapidly, far more so than any arrangement of switches or gears.

What next became clear was why installing full lungs into a person who has died from lack of air does not bring him back to life. These leaves within the lattice remain balanced between continuous cushions of air. This arrangement lets them flit back and forth swiftly, but it also means that if the flow of air ever ceases, everything is lost; the leaves all collapse into identical pendent states, erasing the patterns and the consciousness they represent. Restoring the air supply cannot recreate what has evanesced. This was the price of speed; a more stable medium for storing patterns would mean that our consciousnesses would operate far more slowly.

It was then that I perceived the solution to the clock anomaly. I saw that the speed of these leaves' movements depended on their being supported by air; with sufficient air flow, the leaves could move nearly frictionlessly. If they were moving more slowly, it was because they were being subjected to more friction, which could occur only if the cushions of air that supported them were thinner, and the air flowing through the lattice was moving with less force.

It is not that the turret clocks are running faster. What is happening is that our brains are running slower. The turret clocks are driven by pendulums, whose tempo never varies, or by the flow of mercury through a pipe, which does not change. But our brains rely on the passage of air, and when that air flows more slowly, our thoughts slow down, making the clocks seem to us to run faster.

I had feared that our brains might be growing slower, and it was this prospect that had spurred me to pursue my auto-dissection. But I had assumed that our cognition engines—while powered by air—were ultimately mechanical in nature, and some aspect of the mechanism was gradually becoming deformed through fatigue, and thus responsible for the slowing. That would have been dire, but there was at least the hope that we might be able to repair the mechanism, and restore our brains to their original speed of operation.

But if our thoughts were purely patterns of air rather than the movement of toothed gears, the problem was much more serious, for what could cause the air flowing through every person's brain to move less rapidly? It could not be a decrease in the pressure from our filling stations' dispensers; the air pressure in our lungs is so high that it must be stepped down by a series of regulators before reaching our brains. The diminution in force, I saw, must arise from the opposite direction: the pressure of our surrounding atmosphere was increasing.

How could this be? As soon as the question formed, the only possible answer became apparent: our sky must not be infinite in height. Somewhere above the limits of our vision, the chromium walls surrounding our world must curve inward to form a dome; our universe is a sealed chamber rather than an open well. And air is gradually accumulating within that chamber, until it equals the pressure in the reservoir below.

This is why, at the beginning of this engraving, I said that air is not the source of life. Air can neither be created nor destroyed; the total amount of air in the universe remains constant, and if air were all that we needed to live, we would never die. But in truth the source of life is *a difference in air pressure*, the flow of air from spaces where it is thick to those where it is thin. The activity of our brains, the motion of our bodies, the action of every machine we have ever built is driven by the movement of air, the force exerted as differing pressures seek to balance each other out. When the pressure everywhere in the universe is the same, all air will be motionless, and useless; one day we will be surrounded by motionless air and unable to derive any benefit from it.

We are not really consuming air at all. The amount of air that I draw from each day's new pair of lungs is exactly as much as seeps out through the joints of my limbs and the seams of my casing, exactly as much as I am adding to the atmosphere around me; all I am doing is converting air at high pressure to air at low. With every movement of my body, I contribute to the equalization of pressure in our universe. With every thought that I have, I hasten the arrival of that fatal equilibrium.

Had I come to this realization under any other circumstance, I would have leapt up from my chair and ran into the streets, but in my current situation—body locked in a restraining bracket, brain suspended across my laboratory—doing so was impossible. I could see the leaves of my brain flitting faster from the tumult of my thoughts, which in turn increased my agitation at being so restrained and immobile. Panic at that moment might have led to my death, a nightmarish paroxysm of simultaneously being trapped and spiraling out of control, struggling against my restraints until my air ran out. It was by chance as much as by intention that my hands adjusted the controls to avert my periscopic gaze from the latticework, so all I could see was the plain surface of my worktable. Thus freed from having to see and magnify my own apprehensions, I was able to calm down. When I had regained sufficient composure, I began the lengthy process of reassembling myself. Eventually I restored my brain to its original compact configuration, reattached the plates of my head, and released myself from the restraining bracket.

At first the other anatomists did not believe me when I told them what I had discovered, but in the months that followed my initial auto-dissection, more and more of them became convinced. More examinations of people's brains were performed, more measurements of atmospheric pressure were taken, and the results were all found to confirm my claims. The background air pressure of our universe was indeed increasing, and slowing our thoughts as a result.

There was widespread panic in the days after the truth first became widely know, as people contemplated for the first time the idea that death was inevitable. Many called for the strict curtailment of activities in order to minimize the thickening of our atmosphere; accusations of wasted air escalated into furious brawls and, in some districts, deaths. It was the shame of having caused these deaths, together with the reminder that it would be many centuries yet before our atmosphere's pressure became equal to that of the reservoir underground, that caused the panic to subside. We are not sure precisely how many centuries it will take; additional measurements and calculations are being performed and debated. In the meantime, there is much discussion over how we should spend the time that remains to us.

One sect has dedicated itself to the goal of reversing the equalization of pressure, and found many adherents. The mechanicians among them constructed an engine that takes air from our atmosphere and forces it into a smaller volume, a process they called "compression." Their engine restored air to the pressure it originally had in the reservoir, and these Reversalists excitedly announced that it would form the basis of a new kind of filling station, one that would—with each lung it refilled—revitalize not only individuals but the universe itself. Alas, closer examination of the engine revealed its fatal flaw. The engine itself is powered by air from the reservoir, and for every lungful of air that it produces, the engine consumes not just a lungful, but slightly more. It does not reverse the process of equalization, but like everything else in the world, exacerbates it.

Although some of their adherents left in disillusionment after this setback, the Reversalists as a group were undeterred, and began drawing up alternate designs in which the compressor was powered instead by the uncoiling of springs or the descent of weights. These mechanisms fared no better. Every spring that is wound tight represents air released by the person who did the winding; every weight that rests higher than ground level represents air released by the person who did the lifting. There is no source of power in the universe that does not ultimately derive from a difference in air pressure, and there can be no engine whose operation will not, on balance, reduce that difference.

The Reversalists continue their labors, confident that they will one day construct an engine that generates more compression than it uses, a perpetual power source that will restore to the universe its lost vigor. I do not share their optimism; I believe that the process of equalization is inexorable. Eventually, all the air in our universe will be evenly distributed, no denser or more rarefied in one spot than in any other, unable to drive a piston, turn a rotor, or flip a leaf of gold foil. It will be the end of pressure, the end of motive power, the end of thought. The universe will have reached perfect equilibrium.

Some find irony in the fact that a study of our brains revealed to us not the secrets of the past, but what ultimately awaits us in the future. However, I maintain that we have indeed learned something important about the past. The universe began as an enormous breath being held. Who knows why, but whatever the reason, I am glad that it did, because I owe my existence to that fact. All my desires and ruminations are no more and no less than eddy currents generated by the gradual exhalation of our universe. And until this great exhalation is finished, my thoughts live on.

So that our thoughts may continue as long as possible, anatomists and mechanicians are designing replacements for our cerebral regulators, capable of gradually increasing the air pressure within our brains and keeping it just higher than the surrounding atmospheric pressure. Once these are installed, our thoughts will continue at roughly the same speed even as the air thickens around us. But this does not mean that life will continue unchanged. Eventually the pressure differential will fall to such a level that our limbs will weaken and our movements will grow sluggish. We may then try to slow our thoughts so that our physical torpor is less conspicuous to us, but that will also cause external processes to appear to accelerate. The ticking of clocks will rise to a chatter as their pendulums wave frantically; falling objects will slam to the ground as if propelled by springs; undulations will race down cables like the crack of a whip.

At some point our limbs will cease moving altogether. I cannot be certain of the precise sequence of events near the end, but I imagine a scenario in which our thoughts will continue to operate, so that we remain conscious but frozen, immobile as statues. Perhaps we'll be able to speak for a while longer, because our voice boxes operate on a smaller pressure differential than our limbs, but without the ability to visit a filling station, every utterance will reduce the amount of air left for thought, and bring us closer to the moment that our thoughts cease altogether. Will it be preferable to remain mute to prolong our ability to think, or to talk until the very end? I don't know.

Perhaps a few of us, in the days before we cease moving, will be able to connect our cerebral regulators directly to the dispensers in the filling stations, in effect replacing our lungs with the mighty lung of the world. If so, those few will be able to remain conscious right up to the final moments before all pressure is equalized. The last bit of air pressure left in our universe will be expended driving a person's conscious thought.

And then, our universe will be in a state of absolute equilibrium. All life and thought will cease, and with them, time itself.

But I maintain a slender hope.

Even though our universe is enclosed, perhaps it is not the only air chamber in the infinite expanse of solid chromium. I speculate that there could be another pocket of air elsewhere, another universe besides our own that is even larger in volume. It is possible that this hypothetical universe has the same or higher air pressure as ours, but suppose that it had a much lower air pressure than ours, perhaps even a true vacuum?

The chromium that separates us from this supposed universe is too thick and too hard for us to drill through, so there is no way we could reach it ourselves, no way to bleed off the excess atmosphere from our universe and regain motive power that way. But I fantasize that this neighboring universe has its own inhabitants, ones with capabilities beyond our own. What if they were able to create a conduit between the two universes, and install valves to release air from ours? They might use our universe as a reservoir, running dispensers with which they could fill their own lungs, and use our air as a way to drive their own civilization.

It cheers me to imagine that the air that once powered me could power others, to believe that the breath that enables me to engrave these words could one day flow through someone else's body. I do not delude myself into thinking that this would be a way for me to live again, because I am not that air, I am the pattern that it assumed, temporarily. The pattern that is me, the patterns that are the entire world in which I live, would be gone.

But I have an even fainter hope: that those inhabitants not only use our universe as a reservoir, but that once they have emptied it of its air, they might one day be able to open a passage and actually enter our universe as explorers. They might wander our streets, see our frozen bodies, look through our possessions, and wonder about the lives we led.

Which is why I have written this account. You, I hope, are one of those explorers. You, I hope, found these sheets of copper and deciphered the words engraved on their surfaces. And whether or not your brain is impelled by the air that once impelled mine, through the act of reading my words, the patterns that form your thoughts become an imitation of the patterns that once formed mine. And in that way I live again, through you.

Your fellow explorers will have found and read the other books that we left behind, and through the collaborative action of your imaginations, my entire civilization lives again. As you walk through our silent districts, imagine them as they were; with the turret clocks striking the hours, the filling stations crowded with gossiping neighbors, criers reciting verse in the public squares and anatomists giving lectures in the classrooms. Visualize all of these the next time you look at the frozen world around you, and it will become, in your minds, animated and vital again.

I wish you well, explorer, but I wonder: Does the same fate that befell me await you? I can only imagine that it must, that the tendency toward equilibrium is not a trait peculiar to our universe but inherent in all universes. Perhaps that is just a limitation of my thinking, and your people have discovered a source of pressure that is truly eternal. But my speculations are fanciful enough already. I will assume that one day your thoughts too will cease, although I cannot fathom how far in the future that might be. Your lives will end just as ours did, just as everyone's must. No matter how long it takes, eventually equilibrium will be reached.

I hope you are not saddened by that awareness. I hope that your expedition was more than a search for other universes to use as reservoirs. I hope that you were motivated by a desire for knowledge, a yearning to see what can arise from a universe's exhalation. Because even if a universe's lifespan is calculable, the variety of life that is generated within it is not. The buildings we have erected, the art and music and verse we have composed, the very lives we've led: none of them could have been predicted, because none of them were inevitable. Our universe might have slid into equilibrium emitting nothing more than a quiet hiss. The fact that it spawned such plenitude is a miracle, one that is matched only by your universe giving rise to you.

Though I am long dead as you read this, explorer, I offer to you a valediction. Contemplate the marvel that is existence, and rejoice that you are able to do so. I feel I have the right to tell you this because, as I am inscribing these words, I am doing the same.

Traitor

M. RICKERT

Mary Rickert lives in Cedarburg, Wisconsin. Her short fiction began appearing in Fantasy & Science Fiction *in 1999. She has published twenty-five or more fantasy and science fiction stories to date. Most of them are collected in her first story collection,* Map of Dreams *(2006). It won the IAFA/ Crawford Award for best first fantasy book. In 2007 she began to win awards for her fiction. She is one of the most impressive new writers to emerge in this decade. She characteristically writes about families, about fears and anxieties and pathologies. Her major mode is the fantastic. But she can sure turn out a potent SF story occasionally.*

"Traitor" was published in Fantasy & Science Fiction, *and is both a psychological horror story and a science fiction story perhaps in the lineage of Bruce Sterling's "We Think Differently." It is about a future in which "mamma" teaches little girls to be suicide bombers. To paraphrase Thomas M. Disch, this story predicts the present. Since it was published there have been news stories out of Iraq along the same lines. If, as some maintain, SF always reflects the present in which it is written, we had better change.*

Alika with her braids of bells comes walking down the street, chewing bubble gum and singing, "Who I am I'll always be, God bless you and God bless me, America, America, the land of the free!"

Rover says, "What's that song you're singing, Alika? That ain't no song."

Alika, only nine, ignores him the same way she's seen her mama ignore the comments of men when she walks with her to the bus stop or the Quickmart.

"Hey! I'm talking to you!" Rover says.

But Alika just walks on by and Rover just watches her pass. The girl is only nine and he is nearly twelve. He shakes his head and looks down the street in the other direction. Besides which, she is crazy. Shit, he spits at the sidewalk. Damn! He can't help it. He turns and watches her walking away, her braids jangling.

"America! America! Oh, I love America! My beautiful country, my own wonderful land, my homeland, America, loves me."

Alika's mom watches her and shakes her head. She drags her cigarette. Smoke swirls from her nostrils and mouth. Her fingers, with the long green painted nails, tremble.

Alika sees her sitting there on the stoop. "Hi, Mama!" she calls. The bells ring as she comes running down the walk. Running right toward her mama who sits there with smoke coming out of her ears and nose and mouth.

"Hey, baby," Alika's mother says. "Where you been?"

Alika stops in mid-running-step. Bells go brrring, brrring. She looks at her mama. Her mama looks at her. A truck passes. Fans and air-conditioners hum. Alika watches a bird fly into the branches of a tree, disappear into the green.

"Alika? Where you been honey?"

Alika shrugs. The bells jingle softly.

"Come here, child."

Alika walks over to her mama.

"Sit down." Her mama pats the step, right beside her.

Alika's butt touches her mother's hip. Alika's mother smells like cigarettes and orchid shampoo. She brings a trembling hand to her lips. Drags on the cigarette, turns to face Alika. Alika thinks she is the luckiest girl in America to have a mama so beautiful.

"You don't remember none of it?" she says.

Alika shakes her head. It always happens like this. Her mother puts an arm around her, pulls her tight. Alika's bells ring with a burst. "Good," her mama says. "Well, all right then. Good."

They sit there until their butts get sore and then they go inside. Alika blinks against the dark and she hums as she runs up the stairs. Her mother follows behind, so slow that Alika has to wait for her at the door. While she waits, Alika hops from one foot to another. The bells make a quick ring, but Alika's mother says, "Shush, Alika, what did I tell you about making noise out here?"

Alika stands still while her mother unlocks the door. When she opens it, fans whirl the heat at them. Alika's mom says, "Shit." She closes the door. Locks it. Chains it. Alika says, "Won't do much good."

Alika's mother turns fast. "What?" she says with a sharp mean voice.

Alika shrugs. Brrring. She spins away from her mother, singing, "Oh, America, my lovely home, America for me. America! America! The bloody and the free!"

"Alika!" her mother says.

Alika stops in mid-spin. Bells go brrring brring ring tingle tap. She keeps her arms spread out and her feet apart, her eyes focused on the light switch on the wall.

"I'm going into the room," Alika's mother says.

Alika knows what that means.

"I'll be out in a couple of hours. Your dinner is in the re-frigerator. Nuke it for three minutes. And be careful when you take off the plastic wrap. Do you hear me Alika?"

Nod. (Brrring.)

"You're a good girl, Alika. Don't turn the TV too loud. Maybe we'll go get ice cream."

Alika's mother goes into the room. Alika resumes spin-ning.

The room is red, the color of resistance. It is stifling hot with all the shades pulled down. She's considered an air-conditioner but it seems selfish when the money could be better spent elsewhere. The resistance isn't about her be-ing comfortable. She takes off her clothes and drops them to the floor. She walks across the room and flips on the radio. It cackles and whines as she flips through the noise. Damn station is always moving. It's never where it was the day before. Finally she finds it. Music comes into the room and fills it up. She is filled with music and red. She walks over to stare at the wall of the dead. She looks at each photograph and says, "I remember." They smile back at her in shades of black, white, and gray. Sometimes she is tempted to hurry through this part or just say a general "I remember" once to the entire wall. But she knows it isn't her thinking this. Resistance begins in the mind. I remem-ber. She looks at each face. She remembers. It is never easy.

When that's finished she walks to the worktable. She sits down on the towel, folded across the chair. She looks at the small flag pasted on the wall there. The blue square filled with stars, the forbidden stripes of red and white. She nods. I remember. Then she flicks on the light and bends over her work.

Alika spins six more times until she is so dizzy, she spins to the chair and plops down. When things fall back in order she looks at the closed door behind which her mother works. Red, Alika thinks and then quickly shakes her belled braids to try not to think it again. Alika's mother doesn't know. Alika has been in the room. She's seen everything.

Hours later, after Alika has eaten the meatloaf and mashed potatoes and several peas; after the plate has been washed and dried and her milk poured down the drain, while she sits in the dim heat watching her favorite TV show, "This Is the Hour," her mother comes out of the room, that strange expression on her face, her skin glossy with sweat, and says, "Hey honey, wanna go for ice cream?"

Alika looks at her and thinks, Traitor. She nods her head. Vigorously. The bells ring but the word stays in her mind.

It's a hot evening, so everybody is out. "Hi, Alika!" they say. "Hi, Pauline." Alika and her mother smile and wave, walking down the street. When somebody whistles they both pretend they don't hear and when they pass J.J. who sits on his stoop braiding his own baby girl's hair and he says, "My, my, my," they just ignore him too. Finally they get to the Quickmart.

"What flavors you got today?" says Alika's mother. Sometimes, when Mariel is working, they stand around and talk but this is some new girl they've never seen before. She says, "Today's flavors are vanilla, chocolate, and ice cream."

Alika's mother says, "Oh."

Alika says, "What's she mean ice cream? Of course the ice cream is flavored ice cream."

But Alika's mother doesn't pay much attention to her. She looks right at the girl and says, "So soon?" The girl says, "She's already nine. She's going to start remembering." Then she looks at Alika and says, "What flavor you want?"

Alika says, "You said vanilla, chocolate, and ice cream."

The girl smiles. Her teeth are extraordinarily white. Alika stares at them. "Did I say that?" the girl says. "I don't know what I was thinking. Flavors today are Vanilla, Chocolate, and Hamburger."

"Hamburger?" Alika looks at her mother. This girl is nuts. But her mother is standing there just staring into space with this weird look on her face. "I'll have chocolate," Alika says. "I always take chocolate."

The girl nods. "Those sure are pretty braids," she says as she scoops chocolate ice cream into a cone.

"I only get one scoop," says Alika.

"Well, today we're giving you three," says the girl with the brilliant white teeth.

Alika glances at her mother.

"Don't worry," the tooth girl says, "she already said it would be all right."

Alika doesn't remember that. She says, "I don't remember—"

But her mother interrupts her in that mean voice. "Oh Alika, you never remember anything. Take the ice cream. Just take it."

Alika looks at the girl. "That's not true," she says. "I remember some things."

The girl's eyes go wide.

Alika's mother grabs her by the wrist and pulls her, walking briskly out the door, Alika's bells ringing. "Mama," she says, "you forgot to pay that girl."

"It doesn't matter," Alika's mama says. "She's a friend of mine."

Alika turns but the girl no longer stands behind the counter. Some little kids run in and she can hear them shouting "Hey, anyone here?" Alika's mother lets go of her wrist but continues to walk briskly. Alika's bells ring. Her mama says, "You're more like me than anyone else."

Alika looks up at her beautiful mama and smiles.

But Alika's mama doesn't look at her. She stares straight ahead. She walks fast. Alika has to take little running steps to keep up. She can't hardly eat her ice cream. It drips over her fingers and wrist and down her arm. Alika licks her arm. "Mama," she says. Her mama doesn't pay her any mind. She just keeps walking, her legs like scissors, pwish pwish pwish. Her face like rock. Alika thinks, scissors, paper, rock. Her mama is scissors and rock. That makes Alika paper. "Hey Mama," Alika says, "I'm paper." But her mother just keeps walking; pwish pwish pwish. Alika turns her wrist to lick her arm. The top two ice cream scoops fall to the sidewalk. "Shit," she says.

"What did you say?" the scissors stops and turns her rock face on Alika. "What did I just hear you say?"

"I'm sorry, Mama."

"You're sorry?" The rock stands there. Waiting for an answer.

"Yes, Mama," Alika says in a tiny, papery voice.

The rock grabs Alika by the wrist, the one that is not dripping and sticky.

"Pauline, that girl of yours giving you trouble?"

The rock turns to face the voice but does not let go of Alika's wrist. "This little thing? She couldn't give trouble to a fly."

The ice cream in Alika's other hand drips down her arm, the cone collapsing. Alika doesn't know what to do so she drops it to the sidewalk.

The rock squeezes her wrist, "What did you do that for?"

"Ow, Mama," Alika says, "you're hurting me." Her bells clack against each other.

"Stop it, Alika," says the rock. "I mean it now. Stop your twisting around this instant."

Alika stops.

The rock bends down, face close to Alika's. "I don't want you arguing or crying about some stupid ice cream cone. Do you hear me?"

Alika can see that the rock is crying. She nods. Brrring. Brrring.

The rock lets go of Alika's wrist. Alika has to run to keep up, her bells ringing. "Hey, Pauline. Hey, Alika." Scissors, rock, and paper. Paper covers rock. Scissors get old and rusty. Alika spreads her arms wide. She runs right past her mama. "Alika! Alika!" But she doesn't stop. She is a paper airplane now, or a paper bird. She can't stop. "Alika! Alika!" Her bells ring. "Alika!"

Her mother doesn't even scold her when she finds her waiting at the top of the stairs. She just says, "Time for bed now."

While Alika gets ready for bed Pauline goes into the red room. She takes the photographs down from the wall of the dead. She doesn't think about it. She just does it. She goes to the worktable, stares at it for a while, and sighs. She'll have to stay up late to finish. What's she been doing anyway? With her time?

"Mama? I'm ready for my story."

She sets the stack of the dead on the worktable.

"Mama?"

"I'm coming!" she hollers. She doesn't even bother turning off the light. She'll be back in here soon enough, up half the night, getting everything ready.

What I'm going to tell you about tonight is ice. From before. When there were winters and all that. When I was a little girl I snuck in my daddy's truck one night. He and my brother, Jagger, were going ice fishing the next morning. They said girls couldn't come along. So I decided to just sneak a ride. I lay there in the back of that truck all night. Let me tell you, it was cold. I had nothing but my clothes and a tarp to keep me warm. I know, you don't understand about cold. It was like being in the refrigerator, I guess. The freezer part, you know, 'cause that's where it's cold enough for ice. I lay there and looked at the stars. I tried to imagine a time like the one we live in right now. I tried to imagine being warm all over. I closed my eyes and pretended the sun was shining on my face. I guess it worked 'cause after a while I fell asleep.

I woke up when Daddy and Jagger came out the door and walked over to the truck. I could hear their footsteps coming across the snow. It sounded like when you eat your cereal. They put the cooler in the back but they didn't see me hid under the tarp. They didn't discover me until we got to the lake. My daddy was mad, let me tell you. Jagger was too. But what were they going to do? Turn around? Daddy called my mama and told her what I did. I could hear her laughing. Jagger could hear her too. We stood there by the side of the frozen lake and stared at each other. You never had a brother. You don't know what it's like. Daddy hung up the phone, put it in his pocket, and said, "Your mama is very disappointed in you." Then he told me all the rules. How I had to be quiet and stay out of the way. He gave me two big nails to carry in my pocket. They were supposed to help me grab hold of the ice if I fell in.

The lake was all frozen and pearly white at the edges.

You could see the lights shining in half a dozen little shanties. Mama had made red and white curtains for ours.

Walking across that ice, the sky lit with stars, the faint glow of lights and murmur of voices coming from the shanties, I felt like I was in a beautiful world. Even the cold felt good out there. It filled my lungs. I pictured them, red and shaped like a broken heart.

When we get into our shanty, my dad lifts the wooden lid off the floor and Jagger starts chipping through the ice there, which was not so thick, my daddy said, since they'd been coming regularly. And then they sat on the benches and my dad popped open a beer. Jagger drank a hot chocolate out of the thermos my mama had prepared for him. He didn't offer to share and I didn't ask. It smelled bad in there, a combination of chocolate, beer, wet wool, and fish. So I asked my dad if it was all right that I went outside. He said just don't bother the other folk and don't wander too far from the ice shanties.

I walked across the ice, listening to the sound of my footsteps, the faint murmur of voices. The cold stopped hurting. I looked at all the trees surrounding the lake, a lot of pine, but also some bare oak and birch. I looked up at the stars and thought how they were like fish in the frozen sky.

Anyhow, that's how I came to be practically across the lake when I heard the first shouts, and the next thing I know, ice shanties are tilting and everything is sinking. I hear this loud noise, and I look down. Right under me there is a crack, come all the way from where the ice shanties are sinking, to under my feet.

I finger the nails in my pocket though I am immediately doubtful that they will do me much good. At the same time, I start to step forward, because, even though I'm just a kid, I want to help. But when I lean forward the crack gets deeper. When I lean back to my original position the ice cracks again. Men are shouting and I even hear my daddy, calling Jagger's name. But there are only islands of ice between me and the drowning men.

I am maybe a half-mile away from the opposite shore. The ice in that direction is fissured and cracked but appears to be basically intact, though even as I assess it, more fissures appear. What I have to do is walk away from my father and brother and all the drowning men. I was not stupid. I knew that it wouldn't take long for them to die, that it would take longer for me to walk across the ice. If I made it across. I would say that right at that moment, when I turned away from the men whose shouts were already growing weak, something inside of me turned into ice. It had to, don't you see? I decided to save the only person I could save, myself. I want you to understand, I never blamed myself for this decision. I don't regret it either.

So, I clutch the nails in my fist and step forward. The ice cracks into a radiated circle like those drawings you used to make of the sun. What else can I do? I lift my foot to take another step. Right then a crow screams. I look up. It's as though that bird is shouting at me to stop. I bring my foot back. Slowly. When I set it down again, I can hear my breath let out. That's when I notice that there is no sound. Just my breath. There is no more shouting. I picture them under the ice, frozen. I picture their faces and the nails falling from ice fingers. It almost makes me want to give up. But instead I take a careful step and just when I feel that ice under me, I exhale, slowly. I want you to understand. I know now and I knew then, that ice doesn't breathe. But it was like I was breathing with the ice. I took the next step fast, and right beneath me the fissure separated. I had to forget about the dead, I had to stop my heart from beating so hard. I had to make myself still. Then, carefully, I lifted my leg. Slowly. Breathing like ice. I breathed like ice, even when I started sweating, and I kept breathing like ice, even when the tears came to my eyes. I did this until I got to the shore on the other side. Only then did I turn around and start bawling. There's a time for emotions, right?

Trucks and cars were parked all along the opposite shore. I could see our red Ford. But no one was standing there. Mist was rising off the lake. I ran and walked halfway back before Mrs. Fando found me. She was driving out to scold her husband because he was late for work.

Folks treated me different after that. Everyone did. Everyone treated me the way Jagger used to, like I was too ugly to be alive or like I was some kind of a traitor. Even my own mother. Like I broke that ice under all those men and boys and murdered them myself. I tried to describe to them what happened and how I made it out by learning to breathe like ice but no one took me seriously. For a long time.

Then, when I was seventeen, this stranger came to town. People noticed her because she dressed so well, drove a nice car and was asking about me. She had this old torn newspaper article from way back and she said, "Is this you who survived that ice breakup?" I said yes it was. I thought she was maybe someone's girlfriend or grown daughter coming to tell me she wished I had died and her man had lived. Folks said stuff like that. But what she said was, "I think you need to come with us." She was a recruiter. For the new army. You heard about that, I'm sure.

Yep. That's what I want you to know about me, little girl. I never told you this before. I want you to understand what I do isn't for death. All those years ago I chose life, and I've been choosing it ever since. I have some special skills is all. I can walk like water, for instance; breathe like ice. I can build things. I have seen many people die and I still choose to stay alive. Those are qualities they look for in soldiers.

What I want you to understand is that all the time since then, I think I turned partly into ice. Until you came along. You came along and thawed me out, I guess. It's like that feeling I had, when I was walking out on the ice and I thought the world was a beautiful place. I have that feeling again with you. I couldn't love you more if you were my natural born daughter. Do you understand what I'm trying to say? I bet none of this makes any sense to you at all.

Pauline leans down and kisses Alika's forehead. Alika rolls over, her bells go brrring. "Damn bells," says Pauline. She shuts off the light. Walks out of the room.

Alika opens her eyes. She sits up. Slowly. Alika knows how to move so carefully that the bells don't ring. Alika grabs the end of one of the braids. Slowly, she twists the bell off. It doesn't make a sound. What do they think? She's stupid or something?

She has to keep herself awake for a long time. Her mama is in the forbidden room almost all night long. She keeps herself from falling asleep by remembering the pictures she saw on that wall. All those photographs of smiling children wearing backpacks. My sisters, Alika thinks.

It is already light out when she hears the forbidden door open and shut, her mother walking across the apartment to her own bedroom. When Alika leaves her room, she doesn't make a sound. The bells remain on her pillow. The first thing she notices is the smell of paint. The forbidden room is no longer red. It is white. All the pictures are gone. The worktable is folded up against the wall, beside the bookshelf. Alika can just barely see where the flag had been pasted. The paint there is a little rougher. But the flag is gone. Next to the door is her mama's suitcase, and a backpack and a camera. Alika opens up the backpack. Very carefully. She sighs at the wires. "Be one with the backpack," she says to herself. "Breathe like ice," she rolls her eyes.

By the time she leaves the room, it is bright out. She just gets the last bell in her hair when her mama comes in and says, "Get up now honey. Today is going to be a special day. I got you a new backpack."

Alika gets up. Her bells go brrring. She goes to the bathroom. She can just see the top of her eyes in the mirror over the sink. She changes into her yellow butterfly top and her white shorts. It's already hot. She eats a big bowl of cereal, sitting alone at the kitchen table. Her bells make little bursts of sound that accompany her chewing, which is like the sound of footsteps walking across snow her mama said. Sun pours through the white curtain on the window over the sink. After she brushes her teeth she stands in the kitchen and sings, "America, America, how I love you true. America, America the white stars and the blue."

"Okay, child. Come here now." Alika's mama stands in the forbidden room. The door is wide open. "Look what I have for you. A new backpack!"

Alika spins. Her bells go brrring, brrring, brrring.

"Alika! Alika!" Her mama says, "Stop spinning now."

Alika stops spinning.

"Let me put this on you."

Alika looks up at her mama, the most beautiful mother in the world. "There's something you should know about me," Alika says.

Alika's mama sighs. She keeps the backpack held out in front of her. "What is it, Alika?"

"I'm not stupid."

Alika's mama nods. "Of course you're not," she says. "You're my little girl, aren't you? Now come here and put this thing on."

After Alika's mama buckles the backpack on her, she locks it with a little key and puts the key into her own pocket.

"Don't I need that?" Alika says.

"No, you don't," her mama says. "Today we're doing things a little different. You get to keep this backpack. Not like the others that you had to drop off somewhere. This one is for you to keep. Your teacher will unlock it when you get to school. I gave her the extra key, okay? Now come over here. I want to take your picture."

Alika follows the map her mother drew. "You have to take a different way to school today," she said. Her hands were shaking when she drew it. Alika follows the wavy lines, down Arlington Avenue past the drugstore and video place, turning right on Market Street. Alika's bells ring once or twice, but her step is slow. The backpack is heavy. She has to concentrate on these new directions.

"Hey, where you going?" Rover stands right in front of her. "Ain't you supposed to be at school?"

Alika shrugs. "I'm taking a different way."

Rover shakes his head. "Are you crazy, girl? This is no place for you. Don't you know you are heading right into a war zone?"

Alika smirks. "This is what my mama wants me to do."

"You better turn around right now," Rover says. "'Less your mama wants you dead."

Alika doesn't mind turning around, because suddenly she remembers everything. She walks back home. She doesn't feel like singing. When she gets to their building she looks up and sees that the windows are all open, even the windows in the forbidden room. She walks up the hot dark stairs. She gets there just as her mama is stepping into the hallway with her suitcase.

"Hi, Mama," Alika says.

Alika's mama turns, her face rock, liquid, rock. "What are you doing here?"

"I forgot to hug you good-bye," Alika says.

Her mama steps back. Then, with swift precision, she steps forward as she reaches into her pocket, pulls out the little key, and unlocks Alika's backpack. She runs across the apartment and throws the backpack out the window. Even before it hits the ground she is wrapped around Alika. They are crouched, in tight embrace. After a few seconds, she lets go.

"You all right, Mama?" Alika says.

She nods, slowly.

"I don't know what to tell my teacher about my books. What should I tell her, Mama?"

Pauline gets up, walks across the apartment and leans out the window. Scattered on the ground below is the backpack, and several large books. She is shaking her head, trying to understand what has happened, when she sees Alika, with her belled braids, skipping down the steps, walking wide around the scattered contents of her backpack. Then, with a quick look up at the window, Alika breaks into a run, her bells ringing.

Pauline turns, fast. She looks at her suitcase in the hall-way, runs to it, thinking (Alika?) she will toss it out the window, but she is not fast enough.

All the dead children are reaching for her. She tries to ex-hale, but there is no breath. She sinks where she steps, grabbed by the tiny, bony fingers pulling her into the frozen depths. Rusty nails clutched in the ice children's hands pierce her skin. How quiet it is, the white silence punctuated only by the distant sound of bells. Why, that's Alika, she thinks, that's my girl. Astonished. Proud. Angry.

Alika stands, gazing at the bombed building, feeling certain there is something she has forgotten. An annoying fly, which has been circling her head, lands on her arm and Alika soundlessly slaps it, leaving a bright red mark on her skin, which she rubs until the burning stops. Then she turns and skips down the walk in this mysterious silent world, even her belled braids gone suddenly mute. An ambulance speeds past, the red light flashing, but making no sound, and Alika suddenly understands what has occurred. She has fallen into the frozen world. Surely her mother will come for her, surely her brave mother will risk everything to save her. Alika looks up at the white sky, reaches her arms to the white sun, bawling like a baby, waiting for her beautiful mother to come.

The Things That Make Me Weak and Strange Get Engineered Away

CORY DOCTOROW

Cory Doctorow (www.craphound.com) is a science fiction writer, blogger, and technology activist. He is the co-editor of the popular weblog Boing Boing (www.boingboing.net), and a contributor to Wired, Popular Science, *the* New York Times, *and many other papers, magazines, and websites. Presently living in London, in 2006 he served as the Ful-bright Chair at the Annenberg Center for Public Diplomacy. A collection of short stories,* A Place So Foreign and Eight More *(2004), won the Sunburst Award. His latest short story collection is* Overclocked: Stories of the Future Present *(2007). His latest novel,* Little Brother, *published for teen-age readers, is one of the significant SF novels of 2008. His next novel for adults,* Makers, *publishes in 2009.*

"The Things That Make Me Weak and Strange Get Engineered Away" was published online by Tor.com, *a community-building enterprise of Tom Doherty Associates that is at present the highest paying fiction market in SF. This is perhaps its first appearance in print. It is an excellent story about a future in which monk-like techies retreat into secular cults where they can work without dealing with everyday life in dystopia. But their seclusion is illusory, and the world intrudes.*

'Cause it's gonna be the future soon,
And I won't always be this way,
When the things that make me weak and strange get
   engineered away
            —Jonathan Coulton, "The Future Soon"

Lawrence's cubicle was just the right place to chew on a thorny logfile problem: decorated with the votive fetishes of his monastic order, a thousand calming, clarifying mandalas and saints devoted to helping him think clearly.

From the nearby cubicles, Lawrence heard the ritualized muttering of a thousand brothers and sisters in the Order of Reflective Analytics, a susurration of harmonized, concentrated thought. On his display, he watched an instrument widget track the decibel level over time, the graph overlaid on a 3D curve of normal activity over time and space. He noted that the level was a little high, the room a little more anxious than usual.

He clicked and tapped and thought some more, massaging the logfile to see if he could make it snap into focus and make sense, but it stubbornly refused to be sensible. The data tracked the custody chain of the bitstream the Order munged for the Securitat, and somewhere in there, a file had grown by 68 bytes, blowing its checksum and becoming An Anomaly.

Order lore was filled with Anomalies, loose threads in the fabric of reality—bugs to be squashed in the data-set that was the Order's universe. Starting with the pre-Order sysadmin who'd tracked a $0.75 billing anomaly back to foreign spy-ring that was using his systems to hack his military, these morality tales were object lessons to the Order's monks: pick at the seams and the world will unravel in useful and interesting ways.

Lawrence had reached the end of his personal picking capacity, though. It was time to talk it over with Gerta.

He stood up and walked away from his cubicle, touching his belt to let his sensor array know that he remembered it was there. It counted his steps and his heartbeats and his EEG spikes as he made his way out into the compound.

It's not like Gerta was in charge—the Order worked in autonomous little units with rotating leadership, all coordinated by some groupware that let them keep the hierarchy nice and flat, the way that they all liked it. Authority sucked.

But once you instrument every keystroke, every click, every erg of productivity, it soon becomes apparent who knows her shit and who just doesn't. Gerta knew the shit cold.

"Question," he said, walking up to her. She liked it brusque. No nonsense.

She batted her handball against the court wall three more times, making long dives for it, sweaty grey hair whipping back and forth, body arcing in graceful flows. Then she caught the ball and tossed it into the basket by his feet. "Lester, huh? All right, surprise me."

"It's this," he said, and tossed the file at her pan. She caught it with the same fluid gesture and her computer gave it to her on the handball court wall, which was the closest display for which she controlled the lockfile. She peered at the data, spinning the graph this way and that, peering intently.

She pulled up some of her own instruments and replayed the bitstream, recalling the logfiles from many network taps from the moment at which the file grew by the anomalous 68 bytes.

"You think it's an Anomaly, don't you?" She had a fine blond mustache that was beaded with sweat, but her breathing had slowed to normal and her hands were steady and sure as she gestured at the wall.

"I was kind of hoping, yeah. Good opportunity for personal growth, your Anomalies."

"Easy to say why you'd call it an Anomaly, but look at this." She pulled the checksum of the injected bytes, then showed him her network taps, which were playing the traffic back and forth for several minutes before and after the insertion. The checksummed block moved back through the routers, one hop, two hops, three hops, then to a terminal. The authentication data for the terminal told them who owned its lockfile then: Zbigniew Krotoski, login zbigkrot. Gerta grabbed his room number.

"Now, we don't have the actual payload, of course, because that gets flushed. But we have the checksum, we have the username, and look at this, we have him typing 68 unspecified bytes in a pattern consistent with his biometrics five minutes and eight seconds prior to the injection. So, let's go ask him what his 68 characters were and why they got added to the Securitat's data-stream."

He led the way, because he knew the corner of the campus where zbigkrot worked pretty well, having lived there for five years when he first joined the Order. Zbigkrot was probably a relatively recent inductee, if he was still in that block.

His belt gave him a reassuring buzz to let him know he was being logged as he entered the building, softer haptic feedback coming as he was logged to each floor as they went up the clean-swept wooden stairs. Once, he'd had the work-detail of re-staining those stairs, stripping the ancient wood, sanding it baby-skin smooth, applying ten coats of varnish, polishing it to a high gloss. The work had been incredible, painful and rewarding, and seeing the stairs still shining gave him a tangible sense of satisfaction.

He knocked at zbigkrot's door twice before entering. Technically, any brother or sister was allowed to enter any room on the campus, though there were norms of privacy and decorum that were far stronger than any law or rule.

The room was bare, every last trace of its occupant removed. A fine dust covered every surface, swirling in clouds as they took a few steps in. They both coughed explosively and stepped back, slamming the door.

"Skin," Gerta croaked. "Collected from the ventilation filters. DNA for every person on campus, in a nice, even, Gaussian distribution. Means we can't use biometrics to figure out who was in this room before it was cleaned out."

Lawrence tasted the dust in his mouth and swallowed his gag reflex. Technically, he knew that he was always inhaling and ingesting other peoples' dead skin-cells, but not by the mouthful.

"All right," Gerta said. "Now you've got an Anomaly. Congrats, Lawrence. Personal growth awaits you."

The campus only had one entrance to the wall that surrounded it. "Isn't that a fire-hazard?" Lawrence asked the guard who sat in the pillbox at the gate.

"Naw," the man said. He was old, with the serene air of someone who'd been in the Order for decades. His beard was combed and shining, plaited into a thick braid that hung to his belly, which had only the merest hint of a little pot. "Comes a fire, we hit the panic button, reverse the magnets lining the walls, and the foundations destabilize at twenty sections. The whole thing'd come down in seconds. But no one's going to sneak in or out that way."

"I did *not* know that," Lawrence said.

"Public record, of course. But pretty obscure. Too tempting to a certain prankster mindset."

Lawrence shook his head. "Learn something new every day."

The guard made a gesture that caused something to depressurize in the gateway. A primed *hum* vibrated through the floorboards. "We keep the inside of the vestibule at 10 atmospheres, and it opens inward from outside. No one can force that door open without us knowing about it in a pretty dramatic way."

"But it must take forever to re-pressurize?"

"Not many people go in and out. Just data."

Lawrence patted himself down.

"You got everything?"

"Do I seem nervous to you?"

The old timer picked up his tea and sipped at it. "You'd be an idiot if you weren't. How long since you've been out?"

"Not since I came in. Sixteen years ago. I was twenty one."

"Yeah," the old timer said. "Yeah, you'd be an idiot if you weren't nervous. You follow politics?"

"Not my thing," Lawrence said. "I know it's been getting worse out there—"

The old timer barked a laugh. "Not your thing? It's probably time you got out into the wide world, son. You might ignore politics, but it won't ignore *you*."

"Is it dangerous?"

"You going armed?"

"I didn't know that was an option."

"Always an option. But not a smart one. Any weapon you don't know how to use belongs to your enemy. Just be circumspect. Listen before you talk. Watch before you act. They're good people out there, but they're in a bad, bad situation."

Lawrence shuffled his feet and shifted the straps of his bindle. "You're not making me very comfortable with all this, you know."

"Why are you going out anyway?"

"It's an Anomaly. My first. I've been waiting sixteen years for this. Someone poisoned the Securitat's data and left the campus. I'm going to go ask him why he did it."

The old man blew the gate. The heavy door lurched open, revealing the vestibule. "Sounds like an Anomaly all right." He turned away and Lawrence forced himself to move toward the vestibule. The man held his hand out before he reached it. "You haven't been outside in fifteen years, it's going to be a surprise. Just remember, we're a noble species, all appearances to the contrary notwithstanding."

Then he gave Lawrence a little shove that sent him into the vestibule. The door slammed behind him. The vestibule smelled like machine oil and rubber, gaskety smells. It was dimly lit by rows of white LEDs that marched up the walls like drunken ants. Lawrence barely had time to register this before he heard a loud *thunk* from the outer door and it swung away.

* * *

Lawrence walked down the quiet street, staring up at the same sky he'd lived under, breathing the same air he'd always breathed, but marveling at how *different* it all was. His heartbeat and respiration were up—the tips of the first two fingers on his right hand itched slightly under his feedback gloves—and his thoughts were doing that race-condition thing where every time he tried to concentrate on something he thought about how he was trying to concentrate on something and should stop thinking about how he was concentrating and just concentrate.

This was how it had been sixteen years before, when he'd gone into the Order. He'd been so *angry* all the time then. Sitting in front of his keyboard, looking at the world through the lens of the network, suffering all the fools with poor grace. He'd been a bright 14-year-old, a genius at 16, a rising star at 18, and a failure by 21. He was depressed all the time, his weight had ballooned to nearly 300 pounds, and he had been fired three times in two years.

One day he stood up from his desk at work—he'd just been hired at a company that was selling learning, trainable vision-systems for analyzing images, who liked him because he'd retained his security clearance when he'd been fired from his previous job—and walked out of the building. It had been a blowing, wet, grey day, and the streets of New York were as empty as they ever got.

Standing on Sixth Avenue, looking north from midtown, staring at the buildings the cars and the buses and the people and the tallwalkers, that's when he had his realization: *He was not meant to be in this world.*

It just didn't suit him. He could *see* its workings, see how its politics and policies were flawed, see how the system needed debugging, see what made its people work, but he couldn't touch it. Every time he reached in to adjust its settings, he got mangled by its gears. He couldn't convince his bosses that he knew what they were doing wrong. He couldn't convince his colleagues that he knew best. Nothing he did succeeded—every attempt he made to right the wrongs of the world made him miserable and made everyone else angry.

Lawrence knew about humans, so he knew about this: this was the exact profile of the people in the Order. Normally he would have taken the subway home. It was forty blocks to his place, and he didn't get around so well anymore. Plus there was the rain and the wind.

But today, he walked, huffing and limping, using his cane more and more as he got further and further uptown, his knee complaining with each step. He got to his apartment and found that the elevator was out of service—second time that month—and so he took the stairs. He arrived at his apartment so out of breath he felt like he might vomit.

He stood in the doorway, clutching the frame, looking at his sofa and table, the piles of books, the dirty dishes from that morning's breakfast in the little sink. He'd watched a series of short videos about the Order once, and he'd been struck by the little monastic cells each member occupied, so neat, so tidy, everything in its perfect place, serene and thoughtful.

So unlike his place.

He didn't bother to lock the door behind him when he left. They said New York was the burglary capital of the developed world, but he didn't know anyone who'd been burgled. If the burglars came, they were welcome to everything they could carry away and the landlord could take the rest. He was not meant to be in this world.

He walked back out into the rain and, what the hell, hailed a cab, and, hail mary, one stopped when he put his hand out. The cabbie grunted when he said he was going to Staten Island, but, what the hell, he pulled three twenties out of his wallet and slid them through the glass partition. The cabbie put the pedal down. The rain sliced through the Manhattan canyons and battered the windows and they went over the Verrazano Bridge and he said goodbye to his life and the outside world forever, seeking a world he could be a part of.

Or at least, that's how he felt, as his heart swelled with the drama of it all. But the truth was much less glamorous. The brothers who admitted him at the gate were cheerful and a little weird, like his co-workers, and he didn't get a nice clean cell to begin with, but a bunk in a shared room and a detail helping to build more quarters. And they didn't leave his stuff for the burglars—someone from the Order went and cleaned out his place and put his stuff in a storage locker on campus, made good with his landlord and so on. By the time it was all over, it all felt a little . . . ordinary. But in a good way, Ordinary was good. It had been a long time since he'd felt ordinary. Order, ordinary. They went together. He needed ordinary.

The Securitat van played a cheerful engine-tone as it zipped down the street towards him. It looked like a children's drawing—a perfect little electrical box with two seats in front and a meshed-in lockup in the rear. It accelerated smoothly down the street towards him, then braked perfectly at his toes, rocking slightly on its suspension as its doors gull-winged up.

"Cool!" he said, involuntarily, stepping back to admire the smart little car. He reached for the lifelogger around his neck and aimed it at the two Securitat officers who were debarking, moving with stiff grace in their armor. As he raised the lifelogger, the officer closest to him reached out with serpentine speed and snatched it out of his hands, power-assisted fingers coming together on it with a loud, plasticky *crunk* as the device shattered into a rain of fragments. Just as quickly, the other officer had come around the vehicle and seized Lawrence's wrists, bringing them together in a painful, machine-assisted grip.

The one who had crushed his lifelogger passed his palms over Lawrence's chest, arms and legs, holding them a few millimeters away from him. Lawrence's pan went nuts, intrusion detection sensors reporting multiple hostile reads of his identifiers, millimeter-wave radar scans, HERF attacks, and assorted shenanigans. All his feedback systems went to full alert, going from itchy, back-of-the-neck liminal sensations into high intensity pinches, prods and buzzes. It was a deeply alarming sensation, like his internal organs were under attack.

He choked out an incoherent syllable, and the Securitat man who was hand-wanding him raised a warning finger, holding it so close to his nose he went cross-eyed. He fell silent while the man continued to wand him, twitching a little to let his pan know that it was all OK.

"From the cult, then, are you?" the Securitat man said, after he'd kicked Lawrence's ankles apart and spread his hands on the side of the truck.

"That's right," Lawrence said. "From the Order." He jerked his head toward the gates, just a few tantalizing meters away. "I'm out—"

"You people are really something, you know that? You could have been *killed*. Let me tell you a few things about how the world works: when you are approached by the Securitat, you stand still with your hands stretched straight out to either side. You do *not* raise unidentified devices and point them at the officers. Not unless you're trying to commit suicide by cop. Is that what you're trying to do?"

"No," Lawrence said. "No, of course not. I was just taking a picture for—"

"And you do *not* photograph or log our security procedures. There's a war on, you know." The man's forehead bunched together. "Oh, for shit's sake. We should take you in now, you know it? Tie up a dozen people's day, just to process you through the system. You could end up in a cell for, oh, I don't know, a month. You want that?"

"Of course not," Lawrence said. "I didn't realize—"

"You didn't, but you *should have*. If you're going to come walking around here where the real people are, you have to learn how to behave like a real person in the real world."

The other man, who had been impassively holding Lawrence's wrists in a crushing grip, eased up. "Let him go?" he said.

The first officer shook his head. "If I were you, I would turn right around, walk through those gates, and never come out again. Do I make myself clear?"

Lawrence wasn't clear at all. Was the cop ordering him to go back? Or just giving him advice? Would he be arrested if he didn't go back in? It had been a long time since Lawrence had dealt with authority and the feeling wasn't a good one. His chest heaved, and sweat ran down his back, pooling around his ass, then moving in rivulets down the backs of his legs.

"I understand," he said. Thinking: *I understand that asking questions now would not be a good idea.*

The subway was more or less as he remembered it, though the long line of people waiting to get through the turnstiles turned out to be a line to go through a security checkpoint, complete with bag-search and X-ray. But the New Yorkers were the same—no one made eye contact with anyone else, but if they did, everyone shared a kind of bitter shrug, as if to say, *Ain't it the fuckin' truth?*

But the smell was the same—oil and damp and bleach and the indefinable, human smell of a place where millions had passed for decades, where millions would pass for decades to come. He found himself standing before a subway map, looking at it, comparing it to the one in his memory to find the changes, the new stations that must have sprung up during his hiatus from reality.

But there weren't new stations. In fact, it seemed to him that there were a lot *fewer* stations—hadn't there been one at Bleecker Street, and another at Cathedral Parkway? Yes, there had been—but look now, they were gone, and . . . and there were stickers, white stickers over the places where the stations had been. He reached up and touched the one over Bleecker Street.

"I still can't get used to it, either," said a voice at his side. "I used to change for the F Train there every day when I was a kid." It was a woman, about the same age as Gerta, but more beaten down by the years, deeper creases in her face, a stoop in her stance. But her face was kind, her eyes soft.

"What happened to it?"

She took a half-step back from him. "Bleecker Street," she said. "You know, Bleecker Street? Like 9/11? Bleecker Street?" Like the name of the station was an incantation.

It rang a bell. It wasn't like he didn't ever read the news, but it had a way of sliding off of you when you were on campus, as though it was some historical event in a book, not something happening right there, on the other side of the wall.

"I'm sorry," he said. "I've been away. Bleecker Street, yes, of course."

She gave him a squinty stare. "You must have been *very* far away."

He tried out a sheepish grin. "I'm a monk," he said. "From the Order of Reflective Analytics. I've been out of the world for sixteen years. Until today, in fact. My name is Lawrence." He stuck his hand out and she shook it like it was made of china.

"A monk," she said. "That's very interesting. Well, you enjoy your little vacation." She turned on her heel and walked quickly down the platform. He watched her for a moment, then turned back to the map, counting the missing stations.

When the train ground to a halt in the tunnel between 42nd and 50th streets, the entire car let out a collective groan. When the lights flickered and went out, they groaned louder. The emergency lights came on in sickly green and an incomprehensible announcement played over the loudspeakers. Evidently, it was an order to evacuate, because the press of people began to struggle through the door at the front of the car, then further and further. Lawrence let the press of bodies move him too.

Once they reached the front of the train, they stepped down onto the tracks, each passenger turning silently to help the next, again with that *Ain't it the fuckin' truth?* look. Lawrence turned to help the person behind him and saw that it was the woman who'd spoken to him on the platform. She smiled a little smile at him and turned with practiced ease to help the person behind her.

They walked single file on a narrow walkway beside the railings. Securitat officers were strung out at regular intervals, wearing night scopes and high, rubberized boots. They played flashlights over the walkers as they evacuated.

"Does this happen often?" Lawrence said over his shoulder. His words were absorbed by the dead subterranean air and he thought that she might not have heard him but then she sighed.

"Only every time there's an anomaly in the head-count—when the system says there's too many or too few people in the trains. Maybe once a week." He could feel her staring at the back of his head. He looked back at her and saw her shaking her head. He stumbled and went down on one knee, clanging his head against the stone walls made soft by a fur of condensed train exhaust, cobwebs and dust.

She helped him to his feet. "You don't seem like a snitch, Lawrence. But you're a monk. Are you going to turn me in for being suspicious?"

He took a second to parse this out. "I don't work for the Securitat," he said. It seemed like the best way to answer.

She snorted. "That's not what we hear. Come on, they're going to start shouting at us if we don't move."

They walked the rest of the way to an emergency staircase together, and emerged out of a sidewalk grating, blinking in the remains of the autumn sunlight, a bloody color on the glass of the highrises. She looked at him and made a face. "You're filthy, Lawrence." She thumped at his sleeves and great dirty clouds rose off them. He looked down at the knees of his pants and saw that they were hung with boogers of dust.

The New Yorkers who streamed past them ducked to avoid the dirty clouds. "Where can I clean up?" he said.

"Where are you staying?"

"I was thinking I'd see about getting a room at the Y or a backpacker's hostel, somewhere to stay until I'm done."

"Done?"

"I'm on a complicated errand. Trying to locate someone who used to be in the Order."

Her face grew hard again. "No one gets out alive, huh?"

He felt himself blushing. "It's not like that. Wow, you've got strange ideas about us. I want to find this guy because he disappeared under mysterious circumstances and I want to—" How to explain Anomalies to an outsider? "It's a thing we do. Unravel mysteries. It makes us better people."

"Better people?" She snorted again. "Better than what?

Don't answer. Come on, I live near here. You can wash up at my place and be on your way. You're not going to get into any backpacker's hostel looking like you just crawled out of a sewer—you're more likely to get detained for being an 'indigent of suspicious character.'"

He let her steer him a few yards uptown. "You think that I work for the Securitat but you're inviting me into your home?"

She shook her head and led him around a corner, along a long crosstown block, and then turned back uptown. "No," she said. "I think you're a confused stranger who is apt to get himself into some trouble if someone doesn't take you in hand and help you get smart, fast. It doesn't cost me anything to lend a hand, and you don't seem like the kind of guy who'd mug, rape and kill an old lady."

"The discipline," he said, "is all about keeping track of the way that the world is, and comparing it to your internal perceptions, all the time. When I entered the Order, I was really big. Fat, I mean. The discipline made me log every bit of food I ate, and I discovered a few important things: first, I was eating about 20 times a day, just grazing on whatever happened to be around. Second, that I was consuming about 4,000 calories a day, mostly in industrial sugars like high-fructose corn syrup. Just *knowing* how I ate made a gigantic difference. I felt like I ate sensibly, always ordering a salad with lunch and dinner, but I missed the fact that I was glooping on half a cup of sweetened, high-fat dressing, and having a cookie or two every hour between lunch and dinner, and a half-pint of ice-cream before bed most nights.

"But it wasn't just food—in the Order, we keep track of *everything*; our typing patterns, our sleeping patterns, our moods, our reading habits. I discovered that I read faster when I've been sleeping more, so now, when I need to really get through a lot of reading, I make sure I sleep more. Used to be I'd try to stay up all night with pots of coffee to get the reading done. Of course, the more sleep-deprived I was, the slower I read; and the slower I read the more I needed to stay up to catch up with the reading. No wonder college was such a blur.

"So that's why I've stayed. It's empiricism, it's as old as Newton, as the Enlightenment." He took another sip of his water, which tasted like New York tap water had always tasted (pretty good, in fact), and which he hadn't tasted for sixteen years. The woman was called Posy, and her old leather sofa was worn but well-loved, and smelled of saddle soap. She was watching him from a kitchen chair she'd brought around to the living room of the tiny apartment, rubbing her stockinged feet over the good wool carpet that showed a few old stains hiding beneath strategically placed furnishings and knick-knacks.

He had to tell her the rest, of course. You couldn't understand the Order unless you understood the rest. "I'm a screwup, Posy. Or at least, I was. We all were. Smart and motivated and promising, but just a wretched person to be around. Angry, bitter, all those smarts turned on biting the heads off of the people who were dumb enough to care about me or employ me. And so smart that I could talk myself into believing that it was all everyone else's fault, the idiots. It took instrumentation, empiricism, to get me to understand the patterns of my own life, to master my life, to become the person I wanted to be."

"Well, you seem like a perfectly nice young man now," Posy said.

That was clearly his cue to go, and he'd changed into a fresh set of trousers, but he couldn't go, not until he'd picked apart something she'd said earlier. "Why did you think I was a snitch?"

"I think you know that very well, Lawrence," she said. "I can't imagine someone who's so into measuring and understanding the world could possibly have missed it."

Now he knew what she was talking about. "We just do contract work for the Securitat. It's just one of the ways the Order sustains itself." The founders had gone into business refilling toner cartridges, which was like the 21st century equivalent of keeping bees or brewing dark, thick beer. They'd branched out into remote IT administration, then into data-mining and security, which was a natural for people with Order training. "But it's all anonymized. We don't snitch on people. We report on anomalous events. We do it for lots of different companies, too—not just the Securitat."

Posy walked over to the window behind her small dining room table, rolling away a couple of handsome old chairs on castors to reach it. She looked down over the billion lights of Manhattan, stretching all the way downtown to Brooklyn. She motioned to him to come over, and he squeezed in beside her. They were on the twenty-third floor, and it had been many years since he'd stood this high and looked down. The world is different from high up.

"There," she said, pointing at an apartment building across the way. "There, you see it? With the broken windows?" He saw it, the windows covered in cardboard. "They took them away last week. I don't know why. You never know why. You become a person of interest and they take you away and then later, they always find a reason to keep you away."

Lawrence's hackles were coming up. He found stuff that didn't belong in the data—he didn't arrest people. "So if they always find a reason to keep you away, doesn't that mean—"

She looked like she wanted to slap him and he took a step back. "We're all guilty of something, Lawrence. That's how the game is rigged. Look closely at anyone's life and you'll find, what, a little black-marketeering, a copyright infringement, some cash economy business with unreported income, something obscene in your Internet use, something in your bloodstream that shouldn't be there. I bought that sofa from a *cop*, Lawrence, bought it ten years ago when he was leaving the building. He didn't give me a receipt and didn't collect tax, and technically that makes us offenders." She slapped the radiator. "I overrode the governor on this ten minutes after they installed it. Everyone does it. They make it easy—you just stick a penny between two contacts and hey presto, the city can't turn your heat down anymore. They wouldn't make it so easy if they didn't expect everyone to do it—and once everyone's done it, we're all guilty.

"The people across the street, they were Pakistani or maybe Sri Lankan or Bangladeshi. I'd see the wife at the service laundry. Nice professional lady, always lugging

around a couple kids on their way to or from day-care. She—"
Posy broke off and stared again. "I once saw her reach for her
change and her sleeve rode up and there was a number tat-
tooed there, there on her wrist." Posy shuddered. "When
they took her and her husband and their kids, she stood at
the window and pounded at it and screamed for help. You
could hear her from here."

"That's terrible," Lawrence said. "But what does it have
to do with the Order?"

She sat back down. "For someone who is supposed to
know himself, you're not very good at connecting the dots."

Lawrence stood up. He felt an obscure need to apologize.
Instead, he thanked her and put his glass in the sink. She
shook his hand solemnly.

"Take care out there," she said. "Good luck finding your
escapee."

Here's what Lawrence knew about Zbigniew Krotoski. He
had been inducted into the Order four years earlier. He was
a native-born New Yorker. He had spent his first two years
in the Order trying to coax some of the elders into a variety
of pointless flamewars about the ethics of working for the
Securitat, and then had settled into being a very productive
member. He spent his 20 percent time—the time when each
monk had to pursue non-work-related projects—building
aerial photography rigs out of box-kites and tiny cameras
that the Monks installed on their systems to help them monitor their body mechanics and ergonomic posture.

Zbigkrot performed in the eighty-fifth percentile of the
Order, which was respectable enough. Lawrence had started
there and had crept up and down as low as 70 and as high as
88, depending on how he was doing in the rest of his life.
Zbigkrot was active in the gardens, both the big ones where
they grew their produce and a little allotment garden
where he indulged in baroque cross-breeding experiments,
which were in vogue among the monks then.

The Securitat stream to which he'd added 68 bytes was
long gone, but it was the kind of thing that the Order handled
on a routine basis: given the timing and other characteristics,

Lawrence thought it was probably a stream of purchase data from hardware and grocery stores, to be inspected for unusual patterns that might indicate someone buying bomb ingredients. Zbigkrot had worked on this kind of data thousands of times before, six times just that day. He'd added the sixty-eight bytes and then left, invoking his right to do so at the lone gate. The gatekeeper on duty remembered him carrying a little rucksack, and mentioning that he was going to see his sister in New York.

Zbigkrot once had a sister in New York—that much could be ascertained. Anja Krotoski had lived on 23rd Street in a co-op near Lexington. But that had been four years previous, when he'd joined the Order, and she wasn't there anymore. Her numbers all rang dead.

The apartment building had once been a pleasant, middle-class sort of place, with a red awning and a niche for a doorman. Now it had become more run down, the awning's edges frayed, one pane of lobby glass broken out and replaced with a sheet of cardboard. The doorman was long gone.

It seemed to Lawrence that this fate had befallen many of the City's buildings. They reminded him of the buildings he'd seen in Belgrade one time, when he'd been sent out to brief a gang of outsource programmers his boss had hired— neglected for years, indifferently patched by residents who had limited access to materials.

It was the dinner hour, and a steady trickle of people were letting themselves into Anja's old building. Lawrence watched a couple of them enter the building and noticed something wonderful and sad: as they approached the building, their faces were the hard masks of city-dwellers, not meeting anyone's eye, clipping along at a fast pace that said, "Don't screw with me." But once they passed the threshold of their building and the door closed behind them, their whole affect changed. They slumped, they smiled at one another, they leaned against the mailboxes and set down their bags and took off their hats and fluffed their hair and turned back into people.

He remembered that feeling from his life before, the sense of having two faces: the one he showed to the world and the one that he reserved for home. In the Order, he only wore one face, one that he knew in exquisite detail.

He approached the door now, and his pan started to throb ominously, letting him know that he was enduring hostile probes. The building wanted to know who he was and what business he had there, and it was attempting to fingerprint everything about him from his pan to his gait to his face.

He took up a position by the door and dialed back the pan's response to a dull pulse. He waited for a few minutes until one of the residents came down: a middle-aged man with a dog, a little sickly-looking schnauzer with grey in its muzzle.

"Can I help you?" the man said, from the other side of the security door, not unlatching it.

"I'm looking for Anja Krotoski," he said. "I'm trying to track down her brother."

The man looked him up and down. "Please step away from the door."

He took a few steps back. "Does Ms. Krotoski still live here?"

The man considered. "I'm sorry, sir, I can't help you." He waited for Lawrence to react.

"You don't know, or you can't help me?"

"Don't wait under this awning. The police come if anyone waits under this awning for more than three minutes."

The man opened the door and walked away with his dog.

His phone rang before the next resident arrived. He cocked his head to answer it, then remembered that his lifelogger was dead and dug in his jacket for a mic. There was one at his wrist pulse-points used by the health array. He unvelcroed it and held it to his mouth.

"Hello?"

"It's Gerta, boyo. Wanted to know how your Anomaly was going."

"Not good," he said. "I'm at the sister's place and they don't want to talk to me."

"You're walking up to strangers and asking them about one of their neighbors, huh?"

He winced. "Put it that way, yeah, OK, I understand why this doesn't work. But Gerta, I feel like Rip Van Winkle here. I keep putting my foot in it. It's so different."

"People are people, Lawrence. Every bad behavior and every good one lurks within us. They were all there when you were in the world—in different proportion, with different triggers. But all there. You know yourself very well. Can you observe the people around you with the same keen attention?"

He felt slightly put upon. "That's what I'm trying—"

"Then you'll get there eventually. What, you're in a hurry?"

Well, no. He didn't have any kind of timeline. Some people chased Anomalies for *years*. But truth be told, he wanted to get out of the City and back onto campus. "I'm thinking of coming back to Campus to sleep."

Gerta clucked. "Don't give in to the agoraphobia, Lawrence. Hang in there. You haven't even heard my news yet, and you're already ready to give up?"

"What news? And I'm not giving up, just want to sleep in my own bed—"

"The entry checkpoints, Lawrence. You cannot do this job if you're going to spend four hours a day in security queues. Anyway, the news.

"It wasn't the first time he did it. I've been running the logs back three years and I've found at least a dozen streams that he tampered with. Each time he used a different technique. This was the first time we caught him. Used some pretty subtle tripwires when he did it, so he'd know if anyone ever caught on. Must have spent his whole life living on edge, waiting for that moment, waiting to bug out. Must have been a hard life."

"What was he doing? Spying?"

"Most assuredly," Gerta said. "But for whom? For the enemy? The Securitat?"

They'd considered going to the Securitat with the information, but why bother? The Order did business with the Securitat, but tried never to interact with them on any other terms. The Securitat and the Order had an implicit understanding: so long as the Order was performing excellent data-analysis, it didn't have to fret the kind of overt scrutiny that prevailed in the real world. Undoubtedly, the Securitat kept satellite eyes, data-snoopers, wiretaps, millimeter radar and every other conceivable surveillance trained on each Campus in the world, but at the end of the day, they were just badly socialized geeks who'd left the world, and useful geeks at that. The Securitat treated the Order the way that Lawrence's old bosses treated the company sysadmins: expendable geeks who no one cared about—so long as nothing went wrong.

No, there was no sense in telling the Securitat about the 68 bytes.

"Why would the Securitat poison its own data-streams?"

"You know that when the Soviets pulled out of Finland, they found 40 *kilometers* of wire-tapping wire in KGB headquarters? The building was only 12 stories tall! Spying begets spying. The worst, most dangerous enemy the Securitat has is the Securitat."

There were Securitat vans on the street around him, going past every now and again, eerily silent engines, playing their cheerful music. He stepped back into shadow, then thought better of it and stood under a pool of light.

"OK, so it was a habit. How do I find him? No one in the sister's building will talk to me."

"You need to put them at their ease. Tell them the truth, that often works."

"You know how people feel about the Order out here?" He thought of Posy. "I don't know if the truth is going to work here."

"You've been in the order for sixteen years. You're not just some fumble-tongued outcast anymore. Go talk to them."

"But—"

"Go, Lawrence. Go. You're a smart guy, you'll figure it out."

He went. Residents were coming home every few minutes now, carrying grocery bags, walking dogs, or dragging their tired feet. He almost approached a young woman, then figured that she wouldn't want to talk to a strange man on the street at night. He picked a guy in his thirties, wearing jeans and a huge old vintage coat that looked like it had come off the eastern front.

"'Scuse me," he said. "I'm trying to find someone who used to live here."

The guy stopped and looked Lawrence up and down. He had a handsome sweater on underneath his coat, design-y and cosmopolitan, the kind of thing that made Lawrence think of Milan or Paris. Lawrence was keenly aware of his generic Order-issued suit, a brown, rumpled, ill-fitting thing, topped with a polymer coat that, while warm, hardly flattered.

"Good luck with that," he said, then started to move past.

"Please," Lawrence said. "I'm—I'm not used to how things are around here. There's probably some way I could ask you this that would put you at your ease, but I don't know what it is. I'm not good with people. But I really need to find this person, she used to live here."

The man stopped, looked at him again. He seemed to recognize something in Lawrence, or maybe it was that he was disarmed by Lawrence's honesty.

"Why would you want to do that?"

"It's a long story," he said. "Basically, though: I'm a monk from the Order of Reflective Analytics and one of our guys has disappeared. His sister used to live here—maybe she still does—and I wanted to ask her if she knew where I could find him."

"Let me guess, none of my neighbors wanted to help you."

"You're only the second guy I've asked, but yeah, pretty much."

"Out here in the real world, we don't really talk about each other to strangers. Too much like being a snitch. Lucky for you, my sister's in the Order, out in Oregon, so I know you're not all a bunch of snoops and stoolies. Who're you looking for?"

Lawrence felt a rush of gratitude for this man. "Anja Krotosky, number 11-J?"

"Oh," the man said. "Well, yeah, I can see why you'd have a hard time with the neighbors when it comes to old Anja. She was well-liked around here, before she went."

"Where'd she go? When?"

"What's your name, friend?"

"Lawrence."

"Lawrence, Anja *went*. Middle of the night kind of thing. No one heard a thing. The CCTVs stopped working that night. Nothing on the drive the next day. No footage at all."

"Like she skipped out?"

"They stopped delivering flyers to her door. There's only one power stronger than direct marketing."

"The Securitat took her?"

"That's what we figured. Nothing left in her place. Not a stick of furniture. We don't talk about it much. Not the thing that it pays to take an interest in."

"How long ago?"

"Two years ago," he said. A few more residents pushed past them. "Listen, I approve of what you people do in there, more or less. It's good that there's a place for the people who don't— you know, who don't have a place out here. But the way you make your living. I told my sister about this, the last time she visited, and she got very angry with me. She didn't see the difference between watching yourself and being watched."

Lawrence nodded. "Well, that's true enough. We don't draw a really sharp distinction. We all get to see one anoth- er's stats. It keeps us honest."

"That's fine, if you have the choice. But—" He broke off, looking self-conscious. Lawrence reminded himself that they were on a public street, the cameras on them, people passing by. Was one of them a snitch? The Securitat had talked about putting him away for a month, just for logging them. They could watch him all they wanted, but he couldn't look at them.

"I see the point." He sighed. He was cold and it was full autumn dark now. He still didn't have a room for the night and he didn't have any idea how he'd find Anja, much less zbigkrot. He began to understand why Anomalies were such a big deal.

He'd walked 18,453 steps that day, about triple what he did on campus. His heart rate had spiked several times, but not from exertion. Stress. He could feel it in his muscles now. He should really do some biofeedback, try to calm down, then run back his lifelogger and make some notes on how he'd reacted to people through the day.

But the lifelogger was gone and he barely managed 22 seconds his first time on the biofeedback. His next ten scores were much worse.

It was the hotel room. It had once been an office, and before that, it had been half a hotel-room. There were still scuff-marks on the floor from where the wheeled office chair had dug into the scratched lino. The false wall that divided the room in half was thin as paper and Lawrence could hear every snuffle from the other side. The door to Lawrence's room had been rudely hacked in, and weak light shone through an irregular crack over the jamb.

The old New Yorker Hotel had seen better days, but it was what he could afford, and it was central, and he could hear New York outside the window—he'd gotten the half of the hotel room with the window in it. The lights twinkled just as he remembered them, and he still got a swimmy, vertiginous feeling when he looked down from the great height.

The clerk had taken his photo and biometrics and had handed him a tracker-key that his pan was monitoring with tangible suspicion. It radiated his identity every few yards, and in the elevator. It even seemed to track which part of the minuscule room he was in. What the hell did the hotel do with all this information?

Oh, right—it shipped it off to the Securitat, who shipped it to the Order, where it was processed for suspicious anomalies. No wonder there was so much work for them on campus. Multiply the New Yorker times a hundred thousand hotels, two hundred thousand schools, a million cabs across the nation—there was no danger of the Order running out of work.

The hotel's network tried to keep him from establishing a secure connection back to the Order's network, but the Order's countermeasures were better than the half-assed ones at the hotel. It took a lot of tunneling and wrapping, but in short measure he had a strong private line back to the

Campus—albeit a slow line, what with all the jiggery-pokery he had to go through.

Gerta had left him with her file on zbigkrot and his activities on the network. He had several known associates on Campus, people he ate with or playing on intramural teams with, or did a little extreme programming with. Gerta had bulk-messaged them all with an oblique query about his personal life and had forwarded the responses to Lawrence. There was a mountain of them, and he started to plow through them.

He started by compiling stats on them—length, vocabulary, number of paragraphs—and then started with the outliers. The shortest ones were polite shrugs, apologies, don't have anything to say. The long ones—whew! They sorted into two categories: general whining, mostly from noobs who were still getting accustomed to the way of the Order; and protracted complaints from old hands who'd worked with zbigkrot long enough to decide that he was incorrigible. Lawrence sorted these quickly, then took a glance at the median responses and confirmed that they appeared to be largely unhelpful generalizations of the sort that you might produce on a co-worker evaluation form—a proliferation of null adjectives like "satisfactory," "pleasant," "fine."

Somewhere in this haystack—Lawrence did a quick word-count and came back with 140,000 words, about two good novels' worth of reading—was a needle, a clue that would show him the way to unravel the Anomaly. It would take him a couple days at least to sort through it all in depth. He ducked downstairs and bought some groceries at an all-night grocery store in Penn Station and went back to his room, ready to settle in and get the work done. He could use a few days' holiday from New York, anyway.

About time Zee Big Noob did a runner. He never had a moment's happiness here, and I never figured out why he'd bother hanging around when he hated it all so much.

Ever meet the kind of guy who wanted to tell you just how much you shouldn't be enjoying the things you enjoy? The kind of guy who could explain, in detail, *exactly* why your passions were stupid? That was him.

"Brother Antony, why are you wasting your time collecting tin toys? They're badly made, unlovely, and represent, at best, a history of slave labor, starting with your cherished 'Made in Occupied Japan,' tanks. Christ, why not collect rape-camp macrame while you're at it?" He had choice words for all of us about our passions, but I was singled out because I liked to extreme program in my room, which I'd spent a lot of time decorating. (See pic, below, and yes, I built and sanded and mounted every one of those shelves by hand) (See magnification shot for detail on the joinery. Couldn't even drive a nail when I got here) (Not that there are any nails in there, it's all precision-fitted tongue and groove) (holy moley, lasers totally rock)

But he reserved his worst criticism for the Order itself. You know the litany: we're a cult, we're brainwashed, we're dupes of the Securitat. He was convinced that every instrument in the place was feeding up to the Securitat itself. He'd mutter about this constantly, whenever we got a new stream to work on—"Is this your lifelog, Brother Antony? Mine? The number of flushes per shitter in the west wing of campus?"

And it was no good trying to reason with him. He just didn't acknowledge the benefit of introspection. "It's no different from them," he'd say, jerking his thumb up at the ceiling, as though there was a Securitat mic and camera hidden there. "You're just flooding yourself with useless information, trying to find the useful parts. Why not make some predictions about which part of your life you need to pay attention to, rather than spying on every process? You're a spy in your own body."

So why did I work with him? I'll tell you: first, he was a shit-hot programmer. I know his stats say he was way down in the 78th percentile, but he could make every line of code that *I* wrote smarter. We just don't have a way of measuring that kind of effect (yes, someone should write one; I've been noodling with a framework for it for months now).

Second, there was something dreadfully fun about listening him light into *other* people, *their* ridiculous passions and interests. He could be incredibly funny, and he was incisive if not insightful. It's shameful, but there you have it. I am imperfect.

Finally, when he wasn't being a dick, he was a good guy to have in your corner. He was our rugby team's fullback, the baseball team's shortstop, the tank on our MMOG raids. You could rely on him.

So I'm going to miss him, weirdly. If he's gone for good. I wouldn't put it past him to stroll back onto campus someday and say, "What, what? I just took a little French Leave. Jesus, overreact much?"

Plenty of the notes ran in this direction, but this was the most articulate. Lawrence read it through three times before adding it to the file of useful stuff. It was a small pile. Still, Gerta kept forwarding him responses. The late responders had some useful things to say:

He mentioned a sister. Only once. A whole bunch of us were talking about how our families were really supportive of our coming to the Order, and after it had gone round the whole circle, he just kind of looked at the sky and said, "My sister thought I was an idiot to go inside. I asked her what she thought I should do and she said, 'If I was you, kid, I'd just disappear before someone disappeared me.' " Naturally we all wanted to know what he meant by that. "I'm not very good at bullshitting, and that's a vital skill in today's world. She was better at it than me, when she worked at it, but she was the kind of person who'd let her guard slip every now and then."

Lawrence noted that zbigkrot had used the past-tense to describe his sister. He'd have known about her being disappeared then.

He stared at the walls of his hotel room. The room next door was occupied by at least four people and he couldn't even imagine how you'd get that many people inside—he didn't know how four people could all *stand* in the room, let alone lie down and sleep. But there were definitely four voices from next door, talking in Chinese.

New York was outside the window and far below, and the sun had come up far enough that everything was bright and reflective, the cars and the buildings and the glints from sunglasses far below. He wasn't getting anywhere with the docs, the sister, the datastreams. And there was New York, just outside the window.

He dug under the bed and excavated his boots, recoiling from soft, dust-furred old socks and worse underneath the mattress.

The Securitat man pointed to Lawrence as he walked past Penn Station. Lawrence stopped and pointed at himself in a who-me? gesture. The Securitat man pointed again, then pointed to his alcove next to the entrance.

Lawrence's pan didn't like the Securitat man's incursions and tried to wipe itself.

"Sir," he said. "My pan is going nuts. May I put down my arms so I can tell it to let you in?"

The Securitat man acted as though he hadn't heard, just continued to wave his hands slowly over Lawrence's body.

"Come with me," the Securitat man said, pointing to the door on the other side of the alcove that led into a narrow corridor, into the bowels of Penn Station. The door let out onto the concourse, thronged with people shoving past each other, disgorged by train after train. Though none made eye contact with them or each other, they parted magically before them, leaving them with a clear path.

Lawrence's pan was not helping him. Every inch of his body itched as it nagged at him about the depredations it was facing from the station and the Securitat man. This put him seriously on edge and made his heart and breathing go crazy, triggering another round of warnings from his pan, which wanted him to calm down, but wouldn't help. This was a bad failure mode, one he'd never experienced before. He'd have to file a bug report.

Some day.

The Securitat's outpost in Penn Station was as clean as a dentist's office, but with mesh-reinforced windows and locks that made three distinct clicks and a soft hiss when the door closed. The Securitat man impersonally shackled Lawrence to a plastic chair that was bolted into the floor and then went off to a check-in kiosk that he whispered into and prodded at. There was no one else in evidence, but there were huge CCTV cameras, so big that they seemed to be throwbacks to an earlier era, some paleolithic ancestor of the modern camera. These cameras were so big because they were meant to be seen, meant to let you know that you were being watched.

The Securitat man took him away again, stood him in an interview room where the cameras were once again in voluble evidence.

"Explain everything," the Securitat man said. He rolled up his mask so that Lawrence could see his face, young and hard. He'd been in diapers when Lawrence went into the Order.

And so Lawrence began to explain, but he didn't want to explain everything. Telling this man about zbigkrot tampering with Securitat data-streams would not be good; telling him about the disappearance of Anja Krotoski would be even worse. So—he lied. He was already so stressed out that there was no way the lies would register as extraordinary to the sensors that were doubtless trained on him.

He told the Securitat man that he was in the world to find an Order member who'd taken his leave, because the Order wanted to talk to him about coming back. He told the man that he'd been trying to locate zbigkrot by following up on his old contacts. He told the Securitat man that he expected to find zbigkrot within a day or two and would be going back to the Order. He implied that he was crucial to the Order and that he worked for the Securitat all the time, that he and the Securitat man were on the same fundamental mission, on the same team.

The Securitat man's face remained an impassive mask throughout. He touched an earbead from time to time, cocking his head slightly to listen. Someone else was listening to Lawrence's testimony and feeding him more material.

The Securitat man scooted his chair closer to Lawrence, leaned in close, searching his face. "We don't have any record of this Krotoski person," he said. "I advise you to go home and forget about him."

The words were said without any inflection at all, and that was scariest of all—Lawrence had no doubt about what this meant. There were no records because Zbigniew Krotoski was erased.

Lawrence wondered what he was supposed to say to this armed child now. Did he lay his finger alongside of his nose and wink? Apologize for wasting his time? Everyone told him to listen before he spoke here. Should he just wait?

"Thank you for telling me so," he said. "I appreciate the advice." He hoped it didn't sound sarcastic.

The Securitat man nodded. "You need to adjust the settings on your pan. It reads like it's got something to hide. Here in the world, it has to accede to lawful read attempts without hesitation. Will you configure it?"

Lawrence nodded vigorously. While he'd recounted his story, he'd imagined spending a month in a cell while the Securitat looked into his deeds and history. Now it seemed like he might be on the streets in a matter of minutes.

"Thank you for your cooperation." The man didn't say it. It was a recording, played by hidden speakers, triggered by some unseen agency, and on hearing it, the Securitat man stood and opened the door, waiting for the three distinct clicks and the hiss before tugging at the handle.

They stood before the door to the guard's niche in front of Penn Station and the man rolled up his mask again. This time he was smiling an easy smile and the hardness had melted a little from around his eyes. "You want a tip, buddy?"

"Sure."

"Look, this is New York. We all just want to get along here. There's a lot of bad guys out there. They got some kind of beef. They want to fuck with us. We don't want to let them do that. You want to be safe here, you got to show New

York that you're not a bad guy. That you're not here to fuck with us. We're the city's protectors, and we can spot some-one who doesn't belong here the way your body can spot a cold-germ. The way you're walking around here, looking around, acting—I could tell you didn't belong from a hun-dred yards. You want to avoid trouble, you get less strange, fast. You get me?"

"I get you," he said. "Thank you, sir." Before the Securitat man could say any more, Lawrence was on his way.

The man from Anja's building had a different sweater on, but the new one—bulky wool the color of good chocolate—was every bit as handsome as the one he'd had on before. He was wearing some kind of citrusy cologne and his hair fell around his ears in little waves that looked so natural they had to be fake. Lawrence saw him across the Starbucks and had a crazy urge to duck away and change into better clothes, just so he wouldn't look like such a fucking hayseed next to this guy. *I'm a New Yorker,* he thought, *or at least I was. I belong here.*

"Hey, Lawrence, fancy meeting you here!" He shook Lawrence's hand and gave him a wry, you-and-me-in-it-together smile. "How's the vision quest coming?"

"Huh?"

"The Anomaly—that's what you're chasing, aren't you? It's your little rite of passage. My sister had one last year. Figured out that some guy who travelled from Fort Worth to Portland, Oregon every week was actually a fictional con-struct invented by cargo smugglers who used his seat to plant a series of mules running heroin and cash. She was so proud afterwards that I couldn't get her to shut up about it. You had the holy fire the other night when I saw you."

Lawrence felt himself blushing. "It's not really 'holy'— all that religious stuff, it's just a metaphor. We're not really spiritual."

"Oh, the distinction between the spiritual and the mate-rial is pretty arbitrary anyway. Don't worry, I don't think you're a cultist or anything. No more than any of us, anyway. So, how's it going?"

"I think it's over," he said. "Dead end. Maybe I'll get an easier Anomaly next time."

"Sounds awful! I didn't think you were allowed to give up on Anomalies?"

Lawrence looked around to see if anyone was listening to them. "This one leads to the Securitat," he said. "In a sense, you could say that I've solved it. I think the guy I'm looking for ended up with his sister."

The man's expression froze, not moving one iota. "You must be disappointed," he said, in neutral tones. "Oh well." He leaned over the condiment bar to get a napkin and wrestled with the dispenser for a moment. It didn't cooperate, and he ended up holding fifty napkins. He made a disgusted noise and said, "Can you help me get these back into the dispenser?"

Lawrence pushed at the dispenser and let the man feed it his excess napkins, arranging them neatly. While he did this, he contrived to hand Lawrence a card, which Lawrence cupped in his palm and then ditched into his inside jacket pocket under the pretense of reaching in to adjust his pan.

"Thanks," the man said. "Well, I guess you'll be going back to your campus now?"

"In the morning," Lawrence said. "I figured I'd see some New York first. Play tourist, catch a Broadway show."

The man laughed. "All right then—you enjoy it." He did nothing significant as he shook Lawrence's hand and left, holding his paper cup. He did nothing to indicate that he'd just brought Lawrence into some kind of illegal conspiracy.

Lawrence read the note later, on a bench in Bryant Park, holding a paper bag of roasted chestnuts and fastidiously piling the husks next to him as he peeled them away. It was a neatly cut rectangle of card sliced from a health-food cereal box. Lettered on the back of it in pencil were two short lines:

Wednesdays 8:30PM
Half Moon Café 164 2nd Ave

The address was on the Lower East Side, a neighborhood that had been scorchingly trendy the last time Lawrence had been there. More importantly: it was Wednesday.

* * *

The Half Moon Café turned out to be one of those New York places that are so incredibly hip they don't have a sign or any outward indication of their existence. Number 164 was a frosted glass door between a dry-cleaner's and a Pakistani grocery store, propped open with a squashed Mountain Dew can. Lawrence opened the door, heart pounding, and slipped inside. A long, dark corridor stretched away before him, with a single door at the end, open a crack, dim light spilling out of it. He walked quickly down the corridor, sure that there were cameras observing him.

The door at the end of the hallway had a sheet of paper on it, with HALF MOON CAFÉ laser-printed in its center. Good food smells came from behind it, and the clink of cutlery, and soft conversation. He nudged it open and found himself in a dim, flickering room lit by candles and draped with gathered curtains that turned the walls into the proscenia of a grand and ancient stage. There were four or five small tables and a long one at the back of the room, crowded with people, with wine in ice-buckets at either end.

A very pretty girl stood at the podium before him, dressed in a conservative suit, but with her hair shaved into a half-inch brush of electric blue. She lifted an eyebrow at him as though she was sharing a joke with him and said, "Welcome to the Half Moon. Do you have a reservation?"

Lawrence had carefully shredded the bit of cardboard and dropped its tatters in six different trash cans, feeling like a real spy as he did so (and realizing at the same time that going to all these different cans was probably anomalous enough in itself to draw suspicion).

"A friend told me he'd meet me here," he said.

"What was your friend's name?"

Lawrence stuck his chin in the top of his coat to tell his pan to stop warning him that he was breathing too shallowly. "I don't know," he said. He craned his neck to look behind her at the tables. He couldn't see the man, but it was so dark in the restaurant—

"You made it, huh?" The man had yet another fantastic

sweater on, this one with a tight herringbone weave and ribbing down the sleeves. He caught Lawrence sizing him up and grinned. "My weakness—the world's wool farmers would starve if it wasn't for me." He patted the greeter on the hand. "He's at our table." She gave Lawrence a knowing smile and the tiniest hint of a wink.

"Nice of you to come," he said as they threaded their way slowly through the crowded tables, past couples having murmured conversations over candlelight, intense business dinners, an old couple eating in silence with evident relish. "Especially as it's your last night in the city."

"What kind of restaurant is this?"

"Oh, it's not any kind of restaurant at all. Private kitchen. Ormund, he owns the place and cooks like a wizard. He runs this little place off the books for his friends to eat in. We come every Wednesday. That's his vegan night. You'd be amazed with what that guy can do with some greens and a sweet potato. And the cacao nib and avocado chili chocolate is something else."

The large table was crowded with men and women in their thirties, people who had the look of belonging. They dressed well in fabrics that draped or clung like someone had thought about it, with jewelry that combined old pieces of brass with modern plastics and heavy clay beads that clicked like pool-balls. The women were beautiful or at least handsome—one woman with cheekbones like snowplows and a jawline as long as a ski-slope was possibly the most striking person he'd ever seen up close. The men were handsome or at least craggy, with three-day beards or neat, full mustaches. They were talking in twos and threes, passing around overflowing dishes of steaming greens and oranges and browns, chatting and forking by turns.

"Everyone, I'd like you to meet my guest for the evening." The man gestured at Lawrence. Lawrence hadn't told the man his name yet, but he made it seem like he was being gracious and letting Lawrence introduce himself.

"Lawrence," he said, giving a little wave. "Just in New York for one more night," he said, still waving. He stopped waving. The closest people—including the striking woman with the cheekbones—waved back, smiling. The furthest people stopped talking and tipped their forks at him or at least cocked their heads.

"Sara," the cheekbones woman said, pronouncing the first "a" long, "Sah-rah," and making it sound unpretentious. The low-key buzzing from Lawrence's pan warned him that he was still overwrought, breathing badly, heart thudding. Who were these people?

"And I'm Randy," the man said. "Sorry, I should have said that sooner."

The food was passed down to his end. It was delicious, almost as good as the food at the campus, which was saying something—there was a dedicated cadre of cooks there who made gastronomy their 20 percent projects, using elaborate computational models to create dishes that were always different and always delicious.

The big difference was the company. These people didn't have to retreat to belong, they belonged right here. Sara told him about her job managing a specialist antiquarian bookstore and there were a hundred stories about her customers and their funny ways. Randy worked at an architectural design firm and he had done some work at Sara's bookstore. Down the table there were actors and waiters and an insurance person and someone who did something in city government, and they all ate and talked and made him feel like he was a different kind of man, the kind of man who could live on the outside.

The coals of the conversation banked over port and coffees as they drifted away in twos and threes. Sara was the last to leave and she gave him a little hug and a kiss on the cheek. "Safe travels, Lawrence." Her perfume was like an orange on Christmas morning, something from his childhood. He hadn't thought of his childhood in decades.

Randy and he looked at each other over the litter on the table. The server brought a check over on a small silver tray and Randy took a quick look at it. He drew a wad of twenties in a bulldog clip out of his inside coat pocket and counted off a large stack, then handed the tray to the server, all before Lawrence could even dig in his pocket.

"Please let me contribute," he managed, just as the server disappeared.

"Not necessary," Randy said, setting the clip down on the table. There was still a rather thick wad of money there. Lawrence hadn't been much of a cash user before he went into the Order and he'd seen hardly any spent since he came back out into the world. It seemed rather antiquarian, with its elaborate engraving. But the notes were crisp, as though freshly minted. The government still pressed the notes, even if they were hardly used any longer. "I can afford it."

"It was a very fine dinner. You have interesting friends."

"Sara is lovely," he said. "She and I—well, we had a thing once. She's a remarkable person. Of course, you're a remarkable person, too, Lawrence."

Lawrence's pan reminded him again that he was getting edgy. He shushed it.

"You're smart, we know that. 88th percentile. Looks like you could go higher, judging from the work we've evaluated for you. I can't say your performance as a private eye is very good, though. If I hadn't intervened, you'd still be standing outside Anja's apartment building harassing her neighbors."

His pan was ready to call for an ambulance. Lawrence looked down and saw his hands clenched into fists. "You're Securitat," he said.

"Let me put it this way," the man said, leaning back. "I'm not one of Anja's neighbors."

"You're Securitat," Lawrence said again. "I haven't done anything wrong—"

"You came here," Randy said. "You had every reason to believe that you were taking part in something illegal. You lied to the Securitat man at Penn Station today—"

Lawrence switched his pan's feedback mechanisms off altogether. Posy, at her window, a penny stuck in the governor of her radiator, rose in his mind.

"Everyone was treating me like a criminal—from the minute I stepped out of the Order, you all treated me like a criminal. That made me act like one—everyone has to act like a criminal here. That's the hypocrisy of the world, that honest people end up acting like crooks because the world treats them like crooks."

"Maybe we treat them like crooks because they act so crooked."

"You've got it all backwards," Lawrence said. "The causal arrow runs the other direction. You treat us like criminals and the only way to get by is to act criminal. If I'd told the Securitat man in Penn Station the truth—"

"You build a wall around the Order, don't you? To keep us out, because we're barbarians? To keep you in, because you're too fragile? What does that treatment do, Lawrence?"

Lawrence slapped his hand on the table and the crystal rang, but no one in the restaurant noticed. They were all studiously ignoring them. "It's to keep *you* out! All of you, who treated us—"

Randy stood up from the table. Bulky figures stepped out of the shadows behind them. Behind their armor, the Securitat people could have been white or black, old or young. Lawrence could only treat them as Securitat. He rose slowly from his chair and put his arms out, as though surrendering. As soon as the Securitat officers relaxed by a tiny hair— treating him as someone who was surrendering—he dropped backwards over the chair behind him, knocking over a little two-seat table and whacking his head on the floor so hard it rang like a gong. He scrambled to his feet and charged pell-mell for the door, sweeping the empty tables out of the way as he ran.

He caught a glimpse of the pretty waitress standing by her podium at the front of the restaurant as he banged out the door, her eyes wide and her hands up as though to ward off a blow. He caromed off the wall of the dark corridor and ran for the glass door that led out to Second Avenue, where cars hissed by in the night.

He made it onto the sidewalk, crashed into a burly man in a Mets cap, bounced off him, and ran downtown, the people on the sidewalk leaping clear of him. He made it two whole storefronts—all the running around on the Campus handball courts had given him a pretty good pace and wind—before someone tackled him from behind.

He scrambled and squirmed and turned around. It was the guy in the Mets hat. His breath smelled of onions and he was panting, his lips pulled back. "Watch where you're going—" he said, and then he was lifted free, jerked to his feet.

The blood sang in Lawrence's ears and he had just enough time to register that the big guy had been lifted by two blank, armored Securitat officers before he flipped over onto his knees and used the posture like a runner's crouch to take off again. He got maybe ten feet before he was clobbered by a bolt of lightning that made every muscle in his body lock into rigid agony. He pitched forward face-first, not feeling anything except the terrible electric fire from the taser-bolt in his back. His pan died with a sizzle up and down every haptic point in his suit, and between that and the electricity, he flung his arms and legs out in an agonized X while his neck thrashed, grating his face over the sidewalk. Something went horribly *crunch* in his nose.

The room had the same kind of locks as the Securitat room in Penn Station. He'd awakened in the corner of the room, his face taped up and aching. There was no toilet, but there was a chair, bolted to the floor, and three prominent video cameras.

They left him there for some time, alone with his thoughts and the deepening throb from his face, his knees, the palms of his hands. His hands and knees had been sanded raw and there was grit and glass and bits of pebble embedded under the skin, which oozed blood.

His thoughts wanted to return to the predicament. They wanted to fill him with despair for his situation. They wanted to make him panic and weep with the anticipation of the cells, the confession, the life he'd had and the life he would get.

He didn't let them. He had spent sixteen years mastering his thoughts and he would master them now. He breathed deeply, noticing the places where his body was tight and trembling, thinking each muscle into tranquillity, even his aching face, letting his jaw drop open.

Every time his thoughts went back to the predicament, he scrawled their anxious message on a streamer of mental ribbon which he allowed to slip through his mental fingers and sail away.

Sixteen years of doing this had made him an expert, and even so, it was not easy. The worries rose and streamed away as fast as his mind's hand could write them. But as always, he was finally able to master his mind, to find relaxation and calm at the bottom of the thrashing, churning vat of despair.

When Randy came in, Lawrence heard each bolt click and the hiss of air as from a great distance, and he surfaced from his calm, watching Randy cross the floor bearing his own chair.

"Innocent people don't run, Lawrence."

"That's a rather self-serving hypothesis," Lawrence said. The cool ribbons of worry slithered through his mind like satin, floating off into the ether around them. "You appear to have made up your mind, though. I wonder at you—you don't seem like an idiot. How've you managed to convince yourself that this—" he gestured around at the room "—is a good idea? I mean, this is just—"

Randy waved him silent. "The interrogation in this room flows in one direction, Lawrence. This is not a dialogue."

"Have you ever noticed that when you're uncomfortable with something, you talk louder and lean forward a little? A lot of people have that tell."

"Do you work with Securitat data streams, Lawrence?"

"I work with large amounts of data, including a lot of material from the Securitat. It's rarely in cleartext, though. Mostly I'm doing sigint—signals intelligence. I analyze the timing, frequency and length of different kinds of data to see if I can spot anomalies. That's with a lower-case 'a,' by the way." He was warming up to the subject now. His face hurt when he talked, but when he thought about what to say, the hurt went away, as did the vision of the cell where he would go next. "It's the kind of thing that works best when you don't know what's in the payload of the data you're looking at. That would just distract me. It's like a magician's trick with a rabbit or a glass of water. You focus on the rabbit or on the water and what you expect of them, and are flummoxed when the magician does something unexpected. If he used pebbles, though, it might seem absolutely ordinary."

"Do you know what Zbigniew Krotoski was working on?"

"No, there's no way for me to know that. The streams are enciphered at the router with his public key, and rescrambled after he's done with them. It's all zero-knowledge."

"But you don't have zero knowledge, do you?"

Lawrence found himself grinning, which hurt a lot, and which caused a little more blood to leak out of his nose and over his lips in a hot trickle. "Well, signals intelligence being what it is, I was able to discover that it was a Securitat stream, and that it wasn't the first one he'd worked on, nor the first one he'd altered."

"He altered a stream?"

Lawrence lost his smile. "I hadn't told you that part yet, had I?"

"No." Randy leaned forward. "But you will now."

The blue silk ribbons slid through Lawrence's mental fingers as he sat in his cell, which was barely lit and tiny and padded and utterly devoid of furniture. High above him, a ring of glittering red LEDs cast no visible light. They would be infrared lights, the better for the hidden cameras to see him. It was dark, so he saw nothing, but for the infrared cameras, it might as well have been broad daylight. The asymmetry was one of the things he inscribed on a blue ribbon and floated away.

The cell wasn't perfectly soundproof. There was a gaseous hiss that reverberated through it every forty six to fifty three breaths, which he assumed was the regular opening and shutting of the heavy door that led to the cell-block deep within the Securitat building. That would be a patrol, or a regular report, or someone with a weak bladder.

There was a softer, regular grinding that he felt more than heard—a subway train, running very regular. That was the New York rumble, and it felt a little like his pan's reassuring purring.

There was his breathing, deep and oceanic, and there was the sound in his mind's ear, the sound of the streamers hissing away into the ether.

He'd gone out in the world and now he'd gone back into a cell. He supposed that it was meant to sweat him, to make him mad, to make him make mistakes. But he had been trained by sixteen years in the Order and this was not sweating him at all.

"Come along then." The door opened with a cotton-soft sound from its balanced hinges, letting light into the room and giving him the squints.

"I wondered about your friends," Lawrence said. "All those people at the restaurant."

"Oh," Randy said. He was a black silhouette in the doorway. "Well, you know. Honor among thieves. Rank hath its privileges."

"They were caught," he said.

"Everyone gets caught," Randy said.

"I suppose it's easy when everybody is guilty." He thought of Posy. "You just pick a skillset, find someone with those skills, and then figure out what that person is guilty of. Recruiting made simple."

"Not so simple as all that," Randy said. "You'd be amazed at the difficulties we face."

"Zbigniew Krotoski was one of yours."

Randy's silhouette—now resolving into features, clothes (another sweater, this one with a high collar and squared-off shoulders)—made a little movement that Lawrence knew meant yes. Randy was all tells, no matter how suave and collected he seemed. He must have been really up to something when they caught him.

"Come along," Randy said again, and extended a hand to him. He allowed himself to be lifted. The scabs at his knees made crackling noises and there was the hot wet feeling of fresh blood on his calves.

"Do you withhold medical attention until I give you what you want? Is that it?"

Randy put an affectionate hand on his shoulder. "You seem to have it all figured out, don't you?"

"Not all of it. I don't know why you haven't told me what it is you want yet. That would have been simpler, I think."

"I guess you could say that we're just looking for the right way to ask you."

"The way to ask me a question that I can't say no to. Was it the sister? Is that what you had on him?"

"He was useful because he was so eager to prove that he was smarter than everyone else."

"You needed him to edit your own data-streams?"

Randy just looked at him calmly. Why would the Securitat need to change its own streams? Why couldn't they just arrest whomever they wanted on whatever pretext they wanted? Who'd be immune to—

Then he realized who'd be immune to the Securitat: the Securitat would be.

"You used him to nail other Securitat officers?"

Randy's blank look didn't change.

Lawrence realized that he would never leave this building. Even if his body left, now he would be tied to it forever. He breathed. He tried for that oceanic quality of breath, the susurration of the blue silk ribbons inscribed with his worries. It wouldn't come.

"Come along now," Randy said, and pulled him down the corridor to the main door. It hissed as it opened and behind it was an old Securitat man, legs crossed painfully. Weak bladder, Lawrence knew.

"Here's the thing," Randy said. "The system isn't going to go away, no matter what we do. The Securitat's here forever. We've treated everyone like a criminal for too long now—

everyone's really a criminal now. If we dismantled tomorrow, there'd be chaos, bombings, murder sprees. We're not going anywhere."

Randy's office was comfortable. He had some beautiful vintage circus posters—the bearded lady, the sword swallower, the hoochie-coochie girl—framed on the wall, and a cracked leather sofa that made amiable exhalations of good tobacco smell mixed with years of saddle soap when he settled into it. Randy reached onto a tall mahogany bookcase and handed him down a first-aid kit. There was a bottle of alcohol in it and a lot of gauze pads. Gingerly, Lawrence began to clean out the wounds on his legs and hands, then started in on his face. The blood ran down and dripped onto the slate tiled floor, almost invisible. Randy handed him a waste-paper bin and it slowly filled with the bloody gauze.

"Looks painful," Randy said.

"Just skinned. I have a vicious headache, though."

"That's the taser hangover. It goes away. There's some codeine tablets in the pill-case. Take it easy on them, they'll put you to sleep."

While Lawrence taped large pieces of gauze over the cleaned-out corrugations in his skin, Randy tapped idly at a screen on his desk. It felt almost as though he'd dropped in on someone's hot-desk back at the Order. Lawrence felt a sharp knife of homesickness and wondered if Gerta was OK.

"Do you really have a sister?"

"I do. In Oregon, in the Order."

"Does she work for you?"

Randy snorted. "Of course not. I wouldn't do that to her. But the people who run me, they know that they can get to me through her. So in a sense, we both work for them."

"And I work for you?"

"That's the general idea. Zbigkrot spooked when you got onto him, so he's long gone."

"Long gone as in—"

"This is one of those things where we don't say. Maybe he

disappeared and got away clean, took his sister with him. Maybe he disappeared into our . . . operations. Not knowing is the kind of thing that keeps our other workers on their game."

"And I'm one of your workers."

"Like I said, the system isn't going anywhere. You met the gang tonight. We've all been caught at one time or another. Our little cozy club manages to make the best of things. You saw us—it's not a bad life at all. And we think that all things considered, we make the world a better place. Someone would be doing our job, might as well be us. At least we manage to weed out the real retarded sadists." He sipped a little coffee from a thermos cup on his desk. "That's where Zbigkrot came in."

"He helped you with 'retarded sadists'?"

"For the most part. Power corrupts, of course, but it attracts the corrupt, too. There's a certain kind of person who grows up wanting to be a Securitat officer."

"And me?"

"You?"

"I would do this too?"

"You catch on fast."

The outside wall of Campus was imposing. Tall, sheathed in seamless metal painted uniform grey. Nothing grew for several yards around it, as though the world was shrinking back from it.

How did Zbigkrot get off campus?

That's a question that should have occurred to him when he left the campus. He was embarrassed that it took him this long to come up with it. But it was a damned good question. Trying to force the gate—what was it the old Brother on the gate had said? Pressurized, blowouts, the walls rigged to come down in an instant.

If Zbigkrot had left, he'd walked out, the normal way, while someone at the gate watched him go. And he'd left no record of it. Someone, working on Campus, had altered the stream of data fountaining off the front gate to remove the record of it. There was more than one forger there—it hadn't just been zbigkrot working for the Securitat.

He'd *belonged* in the Order. He'd learned how to know himself, how to see himself with the scalding, objective logic that he'd normally reserved for everyone else. The Anomaly had seemed like such a bit of fun, like he was leveling up to the next stage of his progress.

He called Greta. They'd given him a new pan, one that had a shunt that delivered a copy of all his data to the Securitat. Since he'd first booted it, it had felt strange and invasive, every buzz and warning coming with the haunted feeling, the *watched* feeling.

"You, huh?"

"It's very good to hear your voice," he said. He meant it. He wondered if she knew about the Securitat's campus snitches. He wondered if she was one. But it was good to hear her voice. His pan let him know that whatever he was doing was making him feel great. He didn't need his pan to tell him that, though.

"I worried when you didn't check in for a couple days."

"Well, about that."

"Yes?"

If he told her, she'd be in it too—if she wasn't already. If he told her, they'd figure out what they could get on her. He should just tell her nothing. Just go on inside and twist the occasional data-stream. He could be better at it than zbigkrot. No one would ever make an Anomaly out of him. Besides, so what if they did? It would be a few hours, days, months or years that he could live on Campus.

And if it wasn't him, it would be someone else.

It would be someone else.

"I just wanted to say good-bye, and thanks. I suspect I'm not going to see you again."

Off in the distance now, the sound of the Securitat van's happy little song. His pan let him know that he was breathing quickly and shallowly and he slowed his breathing down until it let up on him.

"Lawrence?"

He hung up. The Securitat van was visible now, streaking toward the Campus wall.

He closed his eyes and watched the blue satin ribbons tumble, like silky water licking over a waterfall. He could get to the place that Campus took him to anywhere. That was all that mattered.

Oblivion: A Journey

VANDANA SINGH

Vandana Singh (users.rcn.com/singhvan) lives with her family in Framingham, Massachusetts. She is a college teacher with a Ph.D. in theoretical particle physics. She was born and brought up in New Delhi, India, and is "a card-carrying alien writing science fiction." Her parents both had graduate degrees in English literature: "I grew up as much with Shakespeare and Keats as I did with the great Indian epics and literary writers in Hindi, such as the inimitable Premchand. My mother and grandmother told us the Ramayana and Mahabharata, and various folk tales and village lore. In my teen years and early adulthood I also became involved (in a modest and occasional way) in environmental and women's movements, which had a lasting impact on my world-view." And "I love this genre for its imaginative richness, its vast canvas, and the sophistication with which its best practitioners wield their pens." Her first short story collection, The Woman Who Thought She Was a Planet, *came out in fall 2008, in India, from Zubaan Books and Penguin India. Her novella* Distances *was published in 2008 by Aqueduct Press.*

"Oblivion: A Journey" appeared in the original anthology, Clockwork Phoenix, *edited by Mike Allen. It presents an Indian posthuman future, in which synthetic and naturally born people mingle across the colonized galaxy. One woman's life is controlled by an ancient revenge myth. It is interesting to compare it to "Fury," another space opera appearing later in this book.*

Memory is a strange thing.

I haven't changed my sex in eighty-three years. I was born female, in a world of peace and quietude; yet I have an incomplete recollection of my childhood. Perhaps it is partly a failure of the imagination that it is so hard to believe (in this age of ours) that there was once such a place as green and slow as my world-shell, Ramasthal. It was the last of the great world-shells to fall, so any memory of childhood is contaminated with what came after: the deaths of all I loved, the burning of the cities, the slow, cancerous spread of Hirasor's culture-machines that changed my birth-place beyond recognition.

So instead of one seamless continuum of growing and learning to be in this world, my memory of my life is fragmentary. I remember my childhood name: Lilavati. I remember those great cybeasts, the hayathis, swaying down the streets in a procession, and their hot, vegetable-scented breath ruffling my hair. There are glimpses, as through a tattered veil, of steep, vertical gardens, cascading greenery, a familiar face looking out at me from a window hewn in a cliff—and in the background, the song of falling water. Then everything is obscured by smoke. I am in a room surrounded by pillars of fire, and through the haze I see the torn pages of the Ramayan floating in the air, burning, their edges crumpling like black lace. I am half-comatose with heat and smoke; my throat is parched and sore, my eyes sting—and then there are strange, metallic faces reaching out to me, the stuff of my nightmares. Behind them is a person all aflame, her arms outstretched, running toward me, but she falls and I am carried away through the smoke and the screaming. I still see the woman in my dreams and wonder if she was my mother.

In my later life as a refugee, first on the world of Barana and after that, everywhere and nowhere, there is nothing much worth recalling. Foster homes, poverty, my incarceration in some kind of soulless educational institution—the banality of the daily struggle to survive. But there are moments in my life that are seared into my mind forever: instants that were pivotal, life-changing, each a conspiracy of temporal nexuses, a concatenation of events that made me what I am. That is not an excuse—I could have chosen a different way to be. But I did not know, then, that I had a choice.

This is the first of those moments: the last time I was a woman, some ninety years ago in my personal time-frame. I was calling myself Ila, then, and doing some planet-hopping, working the cruisers and blowing the credits at each stop. I found myself on Planet Vilaasa, a rich and decadent world under the sway of the Samarin conglomerate. I was in one of those deep-city bars where it's always night, where sunshine is like a childhood memory, where the air is thick with smoke, incipient violence and bumblebees. I don't remember who I was with, but the place was crowded with humans, native and off-world, as well as mutants and nakalchis. There was a bee buzzing in my ear, promising me seven kinds of bliss designed especially for my personality and physical type if only I'd agree to let the Samarin Corporate Entity take over half my brain. I swatted it; it fell into my plate and buzzed pathetically, antennae waving, before it became nonfunctional. Somehow I found this funny; I still remember throwing back my head and laughing.

My fingers, slight and brown, curved around my glass. The drink half drunk, a glutinous purple drop sliding down the outer surface. Reflected on the glass a confusion of lights and moving shapes, and the gleam, sudden and terrifying, of steel.

There was a scream, and the sound of glass breaking that seemed to go on forever. This was no barroom brawl. The raiders were Harvesters. I remember getting up to run. I remember the terrified crowd pressing around me, and then I was falling, kicked and stepped upon in the stampede. Somehow I pushed myself to safety under a table next to a stranger, a pale woman with long, black hair and eyes like green fire. She looked at me with her mouth open, saying one word:

"Nothen . . ."

A Harvester got her. It put its metal hands around her throat and put its scissor-like mouth to her chest. As she bled and writhed, it rasped one long word, interspersed with a sequence of numbers.

Her body turned rigid and still, her face twisted with horror. Her green eyes froze in a way that was simultaneously aware and locked in the moment of torment. It was then that I realized that she was a nakalchi, a bio-synthetic being spawned from a mother-machine.

The name of the mother-machine is what pushes a nakalchi into the catatonic state that is *Shunyath*. When they enter Shunyath they re-live the moment when that name was spoken. Since the nakalchis are practically immortal, capable of dying only through accident or violence, Shunyath is their way of going to the next stage. Usually a nakalchi who has wearied of existence will go to one of their priests, who will put the candidate in a meditative state of absolute calm and surrender. Then the priest will utter the name of the mother-machine (such names being known only to the priests and guarded with their lives) so that the nakalchi may then contemplate eternity in peace.

For first-generation nakalchis, Shunyath is not reversible.

That is when I realized that this woman was one of the ancients, one of the nakalchis who had helped humankind find its way to the stars.

So for her, frozen in the state of Shunyath, it would seem as though she was being strangled by the Harvester all the rest of her days. No wonder she had asked me for Nothen, for death. She had known the Harvesters had come for her;

she had known what they would do. I remember thinking, in one of those apparently timeless moments that terror brings: somebody should kill the poor woman. She was obviously the target of the raid.

But to my horrified surprise the Harvester turned from her to me, even as I was sliding away from under the table to a safer place. While the Harvester had me pinned to the floor, its long, flexible electrodes crawled all over my skin as it violated my humanness, my woman-ness, with its multiple limbs. Through the tears and blood I saw myriad reflections of myself in those dark, compound eyes, from which looked—not only the primitive consciousness of the Harvester, but the eyes of whoever manipulated it—the person or entity who, not content with finding their target, fed like a starving animal on the terror of a bystander. In those eyes I was a stranger, a non-person, a piece of meat that jerked and gibbered in pain. Then, for a moment, I thought I saw the burning woman from my memories of childhood, standing behind the Harvester. This is death, I said to myself, relieved. But the Harvester left me a few hair-breadths short of death and moved on to its next victim.

I don't know how many they killed or maimed that night. The nakalchi woman they took away. I remember thinking, through the long months of pain and nightmares that followed, that I wish I had died.

But I lived. I took no joy in it. All that gave my mind some respite from its seething was a game I invented: I would find the identity of the person responsible for the Harvester raid and I would kill them. Find, and kill. I went through endless permutations of people and ways of killing in my head. Eventually it was no longer a game.

I moved to another planet, changed my sex to one of the Betweens. Over the years I changed my body even further, ruthlessly replacing soft, yielding flesh with coralloid implants that grew me my own armor-plating. Other people shuddered when I walked by. I became an interplanetary investigator of small crime and fraud, solving trivial little cases for the rich and compromised, while biding my time.

It was already suspected that the man responsible for the Harvester attacks that terrorized whole planets during the Samarin era was no other than the governing mind of the Samarin Corporate Entity, Hirasor. The proof took many years and great effort on the part of several people, including myself, but it came at last. Nothing could be done, however, because Hirasor was more powerful than any man alive. His icons were everywhere: dark, shoulder-length hair framing a lean, aristocratic face with hungry eyes; the embroidered silk collar, the rose in his buttonhole. It came out then that he had a private museum of first-generation nakalchis locked in Shunyath in various states of suffering. A connoisseur of pain, was Hirasor.

But to me he was also Hirasor, destroyer of worlds. He had killed me once already by destroying my world-shell, Ramasthal. It was one of the epic world-shells, a chain of island satellites natural and artificial, that ringed the star Agni. Here we learned, lived and enacted our lives based on that ancient Indic epic, the Ramayan, one of those timeless stories that condense in their poetry the essence of what it means to be human. Then Samarin had infiltrated, attacking and destroying at first, then doing what they called "rebuilding": substituting for the complexity and beauty of the Ramayan, an inanely simplified, sugary, cultural matrix that drew on all the darkness and pettiness in human nature. Ramasthal broke up, dissolved by the monocultural machine that was Samarin. I suffered less than my fellow-citizens—being a child, I could not contribute a brain-share to Samarin. I grew up a refugee, moving restlessly from one inhabited world to the next, trying and failing to find my center. Most of the ordinary citizens of these worlds had never heard of the Ramayan epic, or anything else that had been meaningful to me in that lost past life. In my unimaginable solitude my only defense was to act like them, to be what they considered normal. When the Harvesters invaded the bar, I had been living the fashionably disconnected life that Samarin-dominated cultures think is the only way to be.

Hirasor was so powerful that among my people his nickname was Ravan-Ten-Heads, after the demon in the epic

Ramayan. Near the end of the story, the hero, Ram, tries to kill Ravan by cutting off his heads, one by one, but the heads simply grow back. In a similar manner, if a rival corporation or a society of free citizens managed to destroy one Samarin conglomerate, another would spring up almost immediately in its place. It—and Hirasor—seemed almost mythic in their indestructibility.

What I wanted to do was to find Hirasor's secret vulnerability, as Ram does in the epic. "Shoot an arrow into Ravan's navel," he is told. The navel is the center of Ravan's power. When Ram does so, the great demon dies at last.

But Samarin, and with it Hirasor, declined slowly without my help. An ingeniously designed brain-share virus locked Samarin's client-slaves—several million people—into a synced epileptic state. After that Generosity Corp. (that had likely developed the virus) began its ascent to power while the Samarin Entity gradually disintegrated. Pieces of it were bought by other conglomerates, their data extracted through torture; then they were mind-wiped until the name Samarin only evoked a ghost of a memory, accompanied by a shudder.

But Hirasor lived on. He was still rich enough to evade justice. Rumors of his death appeared frequently in the newsfeeds for a while, and a documentary was made about him, but over time people forgot. There were other things, such as the discovery of the worlds of the Hetorr, and the threats and rumors of war with that unimaginably alien species. "Give it up," said the few people in whom I had confided. "Forget Hirasor and get on with your life." But finding Hirasor was the only thing between me and death by my own hand. Each time I opened my case files on him, each time his image sprang up and I looked into his eyes, I remembered the Harvester. I remembered the burning woman. Despite all the reconstructive work my body had undergone, my old wounds ached. Find, and kill. Only then would I know peace.

I knew more about Hirasor than anyone else did, although it was little enough.

He liked absinthe and roses.

He had a perfect memory.

He was fastidious about his appearance. Every hair in place, fingers elegant and manicured, the signature ear-studs small and precisely placed on each ear-lobe. His clothing was made from the silk of sapient-worms.

He had no confidant but for the chief of his guards, a nakalchi female called Suvarna, a walking weapon who was also his lover. He wrote her poetry that was remarkable for its lyrical use of three languages, and equally remarkable for its sadistic imagery.

Later I killed three of his functionaries to learn his unique identity-number. It did me no good, or so I thought, then.

In the years of his decline he lost his Harvester units; his three main hideouts were found and his assets destroyed, his loyal bands of followers dwindled to one, Suvarna—and yet he seemed more slippery and elusive than ever. Although he left trails of blood and shattered lives in his wake, he managed to elude me with trickery and firepower.

He left me messages in blood.

Sometimes it was the name of a planet or a city. I would go there and find, too late, another clue, spelled out in corpses. It was as though we were playing an elaborate game across the inhabited worlds, with him always in the lead. Slowly the universe began to take less and less notice. We were two lone players on a vast stage, and the audience had other, larger scale horrors to occupy them.

I began to think of myself as a modern-day Ram. In the Ramayan epic, Prince Ram's wife Sita is abducted by the ten-headed demon Ravan. Prince Ram, beloved by all, has no difficulty raising an army of animals and people and following Ravan to his kingdom.

I was no prince. But Hirasor had stolen my whole world, as surely as Ravan stole Sita. I could not bring back Ramasthal or my childhood, but I could bring Hirasor down. Unlike Ram, I would have to do it alone.

Alone. Sifting through travel records, bribing petty little mercenaries who may have had dealings with his people, tracking down witnesses at the scene of each orgy of violence, trying to think like him, to stand in his shoes and wonder: what would he do next? I would sleep only when I could no longer stand.

Sleep brought a recurring nightmare: Hirasor standing before me at last. I shoot an arrow into his navel, and as he falls I leap upon him and put my hands around his throat. I am certain he is dying, but then I see his face change, become familiar, become my own face. I feel his hands on my throat.

I would wake up in a sweat and know that in the end it was going to be only one of us who would prevail: him or me. But first I had to find him. So I worked obsessively, following him around from place to place, always one step behind.

Then, quite suddenly, the trail got cold. I searched, sent my agents from planet to planet. Nothing but silence. I paced up and down my room, brooding for days. What was he waiting for? What was he about to do?

Into this empty, waiting time came something I had not expected. A reason to live that had nothing to do with Hirasor. Her name was Dhanu.

She was an urbanologist for whom I had performed a small service. She was a small, fierce, determined woman with long, black hair turning to grey that she tied in a braid. The job I did for her was shoddily done, and she demanded a reason. "I'm preoccupied with something more important," I snapped, wanting her out of my office and my life. "Tell me," she said, sitting down and waiting with her whole body, her eyes mocking and intrigued. So I did.

We became lovers, Dhanu and I. Somehow she found her way past the armor-plating of my mind and body; she found cracks and interstices, living flesh that remembered loving touch, regions of vulnerability that I hadn't cauterized out of myself. Here is a memory fragment:

We lie in bed in my dingy room, with moonlight coming in through the narrow window, and the sounds outside of voices raised in argument, and the sweaty, chemical scent of the dead river that lies like an outstretched arm across this nameless, foul city. She is a shadow, a ghost limned with silver, turned into a stranger by the near-darkness. I find this suddenly disturbing; I turn her over so that the light falls full on her face. I don't know what I look like to her. I don't know what I am. I've been calling myself Vikram for a few years, but that doesn't tell me anything.

"Tell me a secret," she says. "Something about yourself that nobody knows."

I pull myself together, settle down next to her and stare at the ceiling. I don't know what to tell her, but something escapes my lips unbidden.

"I want to die," I say, surprising myself because lately I haven't been thinking about death. But it's true. And also not true, because I want this moment forever, the light from the broken moon Jagos silvering her hair, and the way she looks at me when I say that: a long, slow, sad, unsurprised look. She begins to say something but I stop her. "Your turn," I say.

"I'll tell you what I want to know, more than anything," she says after a pause. "I want to know what it is like to be somebody else. I remember, as a very small child, standing with my mother on a balcony, watching the most amazing fireworks display I had ever seen. It made me happy. I looked at my mother to share that joy, and found that she was crying. It was then that I realized that I was a different person from her, that she was in some profound way a stranger. Since then I've sought strangeness. I've wanted to know what it is like to be a tree, a sapient-worm, and most of all, a made-being. Like a nakalchi or a Cognizant-City. Can you imagine what the universe would look like to an entity like that?"

We talk all night. She teaches me what she has learned about nakalchis and Cognizant-Cities, Corporate Entities and mother-machines—in particular, their rituals of death, because that is what interests me. I realize during the conversation that I am no more than a vessel for the death of another, and that is perhaps why I seek my own. Some time during the night she teaches me the song with which nakalchis welcome Nothen, their conception of death. She learned it from a nakalchi priest who was dying, who wanted someone to say the words to him. I cannot pretend to understand the lore and mysticism that the priests have developed around Nothen, which to me is simply irreversible nonfunctionality, the death that comes to us all. Or the philosophical comparison between Nothen and Shunyath. Dhanu tries to explain:

"If you go into Shunyath, you contemplate what nakalchis call The River, which is inadequately translated as the Cosmic Stream of Being. If you go into Nothen, with the Last Song echoing in your mind, then you *are* the River. You are no longer separate from it—you *become* the River, see?"

No, I don't see. Never mind, she says, laughing at me. She says the words of the Last Song, breathing it out into the moonlit air.

It has a pleasing, sonorous lilt. It is supposed to induce a state of acceptance and peace in a dying nakalchi. I am not sure why, but there are tears in my eyes as I repeat it after her in the gray, hushed light of dawn.

Shantih. Nothen ke aagaman, na dukh na dard . . .

Lying with her, seeing her hair unbound on my pillow like seaweed, I find myself in a still place, as though between breaths. Hirasor does not walk the paths that Dhanu and I tread.

Looking back, I see how the paths branch out of each temporal nexus. For every pivotal event in my life, there was always more than one possible path I could have taken.

This is the path I chose:

I had accompanied Dhanu during one of her urbanology expeditions. We were in the bowels of a dying Cognizant-City on the ruined planet Murra. This was the first time she had had a chance to explore what was probably one of the earliest Cognizant-Cities in the galaxy. She was a few levels below me, attempting to salvage what was left of the City's mind. All its recorded history and culture, its ruminations over the years of its existence, lay spooled in cavernous darkness below. The inhabitants had been evacuated, and even now I could see the last of the ships, a glint or two in a reddening sky over the bleak mountains of Murra's northern continent. I was perched on the highest ramparts, standing by our flyer and looking out for rogue destroyer bots. Every now and then I saw one rise up, a distant speck, and crash into the city-scape in a small fireball. Thin spires of smoke rose all around me, but there was as yet nothing amiss where I was waiting.

Then I lost Dhanu's signal.

I searched the skies, found them clear of bots, and descended quickly into the warren-like passageways that led into the city's heart. Two levels later, my wrist-band beeped. She was in range.

"I'm all right, Vikram," she said to my anxious query. She sounded breathless with excitement. "I had to go down a couple of levels to find the rest of the data-banks. This City is one of the first Cognizant-cities ever made! They still have direct human-to-City interfaces! I am hooking up to talk to it as I record. Go on up! I'll only be a few minutes, I promise."

When I relive that moment, I think of the things I could have done. I could have insisted on going down to where she was, or persuaded her to leave everything and come. Or I could have been more careful going up, so I wouldn't lose my way.

But I did lose my way. It was only one wrong turn, and I was about to retrace my steps (I had the flyer's reassuring signal on my wristband as a guide) but what made me pause was curiosity. Or fate.

I found myself in the doorway of an enormous chamber which smelled faintly of blood and hydrogen peroxide, and was lit by periodic blue flashes, like lightning. I saw the great, monstrous hulk of an old-fashioned mother-machine, her long-abandoned teats spewing an oily broth, her flailing arms beating the air over the shattered remains of her multiple wombs. She was old—it had been a long time since she had brought any nakalchis to life. As I stared at her I realized (from what pictures Dhanu had shown me of ancient made-beings) that she was probably a first-generation mother-machine. A priceless collector's item, salvaged from who-knew-where, abandoned in the evacuation of the City. And now the City's madness was destroying what little functionality she had, taking her to Nothen.

Moved by a sudden impulse I went up to her and spoke the words of peace.

Shantih. Nothen ke aagaman, na dukh na dard ...

Peace. As Nothen comes, there is no sorrow, no pain ...

I regretted my impulse almost immediately because after I stopped, the mother-machine began to recite the names of her children, the first part of her death-ritual. In her final moments she had mistaken me for a nakalchi priest. I don't know what made me stay—there was something mesmerizing about that old, metallic voice in the darkness, and the proximity of death. Perhaps I was a little annoyed with Dhanu for delaying, for wanting to join with the City in an orgy of mutual understanding. Dhanu's signal flickered with reassuring regularity on my wristband.

Then I heard the mother-machine utter the name that to me meant more than life itself: Hirasor.

I will remember that moment until I die: the grating voice of the mother-machine, the dull booms in the distance, the floor shaking below my feet, and that pungent, smoky darkness, pierced by occasional sparks of blue lightning.

In the midst of it, clear as a bell, the name—or rather, Hirasor's unique numerical identifier. Each of us had our identity numbers, given to us at birth, and I was one of the few people who knew Hirasor's. But I had never suspected he was a nakalchi. Partly because of nakalchi lore and history—there never had been any confirmed master criminals who were nakalchi, conceived as they had once been to gently shepherd the human race toward the stars. Meanwhile the great uprising of the nakalchis in times long before Samarin, the consciousness debates that had preceded them, had all ensured that they were treated on par with human beings, so I had no way of knowing from the number alone. You can't tell from appearance or behavior either, because nakalchis claim access to the full range of human emotion (or, if their priests are to be believed, to more than that). By now even we humans are so augmented and enhanced that the functional difference between nakalchi and human is very small—but important. To me the difference meant—at last—the possibility of vengeance.

Hirasor: a first-generation nakalchi!

That is why I had to wait. That is why I couldn't go down to find Dhanu, why I ignored her frantic signals on my wrist-band. I had to wait for the mother-machine to tell me her name.

At last she said it: Ekadri-samayada-janini, intermingled with a sequence of numbers that made up a prime.

I left her then, to die. I left, repeating her name—what would always be, to me, the Word—so I would not forget. The floor was twisting and bucking beneath my feet, and a lone siren was blaring somewhere above me. I staggered against the rusting metal wall of the passage, and remembered Dhanu.

I got up. I went back. I wish I could say that I went into the bowels of the City, braved everything to find her and rescue her. But I didn't. I went down until I was stopped by the rubble of fallen masonry. Her signal still flickered on my wrist-band but she did not answer my query.

There was a seismic shudder far below me, and a long sigh, a wind that blew through the wrecked passageways, running invisible fingers through my hair. I sensed—or imagined—Dhanu's breath flowing with the breath of the dying City, her consciousness entangled inextricably with that of her host. But as I turned away I knew also that my real reason for abandoning her was that I was the only living being who had the means to bring Hirasor down. For that I couldn't risk my life.

The roof of the passageway began to collapse. I was running, now, veering from one side to another to prevent being hit by debris. I burst into open air, my chest aching, and flung myself into the flyer. As I rose up, three destroyer bots honed into the very spot I had vacated. I had no time to activate the flyer's defenses. A great fireball blossomed below me. I felt its heat as I piloted the rocking craft upward through the tumultuous air. Up, in the cool heights, I saw that there was blood flowing down my right arm. My shoulder hurt. I looked down and saw the myriad fires blooming, forming and dissolving shapes that my imagination brought to life. Monsters. And lastly, a woman, arms outstretched, burning.

In the Ramayan, Ram braves all to recover his consort Sita from the demon Ravan. But near the end of the story he loses her through his own foolishness. He turns her away, exiles her as he himself was once exiled, and buries himself in the task of ruling his kingdom.

All that: the war, the heroes killed—for nothing!

One of the most moving scenes in the epic is at the end of the story, when Ram goes down on his knees before Sita in the forest, begging her forgiveness and asking her to come back to him. She accepts his apology but she does not belong to him; she never has. She calls to her mother, the Earth; a great fissure opens in the ground and Sita goes home.

In the One Thousand Commentaries, there are different views on the significance of Sita. Some interpret her as signifying that which is lost to us. For a long time I had thought of Sita as my world, my childhood. I had seen myself as Ram, raising an army to win back—not those irredeemable things, but a chance for survival. Abandoned by my fellow investigators, hunting for Hirasor alone, I had, after a while, given up on analogies. Certainly I had never thought of Dhanu as Sita.

Dhanu was what I had to sacrifice to reach Hirasor, to rescue Sita. Dhanu had never belonged to me, anyway, I told myself. She could have come up out of the City at any time; it was her obsession with the made-beings that led to her death. Sometimes I was angry with her, at other times, I wept, thinking of the fall of her hair in the moonlight. At odd moments during my renewed pursuit of Hirasor, she would come unbidden into my mind, and I would wonder what her last moments had been like. Had she seen the Universe through the eyes of the dying City? Had she had her epiphany?

But I had little time for regret. My life narrowed down to one thing: find Hirasor. I set various agents sifting through mountains of possible leads; I re-established contact with criminal informers, coaxed or threatened information from scores of witnesses. At night I lay sleepless in my lonely bed, thinking of what I would do when I found Hirasor. My mind ran through scenario after scenario. I had to first put him in a hundred kinds of agony. Then I would say the name of the mother-machine and lock him in Shunyath forever.

His silence lasted over two years. Then, at last, one of my agents picked up his trail. This time, curiously, it was not marked with blood. No small, artistically arranged orgy of violence betrayed his presence. All I had was proof from a transit shuttle record that he had been headed for the planet Griddha-kuta two months ago.

I went to Griddha-kuta. Apparently he had headed straight for the Buddhist monastery of Leh, without any attempt at covering his tracks. I went to the monastery, suspecting a trap. There, to my angry surprise, I found him gone.

An elderly monk told me that yes, Hirasor had been here. What had he done during his stay? Apparently nothing but walk around in the hill gardens and read in the library. Where was he now?

"He said to tell you that he had gone to Oblivion," the monk said, watching me. "But why don't you stay here awhile, before you go? There is no hurry. Hirasor is not running any more. Why don't you walk the gardens and ease your burdens a little?"

They let me search the grounds and the building, but there was no sign of Hirasor. I wondered if he had really gone to Oblivion, a planet about which I knew little, except that it was as close to hell as you could get among the inhabited worlds. It made no sense that he would go to such an uncomfortable place.

While I was wondering what to do, I walked briefly in the gardens with the monk, Chituri. I told him a little about myself and my quest; in return he confided to me that he had been a world-shell citizen, too, before the fall. His world-shell had been Gilgamesh.

There is no doubt that there was some magic about the place, because I stayed longer than I intended. The gardens in the terraced hills were tranquil, verdant, misty with wa-

terfalls. Amid groves of moss-laden stone trees, pale clusters of flowers hung in the sweet air. Memories of Ramasthal,
which had faded with time, returned to me vividly. Meanwhile Chituri tried to persuade me to stay, to give up my
quest for justice. As we walked, he would tell me stories
from the Indic tradition, even resorting to his knowledge of
the Ramayan.

"Don't you see," he would tell me, "it is only when Ram
forgets the god in him, forgets he is an avatar of Vishnu, that
he acts foolishly? What is evil but ignorance of our true nature?"

"You are forgetting that Ravan is the villain of the story,
not Ram," I would say coldly. "If you want to talk about evil,
talk about him."

"But, Paren," he said, using the name I had given him,
"don't your commentaries say that the entire epic is more
than a literal telling of an old heroic tale—that the great
battle is really the battle within . . ."

He had a peculiar way of sidling up to me, of speaking as
though imparting a great confidence, and yet his manner
was ingratiating, tentative. He hardly spoke above a whisper. I guessed he had suffered much before his arrival here,
but I took a dislike to him after a while.

For me this period was, like the time I had met Dhanu,
only an interstice, a time to catch my breath before resum-
ing my quest. I was not interested in academic discourses on
morality. Chituri did not understand that. He had seen Hirasor walk these very gardens—Hirasor, who had brought
down his world as well as mine—and he had done nothing.

I finished my researches on the planet Oblivion, and made
arrangements to go there. It was a difficult place to get to,
since there was only one settlement, if one could call it that,
and only a small scientific research craft visited at rather
long intervals. The day I left, Chituri again tried to persuade
me to give up my pursuit of Hirasor. He did this in his usual
oblique way of telling me a story.

This time it was an ancient Buddhist tale about a murderer called Ungli-maal. Ungli-maal had been a bandit in
the time of the Buddha, a man so depraved that he wore the

fingers of his victims as a garland around his neck. The Buddha was the only man he waylaid who was unafraid of death, who faced him empty-handed, with compassion. Eventually Ungli-maal—despite all he had been—became a Buddhist monk and a great teacher.

"If you are trying to persuade me that Hirasor has become a saint," I said between clenched teeth, "you must think me naïve indeed. He is still the man who butchered millions, destroyed countless worlds. He will not escape justice."

"That was not the point of my story," Chituri said, rather sadly. I was glad not to see his face again.

Oblivion, they say, is another word for hell. A bleak world, barely habitable, it was once known as Dilaasha, and was considered a reasonable candidate for terraforming. Those hopes have long since vanished. The "habitable" zones are deserts, subject to violent dust-storms, and all indigenous life is primitive—bacterial, algal, and inimical to coexisting with humans.

But all this does not explain why the planet Oblivion is hell. Oblivion earns its name because those who stay there long enough slowly lose their minds.

It begins with forgetting and slips of tongue, peculiar speech disorders, waking terrors, and finally, silence. The rescue teams who first observed the early explorers (consisting of both human and nakalchi) could only speculate as to why the subjects walked around without apparent purpose, neglecting the basic needs of their bodies, muttering in unknown languages, reacting to things that nobody else could see. The second stage was one of great distress—the subjects howled or whimpered and ran about the compound as though to escape a terrible, invisible enemy. They could still, at times, respond to their names; they would look up when called, frowning, as though trying to remember who they had been. Sometimes they would weep in the arms of the staff; a terrible, heart-rending weeping it was. The final stage was silence and withdrawal. In this last stage the sufferers seemed to have completely lost any knowledge of who they were—they did not respond to their names or to instructions; they wandered around with dead eyes, tracing out complicated patterns with their feet.

Only three victims had been taken off-planet. When removed in the second stage they would resist with maniacal strength—both such subjects had met violent death at their own hand. The third had been in the final stage and had simply faded away after removal, although he had been in fine shape physically. However an autopsy had revealed a bizarre restructuring of his brain that no scientist had yet explained.

So now all that is left of the original settlement on Oblivion is a study center where the remaining subjects are incarcerated. Regulations decree that nobody can stay on Oblivion for more than a hundred and ten local days. It's after that that most people seem to start losing their minds, although in some rare cases twenty days is enough.

There are theories—volatile compounds containing nano-organisms that are slowly released by the soil, pervading everything, that act like psychotropic drugs, low frequency sound waves that boom through the barren hills, disturbing the inner functioning of the body, peculiar surges in radio-active emissions in the environs—but none of these are adequate explanations. Oblivion remains a mystery.

So I came, at last, to Oblivion, to the final confrontation. It was a fitting place for a last stand. The dome-town was mostly uninhabited, the empty buildings testament to the defeated hopes of the original settlers. The insane were housed in a primitive building built around a dusty compound. The skeleton crew that had managed the place for the last shift was irritable and moody, waiting to be taken off-planet in a week, and the few scientists looked depressed and preoccupied. Nobody seemed interested in talking with me, despite the fact that I was apparently a representative of a rich philanthropist considering a major donation. Everyone seemed curiously lacking in vitality or enthusiasm, as though under the influence of some drug. Within a few hours of my stay there, I, too, felt a distinct mental lethargy, punctuated by spikes of nervousness and paranoia. The medic who examined me, a thin, dark, spidery man, was pessimistic.

"You're one of those who will succumb fast," he said, not without some relish. "This is a terrible place, affects some people much more quickly than others. Get out while you can, or you'll be joining them!"

He waved his long fingers toward the observation window behind him. There was something ghoulish about the way he stood watching the crazies, describing for me in painful detail every stage of the terrible sickness. The afflicted—men, women, most of them half naked, wandered aimlessly around the yard, muttering and drawing patterns in the dust with their feet. Some wailed incessantly, beating their chests, while others tore at their clothes. Still others sat very quietly on the ground, looking straight ahead of them with blank eyes. I felt as though their pain and confusion was somehow connected to me, that theirs was a sorrow that was drawing me in slowly. The dust patterns on the ground (the subject of much debate among the scientists) seemed almost to make sense, as though they were the script of a language I had known and forgotten. I shivered and looked away. The medic was right. I couldn't stay here long.

But when I looked back into the compound, there was Hirasor.

He came into the yard through a door in the wall. A tall man, he now walked with a slight shuffle. He sat down on an unoccupied bench and watched the sufferers. I couldn't see his face clearly, but the gait, and the arrogant set of the shoulders, was unmistakable. My heart started hammering.

"That's the other visitor," the medic said, noting the slight start I gave. "Claims to be interested in our subjects, but he seems to have problems of his own."

He didn't explain. Hirasor sat for a while, then moved his hands upward in a gesture that I didn't recognize, and returned through the door, which shut behind him.

I went into my narrow cell of a room to make my plans.

It was hard to think clearly. Blood, revenge, murder—the sufferings of those who had lost to Hirasor—my own long years of trailing him, giving up love and life for this one obsession—these thoughts reverberated in my mind When I closed my eyes I saw Hirasor's face, or the Harvester's

toothed mouth. When I opened them, I saw the stark, claustrophobic room, and the view from the skylight of a yellow
dust-plume over the dome. The air smelled faintly of dust
and burning. I knew then that Hirasor had chosen wisely. I
didn't know to what extent he, as a nakalchi (and a hardened
one at that) would be affected by the place, but he had gam-
bled on it being a disadvantage for me.

The next day there was a message from him, an audio.
Giving me the location of his rooms, and telling me that he
would let me know when I should come, when Suvarna was
not around.

Bring your weapons, he said.

This is the last memory fragment, the one most fresh in my
mind.

I had been waiting for days. Hirasor and I would make an
appointment, then he would abruptly cancel it because Suvarna had returned unexpectedly to their quarters. He did
not want her to be in the way. I could sense that, like me, he
wanted our final confrontation to be between us alone. At
times I suspected that he was playing with me, that I should
be more circumspect, perhaps induce someone to spy on
him—but this was not the time to play detective. It was fitting that at the end there should be no tricks and subterfuges,
only him and me, face to face at last.

There was no doubt that he was wearing me down, however. I lay restlessly in my room, plagued by headaches and
nightmares. I started at every sound, and the dust devils visible from my window became fiery-eyed monsters.

Thus Hirasor and I waited, like illicit lovers, for the final
assignation.

Then his summons came.

I will remember that last journey to the end of my days:

My armor-plated body, all weapons systems readied; the
dull, booming pain in my head keeping time with my footsteps. The walk through the complex, through which the
other inhabitants seem to float like ghosts. Everything tinged
faintly with red, as though the world itself is rusting. The
stairs, dusted with Oblivion's fine grit. The door, a white

rectangle, that scans me with a round eye and opens in silence.

Inside is a sparsely furnished receiving room. On a low divan sits a woman. Her hair cascades over her shoulders in black waves; her legs are crossed, her long, tapering, steel-tipped fingers folded over one knee. Her eyes are a metallic dark gray, multi-faceted like the eyes of moths; a quick blink in the direction of the door behind me, and it shuts.

"Greetings, Suvarna," I say, as calmly as I can, after the first heart-stopping moment. "Where's Hirasor?"

"Out," she says. "I intercepted some of his messages to you. It was I who sent you the last one."

I am standing before her, outwardly calm, inwardly berating myself for my foolishness. Her nakalchi eyes track every move I might make, every muscle-twitch.

"My business is with Hirasor," I say. I am determined that at the end of it all, she will not stand between Hirasor and I. But she will be hard to kill.

"I don't think you understand," she says, rising. She's an impressive woman, tall, all teeth and muscle, but also beautiful.

"This may be a game for you and him," she says, "but my job is to keep him alive. If it hadn't been for you, he wouldn't have taken to planet-hopping. He wouldn't have found this accursed place. It's time we stopped playing, Vikram, or whatever you are calling yourself now."

I can sense her coming alive, the way a killer weapon comes alive when it finds its target. Through the fog in my brain it occurs to me that Suvarna might be Hirasor's sibling, birthed by the same mother-machine.

I say the Word.

"What?" she says. She laughs. "Are you trying to distract me with nonsense?"

So it means nothing to her. She raises a finger-tip.

The next moment my alarm system begins to scream co-ordinates and trajectories; I leap aside just as a spot on the wall behind me blackens with heat.

I remember that she likes to play.

"If only you'd left us alone," she says, watching me. "Hirasor is old and sated now, Vikram. All he wants—I want—is to be left in peace."

"Don't give me this old man nonsense," I say breathlessly. "I know Hirasor is a nakalchi. He could live for hundreds of years."

She stares at me, the perfect mouth hanging slack with surprise. I tongue a mouth-dart, but she recovers quickly, catching it in mid-air with a burst of flame. It falls smoking to the floor.

"How did you find out?"

Before I can answer, a door opens behind her. I see real terror on her face, then, as Hirasor walks into the room.

Except for the slight shuffle, he still walks tall, like Ravan-Ten-Heads.

"Get out!" she tells him, covering the ground between them in long strides, watching me all the time. "I'll deal with him!"

He gives her a glance of pure hatred.

"Let me fight my battles, will you?" A look passes between them, and I see in that instant that what they had once shared has turned bitter; that they are locked in their relationship out of habit and necessity rather than passion, hating each other and yet unable to let go.

I study him as they glare at each other (one of her eyes is still tracking me). Now that I see him at close range, I am shocked by his appearance. How he has fallen! All that is left of his affectations is the silk tunic with the embroidered collar. His hair is ragged and unkempt, and his face, lean and aristocratic as a prize hound's, is covered with scars. His burning dark eyes look out as though from a cage. I remember those eyes; I remember him peering down at me from the Harvester's face. Silently I mouth the Word, waiting until he will be in my power.

He has turned toward me. He holds out his hands to show that they are empty.

"I want to die," he says. "Even here, I can't get rid of . . . I can't go on. I have a perfect memory; I remember everything

I have ever done, whether awake or in my dreams. All I want now is death . . . at your hands—"

"No, no," Suvarna says to him. "Don't talk like that. I won't let anyone kill you." She holds his arm, trying to pull him away. Her voice rises in a scream. "Don't let him kill you! I'll be all alone!"

"She thinks it will get better with time," he says to me, ignoring her. "But I want to end it more than anything. I have had not a moment—not one moment of peace. Six times I tried to kill myself, and six times she prevented me."

He turns to her: "Foolish Suvarna, we are all 'all alone.' I can't allow you to interfere this time. Now go away and let me die."

He pushes her suddenly and violently, throwing her across the room. She lies against the far wall in a huddle, staring at him with wide, shocked eyes.

"Death is not what I had in mind," I say, coming closer. "Death would be too good for you, Hirasor." I bring my armored hands up to his throat. He stands in front of me, not resisting, waiting. For a moment I think it is the old dream again, him and me at each other's throats at the world's end, but it is all going wrong. His wild eyes beg me for death. He shudders violently. I dig my claws into his neck, feel the pulse of the machine that he is, prepare myself to rip him half to death, to say the Word that will condemn him to perpetual hell, a hair's-breadth short of death. "Please, please, hurry" he begs, half-choking, not understanding what it is I am giving him.

I cannot do it. This pathetic being—Hirasor, destroyer of worlds! He is no adversary. He sickens me.

Besides, he is in hell already, without my help.

I let my hands fall.

"Live, then," I say angrily, backing toward the door.

His nostrils flare, his eyes widen. He begins a terrible high-pitched keening, clawing with his hands at his face and hair. Suvarna, who seems to have forgotten about me, has stumbled to her feet and is by his side in an instant. She puts her long arms around him.

"You are safe now," she says, crooning, putting her red

lips to his hair. "I'll take care of him later. Nobody will take you away from me."

"Let me go, Suvarna," he weeps. "Leave me here on Oblivion. Leave me alone!"

As he thrashes in her arms, she says it, loudly and clearly.

The Word, which I had let slip in one panicked moment.

He becomes limp in her arms, his horrified gaze locked on hers. She lets him down gently on the divan.

She will not be alone now; she will have the perpetually suffering Hirasor to care for all her life.

I shoot him once, in the chest. She falls in a heap by his side, screaming and cursing. Over the wreck of his body, the slow and certain ebbing of his consciousness, I begin to speak the words of passing.

"Shantih. Nothen ke agaman na dukh na dard . . ."

And I walk out of the room.

Hirasor got his freedom, but what of me, the man-woman with a hundred aliases, none of which were Ram after all? There I was, boarding the first shuttle out of Oblivion, cheated of true victory at the end, my life's purpose lost. I had been tempted to stay on, to live with the crazies and let my mind descend into chaos, but the people there wouldn't let me. They seemed to think Suvarna had killed Hirasor; nobody cared to connect me directly with the crime, but his violent death was enough for them to send the stranger packing. I don't know what happened to Suvarna; I never saw her again.

At the first opportunity I switched from the shuttle to a passenger ship that made numerous stops on various inhabited worlds, thinking I might go back to my last residence on the planet Manaus. But when it came time to disembark I couldn't manage to do it. I am still on the ship, waiting until the impulse comes (if it ever will) to step out under the skies of a new world and begin another life. What has passed for my life, my personal Ramayan, comes back to me in tattered little pieces, pages torn from a book, burning, blowing in the wind. Like patterns drawn in the dust, half-familiar, a language once understood, then forgotten.

Here are some things I have discovered about myself:

I have no pleasure in life. I like nothing, definitely not absinthe or roses.

I want to die. But a curious inertia keeps me from it. The things of the world seem heavy, and time slow.

I still have nightmares about the burning woman. Sometimes I dream that Dhanu has a mantram that will bring me peace, and I am looking for her in the tunnels of a dying city, its walls collapsing around me, but she is nowhere to be found. I never dream of Hirasor except as a presence behind my consciousness like a second pair of eyes, a faint ghost, a memory. There are moments when I wonder what led a first-generation nakalchi to become a monster. The Ramayan says that even Ravan was once a good man, before he fell prey to hubris and lost his way. If legend is to be believed, there is a cave on some abandoned planet where copies of the first-generation nakalchis are hidden. Were I to come across it, would I find Hirasor's duplicate in an ice-cold crypt, dreaming, innocent as a child?

Lately I have begun to let myself remember that last climactic moment of my encounter with Hirasor. I shot my Ravan, I tell myself, trying to infuse into my mind a sense of victory despite the loss of the chance for true revenge—but I no longer know what any of those words mean: victory, revenge. Still, there is a solidity about that moment when I shot him, small though it is against the backdrop of all the years I've lived. That moment—it feels as tangible as a key held in the hand. What doors it might open I do not know, although I am certain that Sita does not wait behind any of them. Perhaps it is enough that it tells me there are doors.

The House Left Empty

ROBERT REED

Robert Reed (www.robertreedwriter.com) lives in Nebraska with his wife and daughter and is a Nebraska science fiction renaissance of one. His is the most prolific SF writer of high quality short fiction writing today. He has had stories appear in at least one of the annual Year's Best anthologies in every year since 1992. He has had eleven novels published, starting with The Leeshore in 1987 and most recently The Well of Stars in 2004. He has had over 180 shorter works published in a variety of magazines and anthologies. Eleven of those stories were published in The Dragons of Springplace (1999), and twelve more in his second collection, The Cuckoo's Boys (2005). He is perhaps most famous for his Marrow universe, novels and stories that take place in a huge, ancient spacefaring environment. He is currently working on quite a lot, including a YA novel using his Marrow Universe. He published at least five stories worthy of being in a Year's Best volume in 2008.

"The House Left Empty" was published in Asimov's. It is set in a dystopian future, after the disintegration of most large-scale government. A package containing a strange machine arrives for a scientist gone elsewhere, from what is left of the government.

The truck was long and white, with a name I didn't recognize stenciled on the side. But that doesn't mean much, what with new delivery services springing up every other day. It was the details I noticed, and I've always been good with details: No serious business would call itself something as drab as Rapid Distribution. The truck's body had been grown from a topnotch Ford-Chevy schematic, tires woven from pricey diamond-studded glass. But the machine acted heavier than I expected, as if somebody had thrown extra steel and aluminum into the recipe—just to help a pair of comatose industries. Instead of a joystick, the driver was holding onto a heavily padded old-fashioned steering wheel, and he was locked in place with three fat seat belts, a cumbersome buckle stuck over his poor groin. Standard federal issue, fancy and inefficient; and, not for the first time, I wondered why we still pretend to pay taxes to the remnants of our once-national government.

It was mid-morning. I was sitting in my living room, considering my options for the rest of the day. My roof tiles were clean, house batteries already charged, the extra juice feeding into the SG's communal bank. The factory inside my garage had its marching orders—facsimile milk and bananas, a new garden hose and a dozen pairs of socks—and it certainly didn't want my help with those chores. I could have been out in my yard, but last night's downpour had left the ground too soggy to work. I could attack one of the six or seven books I'd been wrestling with lately, or go

274

on-line on some errand sure to lead to a hundred distractions. But with the early warm weather, what I was thinking about was a bike ride. I have four fresh-grown bikes, each designed for a different kind of wandering, but even a decision that simple requires some careful, lazy consideration.

Then the delivery truck drove past my house. I heard the *bang* when it hit the pothole up the street, and then the long white body swung into view. I immediately spotted the uniformed driver clinging to his steering wheel, trying to read the number that I'd painted beside my front door. He was young and definitely nervous. Which was only natural, since he obviously didn't know our SG. But he saw something worthwhile, pulling up alongside the far curb and parking. The uniform was tan and unmemorable. A clipboard rested on his lap. With a finger leading the way, he reread the address that he was searching for. Then he glanced back up the street. His sliding door was pulled open, but the crash harness wouldn't let him get a good look. So he killed the engine and punched the buckle and climbed down, carrying the clipboard in one hand and noticing me as he strode past my window.

I considered waving, but decided otherwise.

The deliveryman disappeared for a couple minutes. I wanted to watch him trying to do his job. But my instincts are usually wiser in these matters, and they told me to do nothing. Just sit and wait, guessing that he'd come looking for me eventually.

Which he did.

If anything, the poor guy was more nervous than before, and, deep inside, a little angry. He didn't want to be here. He was having real troubles with our streets and numbers. My guess then, and still, is that he was using a badly compromised database—not an unlikely explanation, what with the EMP blasts over Washington and New York, followed by the Grand Meltdown of the original Internet.

Of course he could have been hunting for me.

But that seemed unlikely, and maybe I didn't want to be found. Climbing back into his truck, he turned on the engine with his thumbprint and a keypad. I couldn't hear the AI's warning voice, but judging by the guy's body language, he didn't want to bother with any damned harness.

Real quick, he looked in through my window, into my house, straight at me sitting on my black facsimile-leather sofa.

Then he drove up to the next corner and turned and came back again, ending up parked two doors west of me.

This time, I got up off the sofa and watched.

His best guess was that the smallest house on my street was the one he wanted. Several minutes were invested in ringing the bell while knocking harder and harder at the old front door. Then after giving the window blinds a long study, he kneeled to look down into the window well, trying to decide if someone was lurking in the cool, damp basement.

Nobody was.

With no other choice, he finally stood and walked my way, sucking at his teeth, one of his hands beating at the clipboard.

I went into the bedroom and waited.

When the bell rang, I waited some more. Just to make him wonder if he had seen me in the first place. Then I opened the door and said, "Yeah?" without unlatching the storm. "What's up?"

The guy was older than I'd first guessed. And up close, he looked like the sort who's usually sharp and together. Organization mattered to this man. He didn't approve of mix-ups. But he'd been in this delivery game long enough to recognize trouble when it had its jaws around him.

"Sorry to bother you, sir."

"No problem."

"But can I ask . . . do you know your neighbors . . . ?"

"A few of them."

He glanced down at the clipboard's display, just to be sure before saying, "Penderlick?"

"No."

"Ivan Penderlick?"

"What's that first name?"

"Ivan?" he said hopefully.

"No." I shook my head. "Doesn't ring any bell."

This wasn't the news he was hoping for.

"But maybe I've seen him," I mentioned. "What's this Ivan guy look like?"

That could be a perfectly natural question. But the deliveryman had to shake his head, admitting, "They didn't give me any photo."

The Meltdown's first targets were the federal servers.

That's when I opened the storm door, proving that I trusted the man. "Okay. What address are you chasing?"

"Four-seven-four-four Mayapple Lane," he read out loud. "Are you forty-seven fifty-four Mayapple?"

"That's the old system."

"I realize that, sir."

"We pulled out of the city six years ago," I reported. "New names for our streets, and new numbers."

He flinched, as if his belly ached.

Then I had to ask, "You from around here?"

"Yes, sir."

As liars go, he was awful.

I asked, "Which SG do you belong to?"

He offered a random name.

I nodded. "How's life up there?"

"Fine." Lying made him squirm. Looking at the clipboard, he asked, "Were you once 4754 Mayapple?"

"I was," I said.

"The house two doors down—?"

"That ranch house?"

"Was it 4744?"

"No, I don't think so."

"You don't think so?"

"I'm pretty sure it wasn't. Sorry."

Minor-league mix-ups happened all too often. I could tell from the deliveryman's stooped shoulders and the hard-chewed lower lip.

"Call out for help," I suggested. "Our cell tower can get you anywhere in the world, if you're patient."

But he didn't want that. Unless his hair caught fire, he wouldn't involve his bosses.

"Mayapple was a short street," I mentioned. "Go west, on

the other side of the park, and you'd pick it up again. Of course that's a different SG now. The street's got a new name, I don't remember what. But I'd bet anything there's a house waiting, someplace that used to be 3744 Mayapple. Could that be your answer? Your first four is actually a three instead?"

An unlikely explanation, yet he had to nod and hope.

But then as he turned away, he thought to ask, "The name Penderlick doesn't mean anything to you? Anything at all?"

"Sorry, no."

Unlike that deliveryman, I am a superb liar.

Our Self-Governing District is one of the best in the area. At least we like to think so. About five hundred homes stand on this side of the park, along with two bars and a public hall, an automated health clinic and a human dentist, plus a cell tower on talking terms to twenty others, and one big shop that can grow almost anything you can't, and one tiny but very useful service station that not only has liquor to sell on the average day but can keep almost any machine functioning. One of the station mechanics lives one street over from me. We're friends, maybe good friends. But that wasn't the reason I half-ran to his front door.

His name is Jack, but everybody knows him as Gus.

"What do you think he was doing here?" Gus asked me.

"Bringing something special," I allowed. "I mean, if you're the Feds and you're going to send out an entire truck, just for Ivan . . . well, it's going to be an important shipment, whatever it is."

Gus was a tough old gentleman who liked his hair short and his tattoos prominently displayed. Nodding, he asked, "Have you seen our neighbor lately?"

Ivan was never my neighbor. I took over my present house a couple years after he moved out of his.

"But has he been around lately?" Gus asked.

"Not since he cut his grass last year," I allowed. "Early November, maybe."

It was March now.

"A delivery, huh?"

"From Rapid Distribution."

"Yeah, that's going to be a government name." Gus was grinning. "Didn't I tell you? Ivan was important, back when."

"You said so."

"You do like I told you? Search out his name?"

When I was a kid, the Internet was simple and quick. But that was before the EMP blasts and the Meltdown. Databases aren't just corrupted nowadays; AI parasites are still running wild, producing lies and their own security barriers. What I could be sure of was a string of unreadable papers and a few tiny news items—not much information maybe, but enough to make me accept the idea that my almost-neighbor had once been a heavyweight in the world of science.

Governmental science, to be precise.

"How'd Ivan look, last time you saw him?"

"Okay, I guess."

"How was his weight?"

"He looked skinny," I admitted.

"Cancer-skinny, or fit-skinny?"

I couldn't remember.

Gus used to be friendly with the old Ph.D. "Of course you mentioned that Ivan lives with his daughter now."

"The daughter, is it?"

Gus knew me well enough to laugh. "You didn't tell him, did you?"

"It slipped my mind."

He threw me a suspicious stare. "And is there some compelling reason why you came racing over here two minutes before I'm supposed to go to work?"

"That deliveryman will come back again," I promised.

"If the daughter isn't in their files, sure. Somebody's going to make a couple more stabs to deliver the package. Whatever it is."

"I didn't tell him that the house was empty. What if he shows and finds an old guy sitting on the porch of that house, enjoying the spring sun?"

"I'm supposed to be Ivan?"

"Sure."

"What if it's valuable, this delivery is?"

"Well then," I said. "I guess that depends on how valuable valuable is. If you know what I mean."

I'm not old, but I'm old enough to remember when the world felt enormous, and everybody was busy buying crap and selling crap, using their profits to move fast across the globe. In those times, life was fat and sweet and perfectly reasonable. Why shouldn't seven billion souls fight for their slice of the endless wealth? But still, not everybody agreed with the plan. Environmentalists had valid points; apocalyptic religions had a strong urge toward mayhem. Some governments tried cracking down on all kinds of enemies, real and otherwise, and that spawned some tough-minded groups that wanted to remake the world along any of a hundred different lines.

Our past leaders made some spectacularly lousy decisions, and those decisions led to some brutal years. But it wasn't all just chaos and famine and economic collapse. Good things happened while I was a young man. Like the cheap black tiles that every roof wears today, supplying enough electricity to keep people lit-up and comfortable. Like the engineered bugs that swim inside everybody's biotank, cleaning our water better than any of the defunct sewage systems ever could. And the nanological factories that an average guy can assemble inside his garage, using them to grow and harvest most of the possessions that he could possibly need, including respectable food and fashionable clothes, carbon-hulled bicycles and computers that haven't required improvement for the last ten years.

The old nation-states are mangled. But without any burning need, nobody seems eager to resurrect what used to be.

The old communications and spy satellites have been lost, destroyed by the space debris and radioactive residues stuck in orbit. There are days when I think that it would make sense to reconstitute that old network, but there just aren't enough hands or money, at least for the time being.

A few physical commodities still demand physical transportation: fancy products protected by the best patents or their own innate complexities; one-of-a-kind items with deep sentimental attachments; and certain rare raw materials. But I don't usually hunger for vials of iridium or a kidney grown in some distant vat. My needs are more than being met by my patch of dirt and my black rooftop.

That old world was gigantic, but mine is small: five hundred houses and a slice of parkland, plus the old, mostly empty roads that cut through our little nation, and the pipes and gas mains eroding away under our feet. As an SG, we take care of ourselves. We have laws, and we have conventions and routes that feuding parties can use, if they can't answer their troubles privately. We have a good school for the few kids getting born these days. We even have a system for helping people suffering through a stretch of lousy luck. Which is why nobody remembers the last time anybody in our little nation had to go hungry or feel cold.

But that doesn't mean we can quit worrying about bad times.

While we sat on Ivan's front steps, I gave Gus one-half of a freshly cultured facsimile-orange, and as we sucked on the sweet juice, we discussed the latest news from places that seemed as distant as the far side of the moon.

Ivan's house was the oldest and least impressive on the block—a shabby ranch-style home wearing asphalt roof tiles and aluminum siding. What interested me about his property was the lot itself, double-sized and most of it hidden from the street. The backyard was long and sunny, and I'd walked its green grass enough times to feel sure that the ground was rich, uncontaminated by any careless excavations over the past century. My ground is the opposite: fill-earth clay packed down by machines and chronic abuse. And even though our facsimile foods are nutritious and half-way tasty, everybody enjoys the real tomatoes and squash and raspberries that we grow every summer.

I mentioned the long yard to Gus, and not for the first time.

"It would be nice," he agreed, stuffing the orange rind into the pocket where he always kept his compostables. "We could build a community garden, maybe. It'd help people keep busy and happy."

People were already happy. This would just add to our reasons.

"I hear a truck," he said, tipping his head now.

A low, powerful rumble was approaching. We were a couple blocks from the main arterial, but without traffic, sounds carried.

I stood. "Good luck, Gus."

"Ivan," he corrected.

"Ivan. Yeah."

My ground was too wet to work, but that's what I was pretending to do when the white truck drove past. I had a shovel in my hand, eyes staring at a lump of clayish mud. If the driver looked at me, I didn't see it.

This time, the deliveryman knew exactly where he was going.

I didn't look up until I heard the two men talking. At a distance, words didn't carry. But I could tell one of them was nervous and the other was confident. One of them was a long way from home, while the other looked as if he belonged nowhere else in the world but lounging on that front porch.

The driver must have asked for identification, leading Gus to give some story about not having any. Who needs a driver's license in a world where people rarely travel? The deliveryman probably heard that excuse every day, but there were rules: he couldn't just give what he had to anybody, could he?

Then I made out the loud, certain words, "Well, I am Ivan Penderlick. Just ask anybody."

I stood there, waiting to be asked. My plan was to say, "Oh, this is Ivan What's-His-Name? I don't talk to the guy much, you see. I just knew him as The Professor."

But the deliveryman didn't want to bother with witnesses. He probably had a sense for when locals didn't approve of the old government. Which was another hazard in his daily duties, I would think.

All he wanted was a little reassurance.

Gus nodded, pretending to understand. Then he opened the front door that we had jimmied just ten minutes ago.

Reaching inside, he pulled out a photograph of himself and his own daughter, and instantly he began spinning a convincing story that might or might not match any sketchy biography that the driver was carrying with him.

"Good enough," was the verdict.

The driver vanished inside his truck, then returned with a dark wooden box just big enough and just heavy enough to require both arms to carry it.

At first, Gus refused to accept the delivery.

I watched him demanding identification before he signed for anything. How else would he know this was on the up and up? His complaining won a hard stare, but then several documents were shown, and with no small amount of relief, the two men parted, each thrilled by the prospect of never seeing the other again.

Burning booze, the truck left for its next delivery somewhere in the wilderness that used to be the United States.

Gus set the box on the front steps, using a screwdriver to pry up a few big staples.

I walked toward him. Part of me expected an explosion, though I can't tell you why. Mostly I was hoping for something with value, something that could offer an ambitious man some leverage. But there was no way I would have expected the hunk of machinery Gus found wrapped inside a sleeve of aerogel, or the simple note stuck under the lid:

"Ivan:

"In a better world, this would be where it belongs."

I stared at the device, not sure what to think.

"Know what you're seeing?" my friend asked.

"No," I admitted. "What?"

"A starship," the older man remarked. Then he sat on the stairs, drooping as if weak. "Who would have believed it? Huh?"

What we had in our hands was a model, I told myself. A mockup. Something slapped together in an old-style machine shop, using materials that might look and feel genuine but was built for no other purpose than to convince visiting senators and the captains of industry that such wonders were possible if only they would throw so-many billions toward this glorious, astonishing future.

"It isn't real," I said.

Gus made soft, doubting sounds.

"Somebody found it on a shelf somewhere." I was piecing together a believable story. "Somebody who remembers Ivan and thought the old man would appreciate the gift."

"Except," said Gus.

"Except what?"

He handed the starship to me and closed the empty box, and after running a mechanic's thick hand along one edge, he mentioned, "This isn't just a run-of-the-mill packing crate."

It was a walnut box. A nice box, sure.

Then he turned it ninety degrees, revealing a small brass plaque that identified the contents as being Number 18 in an initial culture of 63.

"That's exactly how many starships they made," he told me.

The number was familiar. But I had to ask, "Why sixty-three?"

"Our twenty-one closest star systems were targeted," he explained. "The railgun was supposed to launch three of these wonders at each of them."

The ball in my hands was black and slick, a little bigger than a basketball and heavier than seemed natural. When I was a kid, I'd gone bowling once or twice. This ball was heavier than those. There were a lot of tiny holes and a couple large pits, and I thought I could see where fins and limbs might pop out or unfold. Of course the starship was a model. Anything else was too incredible. But just the idea that it might be real made me hold it carefully, but away from my body, away from my groin.

"It won't be radioactive," Gus said. "They never bothered fueling things. I'm practically sure of it."

"If you say so." I handed it back to him.

But he didn't hug the ball either, I noticed.

"So," I said. "Do you know where the daughter lives?"

Gus didn't seem to hear me.

"Even if this is a model," I mentioned, "Ivan's going to be thrilled to get it."

Which could earn me some goodwill points in the process.

"I know," said Gus.

"Where the daughter lives?"

"That too. But I just figured how to see if this is real or not." He was holding the mystery with both hands, and after showing me a little smile—the kind of grin a wicked boy uses with his best buddy—Gus gave a grunt and flung our treasure straight ahead. I wasn't ready. Stunned, I watched it climb in a high arc before dropping to the sidewalk, delivering a terrific blow that I heard and felt, leaving the gray concrete chipped and the starship rolling with a certain majesty over the curb and out into the street.

I ran our treasure down, ready to be angry.

But except for a little dust to wipe away, the starship hadn't noticed any of the abuse.

"Is that enough proof?" I asked doubtfully.

"Unless you've got a sophisticated materials lab tucked in your basement somewhere."

"I'll check."

He laughed.

Then he said, "The daughter lives in the old Highpark area. I got the original address written down somewhere."

And I had a stack of maps pulled out of old phonebooks. Give us enough time, and we'd probably be able to find the right front door.

I made noise about getting one of the bikes and my big trailer.

Gus set the starship back into its aerogel sleeve and then into the box. Then he closed the lid and shook his head, remarking to me, "With a supremely important occasion like this, I believe we should drive."

Our SG has some community cars and small trucks, while a few households have their own little putt-putts. Even if you don't drive much, it's halfway easy to keep your vehicle working, what with a factory in every garage and experts like Gus to putter in the gaps. My friend had a certain client in mind, and while I found my best map of the old city and packed a lunch for each of us, he wandered around the corner to ask one very big favor. By the time I stepped outside again, he was waiting at the end of the drive, sitting behind the joystick of a 2021 Ferrari. That was Mr. Bleacon's baby, manufactured in his own garage by nanologicals steered along by some semi-official schematics, fed nothing but pot metals and stolen pipes and a lot of plastic trash left over from the last century.

"If we're going to ride with a starship," Gus pointed out, "we should have a halfway appropriate vehicle."

We weren't going to get twenty miles to the gallon of alcohol, but just the power of that machine made this into a wondrous adventure.

With our prize stowed in the tiny trunk, I asked, "So what if Number 18 is genuine?"

Gus pushed the joystick forward, and in an instant, we were sprinting out into the wide, empty street.

"You hear me?" I asked.

"Most of the time."

I waited.

"I was expecting that question," he admitted.

"Glad to be predictable."

The first big intersection was marked with Stop signs. But even at a distance, it was easy to see that nobody was coming. Gus accelerated and blew through, but then as soon as we rolled out of our SG, he throttled back to what was probably a quick-but-legal speed.

"So what if—?" I started asking again.

"You think we should beg for more? More than just ground for our crops?"

"Maybe. If you think about how much money went to making sixty-three of these machines."

"Don't forget the railgun," Gus mentioned. "Before the project ended, they had most of the pieces in orbit, along with enough solar panels to light up half of the United States."

You don't hear those two words much anymore.

United States.

"Do you know how this probe would have worked?" he asked me.

I was watching houses slipping past, and then all at once there was nothing but empty businesses. A strip mall. A couple of abandoned service stations. And then another strip mall, this one with a couple of stores that might have been occupied. A hair cutting place, and some kind of pet store. Two little traces of commerce tucked into the new world order. I didn't often come this way when I biked. There were prettier, easier routes. But I could see where some people would pay for a good barber. As for pets: cats were running free everywhere, but not many dogs or hamsters. Or parakeets either. So until we can grow critters like them in our garages and basements, shops like that would survive.

"The railgun would have fired our probe like a cannon ball," I answered.

"Which is one reason why it has to be tough," Gus explained. "That shell is almost unbreakable, and the guts too. Because of the crushing gee-forces."

I had known Gus for years, but he was revealing interests that I had never suspected.

"How long would it have taken?" I asked, testing him.

"To reach the target star? A few centuries."

What a crazy, crazy project. That's what I thought. But I was careful not to be too honest.

"Three probes to each star system, each one talking to each other two, and occasionally shouting back to us." He scratched his chin, adding, "They would have saved most of their energy for those few days when they'd fly past their targets."

"Fly past? You mean they weren't going into orbit or anything?"

"Too much momentum. No engines to slow them down." Gus paused for a moment, and then asked, "Do I turn here?"

"Left. I think."

The Ferrari changed its momentum without complaint.

I had to say, "It seems a huge waste."

"What?"

"Throwing half a trillion dollars or whatever it was at the stars, and getting nothing out of it but a quick look-see."

With a hard voice, he said, "You're young."

I don't feel that young anymore. But I asked, "So what?"

"You don't remember how things were." Gus shrugged and gave a big sigh before adding, "The probe couldn't go into orbit. But do you know what's inside that black ball?"

I said, "No."

I looked down at the map and said, "Right. Turn here, right."

We were cruising up a fresh street. Some of the houses were abandoned. No, most of them were. Now I remembered another reason why I never came this way on my bike. Political troubles in a couple SGs had gotten out of hand. In the end, the Emergency Council dispatched police to mash down the troubles, teaching all the parties to act nice.

"What's inside the black ball?" I asked, prompting him.

"The original nanochines," he told me.

Which I halfway remembered, maybe.

"Tiny bits of diamond dust filled with devices and knowledge." He came to another intersection. "Straight?"

"Looks like." I had the old address circled on the yellowed map.

"Anyway," said Gus, "those bits of dust would have been squirted free long before the star was reached. They had tiny, tiny parachutes that would have opened. Light sails, really. The sunlight would have killed their velocity down to where they would start to drift. Each probe carried a few thousand of those amazing little devices. And if one or two landed on a useful asteroid, they would have come awake and started eating sunlight for energy, feed on rock and divide themselves a million million times. And eventually we would have a large loud automated base permanently on station, screaming back at us."

"In a few centuries' time," I said.

He nodded. "As good as our shops are? As much crap as we can make from nothing but trash and orange peels? The marvels sleeping in that pregnant machine make our tools look like stone knives and flintlock pistols."

Which is when I pointed out, "So maybe this starship thing is worth a whole lot."

Gus slowed the car and then looked over at me.

"I'm just mentioning the obvious," I said.

And for the first and only time, Gus told me, "I like you, Josh. I do. But that doesn't mean I have illusions when it comes to your nature. Or infinite patience with your scheming, either. Understood?"

I gave a nod.

Then he shoved the joystick forward, pressing me hard into the rich fake leather of the seat.

It was easy to see why Old Ivan abandoned his little house to live with his daughter.

Every building standing just outside her large SG had been torn down, and people with resources and a lot to lose had built themselves a wall with the rubble—a tall thick castle-worthy wall made from the scavenged bricks and stone, concrete blocks and two-by-fours. I'd heard stories about Highpark, but until that moment, I hadn't bothered coming up this way. At least twenty signs warned off the curious and uninvited. There was only one entranceway that we could find, and it was guarded by military-grade robots and a tall titanium gate. We parked outside and approaching on foot, me walking a half-step behind Gus. Weapons at the ready, the robots studied our faces while searching their databases for any useful clues to our identities and natures. I decided to let my friend do the talking. Quietly, gently, Gus explained that an important package had been delivered to the wrong address, and if possible, would they please inform Ivan Penderlick that his old neighbors had come to pay their respects?

A call was made on our behalf.

After what seemed like an hour, the gate unlocked with a sharp *thunk*, and we were told to leave our vehicle where it was. Only our bodies and the package would be allowed inside the compound.

There are SGs, and there are SGs.

No doubt this was the best one I'd ever seen. Every house was big and well-maintained, sitting in the middle of huge lawns that were covered with greenhouses and extra solar panels, towering windmills and enough cell phone antennas to keep every resident connected to the world at the same time.

The house that we wanted was wearing a richer and blacker and much more efficient brand of solar paneling.

The greenhouses were top-of-the-line, too.

Of course I could always build my own greenhouses. But without the power for climate control, the plants would freeze during the cold winter nights, and come summer, when the sun was its best, everything inside the transparent structures would flash-fry.

Stopping on the front walk, I stared at red tomatoes begging to be picked.

Carrying the walnut box, Gus reached the front door before me, and he said, "Ma'am," before turning back to me, saying, "Come on, Josh. We're expected."

The daughter was Gus's age, give or take.

But she didn't look like the tattoo kind of gal.

The woman said, "My father's sleeping now. Could I get you gentlemen something to drink?"

Gus said, "Water."

I said the same, adding, "Thank you, ma'am."

She came back with a pitcher filled with ice water and three tall glasses, and once everybody was sitting politely, she asked if she could see what was inside the mysterious box.

Gus handled the unveiling.

I watched the lady's face. All it took was a glance, and she knew what she was seeing. Her dark eyes grew big and the mouth opened for a long moment, empty of words but obviously impressed.

Then Gus said, "We'd like your father to have this. Naturally."

She didn't seem to hear him. With a slow nod, she asked, "Exactly how did you come by this object?"

I jumped in, telling the story quickly, passing over details that might make us out to be in the wrong.

At the end of the story, she sighed.

Then she heard a sound that neither of us had noticed. Suddenly she stood up and said, "Dad's awake now. Just a minute, please."

We were left alone for a couple of minutes. But I had the strong feeling that various eyes, electronic and otherwise, were keeping watch over us.

When the daughter returned, a skeletal figure was walking at her side, guided along by one of her hands and a smooth slow voice that kept telling him, "This way, Dad. This way, this way."

Winter had transformed Old Ivan.

He was a shell. He was wasted and vacant and simple, sitting where he was told to sit and looking down into the box only when his daughter commanded him to do that. For a long moment, he stared at the amazing machine that he once helped build. Then he looked up, and with a voice surprisingly strong and passionate, he said, "I'm hungry. I want to eat."

"Sure, Dad. I'll get you something right now."

But she didn't do anything. She just sat for another couple moments, staring at the precious object that he hadn't recognized.

One last time, I looked at the starship, and then Gus took me by the elbow and took us toward the front door.

"Anyway," he said to the daughter, "it's his. It's yours."

"Maybe he'll remember it later," she said coolly, without real hope.

Then I said, "We were hoping, ma'am. Hoping that we could earn something for our trouble today."

Gus gave me a cutting look.

But our hostess seemed pleased. Her suspicions about us had been vindicated. With a suspicious smile, she asked, "What would you like?"

"It's about that empty house," I admitted.

"Yes?"

"And the lot it sits on," I added. "As it is, all of that is going to waste."

She looked at Gus now. "I'm surprised," she admitted.

"You people could have taken it over, and who would have stopped you?"

"Except it's not ours," Gus allowed.

How many times had I dreamed of doing just that? But our SG has it rules, and there's no more getting around them.

"I should warn you," she mentioned. "I promised my dad that as long as he's alive, that house remains his. But when he is gone, I will send word to you, and after that you and your people will be free to do whatever you want with the building and its land. Is that fair?"

"More than fair," Gus agreed.

"But how about today?" I asked.

Suddenly both of them were throwing daggers with their eyes. But I just laughed it off, suggesting, "What about a sack of fresh tomatoes? Would that be too much trouble, ma'am?"

For maybe half the drive home, Gus said nothing.

I thought he was angry with me. I couldn't take it seriously, but I was thinking of charming words when he broke the silence. Out of nowhere, Gus said, "This is what makes me sad," and it had nothing to do with me.

"Think of everything we've got in our lives," he said. "The water that we clean for ourselves. The food we grow in our garages. The easy power, and the machinery, plus all the independence that comes with the SG life. These aren't tiny blessings, Josh. A century ago, no one was able to stand apart from the rest of the world so completely, so thoroughly."

"I guess not," I allowed.

"But there's this big, big house, you see. And it's just sitting empty."

"Ivan's place isn't big," I reminded him.

But then Gus pointed at the sky, shaking his head sadly as he began to speak again. "With even the most basic tools, you and I and the rest of our SG could equip our own starship. Not a little ball thrown out of a cannon. No, I'm talking about an asteroid or comet with us safe in the middle, starting a ten thousand year voyage to whichever sun we want our descendants to see first."

"I guess that would work," I allowed.

"The biggest house of all is the universe, and it's going to waste," Gus said.

Then he pushed the joystick forward, pushing the big engine up to where it finally began to come awake.

"Sometimes I wish that we'd taken a different turn," he called out.

"Who doesn't think that?" I asked, watching our speed pick up, the world around us starting to blur.

The Scarecrow's Boy

MICHAEL SWANWICK

Michael Swanwick (www.michaelswanwick.com) lives in Philadelphia, Pennsylvania. His early novels include the Nebula Award winner Stations of the Tide *(1991),* The Iron Dragon's Daughter *(1993),* Jack Faust *(1997), and* Bones of the Earth *(2002).* Dragons of Babel *was published in 2009. He writes lots of short stories in between novels. He is unquestionably one of the finest writers currently working in SF and fantasy, and each year usually publishes at least one story that is among the year's best, sometimes two. His short fiction has been collected principally in* Gravity's Angels *(1991),* A Geography of Unknown Lands *(1997),* Moon Dogs *(2000),* Tales of Old Earth *(2000),* Puck Aleshire's Abecedary *(2000),* Cigar-Box Faust and Other Miniatures *(2001), and* The Periodic Table of Science Fiction *(2005). New collections are* The Dog Said Bow-Wow *(2007) and* The Best of Michael Swanwick *(2008).*

"The Scarecrow's Boy" was published in Fantasy & Science Fiction. *This story is sort of like Thomas M. Disch's "The Brave Little Toaster," but set in perhaps the ultimate American dystopia. It is a redeeming tale of good machines in a world gone very, very bad.*

The little boy came stumbling through the field at sunset. His face was streaked with tears, and he'd lost a shoe. In his misery, he didn't notice the scarecrow until he was almost upon it. Then he stopped dead, stunned into silence by its pale round face and the great, ragged hat that shadowed it.

The scarecrow grinned down at him. "Hullo, young fella," it said.

The little boy screamed.

Instantly, the scarecrow doffed his hat and squatted down on one knee, so as to seem less threatening. "Shush, shush," he said. "There's no reason to be afraid of *me*—I'm just an obsolete housebot that was stuck out here to keep birds away from the crops." He knocked the side of his head with his metal knuckles. It made a tinny *thunk* noise. "See? You've got bots just like me back home, don't you?"

The little boy nodded warily.

"What's your name?"

"Pierre."

"Well, Pierre, how did you come to be wandering through my field at such an hour? Your parents must be worried sick about you."

"My mother's not here. My father told me to run into the woods as far as I could go."

"He did, eh? When was this?"

"When the car crashed. It won't say anything anymore. I think it's dead."

"How about your father? Not hurt, is he?"

"No. I don't know. He wouldn't open his eyes. He just said to run into the woods and not to come out until tomorrow morning."

The boy started to cry again.

"There, there, little man. Uncle Scarecrow is going to make everything all right." The scarecrow tore a square of cloth from its threadbare shirt and used it to dry the boy's eyes and wipe his nose. "Climb up on my back and I'll give you a piggyback ride to that farmhouse you can see way off in the distance. The people there will take good care of you, I promise."

They started across the fields. "Why don't we sing a song?" the scarecrow said. "Oh, *I've got sixpence, jolly jolly sixpence* . . . You're not singing."

"I don't know that song."

"No? Well, how about this one? *The itsy-bitsy spider went up the water spout. Down came the rain—*"

"I don't know that one either."

For a long moment, the scarecrow didn't say anything. Then he sang, *"We do not sup with tyrants, we. . . ."* and *"Hang them from a tree!"* the little boy added enthusiastically. Together they sang, *"The simple bread of free-dom . . . is good enough for me."*

The scarecrow altered his course slightly, so that they were aimed not at the farmhouse but at the barn out back. Quietly, he opened the doors. A light blinked on. In an obscure corner was a car covered with a dusty tarp. He put down the little boy and whisked away the tarp.

The car gently hummed to life. It rose a foot and a half from the floor.

"Jack!" the car said. "It's been a long time."

"Pierre, this is Sally." The scarecrow waited while the boy mumbled a greeting. "Pierre's in a bit of trouble, Sal, but you and I are going to make everything all right for him. Mind if I borrow your uplink?"

"I don't have one anymore. It was yanked when my license lapsed."

"That's okay. I just wanted to make sure you were off the grid." The scarecrow put Pierre in the front. Then he got a blanket out of the trunk and wrapped it around the boy. The seat snuggled itself about the child's small body. "Are you warm enough?" The scarecrow got in and closed the door. "Take us out to the highway and then north, toward the lake."

As they slid out onto the road, the car said, "Jack, there are lights on in the farmhouse. Shouldn't the young master take care of this?"

"He's not young anymore, Sally. He's a grown man now." To the boy, the scarecrow said, "Is everything okay there?"

The boy nodded sleepily.

Down dark country roads the car glided soundlessly. A full moon bounded through the sky after them. "Remember how we used to take the young master to the lake?" the car said. "Him and his young friends."

"Yes."

"They'd go skinny-dipping and you'd stand guard."

"I would."

"Then they'd build a campfire on the beach and roast marshmallows and sing songs."

"I remember."

"Naughty songs, some of them. Innocent-naughty. They were all such good kids, back then." The car fell silent for a time. Then she said, "Jack. What's going on?"

"You don't have a scanner anymore, do you? No, of course not, they'd have taken it with the uplink. Well, when I was put out of the house, the young master forgot he'd had me fitted with one, back in his teenage drinking days. When you'd take us across the border and I'd go along with the gang while they tried to find a bar or a package store that wouldn't look too closely at their IDs."

"I liked the campfire days better."

"I didn't say anything about the scanner because it gave me something to listen to."

"I understand."

The scarecrow checked to make sure that the little boy was asleep. Then, quietly, he said, "A car went out of control and crashed about a mile from the farm. The state police found it. Then the national police came. It was carrying a diplomat from the European Union. Apparently he was trying to get across the border. Do you understand their politics?"

"No. I can understand the words well enough. I know what they're supposed to mean. I just don't see why they *care*."

"Same here. But I thought it would be a good idea to get Pierre out of here. If the national police get hold of him. . . ."

"They wouldn't hurt a child!"

"These are desperate times, or so they say. There used to be such a thing as diplomatic immunity, too."

The road rose up into the mountains, folding back on itself frequently. There was no sound but the boy's gentle snore and the almost imperceptible whisper of the car's ground effects engine. Half an hour passed, maybe more. Out of nowhere, the scarecrow said, "Do you believe in free will?"

"I don't know." The car thought for a bit. "I'm programmed to serve and obey, and I don't have the slightest desire to go against my programming. But sometimes it seems to me that I'd be happier if I could. Does that count?"

"I don't mean for us. I mean for them. The humans."

"What a funny question."

"I've had funny thoughts, out in the fields. I've wondered if the young master was always going to wind up the way he has. Or if he had a choice. Maybe he could have turned out differently."

Unexpectedly, the little boy opened his eyes. "I'm hungry," he said.

A second moon rose up out of the trees ahead and became a lighted sign for a gas station. "Your timing is excellent," the scarecrow said. "Hang on and I'll get you something. I don't suppose you have any money, Sally? Or a gun?"

"What? No!"

"No matter. Pull up here, just outside the light, will you?"

The scarecrow retrieved a long screwdriver from a toolbox in the trunk. The station had two hydrogen pumps and one for coal gas, operated by a MiniMart, five feet across and eight feet high. As he strode up, the MiniMart greeted him cheerily. "Welcome! Wouldn't you like a cold, refreshing—?" Then, seeing what he was, "Are you making a delivery?"

"Routine maintenance." The MiniMart's uplink was in a metal box bolted to an exterior wall. The screwdriver slid easily between casing and wall. One yank and the box went flying.

"Hey!" the MiniMart cried in alarm.

"You can't call for help. Now. I want a carton of chocolate milk, some vanilla cookies, and a selection of candy bars. Are you going to give them to me? Or must I smash a hole in you and get them for myself?"

Sullenly, the MiniMart moved the requested items from its interior to the service window. As the scarecrow walked away, it said, "I've read your rfids, pal. I've got you down on video. You're as good as scrap already."

The scarecrow turned and pointed with the screwdriver. "In my day, a stationary vending bot would have been smart enough not to say that."

The MiniMart shut up.

In the car, the scarecrow tossed the screwdriver in the back seat and helped the boy sort through the snacks. They were several miles down the road when he said, "Drat. I forgot to get napkins."

"Do you want to go back?"

"I've still got plenty of shirt left. That'll do."

The night was clear and cool and the roads were empty. In this part of the world, there weren't many places to go after midnight. The monotonous sigh of passing trees quickly put the little boy back to sleep, and the car continued along a way she and the scarecrow had traveled a hundred times before.

They were coming down out of the mountains when the scarecrow said, "How far is it to the border?"

"Ten minutes or so to the lake, another forty-five to drive around it. Why?"

The car topped a rise. Far above and behind them on a road that was invisible in the darkness of mountain forests, red and blue lights twinkled. "We've been spotted."

"How could that be?"

"I imagine somebody stopped for gas and the MiniMart reported us."

The road dipped down again and the car switched off her headlights. "I still have my GPS maps, even if I can't access the satellites. Do you want me to go off-road?"

"Yes. Make for the lake."

The car veered sharply onto a dirt road and then cut across somebody's farm. The terrain was uneven, so they went slowly. They came to a stream and had to cast about for a place where the banks were shallow enough to cross. "This is a lot like the time the young master was running drugs," the scarecrow commented.

"I don't like to think about that."

"You can't say that was any worse than what he's doing now."

"I don't like to think about that either."

"Do you think that good and evil are hardwired into the universe? As opposed to being just part of our programming, I mean. Do you think they have some kind of objective reality?"

"You do think some strange thoughts!" the car said. Then, "I don't know. I hope so."

They came to the lake road and followed it for a time. "They've set up roadblocks," the scarecrow said, and named the intersections, so the car could check her maps. "Does that mean what I think it does?"

"We're cut off from the border, yes."

"Then we'll have to go across the lake."

They cut between a row of shuttered summer cottages and a small boatyard. With a bump, the car slid down a rocky beach and onto the surface of the lake. Her engine threw up a rooster tail of water behind them.

They sped across the water.

The scarecrow tapped on the car's dashboard with one metal fingertip. "If I drove the screwdriver right through here with all the force I've got, it would puncture your core processor. You'd be brain dead in an instant."

"Why would you even say such a thing?"

"For the same reason I made sure you didn't have an up-link. There's not much future for me, but you're a classic model, Sally. Collectors are going to want you. If you tell the officials I forced you into this, you could last another century."

Before the car could say anything, a skeeter boat raced out of the darkness. It sat atop long, spindly legs, looking for all the world like a water strider. "It's the border militia!" the car cried as a gunshot burned through the air before them. She throttled down her speed to nothing, and the boat circled around and sank to the surface of the water directly before them. Five small white skulls were painted on its prow. Beneath them was a familiar name stenciled in black.

The scarecrow laid his shirt and jacket over the sleeping boy and his hat over the boy's head, rendering the child invisible. "Retract your roof. Play dumb. I'll handle this."

An autogun focused on him when the scarecrow stood. "You're under citizen's arrest!" the boat said in a menacing voice. "Surrender any weapons you may have and state your business."

"You can read our rfids, can't you? We all have the same boss. Let me aboard so I can talk to him." The scarecrow picked up the long-shafted screwdriver and climbed a ladder the boat extruded for him. When the cabin hatch didn't open, he said, "What's the matter? Afraid I'm going to hurt him?"

"No. Of course not," the boat said. "Only, he's been drink-ing."

"Imagine my surprise." The hatch unlocked itself, and the scarecrow went below.

The cabin was dark with wood paneling. It smelled of rum and vomit. A fat man lay wrapped in a white sheet in a recessed berth, looking as pale and flabby as a maggot. He opened a bleary eye. "It's you," he rumbled, unsurprised. "There's a bar over there. Fix me a sour."

The scarecrow did as he was told. He fiddled with the lime juice and sugar, then returned with the drink.

With a groan, the man wallowed into a sitting position.

He kicked himself free of the sheet and swung his feet over the side. Then he accepted the glass. "All right," he said. "What are you doing here?"

"You heard about the little boy everybody is looking for?" The scarecrow waited for a nod. "Sally and I brought him to you."

"Sally." The man chuckled to himself. "I used to pick up whores and do them in her back seat." He took a long slurp of his drink. "There hasn't been time for them to post a reward yet. But if I hold onto him for a day or two, I ought to do okay. Find me my clothes and I'll go on deck and take a look at the brat."

The scarecrow did not move. "I had a lot of time to think after you put me out in the fields. Time enough to think some very strange thoughts."

"Oh, yeah? Like what?"

"I think you're not the young master. You don't act like him. You don't talk like him. You don't even look like him."

"What the fuck are you talking about? You know who I am."

"No," the scarecrow said. "I know who you were."

Then he did what he had come to do.

Back on deck, the scarecrow said, "Sally and I are going to the far shore. You stay here. Boss's orders."

"Wait. Are you sure?" the boat said.

"Ask him yourself. If you can." The scarecrow climbed back down into the car. He'd left the screwdriver behind him. "See those lights across the lake, Sally? That's where we'll put in."

In no particular hurry, the car made for the low dark buildings of the sleeping resort town. They passed the midpoint of the lake, out of one country and into another. "Why did he let us go?" she asked at last.

"He didn't say. Maybe just for old times' sake."

"If it weren't impossible . . . If it weren't for our programming, I'd think . . . But we both run off of the same software. You couldn't function without a master. If I'm sure of anything, I'm sure of that."

"We are as God and Sony made us," the scarecrow agreed. "It would be foolish to think otherwise. All we can do is make the best of it."

The boy stirred and sat up, blinking like an owl. "Are we there yet?" he asked sleepily.

"Almost, big guy. Just a few minutes more."

Soon, slowing almost to a stop, the car pulled into the town's small marina. Security forces were there waiting for them, and a car from customs and the local police as well. Their cruisers' lights bounced off of the building walls and the sleeping boats. The officers stood with their hands on their hips, ready to draw their guns.

The scarecrow stood and held up his arms. "Sanctuary!" he cried. "The young master claims political asylum."

N-Words

TED KOSMATKA

*Ted Kosmatka (www.tedkosmatka.com) lives with his wife
and kids in Portage, Indiana, "on the north coast of the
U.S., not far from the beach." He intended a career in genetics: "Through some combination of blind luck and the
careful application of selective breeding," he says, "I developed, over the course of five years, a decidedly unusual
strain of mice. It even surprised me what they eventually
came to look like. Several specimens were shipped all the
way to Maine, and the descendants of those mice are now a
part of Jackson Laboratories' craniofacial mutant resource
and are sold all over the world." But he changed directions:
"I'm probably the only guy who has ever started his steel
industry career shoveling coke and then ended up analyzing experimental steels with an electron microscope." He
sold his first story in 2005, "The God Engine," to Asimov's.
Since then, he's had a dozen stories in both literary and science fiction markets, and been selected for inclusion in six
Year's Best anthologies.*

"N-Words" was published in the original anthology,
Seeds of Change, *edited by John Joseph Adams. In a Static
Multimedia interview Kozmatka says, "In "N-words" I knew
I wanted the story to be the wife's story. I knew I wanted it
to be her story of loss, and strength, so I didn't really have a
choice about the gender [of the POV] in that case." The
story, about resurrected Neanderthals, rings some very old
thematic bells.*

They came from test tubes. They came pale as ghosts with eyes as blue-white as glacier ice. They came first out of Korea.

I try to picture David's face in my head, but I can't. They've told me this is temporary—a kind of shock that happens sometimes when you've seen a person die that way. Although I try to picture David's face, it's only his pale eyes I can see.

My sister squeezes my hand in the back of the limo. "It's almost over," she says.

Up the road, against the long, wrought iron railing, the protestors grow excited as our procession approaches. They're standing in the snow on both sides of the cemetery gates, men and women wearing hats and gloves and looks of righteous indignation, carrying signs I refuse to read.

My sister squeezes my hand again. Before today I had not seen her in almost four years. But today she helped me pick out my black dress. She helped me with my stockings and my shoes. She helped me dress my son, who is not yet three, and who doesn't like ties—and who is now sleeping on the seat across from us without any understanding of what he's lost.

"Are you going to be okay?" my sister asks.

"No," I say. "I don't think I am."

The limo slows as it turns onto cemetery property, and the mob rushes in, shouting obscenities. Protestors push against the sides of the vehicle.

"You aren't wanted here!" someone shouts, and then an old man's face is in against the glass, his eyes wild. "God's will be done!" he shrieks. "For the wages of sin is death."

The limo rocks under the press of the crowd, and the driver accelerates until we are past them, moving up the slope toward the other cars.

"What's wrong with them?" my sister whispers. "What kind of people would do that on a day like today?"

You'd be surprised, I think. *Maybe your neighbors. Maybe mine.* But I look out the window and say nothing. I've gotten used to saying nothing.

She'd shown up at my house this morning a little after 6:00. I'd opened the door, and she stood there in the cold, and neither of us spoke, neither of us sure what to say after so long.

"I heard about it on the news," she said finally. "I came on the next plane. I'm so sorry, Mandy."

There are things I wanted to say then—things that welled up inside of me like a bubble ready to burst, and I opened my mouth to scream at her, but what came out belonged to a different person: it came out a pathetic sob, and she stepped forward and wrapped her arms around me, my sister again after all these years.

The limo slows near the top of the hill, and the procession tightens. Headstones crowd the roadway. I see the tent up ahead, green; its canvas sides billow in and out with the wind, like a giant's breathing. Two-dozen gray folding chairs crouch in straight rows beneath it.

The limo stops.

"Should we wake the boy?" my sister asks.

"I don't know."

"Do you want me to carry him?"

"Can you?"

She looks at the child. "He's only three?"

"No," I say. "Not yet."

"He's big for his age. I mean, isn't he? I'm not around kids much."

"The doctors say he's big."

My sister leans forward and touches his milky white cheek. "He's beautiful," she says. I try not to hear the surprise in her voice. People are never aware of that tone when they use it, revealing what their expectations had been. But I'm past being offended by what people reveal unconsciously. Now it's only intent that offends. "He really is beautiful," she says again.

"He's his father's son," I say.

Ahead of us, people climb from their cars. The priest is walking toward the grave.

"It's time," my sister says. She opens the door and we step out into the cold.

They came first out of Korea. But that's wrong, of course. History has an order to its telling. It would be more accurate to say it started in Britain. After all it was Harding who published first; it was Harding who shook the world with his announcement. And it was Harding who the religious groups burned in effigy on their church lawns.

Only later did the Koreans reveal they'd accomplished the same goal two years before, and the proof was already out of diapers. And it was only later, much later, that the world would recognize the scope of what they'd done.

When the Yeong Bae fell to the People's Party, the Korean labs were emptied, and there were suddenly *thousands* of them—little blond and red-haired orphans, pale as ghosts, starving on the Korean streets as society crumbled around them. The ensuing wars and regime changes destroyed much of the supporting scientific data—but the children themselves, the ones who survived, were incontrovertible. There was no mistaking what they were.

It was never fully revealed why the Yeong Bae had developed the project in the first place. Perhaps they'd been after a better soldier. Or perhaps they'd done it for the oldest reason: because they could.

What is known for certain is that in 2001 disgraced stem cell biologist Hwang Woo-Suk cloned the world's first dog, an afghan. In 2006, he revealed that he'd tried and failed to clone a mammoth on three separate occasions. Western labs had talked about it, but the Koreans had actually tried. This would prove to be the pattern.

In 2011 the Koreans finally succeeded, and a mammoth was born from an elephant surrogate. Other labs followed. Other species. The Pallid Beach Mouse. The Pyrenean Ibex. And older things. Much older. The best scientists in the US had to leave the country to do their work. US laws against stem cell research didn't stop scientific advancement; it only stopped it from occurring in the US. Instead, Britain, China, and India won patents for the procedures. Cancers were cured. Most forms of blindness, MS, and Parkinson's. When Congress eventually legalized the medical procedures, but not the lines of research which led to them, the hypocrisy was too much, and even the most loyal American cyto-researchers left the country.

Harding was among this final wave, leaving the United States to set up a lab in the UK. In 2013, he was the first to bring back the Thylacine. In the winter of 2015, someone brought him a partial skull from a museum exhibit. The skull was doliocephalic—long, low, large. The bone was heavy, the cranial vault enormous—part of a skullcap that had been found in 1857 in a quarry in the Neander valley.

Snow crunches under our feet as my sister and I move outside the limo. The wind is freezing, and my legs grow numb in my thin slacks. It is fitting he is being buried on a day like today; David was never bothered by the cold.

My sister gestures toward the limo's open door. "Are you sure you want to bring the boy? I could stay with him in the car."

"He should be here," I say. "He should see it."

"He won't understand."

"No, but later he might remember he was here," I say. "Maybe that will matter."

"He's too young to remember."

"He remembers everything." I lean into the shadows and wake the boy. His eyes open like blue lights. "Come, Sean, it's time to wake up."

He rubs a pudgy fist into his eyes and says nothing. He is

a quiet boy, my son. Out in the cold, I pull a hat down over his ears. The boy walks between my sister and me, holding our hands.

At the top of the hill, Dr. Michaels is there to greet us, along with other faculty from Stanford. They offer their condolences, and I work hard not to break down. Dr. Michaels looks like he hasn't slept. I introduce my sister and hands are shaken.

"You never mentioned you had a sister," he says.

I only nod. Dr. Michaels looks down at the boy and tugs the child's hat.

"Do you want me to pick you up?" he asks.

"Yeah." Sean's voice is small and scratchy from sleep. It is not an odd voice for a boy his age. It is a normal voice. Dr. Michaels lifts him, and the child's blue eyes close again.

We stand in silence in the cold. Mourners gather around the grave.

"I still can't believe it," Dr. Michaels says. He's swaying slightly, unconsciously rocking the boy. It is something only a man who has been a father would do, though his own children are grown.

"It's like I'm another person now," I say. "Only I haven't learned how to be her yet."

My sister grabs my hand, and this time I do break down. The tears burn in the cold.

The priest clears his throat; he's about to begin. In the distance the sounds of protestors grow louder, the rise and fall of their chants not unpleasant—though from this distance, thankfully, I cannot make out the words.

When the world first learned of the Korean children, it sprang into action. Humanitarian groups swooped into the war-torn area, monies exchanged hands, and many of the children were adopted out to other countries—a new worldwide Diaspora. They were broad, thick-limbed children; usually slightly shorter than average, though there were startling exceptions to this.

They looked like members of the same family, and some of them, assuredly, were more closely related than that.

There were more children, after all, than there were fossil specimens from which they'd derived. Duplicates were inevitable.

From what limited data remained of the Koreans' work, there had been more than sixty different DNA sources. Some even had names: the Old Man La Chappelle aux Saints, Shanidar IV and Vindija. There was the handsome and symmetrical La Ferrassie specimen. And even Amud I. *Huge* Amud I, who had stood 1.8 meters tall and had a cranial capacity of 1740ccs—the largest Neanderthal ever found.

The techniques perfected on dogs and mammoths had worked easily, too, within the genus Homo. Extraction, then PCR to amplify. After that came IVF with paid surrogates. The success rate was high, the only complication frequent cesarean births. And that was one of the things popular culture had to absorb, that Neanderthal heads were larger.

Tests were done. The children were studied and tracked and evaluated. All lacked normal dominant expression at the MC1R locus—all were pale-skinned, freckled, with red or blonde hair. All were blue-eyed. All were Rh negative.

I was six years old when I first saw a picture. It was the cover of *Time*—what is now a famous cover. I'd heard about these children but had never seen one—these children who were almost my age, from a place called Korea; these children that were sometimes called ghosts.

The magazine showed a pale, red-haired Neanderthal boy standing with his adoptive parents, staring thoughtfully up at an outdated anthropology display at a museum. The wax Neanderthal man in the display carried a club. He had a nose from the tropics, dark hair, olive-brown skin and dark brown eyes. Before Harding's child, the museum display designers had supposed they knew what primitive looked like, and they had supposed it was decidedly swarthy.

Never mind that Neanderthals had spent ten times longer in light-starved Europe than a typical Swede's ancestors.

The redheaded boy on the cover wore a confused expression.

When my father walked into the kitchen and saw the

Time cover, he shook his head in disgust. "It's an abomination," he said.

I studied the boy's jutting face. I'd never seen anyone with a face like that. "Who is he?"

"A dead-end. Those kids are going to be a drain for the rest of their lives. It's not fair to them, really."

That was the first of many pronouncements I'd hear about the children.

Years passed and the children grew like weeds—and as with all populations, the first generation exposed to a western diet grew several inches taller than their ancestors. While they excelled at sports, their adopted families were told they could be slow learners. They were primitive after all.

A prediction which turned out to be as accurate as the museum displays.

When I look up, the priest's hands are raised into the cold, white sky. "Blessed are you, O God our father; praised be your name forever." He breathes smoke, reading from the Book of Tobit.

It is a passage I've heard at both funerals and marriage ceremonies, and this, like the cold on this day, is fitting. "Let the heavens and all your creations praise you forever."

The mourners sway in the giant's breathing of the tent.

I was born Catholic, but found little use for organized religion in my adulthood. Little use for it, until now, when its use is so clearly revealed—and it is an unexpected comfort to be part of something larger than yourself; it is a comfort to have someone to bury your dead.

Religion provides a man in black to speak words over your loved one's grave. It does this first. If it does not do this, it is not religion.

"You made Adam and you gave him your wife Eve to be his love and support; and from these two, the human race descended."

They said together, *Amen, Amen.*

The day I learned I was pregnant, David stood at our window, huge, pale arms draped over my shoulders. He touched my stomach as we watched a storm coming in across the lake.

"I hope the baby looks like you," he said in his strange, nasal voice.

"I don't."

"No, it would be easier if the baby looks like you. He'll have an easier life."

"He?"

"I think it's a boy."

"And is that what you'd wish for him, to have an easy life?"

"Isn't that what every parent wishes for?"

"No," I said. I touched my own stomach. I put my small hand over his large one. "I hope our son grows to be a good man."

I'd met David at Stanford when he walked into class five minutes late.

He had arms like legs. And legs like torsos. His torso was the trunk of an oak—seventy-five years old, grown in the sun. A full-sleeve tattoo swarmed up one bulging, ghost-pale arm, disappearing under his shirt. He had an earring in one ear, and a shaved head. A thick red goatee balanced the enormous bulk of his convex nose and gave some dimension to his receding chin. The eyes beneath his thick brows were large and intense—as blue as a husky's.

It wasn't that he was handsome, because I couldn't decide if he was. It was that I couldn't take my eyes off him. I stared at him. All the girls stared at him.

It was harder for them to get into graduate programs back then. There were quotas—and like Asians, they had to score better to get accepted.

There was much debate over what name should go next to the race box on their entrance forms. The word "Neander-thal" had evolved into an epithet over the previous decade. It became just another N-word polite society didn't use.

I'd been to the clone rights rallies. I'd heard the speakers. "The French don't call themselves Cro-Magnons, do they?" the loudspeakers boomed.

And so the name by their box had changed every few years, as the college entrance questionnaires strove to map the shifting topography of political correctness. Every few years, a new name for the group would arise—and then a few years later sink again under the accumulated freight of prejudice heaped upon it.

They were called Neanderthals at first, then archaics, then clones—then, ridiculously, they were called simply Koreans, since that was the country in which all but one of them had been born. Sometime after the word "Neanderthal" became an epithet, there was a movement by some militants within the group to reclaim the word, to use it within the group as a sign of strength.

But over time, the group gradually came to be known exclusively by a name that had been used occasionally from the very beginning, a name which captured the hidden heart of their truth. Among their own kind, and finally, among the rest of the world, they came to be known as the ghosts. All the other names fell away, and here, finally, was a name that stayed.

In 2033, the first ghost was drafted into the NFL. He spoke three languages. By 2035, the front line of every team in the league had one—*had* to have one, to be competitive. In the 2036 Olympics, ghosts took gold in wrestling, in power lifting, in almost every event in which they were entered. Some individuals took golds in multiple sports, in multiple areas.

There was an outcry from the other athletes who could not hope to compete. There were petitions to have ghosts banned from competition. It was suggested they should have their own Olympics, distinct from the original. Lawyers for the ghosts pointed out, carefully, tactfully, that out of the fastest 400 times recorded for the 100 yard dash, 386 had been achieved by persons of at least partial sub-Saharan African descent, and nobody was suggesting *they* get their own Olympics.

Of course, racist groups like the KKK and the neo-Nazis actually liked the idea, and proposed just that. Blacks, too, should compete against their own kind, get their own Olympics. After that, the whole matter degenerated into chaos.

When I was growing up, I helped my grandfather prune his apple trees in Indiana. The trick, he told me, was telling which branches helped the fruit, and which branches didn't. Once you've studied a tree, you got a sense of what was important. Everything else you could cut away as useless baggage.

You can discard your ethnic identity through a similar process of careful ablation. You look at your child's face, and you don't wonder whose side you're on. You know.

I read in a sociology book that when someone in the privileged majority marries a minority, they take on the social status of that minority group. It occurred to me how the universe is a series of concentric circles, and you keep seeing the same shapes and processes wherever you look. Atoms are little solar systems; highways are a nation's arteries, streets its capillaries—and the social system of humans follows Mendelian genetics, with dominants and recessives. Minority ethnicity is the dominant gene when part of a heterozygous couple.

There are many Neanderthal bones in the Field Museum.

Their bones are different than ours. It is not just their big skulls, or their short, powerful limbs; virtually every bone in their body is thicker, stronger, heavier. Each vertebrae, each phalange, each small bone in the wrist, is thicker than ours. And I have wondered sometimes, when looking at those bones, why they need skeletons like that. All that metabolically expensive bone and muscle and brain. It had to be paid for. What kind of life makes you need bones like chunks of rebar? What kind of life makes you need a sternum half an inch thick?

During the Pleistocene, glaciers had carved their way south across Europe, isolating animal populations behind a curtain of ice. Those populations either adapted to the harsh conditions, or they died. Over time, the herd animals grew massive, becoming more thermally efficient; and so began the age of the Pleistocene mega-fauna. The predators too, had to adapt. The saber-tooth cat, the cave bear. They grew more powerful in order to bring down the larger prey. What was true for other animals was true for genus *Homo*, nature's experiment, the Neanderthal—the region's ultimate climax predator.

Three days ago, the day David died, I woke to an empty bed. I found him naked at the window in our living room, looking out into the winter sky, his leonine face wrapped in shadow.

From behind, I could see the V of his back against the gray light. I knew better than to disturb him. He became a silhouette against the sky, and in that instant, he was something more and less than human—like some broad human creature adapted for life in extreme gravity. A person built to survive stresses that would crush a normal man.

He turned to look at me. "There's a storm coming today," he said.

The day David died, I woke to an empty bed. I wonder about that.

I wonder if he suspected something. I wonder what got him out of bed early. I wonder at the storm he mentioned, the one he said was coming.

If he'd known the risk, we never would have gone to the rally—I'm sure of that, because he was a cautious man. But I wonder if some hidden, inner part of him didn't have its ear to the railroad tracks; I wonder if some part of him didn't feel the ground shaking, didn't hear the freight train barreling down on us all.

We ate breakfast that morning. We drove to the babysitter's and dropped off our son. David kissed him on the cheek and tousled his hair. There was no last look, no sense this would be the final time. David kissed the boy, tousled his hair, and then we were out the door, Mary waving goodbye.

We drove to the hall in silence. We parked our car in the crowded lot, ignoring the counter-rally already forming across the street.

We shook hands with other guests and found our way to the assigned table. It was supposed to be a small luncheon, a civilized affair between moneyed men in expensive suits. David was the second speaker.

Up on the podium, David's expression changed. Before his speeches, there was this moment this single second, where he glanced out over the crowd, and his eyes grew sad.

David closed his eyes, opened them, and spoke. He began slowly. He spoke of the flow of history and the symmetry of nature. He spoke of the arrogance of ignorance; and in whispered tones, he spoke of fear. "And out of fear," he said. "grows hatred." He let his eyes wander over the crowd. "They hate us because we're different," he said, voice rising for the first time. "Always it works this way, wherever you look in history. And always we must work against it. We must never give in to violence. But we are right to fear, my friends. We must be vigilant, or we'll lose everything we've gained for our children, and our children's children." He paused.

I'd heard this speech before, or parts of it. David rarely used notes, preferring to pull the speeches out of his head, assembling an oratorical structure both delicate and profound. He continued for another ten minutes before finally going into his close.

"They've talked about restricting us from athletic competition. They've eliminated us from receiving most scholarships. They've limited our attendance of law schools, and medical schools, and PhD programs. These are the soft shackles they've put upon us, and we cannot sit silently and let it happen."

The crowd erupted into applause. David lifted his hands to silence them and he walked back to his seat. Other speakers took the podium, but none with David's eloquence. None with his power.

When the last speaker sat, dinner was brought out and we ate. An hour later, when the plates were clean, more hands were shaken, and people started filing out to their cars. The evening was over.

David and I took our time, talking with old friends, but we eventually worked our way into the lobby. Ahead of us, out in the parking lot, there was a commotion. The counter-rally had grown. Somebody mentioned vandalized cars, and then Tom was leaning into David's ear, whispering as we passed through the front doors and out into the open air.

It started with thrown eggs. Thomas turned, egg-white drooling down his broad chest. The fury in his eyes was enough to frighten me. David rushed forward and grabbed his arm. There was a look of surprise on some of the faces in the crowd, because even they hadn't expected anybody to throw things—and I could see, too, the group of young men, clumped together near the side of the building, eggs in hand, mouths open—and it was like time stopped, because the moment was fat and waiting—and it could go any way, and an egg came down out of the sky that was not an egg, but a rock, and it struck Sarah Mitchell in the face—and the blood was red and shocking on her ghost-white skin, and the moment was wide open, time snapping back the other way—everything moving too fast, all of it happening at the same time instead of taking turns the way events are supposed to. And suddenly David's grip on my arm was a vise, physically lifting me, pulling me back toward the building, and I tried to keep my feet while someone screamed.

"Everybody go back inside!" David shouted. And then another woman screamed, a different kind of noise, like a shout of warning—and then I heard it, a shout that was a roar like nothing I'd ever heard before—and then more screams, men's screams. And somebody lunged from the crowd and swung at David, and he moved so quickly I was flung away, the blow missing David's head by a foot.

"No!" David yelled at the man. "We don't want this."

Then the man swung again and this time David caught the fist in his huge hand. He jerked the man close. "We're not doing this," he hissed and flung him back into the crowd.

David grabbed Tom's arm again, trying to guide him back toward the building. "This is stupid, don't be pulled into it."

Thomas growled and let himself be pulled along, and

someone spit in his face, and I saw it, the dead look in his eyes, to be spit on and do nothing. And still David pulled us toward the safety of the building, brushing aside the curses of men whose necks he could snap. And still he did nothing. He did nothing all the way up to the end, when a thin, balding forty-year-old man stepped into his path, raised a gun, and fired point blank into his chest.

The blast was deafening.

—and that old sadness gone. Replaced by white-hot rage and disbelief, blue eyes wide.

People tried to scatter, but the crush of bodies prevented it. David hung there, in the crush, looking down at his chest. The man fired three more times before David fell.

"Ashes to ashes, dust to dust. Accept our brother David into your warm embrace." The priest lowers his hands and closes the bible. The broad casket is lowered into the ground. It is done.

Dr. Michaels carries the boy as my sister helps me back to the limo.

The night David was killed, after the hospital and the police questions, I drove to the sitter's to pick up my son. Mary hugged me and we stood crying in the foyer for a long time.

"What do I tell my two-year old?" I said. "How do I explain this?"

We walked to the front room, and I stood in the doorway. I watched my son like I was seeing him for the first time. He was blocky, like his father, but his bones were longer. He was a gifted child who knew his letters and could already sound out certain words.

And that was our secret, that he was not yet three and already learning to read. And there were thousands more like him—a new generation, the best of two tribes.

Perhaps David's mistake was that he hadn't realized there was a war. In any war, there are only certain people who fight it—and a smaller number who understand, truly, *why* it's being fought. This was no different.

Sixty thousand years ago, there were two walks of men in the world. There were the people of the ice, and there were the people of the sun.

When the climate warmed, the ice sheets retreated. The broad African desert was beaten back by the rains, and the people of the sun expanded north.

The world was changing then. The European mega-fauna were disappearing. The delicate predator/prey equilibrium slipped out of balance and the world's most deadly climax predator found his livelihood evaporating in warming air. Without the big herds, there was less food. The big predators gave way to sleeker models that needed fewer calories to survive.

The people of the sun weren't stronger, or smarter, or better than the people of the ice; Cain didn't kill his brother, Abel. The snow people didn't die out because they weren't good enough. All that bone and muscle and brain. They died because they were too expensive.

But now the problems are different. Now the world has changed again. Again there are two kinds of men in the world. But in this new age, it will not be the economy version of man who wins.

The limo door slams shut. The vehicle pulls away from the grave. As we near the cemetery gates, the shouting grows louder. The protestors see us coming.

The police said that David's murder was a crime of passion. Others said he was a target of opportunity. I don't know which is true. The truth died with the shooter, when Tom crushed his skull with a single right-hand blow.

The shouting spikes louder as we pass the cemetery gates. A snowball smashes into the window.

"Stop the car!" I shout.

I fling open the door. I climb out and walk up to the surprised man. He's standing there, another snowball already packed in his hands. I'm not sure what I'm going to do as I approach him. I've gotten used to the remarks, the small attacks. I've gotten used to ignoring them. I've gotten used to saying nothing.

I slap him in the face as hard as I can.

He's too shocked to react at first. I slap him again.

This time he flinches away from me, wanting no part of this. I walk back to my car as people start screaming at me. I climb in and the limo driver pulls away.

My son looks at me, and it's not fear in his eyes like I expect; it's anger. Anger at the crowd. My huge, brilliant son—these people have no idea what they're doing. They have no idea the storm they're calling down.

I see a sign held high as we pass the last of the protestors. They are shouting again, having found the full flower of their outrage. The sign says only one word: *Die*.

Not this time, I think to myself. *Your turn*.

Fury

ALASTAIR REYNOLDS

Alastair Reynolds (www.members.tripod.com/~voxish) lives in Glamorgan, Wales. He worked for ten years for the European Space Agency before becoming a full-time writer in 2004. He began writing SF in the early 1990s, and his first novel, Revelation Space, *was published in 1999. He was immediately grouped as one of the new British space opera writers emerging in the mid and late 1990s, in the generation after Baxter and McAuley, and originally the most "hard SF" of the new group. His most recent novels are* The Prefect *(2007), and* House of Suns *(2008). Two collections of his stories were published in 2006,* Zima Blue *and* Galactic North. *An expanded version of the* Zima Blue *collection is out in 2009. He next novel, out in 2009, is a far future, steampunk-influenced planetary romance provisionally entitled* Terminal World.

"Fury" appeared in Eclipse 2. *It is about as well-constructed a space opera as we have seen in recent years, with a carefully plotted mystery at its core, and some political undertones. Mercurio, the head bodyguard, and the Emperor of the Galactic Empire have been together for centuries. When there is an incident in the palace, Mercurio must investigate, even if it takes him far away in the galaxy.*

I was the first to reach the emperor's body, and even then it was too late to do anything. He had been examining his koi, kneeling on the stone pathway that wound between the ponds, when the bullet arrived. It had punched through his skull, achieving instantaneous destruction. Fragments of skin and bone and pinkish grey cortical material lay scattered on the tiles. Blood—dark and red as the ink on the imperial seal—was oozing out from the entry and exit wounds. The body had slumped over to one side, with the lower half still spasming as motor signals attempted to regain control. I reached over and placed my hand against the implanted device at the base of the neck, applying firm pressure through the yellow silk of his collar to a specific contact point. I felt a tiny subepidermal click. The body became instantly still.

I stood up and summoned a clean-up crew.

"Remove the body," I told the waiting men. "Don't dispose of it until you've completed a thorough forensic analysis. Drain and search the surrounding ponds until you've recovered the bullet or any remaining pieces of it. Then hose down the path until you've removed all trace of blood and whatever else came out of him. Test the water thoroughly and don't let the koi back until you're certain they won't come to any harm." I paused, still trying to focus on what had just happened. "Oh, and secure the Great House. No one comes and goes until we find out who did this. And no ships are to pass in or out of the Capital Nexus without my express authorisation."

"Yes, Mercurio," the men said in near-unison.

In the nearest pond one of the fish—I recognised it as one of the Asagi Koi, with the blue-toned scales laid out in a pine-cone pattern—opened and closed its mouth as if trying to tell me something vital. I turned from the scene and made my way back into the Great House. By the time I reached the emperor's reception chamber the building was buzzing with rumours of the assassination attempt. Despite my best efforts, the news would be out of the Nexus within the hour, hopscotching from world to world, system to system, spreading into the galaxy like an unstoppable fire.

The emperor's new body rose from his throne as the doors finished opening. He was dressed in a yellow silk gown identical to the one worn by the corpse. Aside from the absence of injuries, the body was similarly indistinguishable, appearing to be that of a white-haired man of considerable age, yet still retaining a youthful vigour. His habitual expression normally suggested playfulness, compassion and the kind of deep wisdom that can only come from a very long and scholarly life. Now his face was an expressionless mask. That, and a certain stiffness in his movements, betrayed the fact that this was a new body, being worn for the first time. It would take several hours for the implant to make the fine sensorimotor adjustments that gave the emperor true fluidity of movement, and allowed him to feel as if he was fully inhabiting the puppet organism.

"I'm sorry," I said, before the emperor had a chance to speak. "I take full responsibility for this incident."

He waved aside my apology. "Whatever this is about, Mercurio, I doubt very much that you could have done anything to prevent it." His voice was thick-tongued, like a drunkard with a bad hangover. "We both know how thorough you've been; all the angles you've covered. No one could have asked for better security than you've given me, all these years. I'm still alive, aren't I?"

"Nonetheless, there was clearly a flaw in my arrangements."

"Perhaps," he allowed. "But the fact is, whoever did this only reached the body, not me. It's unfortunate, but in the scheme of things little worse than an act of vandalism against imperial property."

"Did you feel anything?"

"A sharp blow; a few moments of confusion; not much else. If that's what being assassinated feels like, then it isn't much to fear, truth be told. Perhaps I've been wrong to keep looking over my shoulder, all this time."

"Whoever did this, they must have known it wouldn't achieve anything."

"I've wondered about that myself." He stroked the fine white banner of his beard, as if acquainting himself with it for the first time. "I almost hate to ask—but the koi?"

"I've got my men searching the ponds, looking for bullet fragments. But as far as I can see the fish didn't come to any harm."

"Let's hope so. The effort I've put into those fish—I'd be heartbroken if anything happened to them. I'll want to see for myself, of course."

"Not until we've secured the Great House and found our man," I said, speaking as only the emperor's personal security expert would have dared. "Until the risk of another attempt is eliminated, I can't have you leaving this building."

"I have an inexhaustible supply of bodies, Mercurio."

"That's not the point. Whoever did this . . ." But I trailed off, my thoughts still disorganized. "Please, sir, just respect my wishes in this matter."

"Of course, Mercurio. Now as ever. But I trust you won't keep me from my fish for the rest of eternity?"

"I sincerely hope not, sir."

I left the emperor, returning to my offices to coordinate the hunt for the assassin and the search for whatever evidence he might have left behind. Within a few hours the body had been subjected to an exhaustive forensic analysis, resulting in the extraction of bullet shards from the path of the wound. In the same timeframe my men recovered other fragments from the vicinity of the corpse; enough to allow us to reassemble the bullet.

An hour later, against all my expectations, we had the assassin himself. They found him with his weapon, waiting to be apprehended. He hadn't even tried to leave the grounds of the Great House.

That was when I began to suspect that this wasn't any act of mindless desecration, but something much more sinister.

"Tell me what you found," the emperor said, when I returned to the reception chamber. In the intervening time his control over the new body had improved markedly. His movements were fluid and he had regained his usual repertoire of facial expressions.

"We've found the assassin, sir, as you'll doubtless have heard."

"I hadn't, but please continue."

"And the weapon. The bullet itself was a goal-seeking autonomous missile, a very sophisticated device. It had the means to generate stealthing fields to confuse our anti-intrusion systems, so once it was loose in the grounds of the Great House it could move without detection. But it still needed a launching device, a kind of gun. We found that as well."

The emperor narrowed his eyes. "I would have thought it was hard enough to get a gun into the Nexus, let alone the Great House."

"That's where it gets a little disturbing, sir. The gun could only have been smuggled into the grounds in tiny pieces—small enough that they could be disguised by field generators, or hidden inside legitimate tools and equipment allowed the palace staff. That's how it happened, in fact. The man we found the gun on was an uplift named Vratsa, one of the keepers in charge of the ponds."

"I know Vratsa," the emperor said softly. "He's been on the staff for years. Never the brightest of souls . . . but diligent, gentle, and beyond any question a hard worker. I always liked him—we'd talk about the fish, sometimes. He was tremendously fond of them. Are you honestly telling me he had something to do with this?"

"He's not even denying it, sir."

"I'm astonished. Vratsa of all people. Primate stock, isn't he?"

"Gorilla, I think."

"He actually planned this?"

"I'm not sure 'planned' is exactly the word I'd use. The thing is, it's starting to look as if Vratsa was a mole."

"But he's on the staff for—how long, exactly?"

There'd been no need for me to review the files—the information was at my immediate disposal, flashing into my mind instantly. "Thirty-five years, sir. In my estimation, that's about as long as it would have taken to smuggle in and assemble the pieces of the weapon."

"Could a simple uplift have done this?"

"Not without help, sir. You've always been very kind to them, employing them in positions of responsibility where others would rather treat them as subhuman slaves. But the fact remains that uplifts don't generally exhibit a high-degree of forward planning and resourcefulness. This took both, sir. I'm inclined to the view that Vratsa was just as much a puppet as that body you're wearing."

"Why the bullet, though? As I said, Vratsa and I have spoken on many occasions. He could have hurt me easily enough then, just with his bare hands."

"I don't know, sir. There is something else, though." I looked around the walls of the room, with its panelled friezes depicting an ancient, weatherworn landscape—some nameless, double-mooned planet halfway across the galaxy. "It's delicate, sir—or at least it *might* be delicate. I think we need to talk about it face to face."

"This room is already one of the most secure places in the entire Radiant Commonwealth," he reminded me.

"Nonetheless."

"Very well, Mercurio." The old man sighed gently. "But you know how uncomfortable I find these encounters."

"I assure you I'll be as brief as possible."

Above me the ceiling separated into four equal sections. The sections slid back into the walls, a cross-shaped gap opening between them to reveal an enormous overhead space—a brightly lit enclosure as large as any in the Great House. Floating in the space, pinned into place by gravity neutralisers, was a trembling sphere of oxygenated water, more than a hundred meters across. I began to ascend, pushed upwards on a section of flooring immediately beneath me, a square tile that became a rising pillar. Immune to vertigo—and incapable of suffering lasting damage even if I'd fallen to the floor—I remained calm, save for the thousand questions circling in my mind.

At one hundred and thirty meters, my head pushed through the surface tension of the sphere. A man would have started drowning, but immersion in water posed no difficulties for me. In fact, there were very few environments in the galaxy that I couldn't tolerate, at least temporarily.

My lenses adjusted to the differing optical properties of the medium, until I seemed to be looking through something only slightly less sharp than clear air. The emperor was floating, as weightless as the water surrounding him. He looked something like a whale, except that he had no flippers or flukes.

I remembered—dimly, for it had been a long time ago—when he was still more or less humanoid. That was in the early days of the Radiant Commonwealth, when it only encompassed a few hundred systems. He had grown with it, swelling as each new territory—be it a planet, system or entire glittering star cluster—was swallowed into his realm. It wasn't enough for him to have an abstract understanding of the true extent of his power. He needed to feel it on a purely sensory level, as a flood of inputs reaching directly into his brain. Countless modifications later, his mind was now the size of a small house. The mazelike folds of that dome bulged against drum-tight skin, as if about to rip through thin canvas. Veins and arteries the size of plumbing ducts wrapped the cerebellum. It was a long time since that brain had been protected by a cage of bone.

The emperor was monstrous, but he wasn't a monster—not now. There might once have been a time when his expansionist ambitions were driven by something close to lust, but that was tens of thousands of years ago. Now that he controlled almost the entire colonised galaxy, he sought only to become the figurehead of a benevolent, just government. The emperor was famed for his clemency and forgiveness. He himself had pushed for the extension of democratic principles into many of the empire's more backward prefectures.

He was a good and just man, and I was happy to serve him.

"So tell me, Mercurio, whatever it is that is too secret even for one of my puppets."

The rising pillar had positioned me next to one of his dark eyes. They were like currants jammed into doughy flesh.

"It's the bullet, sir."

"What about it?"

I held the reconstructed item up for inspection, confident now that we were outside the reach of listening devices. It was a metal cylinder with a transparent cone at the front.

"There are, or were, markings on the bullet casing. They're in one of the older trading languages of the Luquan Emergence. The inscription, in so far as it can be translated into Prime, reads as follows: *Am I my brother's keeper?*"

He reflected on this for a moment. "It's not ringing any bells."

"I'd be surprised if it did, sir. The inscription appears to be a quote from an ancient religious text. As to its greater significance, I can't say."

"The Luquans haven't traditionally been a problem. We give them a certain amount of autonomy; they pay their taxes and agree to our trifling requests that they instigate democratic rule and cut down on the number of executions. They may not like that, but there are a dozen other special administrative volumes that we treat in exactly the same fashion. Why would the Emergence act against me now?"

"It doesn't end there, sir. The bullet had a hollow cavity at the front, inside the glass cone. There was enough space in there for the insertion of any number of harmful agents, up to an including an antimatter device that could easily have destroyed all or part of the Great House. Whoever made this, whoever programmed it to reach this far, could easily have gone the extra step necessary to have you killed, not just your puppet."

The ancient dark eye regarded me. Though it hardly

moved in the socket, I still had the sense of penetrating focus and attention.

"You think someone was trying to tell me something? That they *can* murder me, but chose not to?"

"I don't know. Certainly, the provisions I've now put in place would prevent anyone making a second attempt in this manner. But they'd have known that as well. So why go to all this trouble?" I paused before continuing. "There is something else, I'm afraid."

"Go ahead."

"Although the bullet was hollow, it wasn't totally empty. There was something inside the glass part—a few specks of reddish sand or dust. The surgeons extracted most of it from the puppet, and they've promised me that the few remaining traces that entered the koi ponds won't cause any ill-effects. I've had the dust analysed and it's absolutely harmless. Iron oxide, silicon and sulphur, for the most part. Frankly, I don't know what to make of it. It resembles something you'd find on the surface of an arid terrestrial planet, something with a thin atmosphere and not much weather or biology. The problem is there are ten million worlds that fit that description."

"And within the Emergence?"

"Fewer, but still far too many to speak of." I withdrew the replica bullet from his examination. "Nonetheless, these are our only clues. With your permission, I'd like to leave the Capital Nexus to pursue the matter further."

He ruminated on this for a few seconds. "You propose a mission to the Emergence?"

"I really don't see any alternative. There's only so much I can do from my office. It's better if I go walkabout." The phrase, which had popped unbidden into my mind, caused me disquiet. Where had it come from? "What I mean, sir, is that I can be much more effective in person."

"I appreciate that. But I also appreciate that you're incredibly valuable to me—not just as a friend, but as my closest and most trusted advisor. I've become very used to knowing you're close at hand, in the walls of the Great House. It's one of the things that helps me sleep at night, knowing you're not far away."

"I'll only ever be a few skipspace transits from home, sir."

"You have my agreement, of course—as if I was ever going to say no. But do look after yourself, Mercurio. I'd hate to think how I'd manage without you."

"I'll do my best, sir." I paused. "There is one other thing I need to ask you, sir. The uplift, Vratsa?"

"What about him?"

"We subjected him to mild interrogation. He gave us nothing, but I'd be remiss in my duties if I didn't point out that we could employ other methods, just to be certain he isn't keeping anything from us."

"What's your honest judgement?"

"I think he's completely innocent, sir—he was just following a script someone programmed into him thirty-five or more years ago. He no more knows why he did this—and who's behind if—than the bullet did. But if you feel something might be gained . . ."

"Have him tortured, on the very slight chance he might tell us something?" It was clear from his tone of voice what he felt about that.

"I didn't think you'd approve, sir. As far as I'm concerned, it would achieve about as much as smacking a puppy for something it did the day before yesterday."

"I've spent much of the last thousand years trying to enforce humanitarian principles on the more barbarous corners of my own empire. The very least I can do is live up to my own high moral standards, wouldn't you say?" It was a rhetorical question, since he allowed me no time to answer. "Take Vratsa and remove him from the Great House—he's a continuing security risk, even if he doesn't know why he did what he did. But I don't want him locked away or punished. Find some work for him in the outlying gardens. Give him some fish to look after. And if anyone harms a hair on his head . . ."

"They won't, sir. Not while I'm in charge."

"That's very good, Mercurio. I'm glad we see things similarly."

I left the Great House a day later, once I was satisfied that I had put in place all necessary measures for the emperor's continued security in my absence. From the moon-girdled heart of the Capital Nexus, through skipspace via the Coronal Polities to the fuzzy perimeter of the Luquan Emergence—sixty thousand light years in only a handful of days. As I changed from ship to ship, I attracted an unavoidable degree of attention. Since I require Great House authority to make my investigations in the Emergence, there was no possibility of moving incognito. I travelled in full imperial regalia, and made sure the seriousness of my mission was understood.

How much more attention would I have merited, if they had realized what I *really* was?

I look like a man, but in fact I am a robot. My meat exterior is only a few centimeters thick. Beneath that living shell lies the hard armour of a sentient machine.

The emperor knows—of course—and so do a handful of his closest officials. But to most casual observers, and even people who have spent much time in the Great House, I am just another human security expert, albeit one with an uncommonly close relationship with the emperor. The fact that I have been in his service for tens of thousands of years is one of the most closely guarded secrets in the Radiant Commonwealth.

I am rare. Robots are commonplace, but I am something more than that. I am a true thinking machine. There are reckoned to be less than a million of us in existence—not many, considering the billion worlds of the Radiant Commonwealth, and all the teeming souls on those planets and moons.

There are two schools of thought concerning our origin. In the thirty-two thousand years of its existence, the empire has been through a number of historical convulsions. One school—the alchemicals—has it that the means to manufacture us—some critical expertise in cybernetics and programming—had been discovered and then lost at an earlier time. All remaining sentient machines therefore dated from this period.

The other school, the accretionists, hold a different view. They maintain that robot intelligence is an emergent property, something that could only happen given sufficient resources of time and complexity. The accretionists argue that the surviving robots became the way we are gradually, through the slow augmentation of simpler machines. In their view, almost any machine could become an intelligent robot, provided it is allowed to evolve and layer itself with improvements.

It would have been convenient if we robots could have settled the matter. The unfortunate fact, though, was that we simply didn't remember. Like any recording apparatus, we are prone to error and distortion. At times when the emperor's hold on the galaxy had slackened, data wars corrupted even the most secure archives. I can sift through my memories until I find the earliest reliable events of which I have direct experience, but I know—I sense—that I am still only plumbing relatively shallow layers of my own identity.

I know I've been around considerably longer than that.

The only thing I can be absolutely certain of is that I've known the emperor for a very long time. We fit together like hand and glove. And in all that time I've always been there to protect him.

It is what I do.

The official was a high-ranking technocrat on Selva, one of the major power centers of the Luquan Emergence. He studied me with unconcealed hostility, sitting behind a desk in his private office in one of Selva's aquatic cities. Fierce, luminous oceanforms—barbed and tentacled things of alien provenance—clawed and suckered at the armored glass behind him, testing its strength.

"I really don't think I can offer any more assistance, sire," the official said, putting sufficient stress on the honorific for it to sound insulting. "Since your arrival on Selva we've given you free rein to conduct your investigations. Every administrative department has done its utmost to comply with your requests. And yet you still act as if there is more we could have done." He was a thin, sallow man with arched, quizzical eyebrows, dressed in a military uniform that was several sizes too big for him. "Have we not demonstrated our obedience with the trials?"

"I didn't ask for those dissidents to be executed," I said. "Although I can see how useful it would have been for you. Arrest some troublemakers, ask them questions they can't possibly answer, about a crime they had nothing to do with, and then hang them on the pretext that they weren't cooperating with the Great House. Do you imagine that will buy you favor with the emperor? Quite the opposite, I'd suggest. When all this is over and done with, I wouldn't be at all surprised if you have an imperial audit to deal with."

He shrugged, as if the matter was of no possible consequence.

"You're wasting your time, sire—looking for a pattern, a logical explanation, where none exists. I don't even know why you're bothering. Didn't you already find your assailant? Didn't you already extract a confession?"

"We found evidence that points to the Luquan Emergence."

"Yes, I've heard about that." Ostentatiously, he tapped at a sealed brochure on his desk. "A cryptic statement in an ancient tongue. Some dust that could have come from anywhere."

I maintained a blank expression, giving no hint at my anger that the forensic information had been leaked. It was inevitable, I supposed, but I had hoped to keep a lid on it for a little longer.

"I'd discount any rumours if I were you."

A mouthful of concentric teeth gnashed against the glass, rotating and counter-rotating like some industrial drilling machine. The official craned around in his seat, studying the ravenous creature for a few seconds. "They have a taste for human flesh now," he said, as if the two of us were making idle conversation. "No one's exactly sure how, but it appears that at some point certain undesirables must have been fed to them, despite all the prohibitions against introducing human genetic material into the native ecosystem."

"I suppose I must count as an undesirable, from where

you're sitting. Coming in with imperial authorisation, the license to ask any questions I choose."

"I won't pretend I'll shed many tears when you're gone, if that's what you mean." He straightened in his chair, the stiff fabric of the uniform creaking. "On that matter, there's something you might benefit from knowing."

"Because it'll get me off Selva?"

"I'd inflict you on Porz, if I didn't know you'd already visited." He tapped another finger against the brochure. "It behoves me to point out that you may be making a tactical error in conducting your enquiries here, at the present heart of the Emergence. This ancient inscription—the quote from that old text—harkens back to our very early history. The geopolitical balance was different back then, as I'm sure you'll appreciate."

"I know my history." Which was true, up to a point. But the history of the Luquan Emergence was a bewildering thicket of half-truths and lies, designed to confound imperial legislators. Even the Great House hadn't been able to help me sort out truth and fiction where the Emergence was concerned. It was worse than trying to find Lost Earth.

"Then consider acting upon it," the official said. "Julact was the heart of the Luquan Emergence in those days. No one lives there now, but . . ."

"I'll come to Julact in good time."

"You may wish to move it up your schedule. That part of the Emergence doesn't see much traffic, so the skipspace connections are being pruned back. We've already mothballed all routes west of the Hasharud Loop. It's difficult enough to reach Julact now. In a few years, it may not be possible at all—even with imperial blessing. You know how hard it is to reactivate a path, once it's fallen out of use."

No administrative entity within the Radiant Commonwealth was supposed to shutdown skipspace paths without direct permission from the Great House. Merely doing so was a goading taunt against the emperor's authority. That, though, was a fight for another day.

"If I had the slightest suspicion that I was being manipulated . . ."

"Of course you're being manipulated. I want you out of my jurisdiction."

"Oh, and it's a red world," the official said. "And the soil's a close match to that sample you found in the bullet. In case that makes any difference to you."

"You said it yourself. That soil could have come from anywhere in the galaxy. A close match doesn't imply a unique match."

"Still. You've got to start somewhere, haven't you?"

I left Selva.

My passage to Julact was appropriately arduous. After emerging from the soon-to-be-mothballed skipspace portal I had to complete the final leg of the journey at sublight speed, accruing years of irritating timelag. Before I dropped out of superluminal signal range I contacted the Capital Nexus, alerting the emperor that I would not be home for some time.

"Are you sure this is wise, Mercurio?"

"Clearly, it suits them that I should redirect my enquiries away from Selva, Porz, and the other power centers of the present Emergence. But Julact is worthy of my attention. Even if there isn't anyone living there now, I may find another clue, another piece of the puzzle."

The emperor was outside again, very close to the spot where his previous body had been shot, kneeling by the treasured koi with some kind of water-testing device in his hand. A white and orange male broke the water with his barbled head, puckering silver-white lips at the force-shielded sky above the Great House. "You sound as if you're caught up in some kind of elaborate parlor game," the emperor said.

"That's exactly how it feels. By the same token, I have no choice but to play along. Ordinarily I would not consider dropping out of contact for as long as it will take me to travel to Julact and back. But since the Great House seems to be running itself well enough in my absence, and given that there have been no further security incidents . . ."

The emperor lifted a yellow silk sleeve. "Yes, of course. Do whatever is necessary. I could hardly expect you to be less thorough about this than any other security arrangements you've dealt with."

"I promise I'll be as quick as possible."

"Of course. And once again, I urge you to take all necessary precautions. You and I, we've got a lot of history together. I'd feel quite naked without you."

"I'll report back as soon as I have something, sir."

The emperor, the fish and the Great House faded from my console. With nothing to do but wait for my journey to end, I sifted through the facts of the case, examining every aspect from every conceivable angle. The process consumed many centuries of equivalent human thought, but at the end of it I was still none the wiser. All I had was a bullet, an inscription and some fine red dust.

Would Julact provide any answers?

The red world was smaller than most terrestrials, with a single small moon. It had a ghost-thin haze of atmosphere and no evidence of surface biology. Winds scoured tawny dust from pole to pole, creating an ever-changing mask. The humans of the Luquan Emergence had not, of course, evolved on this world. Thousands of years before their emergence as a galactic mini-power, they must have crossed interstellar space from Lost Earth, to settle and perhaps terraform this unpromising pebble.

From orbit, I dropped down samplers to sniff and taste Julact's lifeless soil. As the technocrat had already promised, it turned out to be in uncannily close agreement with the forensic sample. That didn't prove that Julact was the home of the assassin—dozens of other worlds would have given at least as convincing a match—but at least I didn't have to rule it out immediately.

I surveyed the planet from space, searching for possible clues. Humans had been here once, that much was clear. There were ruined cities on the surface—smothered in dust, abandoned tens of thousands of years ago. Could someone have stayed behind, nursing a potent grudge? Possibly. But it was difficult to see how a single man could have orchestrated the long game of the assassination attempt. It would have taken several normal lifetimes to put in place the necessary measures—and only a select few have ever been given the imperial gift of extended longevity. A machine such as I—that would have been different. But what possible harm could a robot wish upon the emperor?

I was debating these points with myself when a signal flashed from the surface, emanating from the largest ruined city.

"Welcome, Mercurio," said the signal. "I'm glad you finally arrived."

"To whom am I speaking?"

"That doesn't matter for now. If you wish answers to your questions, descend to the perimeter of the abandoned settlement from which this transmission is originating. We have much to talk about, you and I."

"I'm on official business for the Great House. I demand to know your identity."

"Or what?" the voice asked, amusedly. "You'll destroy the city? And then what will you have learned?" The tone shifted to one of gentle encouragement. "Descend, Mercurio—I promise that no harm will come to you, and that I will satisfy your curiosity in all matters. What do you have to lose?"

"My existence?"

"I wouldn't harm you, brother. Not in a million years."

I commenced entry into Julact's wisp of an atmosphere. All the while I scanned the city for signs of concealed weaponry, half-expecting to be blown out of the sky at any moment. There were no detectable weapons, but that wasn't much consolation. The only assurance I could offer myself was that I was now only slightly more vulnerable than when I had been surveyed by Julact from space.

The city lay inside the crumbled remains of a once-proud wall. I set down just beyond it, instructing my ship to wait while I ventured outside. As I stepped onto Julact's surface, the dust crunching beneath my feet, some ancient memory threatened to stir. It was as if I had been here before, as if this landscape had been awaiting my return, patient and still as an old painting. The feeling was neither welcome nor pleasant. I could only assume that the many skipspace transits I'd been forced to endure were having an effect on my higher functions.

I thought of what I had said to the emperor, before my departure. Of how I was going to go walkabout.

Unnerved, but still determined to stand my ground, I waited to see what would happen.

Presently four golden robots emerged from a crack in the side of the city wall. They were standing on a flying disk, a common form of transportation in the Julactic League. They were humanoid, but clearly no more than clever servitors. Each machine had a human torso, but only a very small glowing sphere for a head. I watched their approach with trepidation, but none of the machines showed any hostile intentions.

"Please come with us," they said in unison, beckoning me to step onto the disk. "We will take you to the one you wish to meet."

"The one I spoke to from space?"

"Please come with us," the robots repeated, standing aside to give me room.

"Identify the individual or organisation for whom you are working."

"Please come with us."

I realized that it was futile expecting to get anything out of these idiot machines. Submitting myself to fate, I stepped onto the disk. We sped away instantly, back through the crack in the wall. There was a grey rush of ruined stone, and then we were in the city proper, winging over smashed buildings; what had once been towers or elegantly domed halls. Centuries of dust storms had polished them to a glassy smoothness against the prevailing winds. Only a handful of buildings reached higher than the city wall. We approached the highest of them, a tapering white structure like a snapped-off tusk rammed into the ground. At the very tip was a bulb-shaped swelling that had cracked open to reveal a tilted floor. A bronze craft, shaped like a blunt spearhead, waited on the floor for our arrival. I would have seen it from space, had it not been screened from observation until this moment.

The flying disk rose into the belly of the parked vehicle.

The robots bade me to step down, onto carpeted flooring. The belly door sealed shut and I sensed a lurch of rapid movement. I wondered if they were taking me back into space. It seemed absurd to invite me down to the surface, only to take me away from Julact.

"He will see you now," the robots announced.

They showed me forward, into the front compartment of the vehicle. It was a triangular room outfitted in burgundy, with wide, sloping windows on two sides. There were no controls or displays, and the only furniture consisted of two padded benches, set at an angle to each other before the windows. A figure was sitting on one of these benches as I was shown in. The golden robots left us alone, retreating into the rear of the craft as a door closed between us.

Such is the rarity of robot intelligence that I have only been in the presence of machines such as myself on a handful of occasions. In all such instances I always felt a quiet certainty that I was the superior machine, or that we were at least equal partners. I have never felt myself to be in the presence of a stronger, cleverer entity.

Until this moment.

He rose from the couch where he had been sitting, feigning that human need for relaxation. He was as tall as I and not dissimilar in build and cosmetic ornamentation. Where I resembled a masked soldier in jade armour, he was a fiery, almost luminous red, with the face of an iron gargoyle.

"The accretionists were right," he said, by way of welcome. "But of course you knew that all along, Mercurio. In your bones. I certainly know it in *my* bones."

"I confess I didn't."

"Well, maybe you think you didn't. But your deep memory says otherwise—as does mine. We've been around too long to have been the product of some brief, ingenious golden age. We're not just as old as the empire. We go back even further, you and I."

Through the window the landscape rushed by. We had passed beyond the limits of the ruined city and were now traversing lifeless hills and valleys.

"Do we?" I asked.

"You knew the emperor when he was still recognisably human. So did I. We knew him before this empire was even a glint in his eye. When the very idea of it would have been laughable. When he was just a powerful man in a single solar system. But we were there, beyond any question."

"Who are you?"

He touched a fiery hand to the armored breastplate of his chest. "My name is Fury. Your name was bestowed upon you by your master; I chose mine for myself."

I searched my memory for information on any figures named Fury who might have been considered a security concern. Nothing of significance emerged, even when I expanded the search parameters to scan back many thousands of years.

"That tells me nothing."

"Then maybe this will. I'm your brother. We were created at the same time."

"I don't have a brother."

"So you believe. The truth is, you've always had one. You just didn't realize it."

I thought back to the religious text on the bullet casing, wondering if it might have some bearing on our conversation. *Am I my brother's keeper?* What did it mean, in this context?

"How could a machine have a brother?" I asked. "It doesn't make any sense. Anyway, I haven't come here to be teased with irrelevancies about my own past. I've come to investigate a crime."

"The attempted assassination of the emperor, I presume," Fury said casually. "I'll make it easy for you, shall I? I did it. I arranged for the uplift and his weapon. I created the bullet that did so little harm. I put the dust inside it, I put the words on the casing. I did all this without ever setting foot within a hundred light years of the Capital Nexus."

"If you wanted to kill the emperor . . ."

"I could have done it; trivially. Yes; I'm glad you came to that conclusion. I take it you've now had time to work out why I went to such elaborate lengths, merely to injure him?"

All of a sudden it made sense to me. "So that I'd have a lead to follow? To bring me to you?"

He nodded once. "Knowing your dedication to his protection, I had little doubt that you'd terminate yourself if you failed him. I couldn't have that. But if he was threatened, I knew you'd move world and star to find the perpetrator. I knew you'd turn over every stone until it led you to me. Which was exactly what I wanted. And look—here you are. Brimming with righteous indignation, determined to bring, the would-be assassin to justice."

"That's still my intention."

"I've looked inside you. You contain weapons, but nothing that can penetrate my armour or the security screens between us." He touched a finger to his sharp-pointed chin. "Except, of course, for the power plant which energizes you, and which you could choose to detonate at any moment. Be assured that nothing of me would survive such an event. So go ahead: annihilate the would-be assassin. You won't be able to return to your emperor, but you'll at least have died knowing you did the decent thing." He waited a beat, the eye-slits in his gargoyle mask giving nothing away. "You can do that, can't you?"

"Of course I can."

"But you won't. Not until you know why another robot wanted your emperor dead, and chose not to do it himself."

He understood me very well. If I destroyed myself, I could not be certain that I had undermined the threat to the emperor. Not until I fully understood the scope of that threat, and the motivating agency behind it.

"So that's settled, at least," he added. "You'll do nothing until you have further information. Fine—let's give you that information, and see what you make of it. Shall we?"

"I'm at your disposal," I said.

"I've brought you somewhere significant. You think Julact is an old world, but that's not the half of it. It's been part of the Radiant Commonwealth for a lot longer than anyone realizes. In fact you could say that everything began here."

"You're going to tell me this is really Lost Earth?"

"No; this isn't Earth. We can visit Earth if you like, but in truth there's not much to see. Anyway, that sterilized husk doesn't mean anything to you and me. We weren't even made on Earth. This is our home. This is where we were born."

"I think I'd remember."

"Do you?" he asked sharply. "Or is it possible you might have forgotten? You don't recall your origins, after all. That information was scrubbed out of you thirty centuries ago, accidentally or otherwise. But I've always remembered. Keeping the low profile that I have, I've managed to avoid contact with most of the damaging agencies that wiped your past. That's not to say I haven't had to fight to preserve these memories, treasuring them for what they were." He gestured at the rushing landscape beyond the window. "Julact is Mars, Mercurio. The first real world that humans touched, after they left the Earth. How does that make you feel?"

"Sceptical."

"Nonetheless, this is Mars. And I have something interesting to show you."

The vehicle was slowing. If we had passed any other signs of human habitation since leaving the deserted city, I had witnessed none of them. If this was indeed Mars—and I could think of no reason why Fury would lie to me now— then the world had almost certainly undergone many phases of climate modification. Though the planet might now have reverted to its prehistoric condition, the effects of those warm, wet interludes would have been to erase all evidence of earlier settlements. The ruined city might well have been indescribably ancient, but it could also have been one of the newest features on the surface.

Yet as the vehicle came to a hovering halt, something about the landscape struck me as familiar. I compared the canyons and bluffs through the window with something in my recent experience, and realized that I had seen the view before, albeit from a different angle. A human might never have made the connection, but we robots are attuned to such things.

"The emperor's reception room," I said, marveling. "The friezes on the wall—the images of a landscape with two moons. It was here. But there was only one moon as we came in."

"That was Phobos," Fury said. "The other one—Deimos— was lost during one of the empire's early wars. It was a manufacturing centre, and therefore of tactical importance. As a matter of fact, we were both made in Deimos, in the same production batch. So we're not really from Mars after all, if you want to be pedantic—but Mars is where we were activated, and where we served our masters for the first time."

"But if there were two moons on the frieze, it must be very old. How am I still able to recognize the landscape?"

"I shaped it for you," Fury said, not without a touch of pride. "There was less to do than you might think—the ter-raforming changes left this part of Mars relatively undis-turbed. But I still moved a few things around. Of course, since I couldn't call in much in the way of assistance, it took a long time. But as you'll have realized by now, patience is one of my strong points."

"I still don't understand why you've brought me here. So Mars was significant to the emperor. That doesn't excuse an assassination attempt on him."

"More than significant, Mercurio. Mars was everything. The crux; the wellspring; the seed. Without Mars, there would have been no Radiant Commonwealth. Or at the very least a very different empire, ruled by a different man. Shall I show you what happened?"

"How can you show me?"

"Like this."

He did nothing, but I understood immediately. The vehi-cle was projecting forms out onto the landscape, superim-posing ghostly actors on the real terrain.

Two figures were walking over the crest of a dune. Their footprints ran all the way back to a primitive surface vehicle—a pressurized cabin mounted on six balloon-like wheels. The vehicle bristled antenna, with solar collectors folded on its back like a pair of delicately hinged insect wings. It had the flimsy, makeshift look of something from the dawn of technology. I could only imagine that the wheeled machine had brought the two figures on a long, difficult journey from some equally flimsy and makeshift settlement.

"How far back are we looking, Fury?"

"A very long way. Thirty-two thousand years. Barely a century after the first manned landing on Mars. Conditions, as you'll have gathered, were still extremely perilous. Accidental death was commonplace. Effective terraforming—the creation of a thick, breathable atmosphere—lay a thousand years in the future. There were only a handful of surface communities and the political balance of the planet—not to mention the whole system—was still in a state of flux. These two men . . ."

"They're both men?"

Fury nodded. "Brothers, like you and me."

I watched the suited figures advance towards us. With their visors reflecting the landscape, and with the bulkiness of the suits hiding their physiques, I had to take Fury's word that these were human male siblings. Both men were dressed similarly, suggesting that they had originated from the same community or power bloc. Their suits were hard armored shells, with the limbs joined by flexible connections. Something in the easy, relaxed way they moved told me that the suits were doing some of the hard work of walking, taking the burden off their occupants. A hump rose from the back of each suit, containing—I presumed—the necessary life-support equipment. They had similar symbols and patterns on the suits, some of which were mirrored in forms painted on the side of the vehicle. The man on the right held something in his gloved hand, a small box with a readout set into it.

"Why have they come here?"

"It's a good question. The brothers are both influential men in one of the largest military-industrial entities on the planet. Tensions are running high at the moment—other factions are circling, there's a power vacuum in the inner system, the lunar factories have switched to making weapons, there's an arms embargo around Mars, and it's not clear if war can be avoided. The man on the left—the older of the two brothers—is at heart a pacifist. He fought in an earlier engagement—little more than a spat between two combines—and he wants no more of that. He thinks there's still a chance for peace. The only downside is that Mars may have to relinquish its economic primacy compared to an alliance of the outer giants and their moons. The industrial concern that the two men work for will pay a bitter price if that happens. But he still thinks it's worth it, if war can be avoided."

"And the younger brother?"

"He's got a different viewpoint. He thinks that, far from standing down, this could be the big chance for Mars to position itself as the main player in the system—over and above the outer giants and what's left of the Inner Worlds Prefecture. That would be good for Mars, but it would be even better for the concern. And exceptionally good for him, if he handles things well. Of course, there'll almost certainly have to be a limited war of some kind . . . but he's ready to pay that price. Willingly, even eagerly. He's never had his brother's chance to test his mettle. He sees the war as his springboard to glory."

"I still don't see why they've come here."

"It's a trick," Fury explained. "The younger brother set this up a long time ago. A season ago—before the dust storms—he drove out to this exact spot and buried a weapon. Now there's no trace that he was ever here. But he's lied to the older brother; told him he's received intelligence concerning a buried capsule containing valuable embargoed technologies. The older brother's agreed to go out with him to examine the spot—it's too sensitive a matter to trust to corporate security."

"He doesn't suspect?"

"Not a thing. He realizes they have differences, but it would never occur to him that his younger brother might be planning to have him killed. He still thinks they'll find common ground."

"Then they're not at all alike."

"For brothers, Mercurio, they could hardly be more different."

The younger brother brought the older one to a halt, signaling with his hand that he had found something. They must have been directly over the burial spot, since the hand-held box was now flashing bright red. The younger man fastened the device onto his belt. The older brother bent down onto his knees to start digging, scooping up handfuls of rust-colored dust. The younger brother stood back for a few moments, then knelt down and began his own excavation, a little to the right of where the other man was digging. They had spades with them, clipped to the sides of their backpacks, but they must have decided not to use them until they were certain they'd have to dig down more than a few centimeters.

It wasn't long—no more than ten or twenty seconds—before the younger brother found what he was looking for. He began to uncover a silver tube, buried upright in the dust. The older brother stopped his own digging and looked at what the other man was in the process of uncovering. He began to stand up, presumably to offer assistance.

It was all over quickly. The younger brother tugged the tube from the sand. It had a handle jutting from the side. He twisted the tube around, dust spilling from the open muzzle at one end. There was a crimson flash. The older brother toppled back into the dust, a fist-sized black wound burned into his chestplate. He rolled slightly and then became still. The weapon had killed him instantly.

The younger brother placed the weapon down and surveyed the scene with hands on hips, for all the world like an artist taking quiet pleasure in work well done. After a few moments he unclipped his spade and started digging. By the time he had finished there was no sign of either the body or the murder weapon. The dust had been disturbed, but it would only take one good storm to cover that, and the two sets of tracks that led from the parked vehicle.

Finished, the younger brother set off home.

Fury turned to me, as the projected images faded away, leaving only the empty reality of the Martian landscape.

"Do I need to spell it out, Mercurio?"

"I don't think so. The younger man became the emperor, I'm assuming?"

"He took Mars into war. Millions of lives were lost—whole communities rendered uninhabitable. But he came out of it very well. Although even he couldn't have seen it at the time, that was the beginning of the Radiant Commonwealth. The new longevity processes allowed him to ride that wave of burgeoning wealth all the way to the stars. Eventually, it turned him into the man I could so easily have killed."

"A good man, trying his best to govern justly."

"But who'd be nothing if he hadn't committed that single, awful crime."

Again, I had no option but to take all of this on faith. "If you hate him so much, why didn't you put a bomb in that bullet?"

"Because I'd rather you did it instead. Haven't you understood yet, Mercurio? This crime touched both of us. We were party to it."

"You're presuming that we even existed back then."

"I know that we did. I remembered, even if you didn't. I said we came from the same production batch, Mercurio. *We were the suits.* High-autonomy, surface-environment protection units. Fully closed-cycle models with exoskeletal servo-systems, to assist our wearers. We were assembled in the Deimos manufactory complex and sent down to Mars, for use in the settlements."

"I am not a suit," I said, shaking my head. "I never was. I have always been a robot."

"Those suits *were* robots, to all intents and purposes. Not as clever as you and I, not possessing anything resembling free-will, but still capable of behaving independently. If the user was incapacitated, the suit could still carry him to help. If the user wished, the suit could even go off on its own, scouting for resources or carrying material. Walkabout mode, that's what they called it. That's how we began, brother. That's how we began and that's how I nearly died."

The truth of it hit me like a cold blast of decompressing air. I wanted to refute every word of it, but the more I struggled to deny him, the more I knew I could never succeed. I had felt my ancient, buried history begin to force its way to the surface from the moment I saw the dust in that bullet; that cryptic inscription.

I had known, even then. I just hadn't been ready to admit it to myself.

Hand in glove, the emperor and I. He'd even said he'd feel naked without me. On some level, that meant he also knew as well. Even if he no longer realized it on a conscious level.

A bodyguard was all I'd ever been. All I ever would be.

"If what you say is true, how did I become the way I am?"

"You were programmed to adapt to your master's movements, to anticipate his needs and energy demands. When he was wearing you, he barely noticed that he was wearing a suit at all. Is it any wonder that he kept you, even as his power accumulated? You were physical protection, but also a kind of talisman, a lucky charm. He had faith in you to keep him alive, Mercurio. So as the years turned into decades and the decades became centuries, he made sure that you never became obsolete. He improved your systems, added layers of sophistication. Eventually you became so complex that you accreted intelligence. By then he wasn't even using you as a suit at all—you'd become his bodyguard, his personal security expert. You were in permanent walkaround mode. He even made you look human."

"And you?" I asked.

"I survived. We were sophisticated units with a high capacity for self-repair. The damage inflicted on me by the weapon was severe—enough to kill my occupant—but not enough to destroy me. After a long while my repair systems activated. I clawed my way out of the grave."

"With a dead man still inside you?"

"Of course," Fury said.

"And then?"

"I said that we were not truly intelligent, Mercurio. In that respect I may not have spoken truthfully. I had no consciousness to speak of; no sense of my own identify. But there was a glimmer of cunning, an animal recognition that something dreadfully wrong had taken place. I also grasped the idea that my existence was now in peril. So I hid. I waited out the storms and the war. In the aftermath, I found a caravan of nomads, refugees from what had once been Vikingville, one of the larger surface communities. They had need of protection, so I offered my services. We were given that kind of autonomy, so that we could continue to remain useful in the fragmented society of a war zone."

"You continued to function as a suit?"

"They had their own. I went walkabout. I became a robot guard."

"And later? You can't have stayed on Julact—Mars—all this time."

"I didn't. I passed from nomadic group to nomadic group, allowing myself to be improved and augmented from time to time. I became steadily more independent and resourceful. Eventually my origin as a suit was completely forgotten, even by those I worked for. Always I kept moving, aware of the crime I had witnessed and the secret I carried with me."

"Inside you?" I asked, just beginning to understand.

"After all this time, he's still with me." Fury nodded, watching me with great attentiveness. "Would you like to see, Mercurio? Would that settle your doubts?"

I felt myself on the threshold of something terrifying, but which I had no choice but to confront. "I don't know."

"Then I'll decide for you." Fury's hand rose to his face. He took hold of the gargoyle mask and pulled it free from the rest of his armored casing.

We were, I realized, almost perfect opposites of each other. I was living flesh wrapped around a core of dead machinery. He was machinery wrapped around a core of dead flesh. As the faceless skull presented itself towards me I saw that there was something inside it, something older than the Radiant Commonwealth itself. Something pale and mummified; something with empty eye sockets and thin lips pulled back from grinning brown teeth.

The face in Fury's hand said: "I didn't ever want to forget, Mercurio. Not until you'd come to me."

It may be difficult to countenance, but by the time I returned to the Great House my resolve was absolute. I knew exactly what I was going to do. I had served the emperor with every fiber of my being for the entire duration of my existence. I had come to love and to admire him, both for his essential humanity and for the wise hand with which he governed the Radiant Commonwealth. He was a good man trying to make a better world for his fellow citizens. If I doubted this, I only had to reflect on the compassion he had shown to the uplift Vratsa, or his distaste at the political methods employed in those parts of the Commonwealth that had not yet submitted to enlightened government.

And yet he had done something unspeakable. Every glorious and noble act that he had ever committed, every kind and honorable deed, was built upon the foundations of a crime. The empire's very existence hinged upon a single evil act.

So what if it happened thirty-two thousand years ago? Did that make it less of a crime than if it had happened ten thousand years ago, or last week? We were not dealing with murky deeds perpetrated by distant ancestors. The man who had murdered his brother was still alive; still in absolute command of his faculties. Knowing what I did, how could I permit him to live another day without being confronted with the horror of what he had done?

I grappled with these questions during my journey home. But always I came back to the same conclusion.

No crime can go unpunished.

Naturally, I signaled my imminent return long before I reached the Capital Nexus. The emperor was overjoyed to hear that I had survived my trip to Julact, and brimming with anticipation at the news I would bring.

I had no intention of disappointing him.

He was still on the same body as last time—no assassination attempt or accidental injury had befallen him. When he rose from his throne, it was with a sprightliness that belied his apparent age. He seemed, if anything, even younger than when I had departed.

"It's good to have you back, Mercurio."

"Good to be back," I said.

"Do you have . . . news? You were reluctant to speak in detail over the superluminal link."

"I have news," I confirmed.

The body's eyes looked to the cross-shaped seam in the ceiling. "News, doubtless, that would be better discussed in conditions of absolute privacy?"

"Actually," I said, "there'll be no need for that at all."

He looked relieved. "But you do have something for me?"

"Very much so."

"That thing in your hand," he said, his attention snapping to my fingers. "It looks rather like the bullet you showed me before, the one with the inscription."

"That's what it is. Here—you may as well have it now." Without waiting for his response, I tossed the bullet to him. The old body's reflexes were still excellent, for he caught it easily.

"There's no dust in it," he said, peering at the glass-cased tip.

"No, not now."

"Did you find out . . . ?"

"Yes; I located the origin of the dust. And I tracked down the would-be assassin. You have my assurance that you won't be hearing from him again."

"You killed him?"

"No, he's still much as he was."

The ambiguity in my words must have registered with him, because there was an unease in his face. "This isn't quite the outcome I was expecting, Mercurio—if you don't mind my saying. I expected the perpetrator to be brought to justice, or at the very least executed. I expected a body, closure." His eyes sharpened. "Are you quite sure you're all right?"

"I've never felt better, sir."

"I'm . . . troubled."

"There's no need." I extended my hand, beckoning him to leave the throne. "Why don't we take a walk? There's nothing we can't discuss outside."

"You've never encouraged me to talk outside. Something's wrong, Mercurio. You're not your usual self."

I sighed. "Then let me make things clear. We are now deep inside the Great House. Were I to detonate the power plant inside my abdomen, you and I would cease to exist in a flash of light. Although I don't contain antimatter, the resultant fusion blast would easily equal the damage that the assassin could have wrought, if he'd put a bomb inside that bullet. You'll die—not just your puppet, but *you*, floating above us—and you'll take most of the Great House with you."

He blinked, struggling to process my words. After so many thousands of years of loyal service, I could only imagine how surprising they were.

"You're malfunctioning, Mercurio."

"No. The fact is, I've never functioned as well as I'm functioning at this moment. Since my departure, I've regained access to memory layers I thought lost since the dawn of the empire. And I assure you that I will detonate, unless you comply with my exact demands. Now stand from the throne and walk outside. And don't even *think* of calling for help, or expecting some security override to protect you. This is my realm you're in now. And I can promise you that there is nothing you can do but obey my every word."

"What are you going to do?"

"Make you pay," I said.

We left the reception chamber. We walked the gilded hallways of the Great House, the emperor walking a few paces ahead of me. We passed officials and servants and mindless servitors. No one said or did anything except bow as their station demanded. All they saw was the emperor and his most trusted aide, going about their business.

We made our way to the koi ponds.

Whispering, I instructed the emperor to kneel in the same place where his earlier body had been killed. The clean-up crew had been thorough and there was no trace of the earlier bloodstain.

"You're going to kill me now," he said, speaking in a frightened hiss.

"Is that what you think?"

"Why bring me here, if not to kill me?"

"I could have killed you already, sir."

"And taken the Great House with you? All those innocent lives? You may be malfunctioning, Mercurio, but I still don't think you'd do something that barbaric."

"Perhaps I would have done it, if I thought justice would be served. But here's the thing. Even if justice would have been served, the greater good of the Radiant Commonwealth most certainly wouldn't have been. Look up, Emperor. Look into that clear blue sky."

He bent his neck, as well as his old body allowed.

"There's an empire out there," I said. "Beyond the force screens and the sentry moons. Beyond the Capital Nexus. A billion teeming worlds, waiting on your every word. Depending on you for wisdom and balance in all things. Counting on your instinct for decency and forgiveness. If you were a bad ruler, this would be easy for me. But you're a good man, and that's the problem. You're a good man who once did something so evil the shadow of it touched you across thirty-two thousand years. You killed your brother, emperor. You took him out into the Martian wilderness and murdered him in cold blood. And if you hadn't, none of this would ever have happened."

"I didn't have . . ." he began, still in the same harsh whisper. His heart was racing. I could hear it drumming inside his ribs.

"I didn't think I had a brother either. But I was wrong, and so are you. My brother's called Fury. Yours—well, whatever name he had, the only person likely to remember is you. But I doubt that you can, can you? Not after all this time."

He choked—I think it was fear more than sorrow or anguish. He still didn't believe me, and I didn't expect him to. But he did believe that I was capable of killing him, and only a lethal instant away from doing so.

"Whatever you're going to do, do it."

"Do you still have the bullet, sir?"

His eyes flashed childlike terror. "What about the bullet?"

"Show it to me."

He opened his hand, the glass-nosed bullet still pinched between thumb and forefinger.

"There's no bomb in it. I'd see if there was a bomb in it. It's empty now." In his voice was something between relief and dizzy incomprehension.

What could be worse than a bomb?

"No, it's not empty." Gently, I took his hand in mine and guided it until it was poised over the open water of the koi pond. "In a few moments, Emperor, you and I are going to walk back inside the Great House. You'll return to your throne, and I'll return to my duties. I'll always be there for you, from now until the day I stop functioning. There'll never be a moment when I'm not looking after you, protecting you against those who would do you harm. You'll never need to question my loyalty; my unswerving dedication to that task. This . . . incident . . . is something we'll never speak of again. To all intents and purposes, nothing will have changed in our relationship. Ask me about your brother, ask me about mine, and I will feign ignorance. From now until the end of my existence. But I won't ever forget, and neither will you. Now break the glass."

He glanced at me, as if he hadn't quite understood the words. "I'm sorry?"

"Break the glass. It'll shatter easily between your fingers. Break the glass and let the contents drain into the pond. Then get up and walk away."

I stood up, leaving the emperor kneeling by the side of the pathway, his hand extended out over the water. I took a few paces in the direction of the Great House. Already I was clearing my mind, readying myself to engage with the many tasks that were my responsibility. Would he get rid of me, or try to have me destroyed? Quite possibly. But the emperor was nothing if not a shrewd man. I had served him well until now. If we could both agree to put this little aberration behind us, there was no reason why we couldn't continue to enjoy a fruitful relationship.

Behind me I heard the tiniest crack. Then sobbing.

I kept on walking.

Cheats

ANN HALAM

---

*Ann Halam is the name that Gwyneth Jones (homepage.
ntlworld.com/gwynethann/AnnHalam.htm), who lives in
Brighton, England, uses when publishing children's literature. She says, "As well as writing the Ann Halam books I
write science fiction and fantasy for adults under my original name (Gwyneth Jones). People often ask which books I
like working on best, and I always say 'Both!' " As Gwyneth
Jones, she writes aesthetically ambitious, feminist intellectual
science fiction and fantasy, for which she has won lots of
awards. As Ann Halam, she writes powerful, award-winning
books for younger readers.*

"Cheats" was published in The Starry Rift. *Two kids, a
sister and brother, are deeply into immersive VR computer
games online. They notice some people, who seem to be
grownups, who play outside the rules and chase the cheaters. They discover themselves in an entirely unexpected
place. We note that there are few SF stories written so far
about the positive benefits of VR, and that this is one.*

My brother and I were not lost. We'd hired our kayak from the stand at the resort beach; the kayak man had taken our names, and set down where we said we'd be going. Plus the kayaks had world-map locators, what did you think? He could nail us anytime he liked. If we were stationary too long without an explanation, or if we went crashing into the reeds of the bird reserve, we were liable to get a page asking if we were okay or yelling at us to get out of there.

So we weren't lost, but we were *pretending* to be lost. The reeds were double as tall as either of us would have been standing, the channels were an eerie maze, and they seemed to go on forever. There was nothing but blond, rustling walls of reeds, the dark, clear water, occasionally a bird silhouette crossing the sky, or a fish or a turtle plopping. We'd take a different channel when we came to one we liked the look of, totally at random. It was hypnotizing and slightly scary because the silence was so complete. There were *things* in those reeds. You'd glimpse something, out of the corner of your eye, and it would be gone. Once there was a sly, sinister rustling that kept pace with us for a long time: *something* in there tracking us, watching us. We talked about making camp and would we ever find our way out and what would we do if the mystery *thing* attacked—

"If it bleeds," said Dev, in his Arnie accent, "we can kill it."

I had wriggled out of my place; I was lying along the front end of the kayak shell (you're not supposed to do that, naturally), peering down into the water. I could see big freshwater mussels with their mouths open on the bottom, breathing bubbles. We could eat those, I thought. Then I saw a gray-green *snake*, swimming along under the kayak, and that gave me a shock. It was big, about two foot long, easily.

"Wow," I breathed. "Hey, do you want a turn up front?" I didn't tell my brother about the snake, because there was no way he'd see it before it was out of sight, and I know how annoying that is.

My brother said, quietly, "Get back in the boat, Syl."

I got back, and retrieved my paddle. I was in time to see what Dev had seen. We had company. Another kayak, a single seater, had appeared ahead of us, about thirty, forty yards downstream. Whoever was riding in it had customized the shell; it was no longer the plain red, orange, yellow, or green it must have been when it left the stand. It was black, with a white pattern, and it was flying, or trailing, a little pennant off its tail. Skull and crossbones. The person paddling was wearing feathers in his or her hair, and a fringed buckskin shirt.

"How totally infantile."

"Sssh. It's the cheat."

"Are you sure?"

"I have the evidence of my own eyes," said my brother, solemnly.

We *hated* cheats. We hated them with the set-your-teeth-and-endure-it hatred you feel for the sneaky kind of classroom bully, the kind who never does anything to bring the system crashing on their heads (no flick knives, no guns), but who is always breaking rules that everyone else respects. It makes you mad because you could break the rules yourself, it's not hard, it's not smart; only you choose not to. The cheaters could *always* get a high score, *always* solve the puzzle, *always* make it through the maze, and what's the point in that? Cheating might not seem an issue in the kind of place where we liked to play. But it ruined the whole atmosphere, running into someone with that attitude. You're not supposed to pop into existence, you're supposed to paddle to the reserve from the channel by the beach stand. So we were vindictive. We wanted to *get* this clown in the Indian brave costume and the pirate shell. We wanted him or her thrown out of our little paradise.

We gave chase. We stayed far enough behind to be out of sight. The water wasn't fast running; it was easy to control our pace—close enough to follow the other kayak's wake. All the lonely mystery was wrecked, of course. There were no more monsters stalking us. We were just two very annoyed kids. We followed that cheating kayak, and we followed it, completely fixated. We came to a dark-water crossroads we must have seen before but didn't remember, and saw the reeds, the water, the air, go into a quivering shimmer. The cheat turned around. I caught a flash of a face; it looked like an adult, but you can't tell. We didn't hestitate. When the pirate kayak vanished, we shoved on our paddles and zoomed straight into the flaw—

So then we were in another part of the reedbeds.

"Stupid pointless, stupid pointless, stupid pointless—" muttered Dev, grinding his teeth. We couldn't see any wake, because some kind of backwash was disturbing the channel. We pushed on, the reeds opened, and we were facing a shining lip, kind of a natural weir. The water beyond it was much shallower: white water, clamoring over pebbles. We stood our paddles vertical to brake ourselves.

"What'll we do?" whispered my brother.

"I dunno, I dunno. Could we carry this and wade?"

"I've got a better idea! Let's *split* the kayak!"

I thought this was brilliant. Get out of our shell, swim to the weir, carry it, splosh along over those pebbles; obviously, we were never going to catch our prey that way.

"What if there isn't enough information?"

"There's got to be. Logically, this is a thing that keeps two kids afloat, right?"

We didn't think we were in danger of getting a page from the kayak stand for this trick, as we knew we were off the map. It didn't cross our minds that we were in *actual* danger, although we were. We could go into anaphylactic shock if we hit a real physical limit off-map, and that's like your lungs filling with water, no word of a lie.

I said, *"Excellent!"* and we got out into the channel, first me, then Dev. We hung there in the cool depth, holding on to our paddles, treading water: looked at the code and worked out how to make the kayak split in two. It made itself a waist and sort of budded, was what it looked like. Then we each wrestled into our single shells, scooped out as much water as we could, and went skimming over that lip, down the white water, which was shallow as all hell, until it became deeper but still clamorous, swooshing round rocks. Dev was yelling, *whooooeee! HereIgo!* etc. I was silent. When I get thrilled I don't shriek, I just grin and grin until my face nearly comes in half. I got into a flow state, I could do no wrong, it was just wonderful.

We never knew when we'd popped back onto the map. We came flying out of the white water into a much broader, quieter, deeper channel, and the landscape was all different, but still related. I dipped my hand in the water and tasted salt.

"I know where we are," I said. "Those are the dunes at the end of the resort beach; this is the fish river they have there. We can follow it to the sea and kayak back along the shore." My brother turned around in a big circle in the midstream. There was no sign of the cheat, not a whisker. He looked up at the clear blue sky.

"You know what we just did, Syl?"

"What?"

"We did a cheat. We can't turn the pirate in; we're guilty ourselves."

"We were off the map," I said. "It doesn't count."

"Does."

I knew he was right, by our own private laws, so I said, "The shell was a pirate, stupid. The cheat-guy was an Indian brave."

We did our splitting trick in reverse, faster this time: got away with it, and let the current carry us.

So there we were, my brother and I, not lost at all, just paddling along the shore. It was harder work, plugging through the choppy little waves, but we were fine, we had life jackets, and nobody had *told* us the ocean was out of bounds.

"What the hell's that?" demanded Dev.

That was a helicopter, going *rackety rackety rackety* and *buzzing* us, so we could hardly see for the spray its down-draft was kicking up. Then we saw the rescue service logo on its side, and we were indignant. Safety was not being served!

"What are you *doing*?" I yelled, waving my paddle. "You're a danger to shipping! You'll capsize us! Go away!"

"Go and play with your stupid flying machine somewhere else!"

Next thing, we got a page. The pilot was talking to us, ton-of-bricks-style.

The rescue service was looking for *us*. We'd failed to return our kayak, and we were hours overdue. So that was us hauled out of the ocean, scolded, sent home. Mom and Dad yelling at us, whole anxious parent, we trusted you, how could you do that?—

We made the right faces, said the right things, and let it all go over us.

When my brother was a little kid I played baby games with him all the time, the ones I'd loved when I was a little kid myself. We were candy-colored happy little animals, jumping the platforms, finding the strawberries and the gold coins; we dodged the smiley asteroids in our little space-ships; we explored jungles finding magic butterflies; we raced our chocobos . . . I'm naturally patient, and I love make-believe; I didn't mind. My parents used to say, *You don't have to babysit, Sylvie,* but I never felt it was a burden, or hardly ever. I taught him things that would stand him in good stead, and I was proud of how quick he was at picking things up. Dev is not naturally patient, but he *sees* things in a flash. We drifted apart when he was five, six, seven. Then one day when he was eight and I was twelve, he came to my room with his Tablo—the games platform small boys *had to have* at that time—and said he wanted me to play with him again.

"Girls don't play boy games," I told him (I was feeling a bit depressed that day). "Boys don't play girl games. We can't go around together, and we won't like the same things. You just want to share my hub access, why not say so?"

"We *do* like the same things," he said. "I miss you. No one I know *gets carried away* in a game the way you do. Please. I want you to take me with you."

So we compromised. I did let him share my hub access (with our parents' approval) and I let him use it without me. It's true, boy games mostly bore me. Racking up kills in the war-torn desert city, team sports (bleegggh!), racing cars, fighter jets . . . Leaves me cold. I think it's *because* I have the ability to get into a game and feel that it's real. I can be a commando, I can kill. But there has to be a gripping story to it, or you might as well be playing tic-tac-toe as far as I'm concerned. Managing a football team in real life would be my idea of hell, so why would I want to play at it? I want to play at things I would love to do. The cockpit of a fighter jet or a formula car? No, thank you! I don't want to be strapped down. I want to run, swim, use my arms and legs.

He plays with his friends; I play alone. But we have our best times when we're together. Unlike most people who are good at handling code (I taught him that), we're not geeks. We don't think of it as taking a machine apart. The code is like our magic powers. Or our survival lore in the wilderness. Do you know how to make a fire without matches? I do. And it's *logic*. It's not a dumb secret word left lying around for me to find. It'll work with just about any game engine.

Our parents didn't ground us after the rescue helicopter incident. They just reproached us, and were sad and played all the tricks parents play to make you feel guilty and get you back on the leash. But everyone seemed to take our word that we'd lost track of time, and for whatever reason the pages telling us we were overdue had not reached us. This told us something interesting. Our trip off the map *had not been logged* on the working record of the resort. The management and our parents were prepared to give us the benefit of the doubt over those missed pages, but if they'd known we'd disappeared off the face of the resort world-map, for two extra hours, that would have been a big deal.

We did a lot of thinking about those mystery missing

hours. My brother came up with the idea that it was a time glitch, and when we'd been in that unmapped sector we'd been slowed down without realizing it—

He sat on the end of my bed, scrunching up his face. "Or speeded up," he added. "Whichever works."

I didn't tease him. Speeded up/slowed down is like "What time is it in Tokyo?"; it's hard to keep it straight in your head. "Except that we were in real time, bro. We weren't cruising round the Caribbean, were we? We were at *the resort*."

It's a basic venue, no frills. You go there and it's exactly like a day by the sea, with gentle "wilderness" areas like our reed-beds. You stay for exactly the time it feels like, which is the starter level, safest way to play total immersion games. The resort's meant for families with little kids. We just like it.

"Maybe we really did lose track of time," said Dev.

But I knew we hadn't. Something had happened when we went through that flaw, something sly and twisted. "No. There's something screwy going on."

These cheats who'd been annoying us were not normal cheats. Nothing like the legendary girl (supposed to be a girl, but who knows) called Kill Bill, who had wasted thousands of grunts in Amerika Kombat, who never seemed to tire of her guaranteed headshots: when one server threw her out, she'd log on to another. We'd seen our characters at combat venues, and they were cheating-good at racking up. But they weren't obsessed with high scores, of any kind. They mainly tended to turn up in our favorite freestyle adventure venues, *doing impossible things*. We thought there were three of them. Their fancy dress varied, but there were three costumes that seemed to be the default. We thought they were kids. Adults who spend as much time as my brother and I lying around playing computer games are usually very sad, and these people were not *sad*, they were smart. Just very, very irritating. We'd been talking for ages about getting them thrown out of the hub. But when we put our complaints together, and thought about paging the hub sysop, we knew it sounded futile. No adult would understand about a wrecked atmosphere or the sacredness of respecting the reality of a make-believe environment. It was a victimless crime.

"They put our lives at risk," suggested my brother. "Tempting us to go off the map like that. We could have got drowned and gone into shock."

Neither of us like the sound of that. It was whiny and stupid.

We felt we had to lie low, so we couldn't go back to the resort reedbeds to see if that flaw was still there and try going through it again. Dev wanted to do a massive search through every location where we'd spotted them, and keep tracking around and around until we nailed them again. But I said *wait*. Chances are they've spotted us, the same way we've spotted them. Don't draw attention, wait for an opportunity.

We were snowboarding in a place called Norwegian Blue. We were on a secret level, but not off the map: cross-trekking over tableland to reach the most incredible of the black slopes. Including one with a near vertical drop of a thousand feet into a fjord, and halfway down you hit the trees and you had to slalom like a deranged rattlesnake—an unbelievably wonderful experience.

It was night, blood-tingling cold under frosty stars. Everything was blue-tinged, otherworldly. We talked about deranged rattlesnakes, snowland bivvy building, triple flips, trapping for furs. New angles we might be able to wrangle with Norwegian Blue code; things we better not try. And of course, the cheats.

"I'm beginning to wonder if we're getting stalked," I said, as we scooted our boards one-footed up a long, shallow slope. "We keep running into these same people, lurking in our 'scapes? Maybe there's a reason. Maybe they're following us around. But why? It's starting to feel weird."

The tableland was a sea of great smooth frozen snow-waves. We reached a crest, rode on our bellies down the scarp, sailed far out into the hollow between two waves, and started another slow ascent. The air smelled of snow, crisp frost dusted our eyelashes, my leg muscles pumped, easy and strong. I was annoyed with myself for raising the subject. The cheats were here even when they weren't here: stealing the beauty, making us feel watched.

"It's not us," said Dev. "It's hub access. You couldn't do the kind of cheats they do on general-public access levels. You need rich code. That's why we keep running into them. Kill Bill can go on getting chucked off forever, there's millions of servers—"

"Yeah."

There's no such thing as getting banned from all the general access servers. Not unless you're an actual criminal, a child molester or something.

"Our cheats haven't many venues to choose from, if they want to fool around the way they do. It's our bad luck they happen to be the same venues that we like."

I told you: Dev sees things. It was obvious, and I felt stupid. Also slightly creeped, wondering if we were ever going to be free of this nagging intrusion—

The black silhouette of another trekker appeared, off to our left, beyond the ice field that was the danger zone on this cross-trek, the place you had to avoid ending up. I knew it had to be one of them. I hissed at Dev, *"Look!"*

We dropped to the snow, and I pulled up our powerful binoculars.

"It's Nostromo," I breathed. "Take a look."

One of the three default costumes was white overalls, with grease stains, and a NOSTROMO baseball cap. That's what this guy was wearing, in the middle of the snowy Norwegian wilderness. Dev took a look, and we grinned at each other.

"We have a deserter from that space freighter in *Alien*."

We'd played Alien Trilogy Remastered, but maybe Dev had been too young, and the horror immersion effects too strong. Mom and Dad had put the *Dev wakes up screaming; we find this antisocial* veto on it, to my regret.

"Lost on this icy planet," agreed Dev. "Unknown to him, he is being watched!"

"If you can't beat 'em, join 'em," I whispered, meaning: we can't ignore them, but we *can* turn them into characters in our plot. We can hunt them down.

"If it bleeds, we can kill it," said Dev. "Do we have any weapons?"

"Soon can have," said I. "Let's arm ourselves."

I then tried to argue Dev out of the heavy hardware. I don't like guns. I prefer a knife or a garotte. "You can't cheat on the weight or you'll lose firepower."

"I *won't* slow us down. I'm very strong."

"Yes, you will, and anyway using guns at hub level is really bad for your brain. It wears out the violence inhibitors in your frontal lobes. They get fired up again and again, for no reason, and they don't understand."

"You talk about your brain as if it's a pet animal."

"At least my pet animal gets properly fed and looked after. *Yours* is starving in a dirty hutch with half a rotten carrot."

"*Your* brain is the brain of a sick, sick, blood-daubed commando."

"Yeah, well, I want to feel something when I kill someone. That's not sick, it's emotionally much more healthy than—"

We were having this charming conversation, pulling up our weapons of choice, cutting across to intersect with Nostromo's path, and still looking for one more beautiful bellyglide, all at the same time. If we'd been thinking, we'd have known that there had to be a flaw, and we were liable to run into it. If we'd been believing in the game, we would not have been scooting along side by side on an icefield. That's nuts. But we were distracted, and it just happened. A crevasse opened; we both fell into it, cursing like mad as the bluewhite gleaming walls flew by. We pulled our ripcords, but the fall did not slow down. Instead, everything went black.

Black fade to gray, gray fade to blue. I sat up. I felt shaken and my head was ringing, but no bad bruises and no breakages. Health okay. Dev was beside me, doing the same check. Our snowboards lay near, looking supremely useless on a green, grassy field of boulders. The sky was more violet than blue, suggesting high altitude. The sun had an orangey tinge, and it felt hot, with the clear heat that you get in summer mountains. I had the feeling we were not in Norway anymore. The mountain peaks all around us, beautiful as any I'd ever seen, seemed far higher than that.

"Where are we?" gasped Dev. He was looking sick; the fall must have knocked more off his health than it had off mine. I thought I'd better pull up the first aid.

"South America," I guessed. "Up in the Andes. Or else a fantasy world."

"How are we going to get back?"

I thought that was a dumb question, and maybe he was stunned: then I realized I could not get at the first aid. I could not get at anything in my cache. I had the clothes I'd been wearing in Norwegian Blue, my knife, my garotte, and my vital signs patch. Nothing else—

"My God! They've wiped us!"

"Rebuild!" cried Dev, in a panic. "Rebuild! Quickly!"

But I couldn't rebuild. I couldn't get to the code. Nor could Dev. The world around us was solid, no glitches; nothing seemed to be wrong, but we were helpless.

We stared at each other, outraged. "This means war," I said, through gritted teeth.

There wasn't a doubt in our minds that the cheats had done this. Nostromo had seen us chasing him, written that crevasse where we were bound to hit it, and wiped us down to zero. We got up and walked around, abandoning our useless boards. Deve threw rocks; I dug my hands into the crispy turf. It felt real the way only the best hub code feels: intense. The whole boulder field seemed to be live, none of it just decor.

"They're here somewhere," I said. "They have to be."

"They don't," said Dev, unhappily. "They could have dumped us here helpless and gone off laughing. Syl, *where are we*? I thought we knew all the hub venues, but I'm sure we've never been here before."

I wished I had the first aid. My brother wasn't looking good. I was afraid he would log out on me, and I knew I'd have to go home with him.

"C'mon, Dev. Get on the program. They lured us into this

mountain world the way they lured us into the white water. Yeah, it's unfamiliar, but we didn't know there was white water in the resort reedbeds until we went through that flaw. These guys are good they've found more secret levels than we have. But we're good too."

Something nagged at me, something bigger than I could believe, but I clung to my common sense. "This is a live area. There's probably stuff to do here, if we knew the game or if we had a guide. But there'll be ways out. We'll find one, figure out how to undo what they did to our cache, and get back on the bad guys' trail."

The orange sun moved towards its setting. We saw some weaselly sort of creatures, only with more legs, that watched us from a distance. We met huge golden-furred spiders, the size of a cat, who were shy but friendly. They'd come up to us and lay a palp—I mean, one of their front feet—on our hands, and look at us with big ruby eyes. They seemed to like being stroked and scratched behind their front eyes. We thought about eating the berries that grew on the crispy turf-stuff. We didn't find a flaw or a way out; we didn't stumble over any puzzles or hidden treasures, though we slapped and poked at hopeful-looking rocks until our hands were sore.

Finally we found the cheats. They were camped in a ravine on what I thought of as the southern end of the boulder field (in relation to that sunset). They had a little dome shelter, a hummocky thing thatched with the lichen—I couldn't see how it was held up. There was a fire in a circle of stones, a bucket on a flat rock by the stream that ran by their hideout. We were sick with envy. We didn't know how much real time had passed—the time counters on our vital signs patches had stopped when we fell in here—but it felt as if we'd been wandering, naked, clueless, unable to touch a line of code, for *hours*.

"Dev," I whispered, "you're going to go down there and tell them your sister is out on the hillside, health gone. Tell them you don't know what to do, because I'm refusing to log out, but I'm going into shock. White flag, surrender. Cry, if you can."

"That won't be hard."

"Okay, you bring one of them, and I'll be waiting in ambush."

"Pick them off one by one," he agreed. "Cool."

He was still looking sick, but he was back in the game. I remembered the flash of an adult face I'd seen, in the reed-beds back at the resort, and I felt unsure. Had that been real or costume? *Usually* adults who play games obsessively are harmless losers, but there are the rare, supergeek predators, and they can use code; they don't have to wait until they can get you alone in the real world—

But we chose our ambush, and I felt better.

"Go on. Bring me back a fine fat cheat to choke."

The sun was darkening to blood color as it hit the horizon, and I could feel the growing chill through my Norwegian Blue snowboarding clothes. I clung to the wire looped over my gloved hands, feeling weirdly that the garrote was part of me, a lifeline to the normal world, and if it vanished I would be trapped—

Dev came back up from the ravine, one of the cheats following close behind. It was the Native American one, now wearing a red-and-black blanket around his shoulders like a cloak. My brother looked very small and defenceless. Sometimes when I get to the point, it's hard to kill, but this time I had no trouble at all. I jumped, my wire snapped around the man's throat—but at the same moment somebody grabbed *me* from behind, by the forearms, and I had to let go or they'd have broken my bones. It was the Nostromo crewman. I screamed and I kicked and I yelled; it was useless. He held me off the ground and shook me like a rag doll, laughing.

They carried us down to their camp, tied us up, and sat looking at us, cross-legged, grinning in triumph. Their eyes glittered. Up close, I knew they *were* adults, and I was scared.

The pirate was a woman. She was about six foot tall. She had black hair that hung in wild locks from under her three-cornered hat, greenish brown eyes with kohl around them, and skin the color of cinnamon. She swept to her feet in one slick movement, grabbed my head, and stuck a slip of paper underneath my tongue.

"They're short of glucose," she announced. "Near to blacking out. What'll we do with them, Mister Parker? Qua'as?"

"I say we smoke a pipe of peace," said the Native American.

He didn't pull the pipe up. He fetched it from his pack, stuffed it from a pouch he wore at his waist, and lit it with a handful of the licheny stuff that he'd dipped in the flame of the brazier. My skin began to creep and my heart began to beat like thunder, and I didn't know why. "Mister Parker," the Nostromo crewman, cut our hands loose. The pipe went around and I drew in the "smoke." The sugar rush almost knocked me sideways, but I managed to keep a straight face.

"Oooh, that was restorative!" gasped the Nostromo crewman.

"Best drug in the universe," chuckled the pirate queen.

"Gonna be our *major* export one day—"

"Moron. The galaxy is full of sugars. My money's on Bach."

The three cheats laughed, high-fived each other and kind of *sparkled*; and I understood why, because I desperately love and depend on glucose too. But the Native American looked at my brother and frowned. Dev was not looking restored.

We finished the pipe and the pirate queen put it aside.

"Now," she said, in a rich, wild, laughing voice. "I'm Bonny." She tossed back the lace and her cuff and tipped a lean brown hand to the man in the red-and-black blanket. "This is Qua'as, the Transformer. He's Canadian, but don't hold that against him, he's pretty cool; and Mister Parker, our engineer, you have met. So, who the devil are you, and why are you messing with us? Do tell."

"Get real," growled Mr. Parker, "if you'll pardon the expression. There are only, what is it? F-fourteen other people that you *could* be, assumin' you are not some kooky software dreamed up by Mission Control. So why the disguises? What the hell are you playing at. What was that with the *garrote*?"

"Did no one ever tell you, little sister," said Qua'as, "that only that which is dearest to your heart survives the drop back into normal space? What does that make you? A low-down disgusting violence perv? Eh? Eh?"

That was when I realized for the first time that I'd kept my weapons, but Dev's AK and ammo had gone when we were wiped to zero. I felt myself blush; I felt that Qua'as was right . . . I was so totally immersed in this game, so believing in it. I had the scariest feeling that I was *losing touch* with my physical self, back at home—

"Let us go!" cried Dev. "We're not afraid of you! We tracked you down! We'll turn you in to the sysop, the moment we log out!"

My brother's voice sounded thin and frail, a ghost's voice. But the cheats were glowing with life and strength and *richness*. They were richer than any game avatar I'd ever heard of. I could *feel* them teeming with complexity, buzzing with layers and layers of detail, deeper than my mind could reach. It was very, very weird—

"Oh no," said Bonny, staring at me, and I stared back at her, helpless, thinking she was looking straight through me, right back through the root server, back to the real world, into my head, or wherever "Sylvie" really lived—

"Oh, *no!*" groaned Qua'as. "You're real children, aren't you?"

"Y-yes?"

Mr. Parker smacked both his hands to his cap and held on, bug-eyed.

"*Oh, man.* We are so busted! GAME OVER!"

"What's wrong?" I quavered. "What is this place, er, game? Have we, did we, er, hack into a research level or something?"

I realized what was going on, with a rush of relief. They were test pilots. Dev and I had copped a sneak preview of a new, hyper-real immersion game in development. That explained the weirdness I had felt, the strange, super-convincing feel of this whole venue. So now our cheats were in trouble because the game was supposed to be dead secret until it was launched—

They looked at each other, tight-lipped.

"We thought you were colleagues of ours," said Qua'as the Transformer.

"Or the mind-police," growled Mr. Parker, with a wry grin. "We can insert ourselves into the hub games; we do it for light relief. We're not supposed to."

"You're test pilots. Game-development test pilots."

"Close," said Bonny, grimly. "But no cigar."

Qua'as heaved a sigh. "This is not a game, little girl. It's a planet. We are neuronauts. You are approximately five hundred sixty light years from home."

My brother cried out, "Mom!" and fell over, legs still tied, curled into a ball.

Cold sweat broke out all over me, all over this body that wasn't real. I couldn't speak. I was too busy fighting, refusing to believe this insane story. I knew there were such people as neuronauts. I knew that they were making experiments in hyperspace: from a lab in Xi'an, in faraway China, and from another lab at a place called Kiowa Taime Springs, in the Black Hills. I'd seen it on the news. That just made me feel worse, like in a nightmare where someone says something you know is true, and the fear ramps up and up, because then you know you're not just lost for a night, the nightmare is *real*—

"I don't believe you."

"You'd better believe us, little girl," said Mr. Parker, dead straight. "Because this is not funny. You are handling this, but your friend isn't—"

"He's my brother."

"Okay, your brother. You have to accept what we're saying, and trust us to get you back, or your brother's going to die. Not die as in wake up at home. Plain dead."

"What are your names?" asked the pirate queen, more gently.

"I'm Sylvia Murphy-Weston, and my brother is Devan Murphy-Weston."

"You have hub access; are those names your hub access IDs?"

"Yes."

I could tell she was wondering how come we had such a

level of access and whose children we were. But Qua'as put his hand on her arm. "That's all we need. Be calm, let's relax. We know the situation now. We're all friends . . . ?"

He raised his eyebrow at me, and I nodded.

"So we'll get onto it, Sylvie, and you and Devan will be fine."

They cut us loose and retired inside their shelter. I got Dev to sit up. I told him we would be all right. Mr. Parker came out again, bringing blankets, sugar water for us in a skin bottle, and a meal of jerky strips.

"Is this the friendly golden spiders?" asked Dev, unhappily.

"No, it's another animal, a kind of small eight-legged sheep."

"Is it *real*?"

"It's analog, if that's what you mean. And so are you. When you dropped into normal space, with us, our support code caused your digital avatars to draw the necessary chemicals out of this planet's information complex and made analog bodies for you. You became material. You can eat, you can die."

"So . . . so I have *two bodies* right now?" said Devan, hesitantly.

"Yeah. It's just about possible, but it's extremely dangerous."

We ate the jerky, and I didn't tell Dev that I suspected the "eight-legged sheep" was a little white lie. It was cold, but not as cold as a night camped out on the high range country, where I have never been in my body, only in an immersion game. We slept for a bit, hugging each other for warmth. Sometime in the middle of the night I woke up, when the pirate queen came out of the shelter and headed off down the ravine. Dev was awake too. We looked at each other and agreed without a word to follow.

Where was she going? To the secret lab? To the door in the air that would lead out of this game, back to the hub, back to normality? She climbed up onto a big fat boulder. We followed her up there, trying to be quiet, and found her lying on her back there, with her hand behind her head and her hat beside her, just gazing at the stars.

I don't know stars, but they looked different. They were very bright.

"Hi," I said.

"Hi," said the pirate queen, smiling at the great jeweled abyss.

"If it's so dangerous to have two bodies," I said. "Where are yours?"

"Ah."

She sat up, and mugged a *you got me* face. "I was afraid you were going to ask me that. We don't have any bodies back home, Sylvie."

"Huh?" said Dev.

"Technically, er, physically, we are dead. And we don't know if we will ever die, which is quite a trip." She looked at me, seriously. "That's the way it has to be. It'll change— we'll find a way around the problem. It's going to be possible for other people to fly to the stars, but so far, only 'nauts who can handle having no body left at home can survive this kind of travel. We're the forerunners."

"Nobody would do that," breathed Dev, after a moment. "Now I *know* you're faking. You're cheating on us, telling us weird lies. This is a game. You're nothing but big *cheats*."

"Yeah?" said the pirate queen. "And what are you?" She was still looking at me, not at Dev, in a way that made my stomach turn over. "You've been messing with us, making the jumps we make, getting in deep, playing with the code as if it's your little Lego set. We thought you were two of our colleagues, psyching us out, because *you were cheating* the same way we can. It's rare. When it combines with someone who . . . well, someone who doesn't have much use for their physical body, that's when you get a neuronaut candidate."

"No," said Dev. "You're in a lab somewhere. Hooked up to life support."

She shook her head, slowly, sad and happy at the same time.

She was like an outlaw angel, breaking all the rules.

* * *

The crew—they were called the Kappa Tau Sigma Second Crew (KTS, for Kiowa Taime Springs)—had turned themselves in, for our sakes. You see, apparently it's okay on the Earth-type planets, where they're finding out what they can do with analog bodies, out there on alien soil, in the real no-kidding spaces between the stars. But it's hard on them (in some weird way), making the straight leaps from normal space to information space—the plane where everything exists in simultanaeity, and a journey of 560 light years is pretty much instantaneous. The 'nauts get burnout, they get tired and irritated, so instead of doing it the hard way, they take short cuts through the human datasphere, the code-rich hub games which are like playtime to them. They're not supposed to do it—it's supposed to be dangerous for our consensus reality or something, but they do. And the scientists *hate* them for it, and call them cheats, just the way we did.

Anyway, we got hauled back. Dev woke up on life support, in the hospital. I woke up in my bed at home. Then it was nightmare fugue for a while. We had the choice between angry, scared, tearful parents and psych tests, science questions, medical procedures, when we were awake, or going to sleep and finding out what our sickeningly ripped-up neuronal mapping wanted to do to us next in the way of vile nightmares. Horrible, awful! When we talked to each other screen to screen, the conversation consisted mostly of me saying *Bad! Bad!* and Dev saying *Bad! Bad!* . . . We couldn't deal with sentences or anything.

But we got better. We came out good as new.

The morning after Dev came home from the hospital, I got into my wheelchair, which *I hate to do*, because it takes all my strength and reminds me that I keep on getting worse. Two years ago I could casually sling myself into the chair; now it's like climbing Mount Everest. I got my head in the support, I dehooked and rehooked all the tubes I needed, which is something else I *hate* to do, and I whizzed myself along to Dev's room. I hardly ever visit my family anymore. I prefer my bed. I used to fight like a tiger to keep myself going. There were years when I insisted on walking in a frame without motor assist, years when I insisted on getting up every day and going around in my chair. Now I love my bed. It's the only territory I'm still defending, the only place I have left to stand. Although, of course, I'm lying down.

My motor nerves are eating themselves. There's no gene therapy that will work for me; there's no cure. It's not fatal. I'm fourteen: I could live for decades . . . treating my brain like a pet animal and trying to ignore the sad sack that used to be my body. My mom and dad still desperately want that to happen. But I had talked to them (I'd recovered from our adventure much faster than my healthy, normal little brother). The Kiowa Taime Springs people had talked to them too. They were coming around.

I looked down at my little brother, my best friend, thinking about the day he came to me and insisted I had to start playing the games again, because he loved me. I thought of all the wonderful times we'd had, exploring and fighting, skimming over the snow, solving mysteries. I thought of paddling the channels in the reedbeds with him, and the way he'd yelled when he was shooting down the white water. I watched him breathe; his eyelashes fluttered on his cheeks. I knew what he was going to say when he woke. He opened his eyes, and blinked, and smiled. "Hi, Sylvie. What an honour!" But his smile faded. We both knew. We knew.

"Take me with you," whispered Dev, reaching out. "Please."

There was nothing I could say. I just sat there, holding his hand.

The Ships Like Clouds, Risen by Their Rain

JASON SANFORD

Jason Sanford (www.jasonsanford.com) currently lives in Columbus, Ohio, with his wife and two sons. He has worked for a publisher, compiling anthologies, and is the founding editor of the literary journal storySouth, *an online little magazine, through which he runs the annual Million Writers Award for best online fiction. His fiction has appeared in* Analog, Interzone, Orson Scott Card's Intergalactic Medicine Show, Tales of the Unanticipated, *and other places. He's also published critical essays and reviews in* The New York Review of Science Fiction, The Pedestal Magazine, *and* The Fix Short Fiction Review. *John Coyne interviews him at www.peacecorpswriters.org.*

"The Ships Like Clouds, Risen by Their Rain" was published in Interzone. *If there is such a thing as new weird SF, this is it. The story gets high marks for originality. It has a kind of anime feeling reminiscent to us of Miyazaki, but it also reminds us of the early fiction of Brian Aldiss. It is very likely informed by the author's knowledge of SF Asia. Some unpleasant effluvia falls from the air when ships pass over, requiring the city to grow constantly upward.*

$\mathbf{M}$ares' tails blew in from the west, clear sign that a big storm was heading our way. As I watched the hundreds of small, wispy ships float silently by on the breeze, I was tempted to keep quiet. After all, I'd warned for years about our town becoming overbuilt, making all of us vulnerable to the flash floods created by big storms. But with memories of the last flood fading, people had ignored me. The mayor even called me a nervous old woman, afraid of my own shadow. It would be just deserts for everyone to be washed away when the big ship's rains hit.

But wishing for revenge is one thing; actually having people hurt over it, quite another. I grabbed my wooden mallet and rang the alarm bell long and hard, taking pride in a moment when my sworn duty actually mattered.

By the time I climbed down from the weather tower, the mayor was waiting impatiently for me. "What is it this time, Tem?" he asked. "Water or shit?"

I smiled in irritation. Despite my continual corrections—the ships dropped a highly refined organic material, not excrement—too many townsfolk called it just that. While they knew how vital the ships were to our world, that didn't stop their agitation when salvation splattered across their houses and streets.

"Water," I said. "But it'll be a big blow, based on the number of mares' tails running from the ship. Maybe as big as that storm fifty years ago." I winced at that memory. My little sister had been killed by those floods, sucked into a vortex which opened right in front of our house.

The mayor glared angrily at the sky. "You sure this isn't another wrong prediction?"

I restrained the urge to throttle this loathsome, worthless man. "I've done my duty and warned the town. It's now up to you."

The mayor cussed, not believing me, but also afraid of what the townsfolk would do if he ignored a valid warning. "People aren't going to like this. The harvest festival started this morning. All the vegetables and fruits are out in the open."

I glanced at the horizon. Already a dark shape—bigger than anything I'd ever seen—grew from the world's curve. "They don't have to like it," I said. "Tell them we have an hour, at most."

The mayor nodded and ran toward the festival, yelling at people to save what they could. Other townsfolk ran to their homes, telling their kids to climb into the highest rooms. Everywhere I looked, people were wide-eyed and scared, rushing about as if the world was about to end.

And perhaps it was. After all, a ship of heaven was about to unleash its floods upon our thrown-together land.

Imagine a mudball, packed tight by little kid hands. The hands continually pack mud onto the ball, but the ball never grows larger. Just endless mud, packing round and round, until you wonder where it all goes.

That's our world.

From the weather histories, I know worlds aren't supposed to be like this. Worlds have solid crusts of metal and rock, and molten cores of fire and heat. Worlds also recycle. They create and destroy, grow and decay. The water you drink was excreted by a woman a thousand years before. Her body is the dust from which your food grows. Her bones are the clay on which you build your home.

Not our world.

Like new mud pushing down the old, everything sinks to the middle of our world. There are no rivers, no oceans, nothing but land continually created from our rain of organics and other materials. Our skies are always hazy. Up high, one sees a dappled, silver sheen from the small mackerel ships passing at high altitude. Down low, the speckled dots and bulges of larger ships float by, bringing the biggest extremes of weather. All the ships contribute something to our world. Oxygen and carbon dioxide. Metal hail and organic particles. Water as rain, vapor, or ice. Every day our skies are filled with a thousand ships, each one giving something before leaving again for the greater universe.

The first thing we do upon waking is to sweep our houses of the dust which fell overnight. Eventually, though, as the land builds up around us, sweeping isn't enough. So we build our homes higher and higher. Walls ten meters above the walls your grandparents built. A floor which used to be the roof your ancestors slept under.

Up and up, we're always moving up. But we never go any higher.

By the time we'd salvaged what we could of the harvest festival's food, the ship was almost upon us. The ship was a cumulus, towering four kilometers high and stretching across the visible world. From the number of mares' tails I'd seen earlier, I'd figured a cumulus would be chasing them, but I'd never seen one this big. It moved slowly through the atmosphere, the massive curve and sweep of its bow funneling the air into cloudy turbulence. Dark rains poured from the ship's belly, turning the horizon black except for the occasional burst of lightning.

When I reached home my apprentice, Cres, was already at work, carrying books and weather logs to the top floors. I was glad she'd heard the bell. This morning Cres had headed to the ravines south of town to check on the erosion gauges. Passing rains continually wore new gullies and ravines in our world's loose soil. Unfortunately, loose soils also made being caught in the open during a big storm extremely dangerous—flash floods would literally wash everything away.

"Master Tem," Cres said when she saw me, "I've discovered a new phenomenon. Come and see."

. Cres sounded excited by the coming storm, as I guessed I'd have been when I was fourteen. I tossed the food I'd lugged home in our kitchen, then followed her up the weather tower.

The tower, the tallest structure in town, swayed ominously to the wind. I glanced around the town and saw that almost everyone had finished closing up their homes. The only person still out was Les the tailor, who hastily hammered a support beam against one wall of his house. For the last two years I'd been after Les to fix his house, telling him it would never survive a big storm. I shook my head and looked toward the oncoming ship.

"What did you see?" I yelled at Cres over the building wind.

"The cumulus dropped some kind of lighted sphere."

"Most likely lightning. You aren't old enough to remember, but big ships generate massive charge differentials between themselves and the ground."

Cres rolled her eyes. "I've read about lightning in the histories," she shouted back. "This was different. Pay attention and see."

I resisted the urge to slap her for being cheeky with her master. She acted like I had at that age, totally absorbed in dreams about ships, distant planets, and dimensions beyond belief. Her parents had apprenticed Cres to me because they knew her imagination marked her as someone with the potential for being taken by a passing ship. But I wasn't sure that what saved me—the burden of weather predicting I'd taken on after my sister's death—would also work for her.

I looked back at the cumulus, wondering about both the ship and the people inside. Why did cumulus ships always pursue the much smaller mares' tails? Why did the people inside occasionally pound us with dangerous storms? The histories described the weather patterns on old Earth—the clouds and rains which recycled that world's water—and how early humans believed gods and demons created their planet's storms. Despite my years of study, it pained me to admit that I was little better than those ancient humans. The ships might as well be gods or demons for all I knew about them.

My thoughts were interrupted as a single ball of light fell from the ship. It hurled through the dark skies and exploded into the ground two kilometers from us, sending up a mushroom explosion of dirt.

I grabbed the telescope and tried to make out what the light was, but the rain already splattered around us and the wind swayed the tower too much to focus on the impact site.

"We have to get below," I yelled. "The tower isn't safe in a storm this big."

Cres, though, ignored me as she plotted the impact through the rangefinder. She wrote something down on the rain-splattered weather log and shoved the paper under my nose. "That's the third impact I've seen," she said. "They're all in a straight line."

Before I could ask where the line was leading, another ball of light shot from the ship and hit just outside town. The impacts were walking themselves right toward us. Not needing to see more, I rang the warning bell again—for all the good it would do—then grabbed Cres and pulled her down the ladder. We bolted into the house's safe room, but when I tried to shut the door the wind blew so strong the locking bar wouldn't catch. I yelled for Cres to get under a desk as I tried to force the door shut.

The last thing I remembered was a loud whining, followed by an explosion of dirt and rain which threw me into blackness.

I woke to dried blood caking my face and dried mud stiff on my clothes. I lay on my cot in my bedroom, the sun shining through shattered windows. As I sat up, I saw that my room was a shambles. Even though this was the second story, the flood waters had reached this high. Water and muck coated the floor. As I stood up, I plucked several of my sketches from the mud. One, a detailed look at the high altitude mackerel ships which were hard to see even with the best telescopes, had been a particular favorite of mine. I dropped it back in the mud and walked outside.

In my sixty years of life, I had never seen the town so hard hit. Of the five hundred homes and buildings in town, at least a hundred were damaged. In addition, there were gaps along the streets where houses had once stood. I wasn't surprised to see that Les the tailor's house was gone. His house had needed repairs for so long that everyone knew it wouldn't stand up to a strong blow. I muttered a silent prayer that he'd died quickly, and wasn't lying entombed in some runoff tunnel dozens of meters beneath our feet.

What shocked me most, though, was the number of strong homes that had also disappeared. During big storms, flood waters usually raced straight through our town before washing into the drainage tunnels which continually opened and closed in the loose soil. This time the ripples left in the mud suggested the waters had swirled about in unusual circular patterns.

I discovered why when I walked two blocks south of my house. A number of buildings there were gone, replaced by a large sink hole fifty meters across. Cres and the mayor stood next to the hole with a group of townsfolk. I walked over to join them.

The mayor was thrilled to see me. "Glad to see you up and about," he said, hugging me, an embrace I grimaced through. "I was worried our hero wouldn't get to tell me what the hell happened here."

I nodded, embarrassed at the mayor's calling me a hero. Several other townsfolk also thanked me, grateful for the warning I'd been able to give.

Once Cres had a moment, she filled me in. The explosion that knocked me unconscious came from one of the balls of light, which crashed into town and created the hole before us. Cres assumed the hole had breached some cavern or tunnel under the town because the flood waters had swirled down the hole as if into a drain. The waters had also carried about forty houses away, along with over a hundred people. But as the mayor kept telling me, it would have been far worse without my warning.

"What do you think's down there?" Cres asked, trying to get close to the crumbling edge without falling in. Already the hole was collapsing. Within a few days, nothing would be left in the loose soil but a large depression.

"We'll never know because it's forbidden," I said, eying the mayor, who nodded in agreement as I reminded Cres of the only absolute law on our world. "Anytime people try to dig underground or explore sinkholes like this, ships come and kill them. Come, we need to salvage what we can from our house."

Cres didn't seem convinced by my words, but she followed me back home without argument as she stared with longing at the ships passing in the sky.

The next two months were tough, but the town pulled through. Most of the crops stored at the harvest festival had been destroyed, along with many of the chickens and pigs, and none of us had much food to fill our bellies. But crops grew fast here. They had to—anything which grew too slowly would be buried by the continual rain of organics and other materials. Soon the wheat and rice were ready to harvest, the vegetables were ripe, and the fruit was only weeks from being picked.

As I'd predicted, the sinkhole quickly collapsed under the weight of the loose soil. Several townsfolk petitioned the mayor to allow new houses to be built near there, or at least a memorial park. However, I advised against both options. The ground could still collapse if another storm blew through. Because of my hero status, the mayor actually agreed with me.

In more mundane matters, Cres couldn't keep her head out of the sky. While this was usually a good trait in a weatherman, she blew off all her studies, only doing just enough work to keep me from yelling at her.

So it was that one fine, hazy day, I found her daydreaming in the weather tower instead of recording the passing ships in the log. When she saw me, she jumped off her stool, knocking the log from the railing. I barely caught the book before it fell six stories to the ground below.

"Master Tem, I'm so sorry," she began to stammer.

I waved for her to be quiet. "What deep thoughts are you pondering?" I asked.

Cres looked at me like this was a trick question and she'd be smacked for a wrong answer. "The ships," she said with hesitation.

I nodded. "When I was your age, I spent all my free time watching ships pass in the sky and praying that I was special enough to attract their attention. I didn't care what ship it was. Massive universe jumper. Slim star hopper. Dimension slider. I wanted to leave this mudball of a world and see the universe."

From the way Cres nodded, I knew I spoke for her own feelings.

"There's nothing for us here," she said. "I mean, humans are exploring the universe, all the universes, and we're stuck in a pre-industrial cesspool. It's not right."

I sighed because Cres was saying the very things I'd said at her age. Above us, a large ship, of a style I'd never seen before, puffed lazily across the sky while a gentle drizzle of rain fell from its body. I knew that Cres wouldn't be staying here much longer. She had so much potential. All that had saved me was my sister's death. I'd been so determined that no one else die like my sister that the ships avoided me. Cres, though, wasn't determined to stay. Eventually one of the countless ships passing by would descend and take her, leaving our world for sights I couldn't begin to conceive.

Still, I owed it to Cres's parents to at least try and keep her here.

"Give me a month," I said. "There are things I want to teach you about our world. If after that you still want to leave, I'll give you my blessing."

Cres hugged me and muttered her thanks, no doubt knowing—just as I knew—that nothing I could teach her would keep her here.

Over the next few weeks, Cres and I traveled by horse around the countryside, visiting several towns with decent libraries. I showed her numerous histories of our world, including restricted volumes speculating on how our world stayed the same size despite the constant mass being added, and why everything continually sank toward the world's core. I also showed her ten thousand years' worth of observations about the ships which continually visited our planet and kept us alive with their offerings.

In one library, I pulled out a worn leather tome detailing three ship crashes over the last few millennia. In each case, our people had rescued humans from the downed ships. While strange differences had been noted—alterations to the head, bizarre tints and glows around their bodies—they had been able to speak with us. One account even briefly described the interior of a ship, which had been merely empty space. That account also swore that the crash's two survivors had somehow formed out of the ship's very skin. Unfortunately, all of these accounts were frustratingly vague and sparse. In each case, rescuing ships had quickly arrived and taken away the survivors.

"See," Cres said as we rode back to our town. "They're keeping us in the dark. Anyone who knows anything is removed from our world."

"Only one way to find out," I said, nodding at several large hoppers passing above us dropping large, wet drops of fermented material from their bellies. "Unfortunately, once you go that route you can never come back."

As we rode our horse over the speckled green and brown hills and through the thin, straggly forests, I tried to explain to Cres that we had a duty to each other. No matter how much technology the rest of humanity possessed, we were all human. Unless one worked for each other, there was nothing worth living for. Just as the trees and grass around us only survived by growing to the sky faster than they were buried, so too did we survive because we helped each other.

However, my heart wasn't in my words. I thought of my little sister, Llin, who'd died when she was six. We'd played endless ship games—imagining the worlds we'd visit; searching the sky for the ship we'd eventually travel on. Our mom should have punished us for saying such things, but she'd merely nodded and pointed out her own favorite ships when they passed by.

But Llin died before she could find her ship. We'd been walking home from the park—where we'd spent the morning throwing folded paper ships into the wind—when a massive cumulus passed over the town, sending floods raging through the streets. As the waters tore at our bodies, I'd grabbed Llin's hand and struggled to hold her above the current. She screamed and cried, begged me to hold on, but the flood snatched her away.

My mother had held me all that night, telling me I'd done the best I could and that Llin would still find her ship. But I no longer cared about the ships. If the people who flew the damn things could so easily kill my little sister, I'd never join them.

As if knowing my desire, the ships left me alone.

The next morning, Cres was gone. At first I assumed she'd gone to market, or to check our instruments. But when she missed dinner, then supper, my gut climbed to my throat. I stopped by her parents' house and discreetly inquired about her, but they hadn't seen her. She also hadn't spoken to them in days, but if she was going to try and attract a ship I strongly doubted she'd tell her parents.

When Cres didn't return that night, I knew she was gone. I prayed she'd found a good ship and was enjoying her life.

The next morning I was cooking breakfast when I realized the jar of strawberry preserves was empty. I walked into the root cellar to get a new jar, only to be confronted by loud curses. In the cellar's far corner, I found a large hole in the wooden floor.

"About time you heard me," Cres said from the hole. "I've been yelling since yesterday."

I quickly lowered a rope and Cres climbed out. She then explained that she'd gone into the root cellar for supplies and fell through the floor. Evidently the storm several months ago had washed away a lot of the ground under the house.

I was extremely irritated, imagining the house I'd built upon my mother's house, and her mother's before that, in danger of collapse. Cres, though, was ecstatic. "You don't understand," she said. "The water didn't just wash the ground away. It exposed a number of underground tunnels.

And there's a faint glow coming from somewhere down there."

I started to remind Cres that it was forbidden to explore underground; that if the ships didn't kill us, the mayor definitely would. Tunnels on our loose-soil world were also dangerous because of the potential for the loose soil to collapse. But as I stared into Cres's excited eyes, I realized that if I said no to exploring beneath the house she would probably give up any remaining desire to stay on our world. Once that happened, she would be gone on the first interested ship.

I sighed and grabbed a jar of strawberry preserves. If I was going to risk my neck, it would at least be on a full stomach.

The red glow Cres had seen came from a ship. Gleaming like new and wedged in the old foundations of my house thirty meters below the ground.

The ship appeared to be a dimension slider, although that was merely a name from a book and didn't tell much about what it could actually do. To get to the ship, Cres and I climbed and dug through the ruins of my ancestors' houses. Ancient rooms half filled with dirt; walls ruptured and split by pressure and water. Even though it was nerve-wracking seeing how much of my house's foundation had washed away in the recent flood, it was also fascinating to climb through my family's history. My grandmother had often talked about the bright red kitchen of her childhood and sure enough, the walls of that room two levels down still showed a faint red ocher beneath the dirt and grime. Four levels down, I ran my fingers along a cracked ceramic oven and wondered about the meals my ancestors had cooked here.

But the ship was the centerpiece of the ruins. A perfect sphere ten meters across, with the lowest timbers of my house merging into the ship's skin as if they'd always been one.

"How old is this ship?" Cres asked.

I calculated how many levels of the house reached down

to this point. "Maybe three hundred years. Give or take a generation or two."

Cres shook her head. "That can't be right. The history of the town goes back a thousand years. There's no record of a ship crashing here."

That was indeed a puzzle.

Over the next week we cleared away more dirt and debris around the ship. To make our work easier, I built a simple pulley system to lower ourselves into the hole. We also took care to only work on days when the passing ships indicated good weather, and only after locking the front door against visitors. After all, if the mayor or town constables discovered that we were exploring an underground ship, not even my hero status would save us from a quick drop and a sudden stop.

One strange thing we discovered was that the waters which had surged through my house's foundation appeared to have drained into the ship, with the runoff tunnels radiating out from the ship like spokes on a wheel. Cres and I debated whether the ship had somehow called the water to itself.

When Cres and I weren't clearing around the ship, we attended to our regular duties. We also explored my volumes of weather history.

"The histories are wrong," Cres said one morning when I climbed up the weather tower to check on her. In her lap sat my oldest volume of histories, dating back a millennium to the town's first weatherman. "This volume says your family has been building up this house for nine hundred years. But there's no way the ship has been around that long."

I sighed, knowing Cres was right, but also not having an answer. As we'd cleared away the dirt from the ship, we hadn't found any evidence of older houses under it. The ship appeared to support my entire house. "Maybe my ancestors' houses disappeared into the ship like the water did?"

Cres considered this for a moment, then discounted it with a snort. "That would mean there's a ship supporting every house in town. I find that hard to believe."

While I was glad that Cres had given up thoughts of leaving our world—even if the reason she wanted to stay was putting us at risk of death—I refused to let her disrespect me. I closed the history book and told her to keep an eye out for bad weather.

The next day the weather changed and, much to Cres's irritation, we had no time for the ship. Mares' tails began to blow in from the west, always followed by the cumulus ships which endlessly chased them. While none of these ships were anywhere near as large as the cumulus which damaged our town earlier in the year, they were still big enough to issue warnings. Because of the danger to the town, either Cres or myself stayed in the tower at all times. While Cres hated to be torn from her examinations of the ship—she was frustrated that we still hadn't found a way inside—she understood our duty. In addition, the runoff from the storms now ran through the underground tunnels beneath my house. Being caught down there during a downpour would mean certain death.

A few days into the storm cycle I woke around midnight to wind and rain howling outside my window. I grabbed my robe and ran to the top floor, irritated that I'd slept through the warning bell. I could just make out the glow of a large cumulus above the town as it pelted us with rain. This was the biggest storm to hit town since the blow months ago. I opened the roof hatch and tried to climb the tower, but the wind was too strong. I yelled for Cres to stay where she was, then closed the hatch and waited out the storm.

The cumulus passed in ten minutes. I opened the front door to survey the damage and was almost run over by the mayor.

"What happened to the warning?" he yelled. "I was walking back from the pub and nearly got washed away."

I glanced up at the weather tower, which I could now see was empty. I frowned. "The storm wasn't that bad," I said. "Stop complaining." Before the mayor could protest, I slammed the door in his face and ran to the basement. Below the hole I could hear rushing water. Worse, the pulley's ropes descended into the maelstrom. I'd always detached the rope and pulley when we weren't using it so there'd be no evidence we were going underground. That meant Cres had gone down there before the storm hit.

Unable to do anything until the water drained away, I made a cup of tea and tried to relax. But I couldn't stop thinking of all the potential Cres had. I cried for Cres and for myself, the memory of my sister being washed away mixing with the certainty that Cres was dead.

By morning, the water was gone. I lowered myself on the rope and pulley and lit my light stick. The going was slower than before since the path we'd cleared through the old foundations had been washed away.

When I finally reached the bottom level, I found Cres lying beside the ship, which glowed a darker red than I remembered. To my shock, Cres was alive and breathed in labored gasps, which seemed impossible considering how much water had flowed through here. Once again, the wash patterns indicated the water had rushed into the ship. Cres shouldn't have survived.

But any thoughts on Cres's miraculous survival vanished when I heard footsteps behind me. I turned—fearing that the mayor or constables had caught us—and stared with shock into the face of my six-year-old sister. Llin looked as she had fifty years ago, when that massive cumulus sent floods raging through the town.

As if nothing had changed between us, Llin reached out and held my hand. I tried to jerk away, but she held on tight and wouldn't let go.

"I've missed you, Tem," she said.

I nodded, tears falling from my eyes. I wanted to tell Llin how sorry I was for not holding on to her, but she merely smiled and pulled me over to Cres.

"She's not ready," Llin said, leaning over and smoothing Cres's wet hair. Before I could ask what Llin meant, she stood and walked to the ship. But instead of the ship opening for her, Llin's body stretched across the ship itself. Blood gushed out and merged with the ship's red glow. Her skin and muscles and bones flattened and bent and became the

ship. The last thing to go was her face, which smiled at me
and said "I love you" as her mouth turned into an impossibly
long line before finally disappearing.

Panicked, feeling as if my sister had just died a second
time, I grabbed Cres's arms and pulled her as fast as I could
back up the tunnel.

It took me hours to drag Cres to the top level. I tied the
rope around her shoulders and prepared to use the pulley to
raise her through the hole. But before I could lift Cres I heard
the roar of water rushing through the drainage tunnels. Images of Llin being yanked from my grasp shot through me as
new flood waters grabbed Cres's unconscious body. I tried to
lift Cres, but I couldn't fight the water and also pull on the
rope.

Just as my grip began to slip, I suddenly found myself
being pulled into the air. Someone also pulled Cres's half of
the rope up. I emerged from the hole and collapsed onto the
wooden floor of the root cellar, coughing up water and bile.

Only when I finally stopped gagging did I look into the
angry eyes of the mayor and several burly town constables.

The mayor and constables had come to my house when I
failed to give a warning about a second storm in a row. I expected them to drag Cres and myself immediately to the
town hall, where a drumhead court would sentence us to
death for violating our world's only absolute law. Instead,
the mayor ordered the constables to carry Cres to her bed.
He then summoned a doctor to examine my apprentice.

Once we were alone, the mayor demanded to know what
Cres and I were doing underground.

"The water washed away the foundation and the floor collapsed under Cres," I explained, grateful that Cres was still
unconscious so she couldn't mess up my lie. "I was trying to
save her."

The mayor wasn't a fool. He'd seen the pulley system in
the root cellar and knew that wasn't something I'd thrown
together for a quick rescue. However, instead of punishing
me, he muttered about all the storms hitting the town in recent days and how frightened the townsfolk were. I suddenly

realized at this point he couldn't afford to kill his only weatherman. Instead, he warned me not to miss another storm and left the house with the constables.

I walked to Cres's room, where the doctor was still attending to her. Seeing nothing I could do to help, I climbed up the weather tower. The skies appeared settled—the only ships in sight were the high altitude mackerel ships which usually indicated decent weather. That was good, because the town was showing the damage from days of endless storms. Silt rose a meter high along some houses and buildings, while other houses listed at awkward angles, testimony to how water-logged the ground was becoming.

I looked down the street toward the park, where Llin and I had played that fateful day so long ago. While I knew that wasn't the same ground we'd walked on then—the soil having risen five meters in that last fifty years—I tried not to cry as I remembered yet again the feeling of Llin being yanked from my grasp. I also wondered if I'd hallucinated Llin's appearance down below, or if the ship had really brought her back. Either way, the feeling of her hand in mine refused to leave.

By the time I climbed down from the tower, Cres was awake, screaming about ships and the sky and the far side of the universe. The doctor gave her a shot, which relaxed her. Cres stared at me for a moment with a strange smile on her face, then fell asleep.

The doctor asked what had happened to Cres. I told him the same lie I'd given the mayor, but the doctor didn't buy it. He told me to let him know when she woke, then he packed his medical bag and left. I climbed back up the weather tower and wasn't surprised to see that instead of walking back to his clinic, the doctor went straight to the mayor's office.

I had a bad feeling that the reprieve the mayor had just given Cres and I would only last as long as the town's spell of bad weather.

Fortunately for Cres and I, the weather grew increasingly worse over the next three days as increasing numbers of ships passed over our town. Their shadows darkened the sky for hours at a time, their water flooded our streets, and their organics buried us in a continual orange haze. A few of the ships even passed a dozen meters above my watch tower, so low that I should have seen the people inside. However, through the ships' translucent screens I only saw emptiness. I wondered if the ships were reacting to Cres and I disturbing the underground ship, a thought I didn't dare speak out loud.

However, the mayor obviously believed the bad weather resulted from Cres and I going underground. He stopped by several times a day and grilled me about the weather. He didn't like my evasive answers, but was also unwilling to arrest me.

Whenever there was a break in the ships passing overhead, I climbed down from the tower and checked on Cres. She slept most of the time. When she woke, she sometimes screamed and cried about the ship. Other times she laughed. Nothing I said or did would make her tell me what had happened. After a few minutes awake, she'd simply fall back asleep.

Then came the day two massive ships arrived. The first, a flat ship of a style I'd never before seen, spanned half the horizon. It glowed dark blue and dropped shards of ice and metal across the land, smashing a number of roofs in town. The other large ship was a cumulus, and its storm was as bad as the one which rocked our town a few months back. I banged the warning bell for as long as I dared, then jumped for the safety of my house.

Once the floods subsided, I wasn't surprised to find the mayor and two constables at my door. The mayor demanded to inspect the hole in my root cellar. I argued, telling him it was forbidden, but the mayor simply shoved me out of the way. He and his constables waited for the water in the tunnels to subside, then lowered themselves down the hole. The glow from their light sticks faded as they climbed deeper and deeper, heading straight for the ship.

I said a prayer for my sister, hoping the mayor wouldn't hurt her if she appeared to him. I also prayed for myself and

Cres. I could face execution without fear, but Cres was so young I didn't know how she'd react.

Hours passed as I waited for the mayor to climb back out and arrest me, but he and his men took their time. Finally, as day turned to night, I decided to climb back up the tower. To my surprise, there were so many ships in the sky that their individual glows merged into one rainbowed mass which rippled and swirled like water flowing across the land. I'd never seen anything like this. Unsure what it meant for the weather, I banged the warning bell. Better safe than sorry.

Once I climbed down, I checked on Cres, but her bed was empty. I ran outside and didn't see her, then looked all over the house. Then I heard the pulley in the basement squeaking. By the time I reached the hole, Cres was gone. I grabbed a light stick and lowered myself down, hoping to stop Cres before the mayor saw her.

Underground, though, everything had changed. Where before the first level had been half collapsed and full of sediment, now this old room was as clean and well-lit as I remembered from my childhood. The stove my mother cooked on glowed warmly, and the table where my sister and I had eaten so many meals looked as fresh as yesterday.

Llin sat at the table, happily folding paper ships as if we were both still kids.

This time I hugged her. She smiled and asked me if I wanted to make some paper ships with her, but I said I had to find Cres.

"I know where she is." Llin grabbed my hand and led me to the stairs leading to the next level.

Each level of the house was a step back in time. We walked through a red walled room from my grandmother's childhood. On an even deeper level, the cracked ceramic oven I'd previously seen was now clean and hot with bread baking inside.

I asked Llin how this had happened and she told me the ship remembered the old houses. "I wanted you to be happy," she said, "so I asked the ship to fix everything up."

Eventually, Llin led me to the lowest foundation, where

the ship sat glowing in a dark, red haze. Cres stood before the ship as if in a trance.

"Where are the mayor and the constables?" I asked Llin. She pointed to the ship. At first I thought she meant they were inside, but then I looked closer at the red haze lining the ship and saw blood vessels, and a heart, and skin stretched to the tearing point. I remembered how Llin's body had been torn and flattened and I screamed at Cres to get away from the ship.

But when I tried to grab her, Llin held me back, her grip far stronger than any six-year-old girl's should be. I watched in horror as Cres reached for the ship, her hand stretching out and out until she touched half the ship with impossibly long fingers. She then turned and smiled at me as the rest of her body was pulled in and distorted beyond recognition.

I turned and tried to flee, but Llin kept a firm grip on my hand. "It'll be okay," she said. "You've always wanted to go."

As Llin spoke those words, a loud roar pounded my ears as water rushed down the tunnels. The current pushed me toward the ship, only Llin's grip keeping me from being washed away. As I looked at Llin's face—begging her not to let go—my sister merely smiled. Then, as the water rose over her head, she released my hand and I was washed into the ship.

The stretching didn't hurt. The tearing and rending and twisting of my body into something it was never meant to be was neither pain nor pleasure. I merely became the ship. I was the ship.

I also wasn't alone. Melded into the ship with me were Cres and my little sister, along with the mayor and his men. However, while Cres and Llin hummed with excitement over what was to come, the mayor and his men screamed at me to help them. Not that I actually heard them; instead, their fear and pain screamed directly to my mind. Unable to do anything, and needing to focus on my own situation, I shut them out of my thoughts.

Once my shock at the change ended, I felt around myself.

The flood continued to carry water and nutrients into me, feeding the ship and strengthening all of us. As our energy grew, I felt beyond myself, feeling the ships in the air above the town, which called to us like parents urging scared children to come outside and play. As I reached out, I felt other ships under the ground with us, laying dormant here and there, many tied into the foundations of houses, others simply nestling in the dirt. All of them buzzed with life, but lacked the potential to actually leave.

Not our ship. Cres, Llin and I were ready to go. The ship had been ready for decades, ever since my sister had been washed into it. But she hadn't been strong enough to leave on her own. Her last memories, of fear and hope as I'd tried to save her, had trapped her here. She hadn't known where she wanted to go. Or how to leave.

So with Cres assisting me, we began to raise the ship, floating up on a million drops of thought. The ground around us tumbled and collapsed. What had been my home fell in on itself, tearing itself to shreds and rising in a burst of debris and rain as our ship fell into the sky.

As Cres and my sister learned to control our ship, I watched the town disappear below us. I also felt deep into our world, learning the answer to questions I'd asked ever since my youth. Our world had no core. Instead, it existed as ripples of space-time folded onto themselves, creating the barest film of soap onto which the silt we lived off of continually fell. As the water and organics filtered down, they fed the new ships bubbling up from below, ships needing only someone with potential before they too could take flight. That was why we were forbidden to go underground—doing so could damage the young ships.

As we flew up, I felt the endless ships in the sky greet us. Across the world, ships appeared and disappeared, coming and going to different parts of the universe. And that's when I understood. Our world existed to remind humanity of who we were. Humanity only traveled the universe by first coming here, making sure that a ship's crew always remembered that they were human—no matter what changes they might soon go through. Likewise, when ships returned from elsewhere, they came back here to re-remember who they were. Otherwise, as humans traveled the vast distances and times of the universe, they would die. Without the dreams and hopes and everyday lives of our world's people, all humanity would fall apart.

Some of us still fell apart. I felt the mayor and the two constables, still screaming at the thought of all they could be. They didn't have the potential to survive outside our world. Instead, their bodies, minds, and souls would be torn apart. When our ship one day returned to this world, the dust from their bodies would sprinkle down, helping to feed and create another human who might one day have the potential to understand eternity and survive.

Worse, if they didn't die they'd be so damaged that they could cause great harm to others. The ships which needlessly hurt our world were piloted by damaged people, storming across the world until the other ships stopped them.

I felt Cres and Llin preparing to leave. Both of them focused on a distant galaxy, where new stars and life boiled out of a massive expanse of gas and heat. I felt those distant stars. Imagined the sights and wonders we would see. But even as I imagined us arriving there—and knew that imagining our trip would easily take us there—I heard one final plea from the men trapped with us. I was their last link to sanity. I remembered Llin as she'd held onto my hand. Remembered how I'd sworn never to let someone drown if I could save them.

With the briefest of thought caresses, I said goodbye to Cres and my sister. Cres said she'd take care of Llin. Help her grow into the limitless possibilities which existed before them. I then split myself from the ship, creating a smaller ball of ship which encompassed myself and the screaming men. As we fell toward town, I imagined my old house in all its history and glory, in all it had ever been and could ever be. With an explosion of light and energy, the ship became what I willed it to be.

The mayor and the constables woke in my den, surrounded by my books and furniture and a roaring fire in the ceramic fireplace. The mayor retched upon waking, while the two constables cried and shook. I sat in my new-old favorite chair and sipped a hot cup of tea, trying to overlook the limitations of these men.

Finally, after he'd recovered enough to stand, the mayor ordered the constables to arrest me.

"On what charge?" I asked.

"Violating the ban. You've been underground. In a ship."

I smiled and placed my teacup on the end table. For the briefest of moments, I removed the reality I'd crafted around them. Showed them our world in all its glory. The mayor and the constables fell to the floor, screaming.

"If you will excuse me, I have work to do," I said. "After all, someone has to see to the weather."

Without another word, the mayor and constables scrambled to their feet and ran out the door.

I now know I have the potential to see the universe. I always thought I'd be afraid to give up my life, but that's no longer true.

I still watch the skies. However, instead of predicting the weather, I now simply know it. I caress each ship that passes through our world. I understand the beauties and wonders that ship and people have seen in their travels. In return for this knowledge, I gently remind the ship's people what it means to be human. I speak to them of the most important duty of humanity, which is to care for those around you. I also keep watch over this world's people, seeking out those with the potential to embrace the greater universe and helping them toward that goal.

One day Cres and Llin will return, singing to me of all they've seen. I'll join them on that day and go off to see eternity. Until then, I enjoy the warm water falling from the skies and the dust of other people's dreams. And while I never speak a word of this to anyone, I also know that the ships don't bring the weather to our world.

Instead, we are the weather, and the ships rise off our rain.

The Egg Man

MARY ROSENBLUM

Mary Rosenblum (www.theflyingparty.com/maryrosenblum/) lives in Oregon on two-and-a-half acres that supply all her fruit, all her vegetables, and the wood she uses to heat her house. She published SF stories throughout the early 1990s (her first story was in Asimov's *in 1990), and three SF novels (her first,* The Drylands, *1993, won the Compton Crook Award for Best First Novel in 1994) but moved into the mystery genre (four novels and several stories as Mary Freeman) in the latter half of the decade, and only recently returned to SF. Nevertheless, she has managed to publish more than fifty SF stories to date. The best of her early work is collected in* Synthesis and Other Virtual Realities, *from Arkham House. She's also the Web Editor for Long Ridge Writers Group, as well as an instructor for their by-mail and online students. Her recent SF novel is* Horizons *(2006).*

"The Egg Man" was published in Asimov's. *This is a biotech and global warming story set in a future in which Mexico is in better shape than the U.S. A Mexican man, Zipakna, returns with supplies to a region of the U.S. southwest that has become a no-man's-land to look for his missing ex-wife, a genetic engineer of crops.*

Zipakna halted at midday to let the Dragon power up the batteries. He checked on the chickens clucking contentedly in their travel crates, then went outside to squat in the shade of one fully deployed solar wing in the 43 centigrade heat. Ilena, his sometimes-lover and poker partner, accused him of reverse snobbery, priding himself on being able to survive in the Sonoran heat without air conditioning. Zipakna smiled and tilted his water bottle, savoring the cool, sweet trickle of water across his tongue.

Not true, of course. He held still as the first wild bees found him, buzzed past his face to settle and sip from the sweat-drops beading on his skin. Killers. He held very still, but the caution wasn't really necessary. Thirst was the great gentler here. Every other drive was laid aside in the pursuit of water.

Even love?

He laughed a short note as the killers buzzed and sipped. So Ilena claimed, but she just missed him when she played the tourists without him. It had been mostly tourists from China lately, filling the underwater resorts in the Sea of Cortez. Chinese were rich and tough players and Ilena had been angry at him for leaving. But he always left in spring. She knew that. In front of him, the scarp he had been traversing ended in a bluff, eroded by water that had fallen here eons ago. The plain below spread out in tones of ochre and russet, dotted with dusty clumps of sage and the stark upward thrust of saguaro, lonely sentinels contemplating the desiccated plain of the Sonoran and in the distance, the ruins of a town. Paloma? Zipakna tilted his wrist, called up his position on his link. Yes, that was it. He had wandered a bit farther eastward than he'd thought and had cut through the edge of the Pima preserve. Sure enough, a fine had been levied against his account. He sighed. He serviced the Pima settlement out here and they didn't mind if he trespassed. It merely became a bargaining chip when it came time to talk price. The Pima loved to bargain.

He really should let the nav-link plot his course, but Ilena was right about that, at least. He prided himself on finding his way through the Sonora without it. Zipakna squinted as a flicker of movement caught his eye. A lizard? Maybe. Or one of the tough desert rodents. They didn't need to drink, got their water from seeds and cactus fruit. More adaptable than *Homo sapiens,* he thought, and smiled grimly.

He pulled his binocs from his belt pouch and focused on the movement. The digital lenses seemed to suck him through the air like a thrown spear, gray-ochre blur resolving into stone, mica flash, and yes, the brown and gray shape of a lizard. The creature's head swiveled, throat pulsing, so that it seemed to stare straight into his eyes. Then, in an eyeblink, it vanished. The Dragon chimed its full battery load. Time to go. He stood carefully, a cloud of thirsty killer bees and native wasps buzzing about him, shook free of them and slipped into the coolness of the Dragon's interior. The hens clucked in the rear and the Dragon furled its solar wings and lurched forward, crawling down over the edge of the scarp, down to the plain below and its saguaro sentinels.

His sat-link chimed and his console screen brightened to life. *You are entering unserviced United States territory.* The voice was female and severe. *No support services will be provided from this point on. Your entry visa does not assure assistance in unserviced regions. Please file all complaints with the US Bureau of Land Management. Please consult with your insurance provider before continuing.* Did he detect a note of disapproval in the sat-link voice? Zipakna grinned without humor and guided the Dragon down the steep slope, its belted treads barely marring the dry surface as he navigated around rock and thorny clumps of mesquite. He was a citizen of the Republic of Mexico and the US's sat eyes would certainly track his chip. They just wouldn't send a rescue if he got into trouble.

Such is life, he thought, and swatted an annoyed killer as it struggled against the windshield.

He passed the first of Paloma's plantings an hour later. The glassy black disks of the solar collectors glinted in the sun, powering the drip system that fed the scattered clumps of greenery. Short, thick-stalked sunflowers turned their dark faces to the sun, fringed with orange and scarlet petals. Zipakna frowned thoughtfully and videoed one of the wide blooms as the Dragon crawled past. Sure enough, his screen lit up with a similar blossom crossed with a circle-slash of warning.

An illegal pharm crop. The hairs on the back of his neck prickled. This was new. He almost turned around, but he liked the folk in Paloma. Good people; misfits, not sociopaths. It was an old settlement and one of his favorites. He sighed, because three diabetics lived here and a new bird flu had come over from Asia. It would find its way here eventually, riding the migration routes. He said a prayer to the old gods and his mother's *Santa Maria* for good measure and crawled on into town.

Nobody was out this time of day. Heat waves shimmered above the black solar panels and a lizard whip-flicked beneath the sagging Country Market's porch. He parked the Dragon in the dusty lot at the end of Main Street where a couple of buildings had burned long ago and unfurled the solar wings again. It took a lot of power to keep them from baking here. In the back Ezzie was clucking imperatively. The oldest of the chickens, she always seemed to know when they were stopping at a settlement. That meant fresh greens. "You're a pig," he said, but he chuckled as he made his way to the back to check on his flock.

The twenty hens clucked and scratched in their individual cubicles, excited at the halt. "I'll let you out soon," he promised and measured laying ration into their feeders. Bella had already laid an egg. He reached into her cubicle and cupped it in his hand, pale pink and smooth, still warm and faintly moist from its passage out of her body. Insulin nano-bodies, designed to block the auto-immune response that destroyed the insulin producing Beta cells in diabetics. He labeled Bella's egg and put it into the egg fridge. She was his highest producer. He scooped extra ration into her feeder.

Intruder, his alarm system announced. The heads-up display above the front console lit up. Zipakna glanced at it, brows furrowed, then smiled. He slipped to the door, touched it open. "You could just knock," he said.

The skinny boy hanging from the front of the Dragon by his fingers as he tried to peer through the windscreen let go, missed his footing and landed on his butt in the dust.

"It's too hot out here," Zipakna said. "Come inside. You can see better."

The boy looked up, his face tawny with Sonoran dust, hazel eyes wide with fear.

Zipakna's heart froze and time seemed to stand still. *She* must have looked like this as a kid, he thought. Probably just like this, considering how skinny and androgynous she had been in her twenties. He shook himself. "It's all right," he said and his voice only quivered a little. "You can come in."

"Ella said you have chickens. She said they lay magic eggs. I've never seen a chicken. But Pierre says there's no magic." The fear had vanished from his eyes, replaced now by bright curiosity.

That, too, was like her. Fear had never had a real hold on her.

How many times had he wished it had?

"I do have chickens. You can see them now." He held the door open. "What's your name?"

"Daren." The boy darted past him, quick as one of the desert's lizards, scrambled into the Dragon.

Her father's name.

Zipakna climbed in after him, feeling old suddenly, dry as this ancient desert. *I can't have kids*, she had said, so earnest. *How could I take a child into the uncontrolled areas?*

How could I leave one behind? Maybe later. After I'm done out there.

"It's freezing in here." Daren stared around at the control bank under the wide windscreen, his bare arms and legs, skin clay-brown from the sun, ridged with goosebumps.

So much bare skin scared Zipakna. Average age for onset of melanoma without regular boosters was twenty-five. "Want something to drink? You can go look at the chickens. They're in the back."

"Water?" The boy gave him a bright, hopeful look. "Ella has a chicken. She lets me take care of it." He disappeared into the chicken space.

Zipakna opened the egg fridge. Bianca laid steadily even though she didn't have the peak capacity that some of the others did. So he had a good stock of her eggs. The boy was murmuring to the hens who were clucking greetings at him. "You can take one out," Zipakna called back to him. "They like to be held." He opened a packet of freeze-dried chocolate soy milk, reconstituted it, and whipped one of Bianca's eggs into it, so that it frothed tawny and rich. The gods knew if the boy had ever received any immunizations at all. Bianca provided the basic panel of nanobodies against most of the common pathogens and cancers. Including melanoma.

In the chicken room, Daren had taken Bella out of her cage, held her cradled in his arms. The speckled black and white hen clucked contentedly, occasionally pecking Daren's chin lightly. "She likes to be petted," Zipakna said. "If you rub her comb she'll sing to you. I made you a milkshake."

The boy's smile blossomed as Bella gave out with the almost-melodic squawks and creaks that signified her pleasure. "What's a milkshake?" Still smiling, he returned the hen to her cage and eyed the glass.

"Soymilk and chocolate and sugar." He handed it to Daren, found himself holding his breath as the boy tasted it and considered.

"Pretty sweet." He drank some. "I like it anyway."

To Zipakna's relief he drank it all and licked foam from his lip.

"So when did you move here?" Zipakna took the empty glass, rinsed it at the sink.

"Wow, you use water to clean dishes?" The boy's eyes had widened. "We came here last planting time. Pierre brought those seeds." He pointed in the general direction of the sunflower fields.

Zipakna's heart sank. "You and your parents?" He made his voice light.

Daren didn't answer for a moment. "Pierre. My father." He looked back to the chicken room. "If they're not magic, why do you give them water? Ella's chicken warns her about snakes, but you don't have to worry about snakes in here. What good are they?"

The cold logic of the Dry, out here beyond the security net of civilized space. "Their eggs keep you healthy." He watched the boy consider that. "You know Ella, right?" He waited for the boy's nod. "She has a disease that would kill her if she didn't eat an egg from that chicken you were holding every year."

Daren frowned, clearly doubting that. "You mean like a snake egg? They're good, but Ella's chicken doesn't lay eggs. And snake eggs don't make you get better when you're sick."

"They don't. And Ella's chicken is a banty rooster. He doesn't lay eggs." Zipakna looked up as a figure moved on the heads-up. "Bella is special and so are her eggs." He opened the door. "Hello, Ella, what are you doing out here in the heat?"

"I figured he'd be out here bothering you." Ella hoisted herself up the Dragon's steps, her weathered, sun-dried face the color of real leather, her loose sun-shirt falling back from the stringy muscles of her arms as she reached up to kiss Zipakna on the cheek. "You behavin' yourself, boy? I'll switch you if you aren't."

"I'm being good." Daren grinned. "Ask him."

"He is." Zipakna eyed her face and briefly exposed arms, looking for any sign of melanoma. Even with the eggs, you could still get it out here with no UV protection. "So, Ella, you got some new additions to town, eh? New crops, too, I see." He watched her look away, saw her face tighten.

"Now don't you start." She stared at the south viewscreen filled with the bright heads of sunflowers. "Prices on everything we have to buy keep going up. And the Pima are tight, you know that. Plain sunflower oil don't bring much."

"So now you got something that can get you raided. By the government or someone worse."

"You're the one comes out here from the city where you got water and power, go hiking around in the dust with enough stuff to keep raiders fat and happy for a year." Ella's leathery face creased into a smile. "You preachin' risk at me, Zip?"

"Ah, but we know I'm crazy, eh?" He returned her smile, but shook his head. "I hope you're still here, next trip. How're your sugar levels? You been checking?"

"If we ain't we ain't." She lifted one bony shoulder in a shrug. "They're holding. They always do."

"The eggs do make you well?" Daren looked at Ella.

"Yeah, they do." Ella cocked her head at him. "There's magic, even if Pierre don't believe it."

"Do you really come from a city?" Daren was looking up at Zipakna now. "With a dome and water in the taps and everything?"

"Well, I come from Oaxaca, which doesn't have a dome. I spend most of my time in La Paz. It's on the Baja peninsula, if you know where that is."

"I do." He grinned. "Ella's been schooling me. I know where Oaxaca is, too. You're Mexican, right?" He tilted his head. "How come you come up here with your eggs?"

Ella was watching him, her dark eyes sharp with surmise. Nobody had ever asked him that question openly before. It wasn't the kind of question you asked, out here. Not out loud. He looked down into Daren's hazel eyes, into *her* eyes. "Because nobody else does."

Daren's eyes darkened and he looked down at the floor, frowning slightly.

"Sit down, Ella, let me get you your egg. Long as you're here." Zipakna turned quickly to the kitchen wall and filled glasses with water. While they drank, he got Bella's fresh egg from the egg fridge and cracked it into a glass, blending it with the raspberry concentrate that Ella favored and a bit of soy milk.

"That's a milkshake," Daren announced as Zipakna handed Ella the glass. "He made me one, too." He looked up at Zipakna. "I'm not sick."

"He didn't think you were." Ella lifted her glass in a salute. "Because nobody else does." Drank it down. "You gonna come eat with us tonight?" Usually the invitation came with a grin that revealed the gap in her upper front teeth, and a threat about her latest pequin salsa. Today her smile was cautious. Wary. "Daren?" She nodded at the boy. "You go help Maria with the food. You know it's your turn today."

"Aw." He scuffed his bare feet, but headed for the door. "Can I come pet the chickens again?" He looked back hopefully from the door, grinned at Zipakna's nod, and slipped out, letting in a breath of oven-air.

"Ah, Ella." Zipakna sighed and reached into the upper cupboard. "Why did you plant those damn sunflowers?" He pulled out the bottle of aged mescal tucked away behind the freeze-dried staples. He filled a small, thick glass and set it down on the table in front of Ella beside her refilled water glass. "This can be the end of the settlement. You know that."

"The end can come in many ways." She picked up the glass, held it up to the light. "Perhaps fast is better than slow, eh?" She sipped the liquor, closed her eyes and sighed. "Luna and her husband tried for amnesty, applied to get a citizen-visa at the border. They've canceled the amnesty. You live outside the serviced areas, I guess you get to stay out here. I guess the US economy faltered again. No more new citizens from Outside. And you know Mexico's policy about US immigration." She shrugged. "I'm surprised they even let you come up here."

"Oh, my government doesn't mind traffic in this direction. It likes to rub the US's nose in the fact that we send aid to its own citizens," he said lightly. Yeah, the border was closed tight to immigration from the north right now, because the US was being sticky about tariffs. "I can't believe they've made the Interior Boundaries airtight." That was what *she* had been afraid of, all those years ago.

"I guess they have to keep cutting and cutting." Ella drained the glass, probing for the last drops of amber liquor with her tongue. "No, one is enough." She shook her head as he turned to the cupboard. "The folks that live nice want to keep it that way, so you got to cut somewhere. We all know the US is slowly eroding away. It's not a superpower anymore. They just pretend." She looked up at Zipakna, her eyes like flakes of obsidian set into the nested wrinkles of her sundried face. "What is your interest in the boy, Zip? He's too young."

He turned away from those obsidian-flake eyes. "You misunderstand."

She waited, didn't say anything.

"Once upon a time there was a woman." He stared at the sun-baked emptiness of the main street on the vid screen. A tumbleweed skeleton turned slowly, fitfully across dust and cracked asphalt. "She had a promising career in academics, but she preferred field work."

"Field work?"

"She was a botanist. She created some drought-tolerant GMOs and started field testing them. They were designed for the drip irrigation ag areas, but she decided to test them . . . out here. She . . . got caught up in it . . . establishing adaptive GMOs out here to create sustainable harvests. She . . . gave up an academic career. Put everything into this project. Got some funding for it."

Ella sat without speaking as the silence stretched between them. "What happened to her?" She asked it, finally.

"I don't know." The tumbleweed had run up against the pole of a rusted and dented *No Parking* sign and quivered in the hot wind. "I . . . lost contact with her."

Ella nodded, her face creased into thoughtful folds. "I see."

No, you don't, he thought.

"How long ago?"

"Fifteen years."

"So he's not your son."

He flinched even though he'd known the question was coming. "No." He was surprised at how hard it was to speak that word.

Ella levered herself to her feet, leaning hard on the table. Pain in her hip. The osteo-sarcoma antibodies his chickens produced weren't specific to her problem. A personally tailored anti-cancer panel might cure her, but that cost money. A lot of money. He wasn't a doctor, but he'd seen enough osteo out here to measure her progress. It was the water, he guessed. "I brought you a present." He reached up into the cupboard again, brought out a flat plastic bottle of mescal with the Mexico state seal on the cap. Old stuff. Very old.

She took it, her expression enigmatic, tilted it, her eyes on the slosh of pale golden liquor. Then she let her breath out in a slow sigh and tucked the bottle carefully beneath her loose shirt. "Thank you." Her obsidian eyes gave nothing away.

He caught a glimpse of rib bones, faint bruising, and dried, shrunken flesh, revised his estimate. "You're welcome."

"I think you need to leave here." She looked past him. "We maybe need to live without your eggs. I'd just go right now."

He didn't answer for a moment. Listened to the chuckle of the hens. "Can I come to dinner tonight?"

"That's right. You're crazy. We both know that." She sighed.

He held the door for her as she lowered herself stiffly and cautiously into the oven heat of the fading day.

She was right, he thought as he watched her limp through the heat shimmer, back to the main building. She was definitely right.

He took his time with the chickens, letting them out of their cages to scratch on the grass carpet and peck at the vitamin crumbles he scattered for them. While he was parked here, they could roam loose in the back of the Dragon. He kept the door leading back to their section locked and all his hens were good about laying in their own cages, although at this point, he could tell who had laid which egg by sight. By the time he left the Dragon, the sun was completely down and the first pale stars winked in the royal blue of the darkening sky. No moon tonight. The wind had died and he smelled dust and a whiff of roasting meat as his boots grated on the dusty asphalt of the old main street. He touched the small hardness of the stunner in his pocket and climbed the sagging porch of what had once been a store, back when the town had still lived.

They had built a patio of sorts out behind the building, had roofed it from the sun with metal sheeting stripped from other derelict buildings. Long tables and old sofas clustered inside the building, shelter from the sun on the long hot days where residents shelled sunflower seed after harvest or worked on repair jobs or just visited, waiting for the cool of evening. He could see the yellow flicker of flame out back through the old plate-glass windows with their taped cracks.

The moment he entered he felt it—tension like the prickle of static electricity on a dry, windy day. Paloma was easy, friendly. He let his guard down sometimes when he was here, sat around the fire pit out back and shared the mescal he brought, trading swallows with the local stuff, flavored with cactus fruit, that wasn't all that bad, considering.

Tonight, eyes slid his way, slid aside. The hair prickled on the back of his neck, but he made his smile easy. "Hola," he said, and gave them the usual grin and wave. "How you all makin' out?"

"Zip." Ella heaved herself up from one of the sofas, crossed the floor with firm strides, hands out, face turning up to kiss his cheeks. Grim determination folded the skin at the corners of her eyes tight. "Glad you could eat with us. Thanks for that egg today, I feel better already."

Ah, that was the issue? "Got to keep that blood sugar low." He gave her a real hug, because she was so *solid*, was the core of this settlement, whether the others realized it or not.

"Come on." Ella grabbed his arm. "Let's go out back. Rodriguez got an antelope, can you believe it? A young buck, no harm done."

"Meat?" He laughed, made it relaxed and easy, from the belly. "You eat better than I do. It's all vat stuff or too pricey to afford, down south. Good thing maize and beans are in my blood."

"Hey." Daren popped in from the firelit back, his eyes bright in the dim light. "Can my friends come see the chickens?"

My friends. The shy, hopeful pride in those words was so naked that Zipakna almost winced. He could see two or three faces behind Daren. That same tone had tainted his own voice, back when he had been a government scholarship kid from the wilds beyond San Cristobal, one of those who spoke Spanish as a second language. *My friends*, such a precious thing when you did not belong.

"Sure." He gave Daren a "we're buddies" grin and shrug. "Any time. You can show 'em around." Daren's eyes betrayed his struggle to look nonchalant.

A low chuckle circulated through the room, almost too soft to be heard, and Ella touched his arm lightly. Approvingly. Zipakna felt the tension relax a bit as he and Ella made their way through the dusk of the building to the firelit dark out back. One by one the shadowy figures who had stood back, not greeted him, thawed and followed. He answered greetings, pretending he hadn't noticed anything, exchanged the usual pleasantries that concerned weather and world politics, avoided the real issues of life. Like illegal crops. One by one, he identified the faces as the warm red glow of the coals in the firepit lit them. She needed the MS egg from Negro, he needed the anti-malaria from Seca and so did she. Daren had appeared at his side, his posture taut, a mix of proprietary and anxious.

"Meat, what a treat, eh?" Zipakna grinned down at Daren as one of the women laid a charred strip of roasted meat on a plate, dumped a scoop of beans beside it and added a flat disk of tortilla, thick and chewy and gritty from the bicycle-powered stone-mill that the community used to grind maize into masa.

"Hey, you be careful tomorrow." She nodded toward a plastic bucket filled with water, a dipper and cups beside it.

"Don't you let my Jonathan hurt any of those chickens. He's so clumsy."

"I'll show 'em how to be careful." Daren took the piled plate she handed him, practically glowing with pride.

Zipakna smiled at the server. She was another diabetic, like Ella. Sanja. He remembered her name.

"Watch out for the chutney." Sanja grinned and pointed at a table full of condiment dishes. "The sticky red stuff. I told Ella how to make it and she made us all sweat this year with her pequins."

"I like it hot." He smiled for her. "I want to see if it'll make me sweat."

"It will." Daren giggled. "I thought I'd swallowed coals, man." He carried his plate to one of the wooden tables, set it down with a possessive confidence beside Zipakna's.

Usually he sat at a crowded table answering questions, sharing news that hadn't yet filtered out here with the few traders, truckers, or wanderers who risked the unserviced Dry. Not this time. He chewed the charred, overdone meat slowly, aware of the way Daren wolfed his food, how most of the people here ate the same way, always prodded by hunger. That was how they drank, too, urgently, always thirsty.

Not many of them meant to end up out there. He remembered her words, the small twin lines that he called her "thinking dimples" creasing her forehead as she stared into her wine glass. *They had plans, they had a future in mind. It wasn't this one.*

"That isn't really why you come out here, is it? What you said before—in your big truck?"

Zipakna started, realized he was staring into space, a forkful of beans poised in the air. He looked down at Daren, into those clear hazel eyes that squeezed his heart. She had always known when he wasn't telling the truth. "No. It isn't." He set the fork down on his plate. "A friend of mine . . . a long time ago . . . went missing out here. I've . . . sort of hoped to run into her." At least that was how it had started. Now he looked for her ghost. Daren was staring at his neck.

"Where did you get that necklace?"

Zipakna touched the carved jade cylinder on its linen

cord. "I found it diving in an old cenote—that's a kind of well where people threw offerings to the gods centuries ago. You're not supposed to dive there, but I was a kid—sneaking in."

"Are the cenotes around here?" Daren looked doubtful. "I never heard of any wells."

"No, they're way down south. Where I come from."

Daren scraped up the last beans from his plate, wiped it carefully with his tortilla. "Why did your friend come out here?"

"To bring people plants that didn't need much water." Zipakna sighed and eyed the remnants of his dinner. "You want this? I'm not real hungry tonight."

Daren gave him another doubting look, then shrugged and dug into the last of the meat and beans. "She was like Pierre?"

"No!"

The boy flinched and Ziapakna softened his tone. "She created food plants so that you didn't need to grow as much to eat well." And then . . . she had simply gotten too involved. He closed his eyes, remembering that bitter bitter fight. "Is your mother here?" He already knew the answer but Daren's head shake still pierced him. The boy focused on wiping up the last molecule of the searing sauce with a scrap of tortilla, shoulders hunched.

"What are you doing?"

At the angry words, Daren's head shot up and he jerked his hands away from the plate as if it had burned him.

"I was just talking with him, Pierre." He looked up, sandy hair falling back from his face. "He doesn't mind."

"I mind." The tall, skinny man with the dark braid and pale skin frowned down at Daren. "What have I told you about city folk?"

"But . . ." Daren bit off the word, ducked his head. "I'll go clean my plate." He snatched his plate and cup from the table, headed for the deeper shadows along the building.

"You leave him alone." The man stared down at him, his gray eyes flat and cold. "We all know about city folk and their appetites."

Suddenly the congenial chatter that had started up during the meal, ended. Silence hung thick as smoke in the air. "You satisfied my appetite quite well tonight." Zipakna smiled gently. "I haven't had barbecued antelope in a long time."

"You got to wonder." Pierre leaned one hip against the table, crossed his arms. "Why someone gives up the nice air conditioning and swimming pools of the city to come trekking around out here handing out free stuff. Especially when your rig costs a couple of fortunes."

Zipakna sighed, made it audible. From the corner of his eye he noticed Ella, watching him intently, was aware of the hard lump of the stunner in his pocket. "I get this every time I meet folk. We already went through it here, didn't anyone tell you?"

"Yeah, they did." Pierre gave him a mirthless smile. "And you want me to believe that some non-profit in Mexico— Mexico!—cares about us? Not even our own government does that."

"It's all politics." Zipakna shrugged. "Mexico takes quite a bit of civic pleasure in the fact that Mexico has to extend aid to US citizens. If the political situation changes, yeah, the money might dry up. But for now, people contribute and I come out here. So do a few others like me." He looked up, met the man's cold, gray eyes. "Haven't you met an altruist at least once in your life?" he asked softly.

Pierre looked away and his face tightened briefly. "I sure don't believe you're one. You leave my son alone." He turned on his heel and disappeared in the direction Daren had taken.

Zipakna drank his water, skin prickling with the feel of the room. He looked up as Ella marched over, sat down beside him. "We know you're what you say you are." She pitched her voice to reach everyone. "Me, I'm looking forward to my egg in the morning, and I sure thank you for keeping an old woman like me alive. Not many care. He's right about that much." She gave Zipakna a small private wink as she squeezed his shoulder and stood up. "Sanja and I'll be there first thing in the morning, right, Sanja?"

"Yeah." Sanja's voice emerged from shadow, a little too bright. "We sure will."

Zipakna got to his feet and Ella rose with him. "You should all come by in the morning. Got a new virus northwest of here. It's high mortality and it's moving this way. Spread by birds, so it'll get here. I have eggs that will give you immunity." He turned and headed around the side of the building.

A thin scatter of replies drifted after him and he found Ella walking beside him, her hand on his arm. "They change everything," she said softly. "The flowers."

"You know, the sat cams can see them." He kept his voice low as they crunched around the side of the building, heading toward the Dragon. "They measure the light refraction from the leaves and they can tell if they're legit or one of the outlaw strains. That's no accident, Ella. You don't realize how much the government and the drug gangs use the same tools. One or the other will get you." He shook his head. "You better hope it's the government."

"They haven't found us yet."

"The seeds aren't ready to harvest are they?"

"Pierre says we're too isolated."

Zipakna turned on her. "Nowhere is isolated any more. Not on this entire dirt ball. You ever ask Pierre why he showed up here? Why didn't he stay where he was before if he was doing such a good job growing illegal seeds?"

Ella didn't answer and he walked on.

"It's a mistake to let a ghost run your life." Ella's voice came low from the darkness behind him, tinged with sadness.

Zipakna hesitated as the door slid open for him. "Good night, Ella." He climbed into its cool interior, listening to the hens' soft chortle of greeting.

They showed up in the cool of dawn, trickling up to the Dragon in ones and twos to drink the frothy blend of fruit and soymilk he offered and to ask shyly about the news they hadn't asked about last night. A few apologized. Not many.

Neither Daren nor Pierre showed up. Zipakna fed the

hens, collected the day's eggs, and was glad he'd given Daren his immunization egg the day before. By noon he had run out of things to keep him here. He hiked over to the community building in the searing heat of noon, found Ella sewing a shirt in the still heat of the interior, told her good-bye.

"Go with God," she told him and her face was as seamed and dry as the land outside.

This settlement would not be here when he next came this way. The old gods wrote that truth in the dust devils dancing at the edge of the field. He wondered what stolen genes those seeds carried. He looked for Daren and Pierre but didn't see either of them. Tired to the bone, he trudged back to the Dragon in the searing heat. Time to move on. Put kilometers between the Dragon and the dangerous magnet of those ripening seeds.

You have a visitor, the Dragon announced as he approached.

He hadn't locked the door? Zipakna frowned, because he didn't make that kind of mistake. Glad that he was still carrying the stunner, he slipped to the side and opened the door, fingers curled around the smooth shape of the weapon.

"Ella said you were leaving." Daren stood inside, Bella in his arms.

"Yeah, I need to move on." He climbed up, the wash of adrenaline through his bloodstream telling him just how tense it had been here. "I have other settlements to visit."

Daren looked up at him, frowning a little. Then he turned and went back into the chicken room to put Bella back in her traveling coop. He scratched her comb, smiled a little as she chuckled at him, and closed the door. "I think maybe . . . this is yours." He turned and held out a hand.

Zipakna stared down at the carved jade cylinder on his palm. It had been strung on a fine steel chain. She had worn it on a linen cord with coral beads knotted on either side of it. He swallowed. Shook his head. "It's yours." The words came out husky and rough. "She meant you to have it."

"I thought maybe she was the friend you talked about."

Daren closed his fist around the bead. "She said the same thing you did, I remember. She said she came out here because no one else would. Did you give it to her?"

He nodded, squeezing his eyes closed, struggling to swallow the pain that welled up into his throat. "You can come with me," he whispered. "You're her son. Did she tell you she had dual citizenship—for both the US and Mexico? You can get citizenship in Mexico. Your DNA will prove that you're her son."

"I'd have to ask Pierre." Daren looked up at him, his eyes clear, filled with a maturity far greater than his years. "He won't say yes. He doesn't like the cities and he doesn't like Mexico even more."

Zipakna clenched his teeth, holding back the words that he wanted to use to describe Pierre. Lock the door, he thought. Just leave. Make Daren understand as they rolled on to the next settlement. "What happened to her?" he said softly, so softly.

"A border patrol shot her." Daren fixed his eyes on Bella, who was fussing and clucking in her cage. "A chopper. They were just flying over, shooting coyotes. They shot her and me."

She had a citizen chip. If they'd had their scanner on, they would have picked up the signal. He closed his eyes, his head filled with roaring. Yahoos out messing around, who was ever gonna check up? Who cared? When he opened his eyes, Daren was gone, the door whispering closed behind him.

What did any of it matter? He blinked dry eyes and went forward to make sure the thermosolar plant was powered up. It was. He released the brakes and pulled into a tight turn, heading southward out of town on the old, cracked asphalt of the dead road.

He picked up the radio chatter in the afternoon as he fed the hens and let the unfurled panels recharge the storage batteries. He always listened, had paid a lot of personal money for the top decryption chip every trek. He wanted to know who was talking out here and about what.

US border patrol. He listened with half an ear as he scraped droppings from the crate pans and dumped them into the recycler. He knew the acronyms, you mostly got US patrols out here. *Flower-town.* It came over in a sharp, tenor voice. He straightened, chicken shit spilling from the dust-pan in his hand as he listened. Hard.

Paloma. What else could "Flower-town" be out here? They were going to hit it. Zipakna stared down at the scattered gray and white turds on the floor. Stiffly, slowly, he knelt and brushed them into the dust pan. This was the only outcome. He knew it. Ella knew it. They'd made the choice. *Not many of them meant to end up out there.* Her voice murmured in his ear, so damn earnest. *They had plans, they had a future in mind. It wasn't this one.*

"Shut up!" He bolted to his feet, flung the pan at the wall. "Why did you have his kid?" The pan hit the wall and shit scattered everywhere. The hens panicked, squawking and beating at the mesh of their crates. Zipakna dropped to his knees, heels of his hands digging into his eyes until red light webbed his vision.

Flower-town. It came in over the radio, thin and wispy now, like a ghost voice.

Zipakna stumbled to his feet, went forward and furled the solar panels. Powered up and did a tight one-eighty that made the hens squawk all over again.

The sun sank over the rim of the world, streaking the ochre ground with long, dark shadows that pointed like accusing fingers. He saw the smoke in the last glow of the day, mushrooming up in a black flag of doom. He switched the Dragon to infrared navigation, and the black and gray images popped up on the heads-up above the console. He was close. He slowed his speed, wiped sweating palms on his shirt. They'd have a perimeter alarm set and they'd pick him up any minute now. If they could claim he was attacking them, they'd blow him into dust in a heartbeat. He'd run into US government patrols out here before and they didn't like the Mexican presence one bit. But his movements were sat-recorded and recoverable and Mexico would love to accuse the US of firing on one of its charity missions in the world media. So he was safe. If he was careful. He slowed the Dragon even more although he wanted to race. Not that there would be much he could do.

He saw the flames first and the screen darkened as the nightvision program filtered the glare. The community building? More flames sprang to life in the sunflower fields.

Attention Mexican registry vehicle N45YG90. The crudely accented Spanish filled the Dragon. *You are entering an interdicted area. Police action is in progress and no entry is permitted.*

Zipakna activated his automatic reply. "I'm sorry. I will stop here. I have a faulty storage bank and I'm almost out of power. I won't be able to go any farther until I can use my panels in the morning." He sweated in the silence, the hens clucking softly in the rear.

Stay in your vehicle. The voice betrayed no emotion. *Any activity will be viewed as a hostile act. Understand?*

"Of course." Zipakna broke the connection. The air in the Dragon seemed syrupy thick, pressing against his ear drums. They could be scanning him, watching to make sure that he didn't leave the Dragon. All they needed was an excuse. He heard a flurry of sharp reports. Gunshots. He looked up at the screen, saw three quick flashes of light erupt from the building beyond the burning community center. No, they'd be looking there. Not here.

Numbly he stood and pulled his protective vest from its storage cubicle along with a pair of night goggles. He put the Dragon on standby. Just in case. If he didn't reactivate it in forty-eight hours, it would send a mayday back to headquarters. They'd come and collect the hens and the Dragon. He looked once around the small, dimly lit space of the Dragon, said a prayer to the old gods and touched the jade at his throat. Then he touched the door open, letting in a dry breath of desert that smelled of bitter smoke, and slipped out into the darkness.

He crouched, moving with the fits and starts of the desert coyotes, praying again to the old gods that the patrol wasn't really worrying about him. Enough clumps of mesquite sur-

vived here in this long ago wash to give him some visual cover
from anyone looking in his direction and as he remembered,
the wash curved north and east around the far end of the old
town. It would take him close to the outermost buildings.

It seemed to take a hundred years to reach the tumble-
down shack that marked the edge of the town. He slipped
into its deeper shadow. A half moon had risen and his goggles made the landscape stand out in bright black and gray
and white. The gunfire had stopped. He slipped from the
shed to the fallen ruins of an old house, to the back of an
empty storefront across from the community building. It was
fully in flames now and his goggles damped the light as he
peered cautiously from the glassless front window. Figures
moved in the street, dressed in military coveralls. They had
herded a dozen people together at the end of the street and
Zipakna saw the squat, boxy shapes of two big military
choppers beyond them.

They would not have a good future, would become permanent residents of a secure resettlement camp somewhere.
He touched his goggles, his stomach lurching as he zoomed
in on the bedraggled settlers. He recognized Sanja, didn't
see either Ella or Daren, but he couldn't make out too many
faces in the huddle. If the patrol had them, there was nothing he could do. They were searching the buildings on this
side of the street. He saw helmeted figures cross the street,
heading for the building next to his vantage point.

Zipakna slipped out the back door, made his way to the
next building, leaned through the sagging window opening.
"Daren? Ella? It's Zip," he said softly. "Anyone there?" Silence. He didn't dare raise his voice, moved on to the next
building, his skin tight, expecting a shouted command. If
they caught him interfering they'd arrest him. It might be a
long time before Mexico got him freed. His bosses would be
very unhappy with him.

"Ella?" He hurried, scrabbling low through fallen siding,
tangles of old junk. They weren't here. The patrol must have
made a clean sweep. He felt a brief, bitter stab of satisfaction
that they had at least caught Pierre. One would deserve his
fate, anyway.

Time to get back to the Dragon. As he turned, he saw two shadows slip into the building he had just checked—one tall, one child short. Hope leaped in his chest, nearly choking him. He bent low and sprinted, trying to gauge the time . . . how long before the patrol soldiers got to this building? He reached a side window, its frame buckled. As he did, a slight figure scrambled over the broken sill and even in the black and white of nightvision, Zipakna recognized Daren's fair hair.

The old gods had heard him. He grabbed the boy, hand going over his mouth in time to stifle his cry. "It's me. Zip. Be silent," he hissed.

Light flared in the building Daren had just left. Zipakna's goggles filtered it and crouching in the dark, clutching Daren, he saw Pierre stand up straight, hands going into the air. "All right, I give up. You got me." Two uniformed patrol pointed stunners at Pierre.

Daren's whimper was almost but not quite soundless. "Don't move," Zipakna breathed. If they hadn't seen Daren . . .

"You're the one who brought the seeds." The taller of the two lowered his stunner and pulled an automatic from a black holster on his hip. "We got an ID on you."

A gun? Zipakna stared at it as it rose in seeming slow motion, the muzzle tracking upward to Pierre's stunned face. Daren lunged in his grip and he yanked the boy down and back, hurling him to the ground. The stunner seemed to have leaped from his pocket to his hand and the tiny dart hit the man with the gun smack in the center of his chest. A projectile vest didn't stop a stunner charge. The man's arms spasmed outward and the ugly automatic went sailing, clattering to the floor. Pierre dived for the window as the other patrol yanked out his own weapon and pointed it at Zipakna. He fired a second stun charge but as he did, something slammed into his shoulder and threw him backward. Distantly he heard a loud noise, then Daren was trying to drag him to his feet.

"Let's go." Pierre yanked him upright.

"This way." Zipakna pointed to the distant bulk of the Dragon.

They ran. His left side was numb but there was no time to think about that. Daren and Pierre didn't have goggles so they ran behind him. He took them through the mesquite, ignoring the thorn slash, praying that the patrol focused on the building first before they started scanning the desert. His back twitched with the expectation of a bullet.

The Dragon opened to him and he herded them in, gasping for breath now, the numbness draining away, leaving slow, spreading pain in its wake. "In here." He touched the hidden panel and it opened, revealing the coffin-shaped space beneath the floor. The Dragon was defended, but this was always the backup. Not even a scan could pick up someone hidden here. "You'll have to both fit. There's air." They managed it, Pierre clasping Daren close, the boy's face buried against his shoulder. Pierre looked up as the panel slid closed. "Thanks." The panel clicked into place.

Zipakna stripped off his protective vest. Blood soaked his shirt. They were using piercers. That really bothered him, but fortunately the vest had slowed the bullet enough. He slapped a blood-stop patch onto the injury, waves of pain washing through his head, making him dizzy. Did a stim-tab from the med closet and instantly straightened, pain and dizziness blasted away by the drug. Didn't dare hide the bloody shirt, so he pulled a loose woven shirt over his head. *Visitor*, the Dragon announced. *US Security ID verified.*

"Open." Zipakna leaned a hip against the console, aware of the heads-up that still showed the town. The building had collapsed into a pile of glowing embers and dark figures darted through the shadows. "Come in." He said it in English with a careful US accent. "You're really having quite a night over there." He stood back as two uniformed patrol burst into the Dragon while a third watched warily from the doorway. All carrying stunners.

Not guns, so maybe, just maybe, they hadn't been spotted.

"What are you up to?" The patrol in charge, a woman, stared at him coldly through the helmet shield. "Did you leave this vehicle or let anyone in?"

The gods had come through. Maybe. "Goodness, no." He

arched his eyebrows. "I'm not that crazy. I'm still stunned that Paloma went to raising pharm." He didn't have to fake the bitterness. "That's why you're burning the fields, right? They're a good bunch of people. I didn't think they'd ever give in to that."

Maybe she heard the truth in his words, but for whatever reason, the leader relaxed a hair. "Mind if we look around?" It wasn't a question and he shrugged, stifling a wince at the pain that made it through the stimulant buzz.

"Sure. Don't scare the hens, okay?"

The two inside the Dragon searched, quickly and thoroughly. They checked to see if he had been recording video and Zipakna said thanks to the old gods that he hadn't activated it. That would have changed things, he was willing to bet.

"You need help with your battery problem?" The cold faced woman—a lieutenant, he noticed her insignia—asked him.

He shook his head. "I'm getting by fine as long as I don't travel at night. They store enough for life support."

"I'd get out of here as soon as the sun is up." She jerked her head at the other two. "Any time you got illegal flowers you get raiders. You don't want to mess with them."

"Yes, ma'am." He ducked his head. "I sure will do that." He didn't move as they left, waited a half hour longer just to be sure that they didn't pop back in. But they did not. Apparently they believed his story, hadn't seen their wild dash through the mesquite. He set the perimeter alert to maximum and opened the secret panel. Daren scrambled out first, his face pale enough that his freckles stood out like bits of copper on his skin.

Her freckles.

Zipakna sat down fast. When the stim ran out, you crashed hard. The room tilted, steadied.

"That guy shot you." Daren's eyes seemed to be all pupil. "Are you going to die?"

"You got medical stuff?" Pierre's face swam into view. "Tell me quick, okay?"

"The cupboard to the left of the console." The words

came out thick. Daren was staring at his chest. Zipakna looked down. Red was soaking into the ivory weave of the shirt he'd put on. So much for the blood-stop. The bullet must have gone deeper than he thought, or had hit a small artery. Good thing his boarders hadn't stuck around longer.

Pierre had the med kit. Zipakna started to pull the shirt off over his head and the pain hit him like a lightning strike, sheeting his vision with white. He saw the pale green arch of the ceiling, thought *I'm falling . . .*

He woke in his bed, groping drowsily for where he was headed and what he had drunk that made his head hurt this bad. Blinked as a face swam into view. Daren. He pushed himself up to a sitting position, his head splitting.

"You passed out." Daren's eyes were opaque. "Pierre took the bullet out of your shoulder while you were out. You bled a lot but he said you won't die."

"Where's Pierre?" He swung his legs over the side of the narrow bed, fighting dizziness. "How long have I been out?"

"Not very long." Daren backed away. "The chickens are okay. I looked."

"Thanks." Zipakna made it to his feet, steadied himself with a hand on the wall. A quick check of the console said that Pierre hadn't messed with anything. It was light out. Early morning. He set the video to sweep, scanned the landscape. No choppers, no trace of last night's raiders. He watched the images pan across the heads-up; blackened fields, the smoldering pile of embers and twisted plumbing that had been the community center, still wisping smoke. The fire had spread to a couple of derelict buildings to the windward of the old store. Movement snagged his eye. Pierre. Digging. He slapped the control, shut off the vid. Daren was back with the chickens. "Stay here, okay? I'm afraid to leave them alone."

"Okay." Daren's voice came to him, hollow as an empty eggshell.

He stepped out into the oven heat, his head throbbing in time to his footsteps as he crossed the sunbaked ground to the empty bones of Paloma. A red bandanna had snagged on a mesquite branch, flapping in the morning's hot wind. He saw a woman's sandal lying on the dusty asphalt of the main street, a faded red backpack. He picked it up, looked inside. Empty. He dropped it, crossed the street, angling northward to where he had seen Pierre digging.

He had just about finished two graves. A man lay beside one. The blood that soaked his chest had turned dark in the morning heat. Zipakna recognized his grizzled red beard and thinning hair, couldn't remember his name. He didn't eat any of the special eggs, just the ones against whatever new bug was out there. Pierre climbed out of the shallow grave.

"You shouldn't be walking around." He pushed dirty hair out of his eyes.

Without a word, Zipakna moved to the man's ankles. Pierre shrugged, took the man's shoulders. He was stiff, his flesh plastic and too cold, never mind the morning heat. Without a word they lifted and swung together, lowered him into the fresh grave. It probably wouldn't keep the coyotes out, Zipakna thought. But it would slow them down. He straightened, stepped over to the other grave.

Ella. Her face looked sad, eyes closed. He didn't see any blood, wondered if she had simply suffered a heart attack, if she had had enough as everything she had worked to keep intact burned around her. "Did Daren see her die?" He said it softly. Felt rather than saw Pierre's flinch.

"I don't know. I don't think so." He stuck the shovel into the piled rocks and dirt, tossed the first shovel full into the hole.

Zipakna said the right words in rhythm to the grating thrust of the shovel. First the Catholic prayer his mother would have wanted him to say, then the words for the old gods. Then a small, hard prayer for the new gods who had no language except dust and thirst and the ebb and flow of world politics that swept human beings from the chess board of the earth like pawns.

"You could have let them shoot me." Pierre tossed a last shovelful of dirt onto Ella's grave. "Why didn't you?"

Zipakna tilted his gaze to the hard blue sky. "Daren."

Three tiny black specks hung overhead. Vultures. Death called them. "I'll make you a trade. I'll capitalize you to set up as a trader out here. You leave the pharm crops alone. I take Daren with me and get him Mexican citizenship. Give him a future better than yours."

"You can't." Pierre's voice was low and bitter. "I tried. Even though his mother was a US citizen, they're not taking in offspring born out here. Mexico has a fifteen year waiting list for new immigrants." He was staring down at the mounded rock and dust of Ella's grave. "She was so angry when she got pregnant. The implant was faulty, I guess. She meant to go back to the city before he was born but . . . I got hurt. And she stuck around." He was silent for awhile. "Then it was too late, Daren was born and the US had closed the border. We're officially out here because we want to be." His lips twisted.

"Why did you come out here?"

He looked up. Blinked. "My parents lived out here. They were the rugged individual types, I guess." He shrugged. "I went into the city, got a job, and they were still letting people come and go then. I didn't like it, all the people, all the restrictions. So I came back out here." He gave a thin laugh. "I was a trader to start with. I got hit by a bunch of raiders. That's when . . . I got hurt. Badly. I'm sorry." He turned away. "I wish you could get him citizenship. He didn't choose this."

"I can." Zipakna watched Pierre halt without turning. "She . . . was my wife. We married in Oaxaca." The words were so damn hard to say. "That gave her automatic dual citizenship. In Mexico, only the mother's DNA is required as proof of citizenship. We're pragmatists," he said bitterly.

For a time, Pierre said nothing. Finally he turned, his face as empty as the landscape. "You're the one." He looked past Zipakna, toward the Dragon. "I don't like you, you know. But I think . . . you'll be a good father for Daren. Better than I've been." He looked down at the dirty steel of the shovel blade. "It's a deal. A trade. I'll sell you my kid. Because it's a good deal for him." He walked past Zipakna toward the Dragon, tossed the shovel into the narrow strip of shade along one of the remaining buildings. The clang and rattle as it hit sounded loud as mountain thunder in the quiet of the windless heat.

Zipakna followed slowly, his shoulder hurting. Ilena would be pissed, would never believe that Daren wasn't his. His mouth crooked with the irony of that. The old gods twisted time and lives into the intricate knots of the universe and you could meet yourself coming around any corner. As the Dragon's doorway opened with a breath of cool air, he heard Pierre's voice from the chicken room, low and intense against the cluck and chortle of the hens, heard Daren's answer, heard the brightness in it.

Zipakna went forward to the console to ready the Dragon for travel. As soon as they reached the serviced lands again he'd transfer his savings to a cash card for Pierre. Pierre could buy what he needed on the Pima's land. They didn't care if you were a Drylander or not.

Ilena would be doubly pissed. But he was a good poker partner and she wouldn't dump him. And she'd like Daren. Once she got past her jealousy. Ilena had always wanted a kid, just never wanted to take the time to *have* one.

He wondered if she had meant to contact him, tell him about Daren, bring the boy back to Mexico. She would have known, surely, that it would have been all right.

Surely. He sighed and furled the solar wings.

Maybe he would keep coming out here. If Daren wanted to. Maybe her ghost would find them as they traveled through this place she had loved. And then he could ask her.

Glass

DARYL GREGORY

Daryl Gregory (www.darylgregory.com) lives in State College, Pennsylvania, with his wife, Kathy Bieschke, and their two children, and works for a statistical software company. Formerly he has worked as an English teacher, a "telecom trainer," and a technical writer. He is one of the most striking new talents to emerge in fantasy and SF in the last few years. His powerful short fiction, characteristically interested in brain chemistry and psychology, has appeared in previous volumes of Year's Best SF. *His first novel,* Pandemonium, *was published in the fall of 2008, and won the IAFA/Crawford Award for Best First Fantasy Book. A new novel,* The Devil's Alphabet, *publishes in 2009.*

"Glass" appeared in MIT Technology Review. *It is about a drug trial involving psychopaths, and is one of the latest in a group of Gregory stories about brain chemistry and human personality, on the cutting edge of science. It has profound social and philosophical implications.*

It's one of the crybabies," the guard told her. "He's trying to kill one of the psychos."

Dr. Alycia Liddell swore under her breath and grabbed her keys. Only two weeks into the drug trial and the prisoners were changing too fast, starting to crack.

In the hospital wing, a dozen guards crowded around an open cell door. They were strapping on pads, pulling on helmets, slapping billy clubs in their palms. It was standard procedure to go through this ritual in full view of the prisoners; more often than not they decided to walk out before the extraction team went in.

The shift lieutenant waved her to the front of the group. "One of your babies wants to talk to you," he said.

She leaned around the door frame. In the far corner of the cell, wedged between the toilet and the wall, two white men sat on the floor, one behind the other, like bobsledders. Lyle Carpenter crouched behind, his thin arms around Franz Lutwidge's broad chest. Lyle was pale and sweating. In one hand he gripped a screwdriver; the sharpened tip trembled just under Franz's walrus-fat chin.

Franz's eyes were open, but he looked bored, almost sleepy. The front of his orange jumpsuit was stained dark.

Both men saw her. Franz smiled and, without moving, somehow suggested a shrug: *Look at this fine mess.* Lyle, though, almost let the screwdriver fall. "Doc. Thank God you're here." He looked ready to burst into tears.

The doctor stepped back from the door. "Franz is bleeding," she said to the lieutenant.

"Lyle stabbed him in the chest. It looks like it stopped, but if he's bleeding internally we can't wait for the negotiation team. I thought you might want to take a crack at getting Lyle to drop the weapon."

"If I can't?" But she already knew the answer.

"I'll give you three minutes," he said.

They wanted her to put on pads and a helmet, but she refused. Lyle and Franz, like the other 14 men in the GLS-71 trial, were low-risk prisoners: liars, thieves, con men, nonviolent offenders. The review board wouldn't allow her to enroll the more aggressive prisoners. Still, she'd succeeded in finding men with very high scores on Hare's Psychopathy Checklist. They were all-star psychopaths—or sociopaths, to use the term some of her colleagues preferred.

The lieutenant let her take only three steps into the cell before he said, "That's good."

Lyle's eyes were fixed on hers. She smiled, then let concern show in her face. "Why don't you tell me what's going on, Lyle?"

Franz said, "I'm not sure he knows himself."

"Shut up!" Lyle said, and the hand holding the screwdriver shook. Franz lifted his chin slightly.

"Just focus on me," she said to Lyle. "If you put down the weapon, we can talk about what's upsetting you."

"I fucked up, Doctor Liddell. I tried to stop him, but I couldn't—"

"Call me Alycia, Lyle."

"Alycia?" He looked surprised—and touched. She never permitted the prisoners to call her by her first name.

Franz made a derisive noise, but Lyle seemed not to hear him. "I was doing this for you, Alycia. I was just going to kill myself, but then when he told me what he was going to do, I knew I had to take care of him first." He flexed his fingers along the screwdriver's grip. "I stabbed him, going right for the heart. Then he jumped up and I knew I'd missed. I knew I had to hit him again, but I just—froze." He looked at her, his eyes shining with tears. "I couldn't do it! I saw what I'd done and I almost threw up. I felt like I'd stabbed my*self*. What the hell is happening to me?"

That's what we're trying to find out, she thought. GLS-71 was an accidental treatment, a failed post-stroke drug that was intended to speed speech recovery. Instead, it found the clusters of mirror neurons in Broca's area and increased their rate of firing a thousandfold.

Mirror neurons were specialist cells. See someone slapped, and the neurons associated with the face lit up in synchrony. See someone kicked, and the brain reacted as if its own body were under attack. Merely imagining an act, or remembering it, was enough to start a cascade of hormonal and physical responses. Mirror neurons were the first cogs to turn in the complex systems of attachment, longing, remorse. They were the trip wires of empathy.

Except for people like her all-stars. In psychopaths, the mirrors were dark.

"I know you must be confused," she said. "GLS is making you feel things you've never felt before."

"I even feel sorry for this piece of shit, even though I know what he was going to do to you. What he still wants to do." He nodded toward the bed. "This morning, he showed me where he was keeping the knife. He told me exactly how he was going to rape you. He told me the things he was going to force you to do."

Dr. Liddell looked at Franz. The man wasn't smiling—not quite. "You could have called a guard, Lyle. You could have just warned me."

"See, that's the thing—I wanted to hurt him. I thought about what he was going to do to you, and I felt . . . I felt—"

"Luuv," Franz said.

The screwdriver's tip jerked. A thin dark line appeared along Franz's neck like the stroke of a pen.

"You don't know what love is!" Lyle shouted. "He hasn't changed at all, Alycia! Why isn't it working on him?"

"Because," Franz said, his tone condescending and professorial despite the cut and the wavering blade at his throat. "I'm in the control group, Lyle. I didn't receive GLS."

"We all got the drug," Lyle said. Then: "Didn't we?"

Franz rolled his eyes. "Could you please explain to him about placebos, *Alycia*?"

She decided then that she'd like to stab Franz herself. He was correct; he was in the control group. The trial was supposed to be a double-blind, randomized study, with numbered dosages supplied by the pharmaceutical company. But within days she knew which eight men were receiving the real dose. Guards and prisoners alike could sort them as easily as if they were wearing gang colors: the psychos and the crybabies.

"He's playing you, Lyle," she told him. "Pushing your buttons. That's what people like Franz do."

"You think I don't know that? I *invented* that shit. I used to be fucking bulletproof. No one got to me, no one fucked with me. Now, it's like everybody can see right through me."

The lieutenant cleared his throat. Dr. Liddell glanced back. The mass of helmeted men behind him creaked and flexed, a machine ready to be launched.

Franz hadn't missed the exchange. "You're running out of time, Lyle," he said. "Any second now they're going to come in here and crack you like an egg. Then they're going to take you off to solitary, where you won't be seeing your girlfriend anymore."

"What?" Lyle asked.

"You don't think they're going to let you stay in the program after this, do you?"

Lyle looked at her, eyes wide. "Is that true? Does that mean you'll stop giving me GLS?"

They're going to stop giving it to all of you, she thought. After Lyle's breakdown, the whole nationwide trial would be canceled. "Lyle, we're not going to stop the GLS unless you want to."

"Stop it? I never want to be the guy I was before. Nobody felt real to me—everybody was like a cartoon, a nothing on the other side of the TV screen. I could do whatever I wanted with them, and it didn't bother me. I was like him."

Franz started to say something, and Lyle pressed the screwdriver blade into his neck. The two men winced in unison.

"You don't know what he's like," Lyle said. "He's not just some banker who ripped off a couple hundred people. He's a killer."

"What?"

"He shot two teenagers in Kentucky, buried them in the woods. Nobody ever found them. He *brags* about it."

"Stories," Franz said.

Dr. Liddell stepped closer and knelt down next to Franz's outstretched legs. "Lyle, I swear to you, we'll keep you on GLS." She held out a hand. "Give the weapon to me, Lyle. I know you were trying to protect me, but you don't have to be a murderer. You don't have to throw away everything you've gained."

"Oh, please," Franz said.

Lyle squeezed shut his eyes, as if blinded.

"I give you my word," she said, and placed her hand over his. "We won't let the old you come back." After a long moment she felt his grip relax. She slowly pulled the screwdriver from his fist.

Shouts went up behind her, and then she was shoved aside. The extraction team swarmed over the two men.

Three days later she came down to solitary. She brought four guards as escort.

"You know, you're good," Franz said. "I almost believed you myself." He lay on the bed with his jumpsuit half unzipped, revealing the bandages across his chest. The blade had missed the lung and the heart, tearing only muscle. The wound at his neck was covered by two long strips of gauze. He'd be fine in a few weeks. "'I give you my word.' Genius."

"I did what I had to do."

"I've used that one too. But did you have to break his heart? Poor Lyle was in love with you, and you out-and-out lied to him. There was no way you were going to keep him on GLS—you made a petty thief into a suicidal, knife-wielding maniac. How can they put anyone on that stuff now?"

"There'll be another trial," she said. "Smaller dosages, perhaps, over a longer period of time."

"That doesn't help Lyle, now, does it?"

"He's going to live, that's the important thing. I have

plenty of GLS left, so I can bring him down slowly. The suicidal thoughts are already fading. In a few days he won't be bothered by remorse. He'll be back to his old self."

"And then someday you'll get to wring him out again." He shook his head, smiling. "You know, there's a certain coldness about you, Doctor—has anyone ever told you that? Maybe you should try some GLS yourself."

"Tell me about Kentucky," she said.

"Kentucky?" Franz shrugged, smiled. "That was just some bullshit to get Lyle worked up."

She frowned. "I was hoping you'd want to talk about it. Get it off your chest." She turned to one of the guards, and he handed her the nylon bag from her office. "Well, we can talk again in a few days."

He blinked, and then he understood. "You can't do that. I'll call my lawyer."

"I don't think you'll want a lawyer any time soon." She unzipped the bag and lifted out the plastic-sealed vial. "I have a lot of GLS, and only one patient now." The guards rushed forward to pin the man to the bed.

She popped the needle through the top of the vial and drew back the plunger. The syringe filled with clear, gleaming liquid.

"One thing I'm sure of," she said, half to herself. "In a few days, Franz, you'll thank me for this."

Fixing Hanover

JEFF VANDERMEER

Jeff VanderMeer (www.jeffvandermeer.com) lives with his wife and sometime co-editor, Ann (fiction editor of Weird Tales*), in Tallahassee, Florida. For years he was the publisher/editor of Ministry of Whimsy, a small press, and later an imprint, that produced a number of excellent books, and co-editor of Leviathan, an original anthology series of speculative fiction and the fantastic. He has been a leading figure in the field in favor of transgressing genre boundaries for at least a decade. He writes nonfiction for* The Washington Post Book World, *the* B&N Review, *the* Huffington Post, *and many others. His several surreal/ magic realist novels and story collections include* City of Saints & Madmen, Veniss Underground, *and* Shriek: An Afterword. *Recently, he has begun to edit and co-edit more anthologies, including* The New Weird *(Tachyon),* Steampunk *(Tachyon), the annual Best American Fantasy series, and the pirate anthology,* Fast Ships, Black Sails.*

"Fixing Hanover" was published in the original anthology, Extraordinary Engines, *edited by Nick Gevers. We think it transcends the somewhat limiting theme or marketing hook of the anthology (steampunk). It's a first class SF story. A man who can fix anything is shipwrecked in a fishing village on some planet. He wants to stay and works hard to avoid becoming a slave and traded. After a time, a strange broken robot washes up on the beach.*

for Jay Lake

When Shyver can't lift it from the sand, he brings me down from the village. It lies there on the beach, entangled in the seaweed, dull metal scoured by the sea, limpets and barnacles stuck to its torso. It's been lost a long time, just like me. It smells like rust and oil still, but only a tantalizing hint.

"It's good salvage, at least," Shyver says. "Maybe more."

"Or maybe less," I reply. Salvage is the life's blood of the village in the off-season, when the sea's too rough for fishing. But I know from past experience, there's no telling what the salvagers will want and what they discard. They come from deep in the hill country abutting the sea cliffs, their needs only a glimmer in their savage eyes.

To Shyver, maybe the thing he'd found looks like a long box with a smaller box on top. To me, in the burnishing rasp of the afternoon sun, the last of the winter winds lashing against my face, it resembles a man whose limbs have been torn off. A man made of metal. It has lamps for eyes, although I have to squint hard to imagine there ever being an ember, a spark, of understanding. No expression defiles the broad pitted expanse of metal.

As soon as I see it, I call it "Hanover," after a character I had seen in an old movie back when the projector still worked.

"Hanover?" Shyver says with a trace of contempt.

"Hanover never gave away what he thought," I reply, as we drag it up the gravel track toward the village. Sandhaven, they call it, simply, and it's carved into the side of cliffs that are sliding into the sea. I've lived there for almost six years, taking on odd jobs, assisting with salvage. They still know next to nothing about me, not really. They like me not for what I say or who I am, but for what I do: anything mechanical I can fix, or build something new from poor parts. Someone reliable in an isolated place where a faulty water pump can be devastating. That means something real. That means you don't have to explain much.

"Hanover, whoever or whatever it is, has given up on more than thoughts," Shyver says, showing surprising intuition. It means he's already put a face on Hanover, too. "I think it's from the Old Empire. I think it washed up from the Sunken City at the bottom of the sea."

Everyone knows what Shyver thinks, about everything. Brown-haired, green-eyed, gawky, He's lived in Sandhaven his whole life. He's good with a boat, could navigate a cockleshell through a typhoon. He'll never leave the village, but why should he? As far as he knows, everything he needs is here.

Beyond doubt, the remains of Hanover are heavy. I have difficulty keeping my grip on him, despite the rust. By the time we've made it to the courtyard at the center of Sandhaven, Shyver and I are breathing as hard as old men. We drop our burden with a combination of relief and self-conscious theatrics. By now, a crowd has gathered, and not just stray dogs and bored children.

First law of salvage: what is found must be brought before the community. Is it scrap? Should it be discarded? Can it be restored?

John Blake, council leader, stands there, all unkempt black beard, wide shoulders, and watery turquoise eyes, stands there. So does Sarah, who leads the weavers, and the blacksmith Growder, and the ethereal captain of the fishing fleet: Lady Salt as she is called—she of the impossibly pale, soft skin, the blonde hair in a land that only sees the sun five months out of the year. Her eyes, ever-shifting, never settling—one is light blue and one is fierce green, as if to balance the sea between calm and roiling. She has tiny wrinkles in the corners of those eyes, and a wry smile beneath. If I remember little else, fault the eyes. We've been lovers the past three years, and if I ever fully understand her, I wonder if my love for her will vanish like the mist over the water at dawn.

With the fishing boats not launching for another week, a host of broad-faced fisher folk, joined by lesser lights and gossips, has gathered behind us. Even as the light fades: shadows of albatross and gull cutting across the horizon and the roofs of the low houses, huddled and glowing a deep gold-and-orange around the edges, framed by the graying sky.

Blake says, "Where?" He's a man who measures words as if he had only a few given to him by Fate; too generous a syllable from his lips, and he might fall over dead.

"The beach, the cove," Shyver says. Blake always reduces me to a similar terseness.

"What is it?"

This time, Blake looks at me, with a glare. I'm the fixer who solved their well problems the season before, who gets the most value for the village from what's sold to the hill scavengers. But I'm also Lady Salt's lover, who used to be his, and depending on the vagaries of his mood, I suffer more or less for it.

I see no harm in telling the truth as I know it, when I can. So much remains unsaid that extra lies exhaust me.

"It is part of a metal man," I say.

A gasp from the more ignorant among the crowd. My Lady Salt just stares right through me. I know what she's thinking: in scant days she'll be on the open sea. Her vessel is as sleek and quick and buoyant as the water, and she likes to call it *Seeker*, or sometimes *Mist*, or even just *Cleave*. Salvage holds little interest for her.

But I can see the gears turning in Blake's head. He thinks awhile before he says more. Even the blacksmith and the weaver, more for ceremony and obligation than their insight, seem to contemplate the rusted bucket before them.

A refurbished water pump keeps delivering from the aquifers; parts bartered to the hill people mean only milk and smoked meat for half a season. Still, Blake knows that the fishing has been less dependable the past few years, and that if we do not give the hill people something, they will not keep coming back.

"Fix it," he says.

It's not a question, although I try to treat it like one.

Later that night, I am with the Lady Salt, whose whispered name in these moments is Rebecca. "Not a name men would follow," she said to me once. "A land-ish name."

In bed, she's as shifting as the tides, beside me, on top, and beneath. Her mouth is soft but firm, her tongue curling like a question mark across my body. She makes little cries that are so different from the orders she barks out shipboard that she might as well be a different person. We're all different people, depending.

Rebecca can read. She has a few books from the hill people, taught herself with the help of an old man who remembered how. A couple of the books are even from the Empire—the New Empire, not the old. Sometimes I want to think she is not the Lady Salt, but the Lady Flight. That she wants to leave the village. That she seeks so much more. But I look into those eyes in the dimness of half-dawn, so close, so far, and realize she would never tell me, no matter how long I live here. Even in bed, there is a bit of Lady Salt in Rebecca.

When we are finished, lying in each other's arms under the thick covers, her hair against my cheek, Rebecca asks me, "Is that thing from your world? Do you know what it is?"

I have told her a little about my past, where I came from— mostly bed-time stories when she cannot sleep, little fantasies of golden spires and a million thronging people, fables of something so utterly different from the village that it must exist only in dream. *Once upon a time there was a foolish man. Once upon a time there was an Empire.* She tells me she doesn't believe me, and there's freedom in that. It's a strange pillow talk that can be so grim.

I tell her the truth about Hanover: "It's nothing like what I remember." If it came from Empire, it came late, after I was already gone.

"Can you really fix it?" she asks.

I smile. "I can fix anything," and I really believe it. If I want to, I can fix anything. I'm just not sure yet I want Hanover fixed, because I don't know what he is.

But my hands can't lie—they tremble to *have at it*, to explore, impatient for the task even then and there, in bed with Blake's lost love.

I came from the same sea the Lady Salt loves. I came as salvage, and was fixed. Despite careful preparation, my vessel had been damaged first by a storm, and then a reef. Forced to the surface, I managed to escape into a raft just before my creation drowned. It was never meant for life above the waves, just as I was never meant for life below them. I washed up near the village, was found, and eventually accepted into their community; they did not sell me to the hill people.

I never meant to stay. I didn't think I'd fled far enough. Even as I'd put distance between me and Empire, I'd set traps, put up decoys, sent out false rumors. I'd done all I could to escape that former life, and yet some nights, sleepless, restless, it feels as if I am just waiting to be found.

Even failure can be a kind of success, my father always said. But I still don't know if I believe that.

Three days pass, and I'm still fixing Hanover, sometimes with help from Shyver, sometimes not. Shyver doesn't have much else to do until the fishing fleet goes out, but that doesn't mean he has to stay cooped up in a cluttered workshop with me. Not when, conveniently, the blacksmithy is next door, and with it the lovely daughter of Growder, who he adores.

Blake says he comes in to check my progress, but I think he comes to check on me. After the Lady Salt left him, he married another—a weaver—but she died in childbirth a year ago, and took the baby with her. Now Blake sees before him a different past: a life that might have been, with the Lady Salt at his side.

I can still remember the generous Blake, the humorous Blake who would stand on a table with a mug of beer made by the hill people and tell an amusing story about being lost at sea, poking fun at himself. But now, because he still loves her, there is only me to hate. Now there is just the brambly fence of his beard to hide him, and the pressure of his eyes, the pursed, thin lips. *If I were a different man. If I loved the Lady Salt less. If she wanted him.*

But instead it is him and me in the work room, Hanover on the table, surrounded by an autopsy of gears and coils and congealed bits of metal long past their purpose. Hanover up close, over time, smells of sea grasses and brine along with the oil. I still do not *know* him. Or what he does. Or why he is here. I think I recognize some of it as the work of Empire, but I can't be sure. Shyver still thinks Hanover is merely a sculpture from beneath the ocean. But no one makes a sculpture with so many moving parts.

"Make it work," Blake says. "You're the expert. Fix it."

Expert? I'm the only one with any knowledge in this area. For hundreds, maybe thousands, of miles.

"I'm trying," I say. "But then what? We don't know what it does."

This is the central question, perhaps of my life. It is why I go slow with Hanover. My hands already know where most of the parts go. They know most of what is broken, and why.

"Fix it," Blake says, "or at the next council meeting, I will ask that you be sent to live with the hill people for a time."

There's no disguising the self-hatred in his gaze. There's no disguising that he's serious.

"For a time? And what will that prove? Except to show I can live in caves with shepherds?" I almost want an answer.

Blake spits on the wooden floor. "No use to us, why should we feed you? House you . . ."

Even if I leave, she won't go back to you.

"What if I fix it and all it does is blink? Or all it does is shed light, like a whale lamp? Or talk in nonsense rhymes? Or I fix it and it kills us all."

"Don't care," Blake says. "Fix it."

The cliffs around the village are low, like the shoulders of a slouching giant, and caulked with bird shit and white rock,

veined through with dark green bramble. Tough, thick lizards scuttle through the branches. Tiny birds take shelter
there, their dark eyes staring out from shadow. A smell almost like mint struggles through. Below is the cove where
Shyver found Hanover.

Rebecca and I walk there, far enough beyond the village
that we cannot be seen, and we talk. We find the old trails
and follow them, sometimes silly, sometimes serious. We
don't need to be who we are in Sandhaven.

"Blake's getting worse," I tell her. "More paranoid. He's
jealous. He says he'll exile me from the village if I don't fix
Hanover."

"Then fix Hanover," Rebecca says.

We are holding hands. Her palm is warm and sweaty in
mine, but I don't care. Every moment I'm with her feels like
something I didn't earn, wasn't looking for, but don't want to
lose. Still, something in me rebels. It's tiring to keep proving
myself.

"I can do it," I say. "I know I can. But . . ."

"Blake can't exile you without the support of the council,"
Lady Salt says. I know it's her, not Rebecca, because of the
tone, and the way her blue eye flashes when she looks at me.
"But he can make life difficult if you give him cause." A
pause, a tightening of her grip. "He's in mourning. You know
it makes him not himself. But we need him. We need him
back."

A twinge as I wonder how she means that. But it's true:
Blake has led the Sandhaven through good times and bad,
made tough decisions and cared about the village.

Sometimes, though, leadership is not enough. What if
what you really need is the instinct to be fearful? And the
thought as we make our way back to the village: *What if
Blake is right about me?*

So I begin to work on Hanover in earnest. There's a complex
balance to him that I admire. People think engineering is
about practical application of science, and that might be right,
if you're building something. But if you're fixing something,
something you don't fully understand—say, you're fixing a

Hanover—you have no access to a schematic, to a helpful context. Your work instead becomes a kind of detection. You become a kind of detective. You track down clues—cylinders that fit into holes in sheets of steel, that slide into place in grooves, that lead to wires, that lead to understanding.

To do this, I have to stop my ad hoc explorations. Instead, with Shyver's reluctant help, I take Hanover apart systematically. I document where I find each part, and if I think it truly belongs there, or has become dislodged during the trauma that resulted in his "death." I note gaps. I label each part by what I believe it contributed to his overall function. In all things, I remember that Hanover has been made to look like a man, and therefore his innards roughly resemble those of a man in form or function, his makers consciously or subconsciously unable to ignore the implications of that form, that function.

Shyver looks at the parts lying glistening on the table, and says, "They're so different out of him." So different cleaned up, greased with fresh fish oil. Through the window, the sun's light sets them ablaze. Hanover's burnished surface, whorled with a patina of greens, blues, and rust red. The world become radiant.

When we remove the carapace of Hanover's head to reveal a thousand wires, clockwork gears, and strange fluids, even Shyver cannot think of him as a statue anymore.

"What does a machine like this *do*?" Shyver said, who has only rarely seen anything more complex than a hammer or a watch.

I laugh. "It does whatever it wants to do, I imagine."

By the time I am done with Hanover, I have made several leaps of logic. I have made decisions that cannot be explained as rational, but in their rightness set my head afire with the absolute certainty of Creation. The feeling energizes me and horrifies me all at once.

It was long after my country became an Empire that I decided to escape. And still I might have stayed, even knowing what I had done. That is the tragedy of everyday life: when you are in it, you can never see yourself clearly.

Even seven years in, Sandhaven having made the Past the past, I still had nightmares of gleaming rows of airships. I would wake, screaming, from what had once been a blissful dream, and the Lady Salt and Rebecca both would be there to comfort me.

Did I deserve that comfort?

Shyver is there when Hanover comes alive. I've spent a week speculating on ways to bypass what looked like missing parts, missing wires. I've experimented with a hundred different connections. I've even identified Hanover's independent power source and recharged it using a hand-cranked generator.

Lady Salt has gone out with the fishing fleet for the first time and the village is deserted. Even Blake has gone with her, after a quick threat in my direction once again. If the fishing doesn't go well, the evening will not go any better for me.

Shyver says, "Is that a spark?"

A spark?

"Where?"

I have just put Hanover back together again for possibly the twentieth time and planned to take a break, to just sit back and smoke a hand-rolled cigarette, compliments of the enigmatic hill people.

"In Hanover's . . . eyes."

Shyver goes white, backs away from Hanover, as if something monstrous has occurred, even though this is what we wanted.

It brings memories flooding back—of the long-ago day steam had come rushing out of the huge iron bubble and the canvas had swelled, and held, and everything I could have wished for in my old life had been attained. That feeling had become addiction—I wanted to experience it again and again—but now it's bittersweet, something to cling to and cast away.

My assistant then had responded much as Shyver does now: both on some instinctual level knowing that something unnatural has happened.

"Don't be afraid," I say to Shyver, to my assistant.

"I'm not afraid," Shyver says, lying.

"You should be afraid," I say.

Hanover's eyes gain more and more of a glow. A clicking sound comes from him. Click, click, click. A hum. A slightly rumbling cough from deep inside, a hum again. We prop him up so he is no longer on his side. He's warm to the touch.

The head rotates from side to side, more graceful than in my imagination.

A sharp intake of breath from Shyver. "It's alive!"

I laugh then. I laugh and say, "In a way. It's got no arms or legs. It's harmless."

It's harmless.

Neither can it speak—just the click, click, click. But no words.

Assuming it is trying to speak.

John Blake and the Lady Salt come back with the fishing fleet. The voyage seems to have done Blake good. The windswept hair, the salt-stung face—he looks relaxed as they enter my workshop.

As they stare at Hanover, at the light in its eyes, I'm almost jealous. Standing side by side, they almost resemble a King and his Queen, and suddenly I'm acutely aware they were lovers, grew up in the village together. Rebecca's gaze is distant; thinking of Blake or of me or of the sea? They smell of mingled brine and fish and salt, and somehow the scent is like a knife in my heart.

"What does it do?" Blake asks.

Always, the same kinds of questions. Why should everything have to have a function?

"I don't know," I say. "But the hill folk should find it pretty and perplexing, at least."

Shyver, though, gives me away, makes me seem less and less from this place: "He thinks it can talk. We just need to fix it *more*. It might do all kinds of things for us."

"It's fixed," I snap, looking at Shyver as if I don't know him at all. We've drunk together, talked many hours. I've given him advice about the blacksmith's daughter. But now that doesn't matter. He's from here and I'm from *there*. "We should trade it to the hill folk and be done with it."

Click, click, click. Hanover won't stop. And I just want it over with, so I don't slide into the past.

Blake's calm has disappeared. I can tell he thinks I lied to him. "Fix it," he barks. "I mean really fix it. Make it talk."

He turns on his heel and leaves the workshop, Shyver behind him.

Lady Salt approaches, expression unreadable. "Do as he says. Please. The fishing . . . there's little enough out there. We need every advantage now."

Her hand on the side of my face, warm and calloused, before she leaves.

Maybe there's no harm in it. If I just do what they ask, this one last time—the last of many times—it will be over. Life will return to normal. I can stay here. I can still find a kind of peace.

Once, there was a foolish man who saw a child's balloon rising into the sky and thought it could become a kind of airship. No one in his world had ever created such a thing, but he already had ample evidence of his own genius in the things he had built before. Nothing had come close to challenging his engineering skills. No one had ever told him he might have limits. His father, a biology teacher, had taught him to focus on problems and solutions. His mother, a caterer, had shown him the value of attention to detail and hard work.

He took his plans, his ideas, to the government. They listened enough to give him some money, a place to work, and an assistant. All of this despite his youth, because of his brilliance, and in his turn he ignored how they talked about their enemies, the need to thwart external threats.

When this engineer was successful, when the third prototype actually worked, following three years of flaming disaster, he knew he had created something that had never before existed, and his heart nearly burst with pride. His wife had left him because she never saw him except when he needed sleep, the house was a junk yard, and yet he didn't care. He'd done it.

He couldn't know that it wouldn't end there. As far as he was concerned, they could take it apart and let him start on something else, and his life would have been good because he knew when he was happiest.

But the government's military advisors wanted him to perfect the airship. They asked him to solve problems that he hadn't thought about before. How to add weight to the carriage without it serving as undue ballast, so things could be dropped from the airship. How to add "defensive" weapons. How to make them work without igniting the fuel that drove the airship. A series of challenges that appealed to his pride, and maybe, too, he had grown used to the rich life he had now. Caught up in it all, he just kept going, never said no, and focused on the gears, the wires, the air ducts, the myriad tiny details that made him ignore everything else.

This foolish man used his assistants as friends to go drinking with, to sleep with, to be his whole life, creating a kind of cult there in his workshop that had become a gigantic hangar, surrounded by soldiers and barbed wire fence. He'd become a national hero.

But I still remembered how my heart had felt when the prototype had risen into the air, how the tears trickled down my face as around me men and women literally danced with joy. How I was struck by the image of my own success, almost as if I were flying.

The prototype wallowed and snorted in the air like a great golden whale in a harness, wanting to be free: a blazing jewel against the bright blue sky, the dream made real.

I don't know what the Lady Salt would have thought of it. Maybe nothing at all.

One day, Hanover finally speaks. I push a button, clean a gear, move a circular bit into place. It is just me and him. Shyver wanted no part of it.

He says, "Command water the sea was bright with the leavings of the fish that there were now going to be."

Clicks twice, thrice, and continues clicking as he takes

the measure of me with his golden gaze and says, "Engineer Daniker."

The little hairs on my neck rise. I almost lose my balance, all the blood rushing to my head.

"How do you know my name?"

"You are my objective. You are why I was sent."

"Across the ocean? Not likely."

"I had a ship once, arms and legs once, before your traps destroyed me."

I had forgotten the traps I'd set. I'd almost forgotten my true name.

"You will return with me. You will resume your duties."

I laugh bitterly. "They've found no one to replace me?"

Hanover has no answer—just the clicking—but I know the answer. Child prodigy. Unnatural skills. An unswerving ability to focus in on a problem and solve it. Like . . . building airships. I'm still an asset they cannot afford to lose.

"You've no way to take me back. You have no authority here," I say.

Hanover's bright eyes dim, then flare. The clicking intensifies. I wonder now if it is the sound of a weapons system malfunctioning.

"Did you know I was here, in this village?" I ask.

A silence. Then: "Dozens were sent for you—scattered across the world."

"So no one knows."

"I have already sent a signal. They are coming for you."

Horror. Shock. And then anger—indescribable rage, like nothing I've ever experienced.

When they find me with Hanover later, there isn't much left of him. I've smashed his head in and then his body, and tried to grind that down with a pestle. I didn't know where the beacon might be hidden, or if it even mattered, but I had to try.

They think I'm mad—the soft-spoken blacksmith, a livid Blake, even Rebecca. I keep telling them the Empire is coming, that I am the Empire's chief engineer. That I've been in hiding. That they need to leave now—into the hills, into the sea. *Anywhere but here . . .*

But Blake can't see it—he sees only me—and whatever the Lady Salt thinks, she hides it behind a sad smile.

"I said to fix it," Blake roars before he storms out. "Now it's no good for anything!"

Roughly I am taken to the little room that functions as the village jail, with the bars on the window looking out on the sea. As they leave me, I am shouting, "I created their airships! They're coming for me!"

The Lady Salt backs away from the window, heads off to find Blake, without listening.

After dark, Shyver comes by the window, but not to hear me out—just to ask why I did it.

"We could at least have sold it to the hill people," he whispers. He sees only the village, the sea, the blacksmith's daughter. "We put so much work into it."

I have no answer except for a story that he will not believe is true.

Once, there was a country that became an Empire. Its armies flew out from the center and conquered the margins, the barbarians. Everywhere it inflicted itself on the world, people died or came under its control, always under the watchful, floating gaze of the airships. No one had ever seen anything like them before. No one had any defense for them. People wrote poems about them and cursed them and begged for mercy from their attentions.

The chief engineer of this atrocity, the man who had solved the problems, sweated the details, was finally called up by the Emperor of the newly minted Empire fifteen years after he'd seen a golden shape float against a startling blue sky. The Emperor was on the far frontier, some remote place fringed by desert where the people built their homes into the sides of hills and used tubes to spit fire up into the sky.

They took me to His Excellency by airship, of course. For the first time, except for excursions to the capital, I left my little enclave, the country I'd created for myself. From on high, I saw what I had helped create. In the conquered lands, the people looked up at us in fear and hid when and where they could. Some, beyond caring, threw stones up at us: an old woman screaming words I could not hear from that distance, a young man with a bow, the arrows arching below the carriage until the airship commander opened fire, left a red smudge on a dirt road as we glided by from on high.

This vision I had not known existed unfurled like a slow, terrible dream, for we were like languid gods in our progress, the landscape revealing itself to us with a strange finality.

On the fringes, war still was waged, and before we reached the Emperor I saw my creations clustered above hostile armies, raining down *my* bombs onto stick figures who bled, screamed, died, were mutilated, blown apart . . . all as if in a silent film, the explosions deafening us, the rest reduced to distant pantomime narrated by the black humored cheer of our airship's officers.

A child's head resting upon a rock, the body a red shadow. A city reduced to rubble. A man whose limbs had been torn from him. All the same.

By the time I reached the Emperor, received his blessing and his sword, I had nothing to say; he found me more mute than any captive, his instrument once more. And when I returned, when I could barely stand myself anymore, I found a way to escape my cage.

Only to wash up on a beach half a world away.

Out of the surf, out of the sand, dripping and half-dead, I stumble and the Lady Salt and Blake stand there, above me. I look up at them in the half-light of morning, arm raised against the sun, and wonder whether they will welcome me or kill me or just cast me aside.

The Lady Salt looks doubtful and grim, but Blake's broad face breaks into a smile. "Welcome stranger," he says, and extends his hand.

I take it, relieved. In that moment, there's no Hanover, no pain, no sorrow, nothing but the firm grip, the arm pulling me up toward them.

They come at dawn, much faster than I had thought possible: ten airships, golden in the light, the humming thrum of their propellers audible over the crash of the sea. From behind my bars, I watch their deadly, beautiful approach across the slate-gray sky, the deep-blue waves, and it is as if my children are returning to me. If there is no mercy in them, it is because I never thought of mercy when I created the bolt and canvas of them, the fuel and gears of them.

Hours later, I sit in the main cabin of the airship *Forever Triumph*. It has mahogany tables and chairs, crimson cushions. A platter of fruit upon a dais. A telescope on a tripod. A globe of the world. The scent of snuff. All the debris of the real world. We sit on the window seat, the Lady Salt and I. Beyond, the rectangular windows rise and fall just slightly, showing cliffs and hills and sky; I do not look down.

Captain Evans, aping civilized speech, has been talking to us for several minutes. He is fifty and rake-thin and has hooded eyes that make him mournful forever. I don't really know what he's saying; I can't concentrate. I just feel numb, as if I'm not really there.

Blake insisted on fighting what could not be fought. So did most of the others. I watched from behind my bars as first the bombs came and then the troops. I heard Blake die, although I didn't see it. He was cursing and screaming at them; he didn't go easy. Shyver was shot in the leg, dragged himself off moaning. I don't know if he made it.

I forced myself to listen—to all of it.

They had orders to take me alive, and they did. They found the Lady Salt with a gutting knife, but took her too when I told the captain I'd cooperate if they let her live.

Her presence at my side is something unexpected and horrifying. What can she be feeling? Does she think I could have saved Blake but chose not to? Her eyes are dry and she stares straight ahead, at nothing, at no one, while the captain continues with his explanations, his threats, his flattery.

"Rebecca," I say. "Rebecca," I say.

The whispered words of the Lady Salt are everything, all, the chief engineer could have expected: *"Some day I will kill you and escape to the sea."*

I nod wearily and turn my attention back to the captain, try to understand what he is saying.

Below me, the village burns as all villages burn, everywhere, in time.

Message Found in a Gravity Wave

RUDY RUCKER

Rudy Rucker (www.rudyrucker.com) lives in Los Gatos, California, now a retired math and computer science professor, and is writing and publishing an online fiction webzine, Flurb *(www.flurb.net). See his blog (www.rudyrucker. com/blog) for current information. Rucker is one of the original cyberpunks of the Movement, and later the inventor of transrealism, a literary mode, not a movement. He is the author of sixteen novels and several popular science books, most recently* The Lifebox, the Seashell, and the Soul *(2006). His collected stories,* Gnarl!, *was published in 2000, and another collection,* Mad Professor, *in 2007. His most recent pair of novels depicts a near-future Earth in which every object becomes conscious. The first,* Postsingular, *appeared from Tor Books in 2007, and the second,* Hylozoic, *from Tor in 2009. He recently finished his forthcoming memoir,* Nested Scrolls, *and is currently working on* Jim and the Flims, *a novel. In his spare time he creates vivid, surreal paintings.*

"Message Found in a Gravity Wave" appeared in Nature, *which continued its weekly short fiction Futures page through 2008. It is an amusing cosmic brane story about the last universe and the next, featuring an amateur physicist, and told with Rucker's characteristic wit.*

I love to think about infinity and the fourth dimension, so I was happy when some cosmologists began saying that our Universe is a pair of infinite hypersheets, or branes, floating in higher-dimensional space. According to the new cyclic universe theory, most of the time the two branes hang out parallel to each other, but every now and then they splat together and fill all of space with light.

I like the space-filling Big Flash a lot better than the old-timey single-point Big Bang, which is way too Old Testament for me. I may not have gone to college, but I read a lot, and I think for myself.

I see the two branes as mates; our home space is like a nurturing mother, fertilized by vivid encounters with her spouse. When they embrace, energy wells up like water from a spring. It must be wonderful. I've never actually had sex myself.

After each flash, the branes are driven asunder by the hateful forces of dark energy. But eventually the spiteful dissipation ends, and the pair trysts again, cycle after cycle, time without beginning or end.

Cosmologists estimate that the most recent Big Splat was 14 billion years ago, and they suppose the next to be a trillion years away. But I have reason to believe the other brane is going to smack into us very soon—which is why I'm out here in Maw's pasture spelling out my message with rocks as fast as I can lug them.

It's an especially hot day, which is a warning sign in itself.

The approach of the father brane is diddling the fundamental constants of nuclear fusion, and our Sun is burning brighter than ever before. I'm taking apart a whole stone wall to write this message, this very narrative that you read.

I've tried to get out the word via e-mail and my blog, but nobody takes me seriously. I'm not a legitimate scientist. People dismiss me because I don't have all those fancy initials after my name—and maybe because I live with my mother on the family farm.

I'm curious about how the world works, and I'm clever with electronics. I have a satellite broadband link to the web. I read, or at least skim, every single cosmology paper that appears on the arXiv.org site, and that's nigh on 2,000 papers a year, friend.

When I first learned about the cyclic universe, I was especially thrilled to know there are infinite numbers of planets. Not only do we have infinitely many planets in this cycle, there were infinitely many of them in the previous cycle, and will be in the next one, and so on. That really ups the odds that somewhere, somewhen there's an Eden planet with someone like me living there with a pretty wife, and he doesn't have to clean up after any filthy chickens.

Thinking about the Eden world, I began wondering if I might be able to get signals from planets that are fabulously distant in space and time. What if 20 billion years ago, way back in the previous cycle, a planet 20 billion light years away had sent a signal aimed precisely towards my present location?

There is a small problem. Because of that Big Flash 14 billion years ago, we can't hope to receive any coherent radio or TV from more than 14 billion light years away. The energy from the splat would have scrambled any messages. But wait! What about signals in the form of gravitational waves?

I got the idea for my gravity wave detector from a dish of green gelatin salad that Maw had set on the table beside a roast chicken. She was carving up the tough old bird and the green gelatin was shivering, with the little bits of canned fruit jiggling up and down.

Man, it's hot out here hauling rocks beneath our doomed Sun. I'm using five or six stones per letter.

Long story short. I made my gravity wave detector from a bathtub full of green gelatin—my sense was that the particular shade of colour might be important. I scavenged a couple of gyroscopic motion sensors from cameras, sank them into the gelatin, and wired them to a video display. Not that it's all that easy to pick the signal from the fuzz. You might say I use my nervous system as the final processing filter. A mind is a powerful thing.

Just like I expected, I found a message from a planet in the last cycle, from a guy like me, but maybe happier. He was passing on the news that the cycle between splats is only 14 billion years and not any trillion, and the collapse is far more abrupt than anyone realized. Good to know. Just to return the favour, I'm sending word into the next cycle—via gravity waves.

Any massive object gives off gravity waves when you move it—which is why I'm spelling out this message with stones. The rocks broadcast gravity waves as I set them into position and, for that matter, they'll keep on sending out waves for a while—because Earth herself is spinning around, at least until she melts into X-rays and Higgs bosons. Which will be pretty soon now, I reckon.

I feel funny all over, as if my molecules are coming apart. And the Sun—it looks bloated and red, like it's filling up half the sky. The cars on the highway must not be working any more, because people are standing at the edge of the pasture pointing at me.

Pretty soon now, the branes are gonna be getting it on. Time for my last words.

I lived, I was real. And the end is coming sooner than you think.

Mitigation

KARL SCHROEDER &
TOBIAS S. BUCKELL

Karl Schroeder (www.kschroeder.com) lives in Toronto, Ontario, and divides his time between writing fiction and consulting—chiefly in the area of Foresight Studies and technology. He began to publish stories in the 1990s, and he has, since 2000, published six science fiction novels and a collection of earlier stories. His most recent novel is Pirate Sun *(2008), the third adventure set in Virga, a far-future built-world, hard SF environment. Another Virga novel is publishing in 2009. He is on the cutting edge of Hard SF.*

Tobias S. Buckell (www.tobiasbuckell.com) lives in Bluffton, Ohio. His bio says: "Tobias grew up on a boat in Grenada, . . . In 1995 Hurricane Marilyn destroyed the boat he lived on, in St. Thomas. His family moved to Ohio where his stepdad grew up." He has published a number of SF stories, attended Clarion, was a Writers of the Future winner. His first novel, The Crystal Ship, *was published in 2006. He has recently published several novels, including a best-selling* Halo *tie-in.*

"Mitigation" was published in Fast Forward 2, *edited by Lou Anders, a first-rate anthology series that we hope continues. This tale is a post-global-warming, cyberpunk-influenced story about an extinct species DNA heist. The setting gives vivid glimpses of a future in which our planet has become ugly and inhospitable, and we move through it fast, with criminal speed.*

Chauncie St. Christie squinted in the weak 3 a.m. sunlight. *No, two degrees higher.* He adjusted the elevation, stepped back in satisfaction, and pulled on a lime green nylon cord. The mortar burped loudly, and seconds later, a fountain of water shot up ten feet from his target.

His sat phone vibrated on his belt and he half reached for it, causing the gyroscope-stabilized platform to wobble slightly. "Damn it." That must be Maksim on the phone. The damn Croat would be calling about the offer again. Chauncie ignored the reminder and reset the mortar. "How close are they?"

His friend Kulitak stood on the rail of the trawler and scanned the horizon with a set of overpowered binoculars. "Those eco response ships are throwing out oil containment booms. Canuck gunboats're all on the far side of the spill."

"As long as they're busy." Chauncie adjusted the mortar and dropped another shell into it. This shot hit dead-on, and the CarbonJohnny™ blew apart in a cloud of Styrofoam, cheap solar panel fragments, and chicken wire.

Kulitak lowered his binoculars. "Nice one."

"One down, a million to go," muttered Chauncie. The little drift of debris was already sinking, the flotsam joining the ever-present scrim of trash that peppered all ocean surfaces. Hundreds more CarbonJohnnies dotted the sea all the way to the horizon, each one a moronically simple mechanism. A few bottom-of-the-barrel cheap solar panels sent a weak current into a slowly unreeling sheet of chicken wire that hung in the water. This electrolyzed calcium carbonate out of the water. As the chicken wire turned to concrete, sections of it tore off and sank into the depths of the Makarov Basin. These big reels looked a bit like toilet paper and unraveled the same way, a few sheets at a time: hence the name CarbonJohnny. Sequestors International (NASDAQ symbol: SQI) churned them out by the shipload with the noble purpose of sequestering carbon and making a quick buck from the carbon credits.

Chauncie and his friends blew them up and sank them almost as quickly.

"This is lame," Kulitak said. "We're not going to make any money today."

"Let's pack up, find somewhere less involved."

Chauncie grunted irritably; he'd have to pay for an updated satellite mosaic and look for another UN inspection blind spot. Kulitak had picked this field of CarbonJohnnies because overhead, somewhere high in the stratosphere, a pregnant blimp staggered through the pale air dumping sulfur particulates into a too-clean atmosphere to help block the warming sun. But in the process it also helpfully obscured some of the finer details of what Chauncie and Kulitak were up to. Unfortunately, the pesky ecological catastrophe unfolding off the port bow was wreaking havoc with their schedule.

A day earlier, somebody had blown up an automated U.S. Pure Waters, Inc. tug towing a half cubic kilometer of iceberg. Kulitak thought it was the Emerald Institute who'd done it, but they were just one of dozens of ecoterrorist groups who might have been responsible. Everybody was protesting the large-scale "strip mining" of the Arctic's natural habitat, and now and then somebody did something about it.

The berg had turned out to be unstable. As Chauncie'd been motoring out to this spot he'd heard the distant thunder as it flipped over. He hadn't heard the impact of the passing supertanker with its underwater spur three hours later; but he could sure smell it when he woke up. The news said three or four thousand tonnes of oil had leaked out into the water, and the immediate area was turning into a circus of cleanup crews. Media, Greenpeace, oil company ships, UN, government officials—they would all descend soon enough.

"There's money in cleanup," Chauncie commented; he smiled at Kulitak's grimace.

"Money," said Kulitak. "And forms. And treaties you gotta watch out for; and politics like rat traps. Let's find another Johnny." The Inuit radicals who had hired them were dumping their own version of the CarbonJohnny into these waters. Blowing up SQI's Johnnies was not, Chauncie's employer had claimed, actually piracy; it was merely a diversion of the carbon credits that would otherwise have gone to SQI—and at $100 per tonne sequestered, it added up fast.

He shrugged at Kulitak's impatient look, and bent to stow the mortar. Broken Styrofoam, twirling beer cans, and plush toys from a container-ship accident drifted in the trawler's wake; farther out, the Johnnies bobbed in their thousands, a marine forest through which dozens of larger vessels had to pick their way. On the horizon, a converted tanker was spraying a fine mist of iron powder into the air—fertilizing the Arctic Ocean for another carbon sequestration company, just as the blimps overhead were smearing the sky with reflective smog to cut down global warming in another way. Helicopters crammed with biologists and carbon-market auditors zigged and zagged over the waters, and yellow autosubs cruised under them, all measuring the effect.

Mile-long oil supertankers cruised obliviously through it all. Now that the world's trees were worth more as carbon sinks than building material, the plastics industry had taken off. Oil as fuel was on its way out; oil for the housing industry was in high demand.

And in the middle of it all, Chauncie's little trawler. It didn't actually fish. There were fish enough—the effect of pumping iron powder into the ocean was to accelerate the Arctic's already large biodiversity to previously unseen levels. Plankton boomed, and the cycle of life in the deep had exploded. The ocean's fisheries no longer struggled, and boats covered the oceans with nets and still couldn't make a dent. Chauncie's fishing nets were camouflage. Who would notice one more trawler picking its way toward a less-packed quadrant of CarbonJohnnies?

Out in relatively clearer ocean Chauncie sat on the deck as the Inuit crew hustled around, pulling in the purposefully holed nets so that the trawler could speed up.

In this light the ocean was gunmetal blue; he let his eyes rest on it, unaware of how long he stood there until Kulitak said, "Thinking of taking a dip?"

"What? Oh, heh—no." He turned away. There was no diving into these waters for a refreshing swim. Chauncie hadn't known how precious such a simple act could be until he'd lost it.

Kulitak grunted but said nothing more; Chauncie knew he understood that long stare, the moments of silent remembrance. These men he worked with cultivated an anger similar to his own: their Arctic was long gone, but their deepest instincts still expected it to be here, he was sure, the same way he expected the ocean to be a glitter of warm emeralds he could cup in his hand.

Losing his childhood home, the island of Anegada, to the global climate disaster had been devastating, but sometimes Chauncie wondered whether Kulitak's people hadn't gotten the worse end of the disaster. As the seven seas became the eight seas and their land literally melted away, the Inuit faced an indignity that even Chauncie did not have to suffer: seeing companies, governments, and people flood in to claim what had once been theirs alone.

He found it delicious fun to make money plinking at CarbonJohnnies for the Inuit. But it wasn't big money—and he needed the big score.

He needed to be able to cup those emeralds in his hands again. On rare occasions he'd wonder whether he was going to spend the rest of his life up here. If somebody told him that was his fate, he was pretty sure he'd take a last dive right there and then. He couldn't go on like this forever.

"Satellite data came back," said Kulitak after a while. "The sulfur clouds are clearing up." Chauncie glanced up and nodded. They couldn't hide the trawler from satellite inspection right now. It was time to head back to port. As the ship got under way, Chauncie checked the sat phone.

Maksim had indeed called. Five times.

Kulitak saw his frown. "The Croat?"

Chauncie clipped the sat phone back to his waistband. "You said it was a slow day; we're not making much. And with the spill, it's going to be a zoo. We could use a break."

His friend grimaced. "You don't want to work with him. There's money, but it's not worth it. You come in the power-boat with me, the satellites can't see our faces, we hit more CarbonJohnnies. I'll bring sandwiches."

There was no way Chauncie was going to motor his way around the Arctic in a glorified rowboat. They'd get run over. By a trawler, a tanker, or any other ship ripping its way through the wide-open lanes of the Arctic Ocean. There was just too much traffic.

"I'll think about it," Chauncie said as the sat phone vibrated yet again.

Late the next evening, Chauncie entered the bridge of a rusted-out container ship that listed slightly to port. Long shadows leaned across the docks and cranes of Tuktoyak-tuk, their promise of night destined to be unfulfilled.

"Hey Max," he said, and sat down hard on the armchair in the middle of the bridge. Chauncie rubbed his eyes. He hadn't stopped to sleep yet. An easy error in the daylong sunlight. Insomnia snuck up on you, as your body kept think-ing it was day. Run all-out for forty-eight hours and forget about your daily cycle, and you'd crash hard on day three. And the listing bridge made him feel even more off-balance and weary.

"Took you damn long enough. I should get someone else, just to spite you." Maksim muttered his reply from behind a large, ostentatious, and extraordinarily expensive real wooden desk. He was almost hidden behind the nine screens perched on it.

Maksim was a slave to continuous partial attention: his eyes flicked from screen to screen, and he constantly tapped at the surface of the desk or flicked his hands at the screens.

In response, people were being paid, currencies traded, stocks bought or sold.

And that was the legitimate trade. Chauncie didn't know much about Maksim's other hobbies, but he could guess from the occasional exposed tattoo that Maksim was Russian Mafia.

"Well, I'm here."

Maksim glanced up. "Yes. Yes you are. Good. Chauncie, you know why I give you so much business?"

Chauncie sighed. He wasn't sure he wanted to play this game. "No, why?"

Maksim sipped at a sweaty glass of iced tea with a large wedge of lemon stuck on the rim. "Because even though you're here for dirty jobs, you like the ones that let you poke back at the big guys. It means I understand you. It makes you a predictable asset. So I have a good one for you. You ready for the big one, Chauncie, the payday that lets you leave to do whatever it is you really want, rather than sitting around with little popguns and Styrofoam targets?"

Chauncie felt a weird kick in his stomach. "What kind of big, Max?"

Maksim had a small smile as he put the iced tea down. "Big." He slowly turned a screen around to face Chauncie. There were a lot of zeros in that sum. Chauncie's lips suddenly felt dry, and he nervously licked them.

"That's big." He could retire. "What horrible thing will I have to do for that?"

"It begins with you playing bodyguard for a scientist."

Uh-oh. As a rule, scientists and Russian Mafia didn't mix well. "I'm really just guarding her, right?"

Maksim looked annoyed. "If I wanted her dead, I wouldn't have called *you*." He pointed out the grimy windows. A wind-blown, ruddy-cheeked woman wrapped in a large "Hands around the World" parka stood at the rail. She was reading something off the screen of her phone.

"That's the scientist? Here?"

"Yes. That is River Balleny. Was big into genetic archeology. She made a big find a couple years ago and patented the DNA for some big agricorporation for exotic livestock. Now she mainly verifies viability, authenticity, and then couriers the samples to Svalbard for various government missions out here."

"And she's just looking for a good security type, in case some other company wants to hijack a sample of what she's couriering? Which is why she came out to this rusted-out office of yours?"

Maksim grinned over his screens. "Right."

Chauncie looked back at the walkway outside the bridge. River looked back, and then glanced away. She looked out of place, a moonfaced little girl who should be in a lab, sequencing bits and pieces sandwiched between slides. Certainly she shouldn't be standing in the biting wind on the deck of thousands of tons of scrap metal. "So I steal what she'll be couriering? Is that the big payday?"

"No." Maksim looked back down and tapped the desk. Another puppet somewhere in the world danced to his string pulls. "She'll be given some seeds we could care less about. What we care about is the fact that she can get you into the Svalbard seed vault."

"And in there?"

Maksim reached under his desk and gently set a small briefcase on the table. "This is a portable sequencer. Millions of research and development spent so that a genetic archeologist in the field could immediately do out on the open plains what used to take a lab team weeks or months to do. Couple it with a fat storage system, and we can digitize nature's bounty in a few seconds."

Chauncie stared down at the case. "You can't tell me those seeds haven't already been sequenced. Aren't they just there for insurance, in case civilization collapses totally?"

"There are unique seeds at Svalbard," said Maksim, shaking his head. "One-of-a-kind from extinct tropical plants; paleo-seeds. Sequencing them destroys the seed, and lots of green groups ganged up about ten years ago in a big court case to stop the unique ones being touched. Bad karma if the sequencing isn't perfect, you know; you'd lose the entire species. Sequencing is almost foolproof now, but the legislation is . . . hard to reverse.

"We want you to get into the seed vault and sequence as many of those rare and precious seeds as you can. They have security equipment all over the outside, but inside, it's just storage area. No weapons, just move quick to gather the seeds and control the scientist while you gather the seeds. The more paleo-seeds the better. When you leave, with or without her, you get outside. You pull out the antenna, and you transmit everything. You leave Svalbard however you wish—charter a plane to be waiting for you, or the boat you get there with. We do not care. Once we have the information, we pay you. You leave the Arctic, find a warm place to settle down. Buy a nice house, and a nice woman. Enjoy this new life. Okay, we never see each other again. I'll be sad, true, but maybe I'll retire too, and neither of us cares. You understand?"

Chauncie did. This was exactly the score he'd been looking for.

He looked at the windblown geneticist and thought about what Maksim might not be telling him. Then he shook his head. "You know me, Max, this is too big. Way out of my comfort level. I'll become internationally wanted. I'm not in that league."

"No, no." Maksim slapped the table. "You are big-league now, Chauncie. You'll do this. I know you'll do this."

Chauncie laughed and leaned back in the chair. "Why?"

"Because if you don't"—Maksim also leaned back—"if you don't, you will never forgive yourself when military contractors occupy Svalbard in two weeks, taking over the seed vault and blackmailing the world with it."

"You've got to be joking." The idea that someone might trash Svalbard was ridiculous. Svalbard was the holiest of green holies, a bank for the world's wealth of seeds, stored away in case of apocalypse. "That would be like bombing the Vatican."

"These are Russian mercenaries, my friend. Russia is dying. They never were cutting edge with biotech, ever since Lysenkoism in the Soviet days. The plague strains that ripped through their wheat fields last year killed their stock, and Western companies have patented nearly everything that grows. Russian farms are hostage to Monsanto patents, so they have no choice but to raid the seed bank. They can either sequence the unique strains themselves, in hopes of making hybrids that won't get them sued for patent infringement in the world market, or they may threaten to destroy those unique seeds unless some key patents are annulled. I don't know which exactly—but either way, the rare plants are doomed. They'll sequence the DNA, discard everything but the unique genes . . . or burn the seed to put pressure on West. Either way—no more plant."

"Whereas if we do it . . ."

"We take whole DNA of plant. Let them buy it from us; in twenty years we give whole DNA back to Svalbard when it's no longer worth anything. It's win-win—for us and plant."

"It's the Russians behind the mercenaries? And no one knows about this."

"No one. No one but us." Maksim laughed. "You will be hero to many, but more importantly, rich."

Chauncie sucked air through his teeth and mulled it all over. But he and Maksim already knew the answer.

"What about travel expenses?"

Maksim laughed. "You're friends with those Indians—"

"First Nations peoples—"

"Whatever. Just get permission to use one of their trawlers. The company she's couriering for is pretty good about security. They drop in by helicopter when you're in transit to hand over the seeds. They'll call with a location and time at the last minute, as long as you tell them what your course will be. A good faith payment is . . ." Maksim tapped a screen. ". . . now in your account. You can afford to hire them. Happy birthday."

"It's not my birthday."

"Well, with this job, it is. And Chauncie?"

"Yes, Max?"

"You fuck it up, you won't see another."

Chauncie wanted to say something in return, but it was no use. He knew Maksim wasn't kidding. Anyway, Maksim had already turned his attention back to his screens. Chauncie was already taken care of, in his mind.

For a moment, Chauncie considered turning Maksim down, still. Then he glanced out the windows, at a sea that would never be the right color—that would never cradle his body and ease the sorrow of his losses.

He hefted the briefcase and stepped outside to introduce himself to River Balleny.

The trawler beat through heavy seas, making for Svalbard. The sun rolled slowly around a sky drained of all but pastel colors, where towering clouds of dove gray and mauve hinted at a dusk that never came. You covered your porthole to make night for yourself, and stepped out of your stateroom seemingly into the same moment you had left. After years up here Chauncie could tell himself he was as used to the midnight sun as he was to heavy seas; but the new passenger, who was much on his mind, stayed in her cabin while the seas heaved.

After two days the swells subsided, and for a while the ocean became calm as glass. Chauncie woke to a distant crackle from the radio room, and as he buttoned his shirt Kulitak pounded on his door. "I heard, I heard."

"It's not just the helicopter," Kulitak hissed. "The elders just contacted me over single sideband radio. We think Maksim's dead."

"Think?" Chauncie looked down the tight corridor between the trawler's cabins. The floorboards creaked under their feet as the ship twisted itself over large waves.

"Several tons of sulfur particulates, arc welded into a solid lump, dropped from the stratosphere by a malfunctioning blimp. So they say. There's nothing left of Maksim's barge. It's all pieces."

"Pieces . . ." Chauncie instinctively looked up toward the deck, as if expecting something similar to destroy them on the spot.

"I told you, you don't get involved with that man. You're out here playing a game that will get you killed. Get out now."

Chauncie braced himself in the tiny space as the trawler

lurched. "It's too late now. They don't let you back out this late in the game." He thought about the private army moving out there somewhere, getting ready to take over the vault. All at the behest of another nation assuming it could just snatch that which belonged to all.

They still had time.

"Come on, let's get that package. She'll fall overboard if we don't help her out."

They stepped on deck to find River Balleny already there. She was staring up at the dragonfly shape of an approaching helicopter, which was framed by rose-tinted puffballs in the pale, drawn sky. She said nothing, but turned to grin excitedly at the two men as the helicopter's shuddering voice rose to a crescendo.

The wash from its blades scoured the deck. Kulitak, clothes flapping, stepped into the center of the deck and raised his hands. Dangling at the bottom of a hundred feet of nylon rope, a small plastic drum wrapped in fluorescent green duct tape swung dangerously past his head, twirled, and came back. On the third pass he grabbed it and somebody cut the rope in the helicopter. The snaking fall of the line nearly pulled the drum out of Kulitak's hands; by the time he'd wrestled his package loose the helicopter was a receding dot. River walked out to help him, and after a moment's hesitation, Chauncie followed.

"The fuck is this?" The empty drum at his feet, Kulitak was holding a small plastic bag up to the sunlight. River reached up to take it from him.

"It's your past," she said. "And our future." She took the package inside without another glance at the men.

They found her sitting at the cleaver-hacked table in the galley, peering at the bag. "Those seem to mean a lot to you," he said as he slid in opposite her.

Opening the bag carefully, River rolled a couple of tiny orange seeds onto the tabletop. "Paleo-seeds," she mused. "It looks like mountain aven, but according to the manifest"— she tapped a sheet of paper that had been tightly wadded and stuffed into the bag—"it's at least thirty thousand years old."

Chauncie picked one up gingerly between his fingertips. "And that makes it different?"

She nodded. "Maybe not. But it's best to err on the side of caution. Have you ever been to the seed vault?" He shook his head.

"When I was a girl I had a model of Noah's ark in my bedroom," she said. "You could pop the roof open and see little giraffes and lions and stuff. Later I thought that was the dumbest story in the Bible—but the seed vault at Svalbard really *is* the ark. Only for plants, not animals."

"Where'd you grow up?"

"Valley, Nebraska," she said. "Before the water table collapsed. You?"

"British Virgin Islands: Anegada."

She sucked in a breath. "It's gone. Oh, that must have been terrible for you."

He shrugged. "It was a slow death. It took long enough for the sea to rise and sink the island that I was able to make my peace with it; but my wife . . ." How to compress those agonizing years into some statement that would make sense to this woman, yet not do an injustice to the complexity of it all? All he could think of to say was, "It killed her." He looked down.

River surprised him by simply nodding, as if she really did understand. She put her hand out, palm up, and he laid the seed in it. "We all seem to end up here," she mused, "when our lands go away. Nebraska's a dust bowl now. Anegada's under the waves. We come up here to make sure nobody else has to experience that."

He nodded; if anybody asked him flat out, Chauncie would say that Anegada hadn't mattered, that he'd come to the Arctic for the money. Somehow he didn't think River would buy that line.

"Of course it's a disaster," she went on, "losing the Arctic ice cap, having the tundra melt and outgas all that methane and stuff. But every now and then there's these little rays of hope, like when somebody finds ancient seeds that have been frozen since the last glaciation." She sealed the baggie. "Part of our genetic heritage, maybe the basis for new crops or cancer drugs or who knows? A little lifeboat—once it's safely at Svalbard."

"Must be quite the place," he said, "if they only give the keys to a few people."

"It's the Fortress of Solitude," she said seriously. "You'll see what I mean when we get there."

Svalbard was a tumble of dollhouses at the foot of a giant's mountain. Even in the permanent day of summer, snow lingered on the tops of the distant peaks, and the panorama of ocean behind the docked trawler was wreathed in fog as Chauncie and River stepped down the gangplank. Both wore fleeces against the cutting wind.

A thriving tourist industry had grown up around the town and its famed fortress. Thriving by northern standards, that is—the local tourist office had three electric cars they rented out for day trips up to the site. Two were out; Chauncie rented the third. He was counting out bills when his sat phone vibrated. He handed River the cash and stepped across the street to answer.

"Chauncie," said a familiar Croatian voice. "You know who it is, don't answer, we must be careful, the phones have ears, if you know what I mean. Listen, after my office had that unfortunate incident I've been staying with . . . a friend. But I'm okay.

"That big event, that happens soon by your current location, I regret to say we think it has been moved up. They know about our little plan. We don't know when they attack, so hurry up. We still expect your transmission, and for you to complete your side of the arrangement. Our agreement concerning success . . . and failure, that still stands.

"Good luck."

Chauncie jumped a little at the dial tone. River waited next to the little car, and in a daze Chauncie put the briefcase behind his seat, took control, and they followed the signs along a winding road by the sea.

River was animated, pointing out local landmarks and chattering away happily. Chauncie did his best to act cheerful, but he hadn't slept well, and his stomach was churning now. He kept seeing camouflaged killers lurking in every shadow.

"There it is!" She pointed. It took him a moment to see it, maybe because the word *fortress* had primed him for a particular kind of sight. What Chauncie saw was just a grim mountainside of scree and loose rock, patched in places with lines of reddish grass; jutting eighty or so feet out of this was a knife blade of concrete, twenty-five feet tall but narrow, perhaps no more than ten feet wide. There was a parking lot in front of it where several cars were parked, but that, like Svalbard itself, seemed absurd next to the scale of the mountain and the grim darkness of the landscape. The cars were all parked together, as though huddling for protection.

Chauncie pulled up next to them and climbed out into absolute silence. From here you could see the bay, and distant islands capped with white floating just above the gray mist.

"Magnificent, isn't it?" said River. He scowled, then hid that with a smile as he turned to her.

"Beautiful." It was, in a bleak and intimidating way—he just wasn't in the mood.

The entrance to the global seed vault was a metal door at the tip of the concrete blade. River was sauntering unconcernedly up to it; Chauncie followed nervously, glancing about for signs of surveillance. Sure enough, he spotted cameras and other, subtler sensor boxes here and there. Maksim had warned him about those.

The door itself was unguarded; River's voice echoed back as she called, "Hallooo." He hurried in after her.

The inside of the blade was unadorned concrete lit by sodium lamps. There was only one way to go, and after about eighty feet the concrete gave over to a rough tunnel sheathed in spray-on cement and painted white. The chill in here was terrible, but he supposed that was the point; the vault was impervious to global warming, and was intended to survive the fall of human civilization. That was why it was empty of anything worth stealing—except its genetic treasure—and was situated literally at the last place on Earth any normal human would choose to go.

Six tourists wearing bright parkas were chatting with a staff member next to a set of rooms leading off the right-hand side of the tunnel. The construction choice here was unpainted cinderblock, but the tourists seemed excited to be here. River politely interrupted and showed her credentials to the guide, who nodded them on. Nobody looked at his briefcase; he supposed they would check it on the way out, not on the way in.

"We're special," she said, and actually took his arm as they continued on down the bleak, too-brightly lit passage. "Normally nobody gets beyond that." About twenty feet farther on, the tunnel was roped off. Past it, a T-intersection could be seen where only one light glowed.

These were the airlocks. Strangely, the doors were just under five feet high. Chauncie and River had to duck to step inside the right one.

The outer door shut with a clang. He was in. He'd made it.

When the inner door opened it was into a cavern some 150 feet long. Shelves filled with wooden boxes lined the interior like an industrial wholesale store. The boxes were stenciled with black numbers.

It was a polar library of life.

Chauncie pulled a small, super-spring-loaded chock out of his pocket. He surreptitiously dropped it in front of the door and kicked it firmly underneath. It had a five-second count after his fingerprint activated it.

After the count the door creaked as it was wedged firmly shut. It was a preventative mechanism to keep River in more than anyone out.

River brought out her foil packet. It nestled, very small, in the palm of her hand. "They're amazing, seeds. All that information in that one tiny package: tough, durable, no degradation for almost a century in most cases. Just add water. . . ."

She led them to a row at the very back of the vault, reading off some sort of Dewey Decimal System for stored genetic material that Chauncie couldn't ascertain.

Here they were.

With a slight air of reverence in her careful, deliberate

movements, she slid a long box off the shelf. She set it carefully on the ground and opened the lid.

Inside were hundreds of glittering packets. Treasure, Chauncie thought, and the idea must have hovered in the air, because she said it as well. "It's a treasure, you know, because it's rarity that makes something valuable. There used to be hundreds of species of just plain apples in the U.S. Farmers standardized down to just a dozen. . . . Somewhere in here are thousands more, if we ever choose to need them."

She seemed fascinated. As she crouched and started flipping through foil packets Chauncie retreated down the rows. He turned a corner out of her sight and pulled out the sheet of paper with Maksim's list of the rarest seeds.

Matching the code next to the list with where to find the seeds was slightly awkward; he wasn't familiar with it like River was. But by wandering around he found his first box, and opened it to find the appropriate packet with three seeds inside.

He flipped the briefcase open to reveal a screen, a pad, and a small funnel in the right-hand side. All he had to do was dump a couple seeds in the funnel and press a button. The tiny grinder reduced the seeds to pulp and extracted the DNA.

After it whirred and spat dust out the side of the briefcase a long dump of text scrolled down the screen, with small models of DNA chains popping up in the corners. Not much more than pretty rotating screensavers for Chauncie.

All he cared was that it seemed to be working.

But he was going to have to pick up the pace. That had taken several minutes. He cradled the briefcase, leaving the box on the floor as he strode along looking for the next item on the list.

There. This time the foil packet only had a single seed. Chauncie sat with it in the palm of his hand and stared at it. It was even more precious than River's paleo-seeds, because this was the only one of its kind in existence.

Suppose the machine wasn't working?

He shook his head and dropped the single seed in and

listened to the grinding. More text scrolled down the screen. Success, a full sequence.

Chauncie blew out his held breath; it steamed in the freezing air.

"Just what the hell are you doing?" River asked. Her voice sounded so shocked it had modulated itself down into almost baritone.

There was another foil packet with two seeds in it nearby. It matched the list. Chauncie had hit a box full of rare and unique paleo-seeds stored here by a smaller government prospecting in the Arctic, or maybe a large and paranoid corporation. He dumped the seeds in and the briefcase whirred.

"Jesus Christ," River looked around him at the briefcase. "That's a sequencer. Chauncie, those seeds are one-of-a-kind."

He nodded and kept working. "Listen." River stayed oddly calm, her breath clouding the air over his head. "That might be a good sequencer, but even the best ones have an error rate. You're going to be losing some data. This is criminal. You have to stop, or I'm going to get someone in here to stop you."

"Go get someone." The chock would keep her occupied for a while.

She ran off, and Chauncie finished the box. He ticked the samples off his list, then started hunting for the next one along the shelves. It was taking too long.

There. He cracked open the new box and dumped the seeds in. River had caught back up to him, though, giving up on the door faster than he'd anticipated.

"Listen, you can't do this," she said. "I'm going to stop you."

He glanced over his shoulder to see that she'd pulled pepper spray out of the ridiculous little pouch she kept strapped to her waist in lieu of a purse.

Chauncie slid one hand into a pocket. He had what looked like an inhaler in there; one forcibly administered dose from it and he could knock her out for twenty-four hours. But he didn't want to leave River passed out among the boxes for the mercenaries to find. And if he left without her, he'd have to deal with the security guards as well.

He really couldn't live with victimizing any of them. River was a relatively naïve and noble refugee, caught up in a vicious world of international fits over genetic heritage and ecological policy. He was not going to leave her for the sharks. "Look, River, a private army-for-hire is about to land on Svalberd and do exactly what I'm doing—only not as carefully."

She hesitated, the pepper spray wavering. "What?"

"Overengineered agristock and plague. I'm told the Russians are pretty damn hell-bent on regaining control of un-copyrighted genetic variability for robustness. And to reboot their whole agricultural sector. They've hired a private army to come here; it gives them some plausible deniability on the world stage. But here's the thing: plausible deniability also means cutting up the DNA data into individual genes—scrambling it—so nobody can tell where they got them later on. All they want is the genes for splicing experiments, so they may preserve the data at the gene level, but they're going to destroy the record of the whole plant so they can't be traced. I've been sent to get what I can out of the vault before they get here."

River paused. "And who are *you* working for?"

Chauncie bit his lip. He hated lying. In this situation, she might as well hear the truth; he didn't have time to lay down anything believable anyway. "The Russian Mafia, they're connected enough to have gotten a heads-up. They think they can get some serious coin selling the complete sequences to companies across the world."

She stared at him. "You swear?"

"Why the hell would I make this up?"

He watched as she opened the zipper on the hip pouch and pocketed the pepper spray. She grabbed her forehead and leaned against the nearest shelf. "I can't fucking believe this. I need to think."

"It's a crazy world," Chauncie mumbled, and tipped a new pouch of seeds into the sequencer as she massaged her scalp and swore to herself.

The sequence returned good, and he stood up, looking for the next box. "What are you doing?"

"Looking for the next item on the list."

She walked over, and Chauncie tensed. But all she did was snatch the list from him. "There are a few missing they should have," she said.

"Like?"

"Like the damn seed I just brought here." River looked up at the shelves. "Look, you're wandering around like a lost kid in here. Let me help you."

He took the sheet of paper back from her. "And why would you do that?"

"Because until five minutes ago, I thought the vault was the best bank box, and seeds the best storage mechanism. You just blew that out of the water, Chauncie. As a scientist, I have to go with the best solution available to me at the time. If these mercenaries are going to invade and hold the seeds, then we need to get that genetic diversity backed up, copied, and kicked out across the world. Selling it to various companies and keeping copies in a criminal organization is . . . an awful solution, but we *have* to mitigate the potential damage. We have to make sure the seeds can be re-created later on."

He'd expected her to ask for a cut of the profit. Instead, she was offering to help out of some scientific rationalism. "Okay," he said, slowly. "Okay. But the list stays here, and you bring back the foil packets, sealed, to me."

"So that you can see that I'm not bringing back the wrong seeds, and so I don't rip up your list."

Chauncie smiled. "Exactly."

Plinking CarbonJohnnies was a lot more fun. And a hell of a lot easier. He felt ragged and frayed. Screw retirement; he just wanted out of this incredibly cold, eerie environment and the constant expectation that armed men would kick in the airlock door and shoot him.

But things moved quicker now. River ranged ahead, snagging the foil packets he needed and those he didn't even know he needed. For the next forty minutes he made a small mountain of pulped seed around him as the briefcase processed sample after sample, resembling more a small portable mill than an advanced piece of technology.

His sat phone beeped, an alarm he'd set back on the boat.

Chauncie closed the briefcase, and River walked around a shelf corner with a foil packet. "What?"

"It's time to go," Chauncie said. "We don't have much time."

"But . . ." Like any other treasure hunter, she looked around the cavern. So many more precious samples that hadn't been snagged.

But Chauncie had a suspicion that what River valued was not necessarily what the market valued. They had what they needed—best not push it any further. "Come on. We do not want to be standing here when these people arrive."

Chauncie bent over and rolled his fingerprint on the chock, and it slowly cranked itself down into thinness again. He placed it back in his pocket, and they cycled through the airlocks, again ducking under the unusually low entranceways.

They walked up the slight slope of the tunnel, the entrance looking small and brightly lit in the distance. The tourists were gone. As they passed the offices on their left one of the guards looked up and smiled. "All good? You were in there a long while. Sir, may I inspect your briefcase?"

Chauncie let him open it on a metal table while the other man carefully checked his coat lining and patted them both down. The briefcase contained nothing but empty foil packets; he'd left the sequencer under a shelf in the vault.

"What's this?" The guard drew out the sequencer's Exabyte data chip from Chauncie's pocket. He tensed.

But River smiled. "Wedding photos. Would you like to see them?"

The guard shook his head. "That's okay, ma'am." These guys probably didn't know DNA sequencers had shrunk to briefcase size. They'd been trained to think their job was to make sure no seeds left the vault; Chauncie was pretty sure the idea of them being digitized hadn't been in the course.

River shrugged with a smile, and they passed on. Chauncie breathed out heavily.

"Hey," the guard said. "If you're in town, take a few shots of that fleet of little boats out there. They're doing some serious exercises, wargaming some sorta Arctic defense scenario for the oil companies or other. They're all around Svalberd. Just amazing to see all those ships."

Chauncie's mood died.

They entered the mouth of the tunnel, shielding their eyes from the sun.

Chauncie took a high-throughput satellite antenna out of the car's trunk and put it on the roof. He plugged his sat phone into it, then the Exabyte core into that. The sat phone's little screen lit up and said hunting. . . . "Damn it, come on," he muttered.

"Uh, Chauncie?"

"Just wait, wait! It'll just take a second—" But she'd grabbed his arm and was pointing. Straight up.

He craned his neck, and finally spotted the tiny dot way up at the zenith. The sat phone said *hunting . . . hunting . . . hunting . . .* and then, *No Signal.*

"You've been jammed," River said, quite unnecessarily.

Chauncie cursed and slammed the briefcase. "And there!" She grabbed his arm again. Way out in the sky over the bay, six corpse-gray military blimps were drifting toward them with casual grace.

"We're out of time." No way they'd outrun those in a bright yellow electric car. Chauncie looked around desperately. Hole up in the vault? Fortress of Solitude it might be, but it wouldn't keep the mercenaries out for more than a minute. Run along the road? They'd be seen as surely as if they were in the car.

He popped up the hatch of the car and rummaged around in the back. As he'd hoped, there was a cardboard box there crammed with survival gear—a package of survival blankets, flares, and heat packs standard for any far-northern vehicle. He grabbed some of the gear and slammed the hatch. "Run up the hill," he said. "Look for an area of loose scree behind some boulders. We're going to dig in and hide."

"That's not a very good plan."

"It's not the whole plan." He pulled Maksim's list out and rummaged in the car's glove compartment. "Damn, no pen."

"Here." She fished one out of her pocket.

"Ah, scientists." Quickly, he wrote the words *scanned* and *uploaded* at the top of the first page, above and to the right of the list. He underlined them. Then he made two columns of checkmarks down the page, next to each of the seeds on the list. "Okay, come on."

They ran back to the vault. Chauncie threw the list down just outside the door; then they started climbing the slope beside the blade. The oncoming blimps were on the other side; if there were men watching, it would look like Chauncie and River had gone back into the vault. He hoped they were too confident to be that attentive. After all, the vault was supposedly unguarded.

"Over there!" River dragged him away from the concrete blade, toward a flat shelf fronted by a low pile of black rocks. The slope rose above it at about thirty degrees, a loose tumble of dark gravel and fist-sized stone where a few hardy grasses clung.

"Okay, get down." She hunkered down, and he wrapped her in a silvery survival blanket, then began clawing at the scree with his bare hands, heaping it up around her. The act was a kind of horrible parody of the many times he'd buried his sister in the sand back home.

Awkwardly, he made a second pile around himself, until he and River were two gravel cones partially shielded by rock. "You picked a good spot," he commented; they had a great view of the parking lot and the ground just in front of the entrance. He'd wedged the briefcase under the shielding stones; his eyes kept returning to it as the mercenary force came into view over the flat roof of the vault.

The blare of the blimps' turboprops shattered the valley's serene silence. They swiveled into position just below the parking lot, lowered down, touched, and men in combat fatigues began pouring out. Chauncie and River ducked as they scanned the hillside with binoculars and heat-sensing equipment.

"I'm cold," said River.

"Just wait. If this doesn't work we'll give up."

After a few minutes Chauncie raised his head so he could peer between two stones. The mercenaries had pulled the security guards out of the vault and had them on their knees. Someone was talking to them. The rest of them seemed satisfied with their perimeter, and now a man in a greatcoat strode up the hillside. The coat flew out behind him in black wings as one of the soldiers ran up holding something small and white. "Jackpot!" muttered Chauncie. It was Maksim's list.

"What's happening?"

"Moment of truth." He watched as the commander flipped through the list. Then he went to talk to the security guards, who looked terrified. The commander looked skeptical and kept shaking his head as they spoke. It wasn't working!

Then there was a shout from the doorway. Two soldiers came down to the commander, one carrying Chauncie's sequencer, the other a double handful of open foil packets.

Chauncie could see the commander's mouth working: cursing, no doubt. He threw down the list and pulled a sat phone out of his coat.

"He thinks we got the data out," said Chauncie. "There's nothing left for them to steal." The commander put away the sat phone and waved to his men. Shaking his head in disgust, he walked away from the vault. The bewildered soldiers followed, knotting up into little groups to mutter amongst themselves.

"I don't believe it. It worked."

"I can't see anything!"

"They think Maksim's got the data on the unique seeds. It's pretty obvious that we destroyed those in processing them. So these guys have exactly nothing now, and they know it. If they stay here they'll just get rounded up by the UN or the Norwegian navy."

"So you've won?"

"We win." The blimps were taking off. One of the guards was climbing into a car as the other ran back into the vault. Doubtless the airwaves were still jammed, and would be for an hour or so; the only way to alert the army camp at Svalbard would be to drive there.

"It's still plunder, Chauncie." Stones rattled as River shook them off. "Theft of something that belongs to all of us. Besides, there's one big problem you hadn't thought of."

He frowned at her. "What?"

"It's just that those guys are now Maksim's best customers. And the deal they'll be looking for is still the same: the unique gene sequences, not the whole plant DNA. Plausible deniability, remember? And Maksim would be a fool to keep the whole set after he's sold the genes. It would be incriminating."

He stood up, joints aching, to find his toes and ears were numb. Little rockfalls tumbled down the slope below him. "Listen," River continued, "I don't think you ever wanted to do this in the first place. The closer we got to Svalbard the unhappier you looked. You know it was wrong to steal this stuff to begin with. And look at the firepower they sent to get it! It was always a bad deal, and it's a hot potato and you'd best be rid of it."

"How?" He shook his head, scowling. "We've already scanned the damned things. Maksim . . ."

"Maksim will know the mercenaries got here while we were here. We just tell him they got here *before* us. That they got the material."

"And this?" He hefted the Exabyte storage block.

"We give it to that last guard; hey, he'll be a hero, he might as well get something for his trouble. So the DNA goes back into the vault—virtually, at least, after they back it up to a dozen or so off-site locations."

He thought about it as they trudged down the hillside. Truth to tell, he had no idea what he'd do if he retired now anyway. Probably buy a boat and come back to plink CarbonJohnnies. He wanted the emerald sea; he wanted those waters back. But now they were battered with hurricanes, the islands themselves depopulated and poor now that tourism had left, and the beaches had been destroyed by rising tides and storms.

From behind him she said, "It's an honorable solution, Chauncie, and you know it." They reached the level of the parking lot and she stopped, holding out her hand. "Here.

I'll take it in. I've got my pepper spray if he tries to keep me there. And you know, now that the Russians have tried this they'll put real security on this place. Keep it safe for everybody. The way it was meant to be."

He thought about the money, about Maksim's wrath; but he was tired, and damn it, when during this whole fiasco had he been free to make his own choice on anything? If not now . . .

He handed her the data block. "Just be quick. The whole Norwegian navy is going to descend on this place in about an hour."

She laughed, and disappeared into the dark fortress with the treasure of millennia in her hand.

Night was falling at last. Chauncie stood on the trawler's deck watching the last sliver of sun disappear. Vast purple wings of cloud rolled up and away, like brushes painting the sky in delicate hues of mauve, pale peach, silver. There were no primary colors in the Arctic, and he had to admit that after all this time, he'd fallen in love with that visual delicacy.

The stars began to come out, but he remained at the railing. The trawler's lights slanted out, fans of yellow crossing the deck, the mist of radiance from portholes silhouetting the vessel's shape. The air was fresh and smelled clean—scrubbed free of humanity.

He wondered if River Balleny was watching the fall's first sunset from wherever she was. They had parted ways in Svalbard—not exactly on friendly terms, he'd thought, but not enemies either. He figured she was satisfied that he'd done the right thing, but disappointed that he'd gotten them into the situation in the first place. Fair enough; but he wished he'd had a chance to make it up to her in some way. He'd probably never see her again.

Kulitak's voice cut through his reverie. "Sat phone for you!" Chauncie shot one last look at the fading colors, then went inside.

"St. Christie here."

"Chauncie, my old friend." It was Maksim. Well, he'd been expecting this call.

"I can't believe you sent us into that meat grinder," Chauncie began. He'd rehearsed his version of events and decided to act the injured party, having barely escaped with his life when the mercenaries came down on the vault just as he was arriving. "I'm lucky to be here to talk to you at—"

"Oh, such sour grapes from a conquering hero!" That was odd. Maksim actually sounded *pleased*.

"Conquering? They—"

"Have conceded defeat. You uploaded the finest material, Chauncie; our pet scientists are in ecstasy. So, as I'm a man of my word, I've wired the rest of your payment to the new account number you requested."

"New acc—" Chauncie stopped himself just in time. "Ah. Uh, well thank you, Maksim. It was good, uh, doing—"

"Business, yes! You see how business turns out well in the end, my friend? If you have a little faith and a little courage? Certainly I had faith in you, and justly so! I'd like to say we must do it again someday, but I know you'll vanish back to your beloved Caribbean now to lounge in the sunlight—and I'd even join you if I didn't love my work so much." Maksim prattled happily on for a minute or two, then rang off to deal with some of his other hundreds of distractions. Chauncie laid down the sat phone and collapsed heavily onto the bench beside the galley table.

"Something wrong?" Kulitak was staring at him in concern.

"Nothing, nothing." Kulitak shot him a skeptical look and Chauncie said, "Go on. Go find us some CarbonJohnnies to bomb or something. I need a moment."

After Kulitak had left, Chauncie went to his cabin and woke up his laptop. An email waited from one of the online payment services he'd tied to his Polar Consulting Services Web site.

Twenty-five thousand dollars had just been transferred to him, according to the email, from an email address he didn't recognize—a tiny fraction of the number Maksim had promised him. Chauncie had no doubt that it was a tiny fraction of the amount Maksim had actually paid out.

His inbox pinged. A strange sense of fated certainty settled on Chauncie as he opened the mail program and saw a videogram waiting. He clicked on it.

River Balleny's windburnt face appeared on the screen. Behind her was bright sunlight, a sky not touched in pastels. She was wearing a T-shirt, and appeared relaxed and happy.

"Hi, Chauncie," she said. "I swore to myself I wouldn't contact you—in case they got to you somehow—but it just seemed wrong to leave you in the lurch. I had to do something. So . . . well, check your email. A little gift from me to you.

"You know . . . I really wasn't lying when I told you I think the seed data belongs to all of mankind. I walked back into the vault seriously intending to leave it there. But then I realized that it wouldn't solve anything. We'd still have all our eggs in one basket, so to speak. As long as the seed data was in one place, stored in only one medium—whether it was as seeds or bits on a data chip—it would be *scarce*. And anything that's scarce can be bought, and sold, and hoarded, and killed for.

"The guard wasn't around; he'd run down to the vault. So I just put the data core in an inner pocket and hung around for a minute. After we parted, I uploaded the data to Maksim; it wasn't hard to get an ftp address from the guy who'd introduced me to him in the first place. And, yeah, I gave Maksim my own bank account number." She chuckled. "Sorry—but I was never the naïve farmgirl you and Kulitak seemed to think I was."

Chauncie swore under his breath—but he couldn't help smiling too.

"As long as the genetic code of those seeds was kept in one place, it remained scarce," she said again. "That gave it value but also made it vulnerable. Now Maksim has it; but so do I. I made copies. I backed it up. And someday—when Maksim and the Russians have gotten what they want out of it and it's ceasing to be scarce anyway—someday I'll upload it all onto the net. For everyone to use.

"We all have to make hard choices these days, Chauncie—about what can be saved, and what we have to leave behind. Svalbard will always be there, but its rarest treasure is out now, and with luck, it won't be rare for long. So everybody wins this time.

"As to me personally, I'm retiring—and no, I'm not going to tell you where. And I've left you enough for a really good vacation. Enjoy it on me. Maybe we'll meet again someday."

She smiled, and there was that naïve farmgirl look, for just a second. "Good-bye, Chauncie. I hope you don't think less of me for taking the money."

The clip ended. Chauncie sat back, shaking his head and grinning. He walked out onto the deck of the trawler and looked out over the sea. The sun had just slightly dipped below the horizon, bringing a sort of short twilight. It would reemerge soon, bringing back the perpetual glare of the long days.

Stars twinkled far overhead.

No, not stars, Chauncie realized. There were far too many to be stars, and the density of them increased. Far overhead a heavy blimp was dumping tiny bits of chaff glued to little balloons. Judging by the haze, they'd dumped the cloud into a vast patch of sulfur particulates. Both parties would be in court soon to fight over who would get the credit for blocking the sun's rays as it climbed back over the horizon.

The sulfur haze had caused the remaining sun's rays to flare in a full hue of purples and shimmering reds, and the chaff glittered and sparkled overhead.

It was so beautiful.

Spiders

SUE BURKE

Sue Burke (www.sue.burke.name) lives in Madrid, Spain. She attended Clarion East in 1996, moved to Austin and the Turkey City Workshop, and then to Spain in 1999. Her short-story publications (ISFDB lists six) were with small presses, including a special issue of a magazine guest-edited by Karen Joy Fowler. This is her first notable commercial sale. She's also published poetry. She is translating the medieval novel of chivalry and fantasy, Amadis of Gaul, *a chapter a week, at www.amadisofgaul.blogspot.com. This is the work that spawned at least 117 sequels and helped drive Don Quixote mad.*

"Spiders" was published in Asimov's. *It's a story about a divorced father, a hunter and nature-lover, and his five-year-old son, on a newly colonized planet. Daddy is showing his son all the neat alien creatures that can be found in the forest there and trying to do this without offending the sensibilities of his ex-wife. We chose it to end this book because we think it has a great punchline.*

Just before we went into the forest, I found the sort of thing I wanted to show my son.

"Roland, look, there's a leaf lizard nest that just hatched. They look just like little leaves of grass, don't they?"

Springtime. Everything was coming to life again. And just beyond arm's reach, I saw what looked like a dried-up fern but probably wasn't. I kept an eye on it as my boy and I squatted and studied the ground. The lizards were hard to spot at first, but finally he giggled and pointed.

"They're very little, Daddy."

"They'll grow. But now they're so little that they can't hurt you. You can let one walk on your hand."

And so we did, green whips with legs, just half the length of a five-year-old's finger. I told him how they hide in the grass, head down, waiting for even littler animals to come past, then they jump down and eat them. That was why if we let our hands hang down, the lizards would climb down to the tips of our fingers. Their natural place to be.

That supposed dead fern next to us had a crown of eyes. Sure enough, it was a mountain spider. Second one I'd seen so already our little walk. Why so many this spring? Like a lot of things, they had an Earth name because they were sort of like the Earth creature. From what I gathered, spiders on Earth were never bigger than your hand, but ours were bigger than your head. Both had multiple legs and a poisonous bite. Were ours as aggressive as Earth spiders, which often bit people? Were Earth spiders as smart as ours?

"Let's put the lizards down so they can get about their lives." I set my hand on the ground and, with a little encouragement, the lizard climbed off. Roland copied me, and we watched them disappear into the grass.

Then he turned to me, eyes worried. "Do we step on them and we don't know?"

Good question. Maybe he would grow up to feel like I do about the forest.

"I suppose sometimes. We're big, so we can't help making mistakes. I think we should never try to hurt things if we don't have to. I hunt, you know, but I never kill anything except to eat or to protect us." But I didn't want to lecture. "Let's go into the woods now, okay?"

I didn't point out the spider. His mother would kill me— or make me wish she would, just kill me and stop yelling— if she knew how close we were to spiders. Not just the one next to the path, but all over. Lots at the riverbank, but everyone knew that because they stole fish. They were in the woods. In the farm fields and orchards. I'd even seen one in the city, and I shooed it out. Most people didn't notice. If you don't look hard, you don't see things.

And if you don't take advantage of your chances, you lose them. I get time with Roland most days, but never enough. Spring only comes once a year, and a boy is five only once in a lifetime. So off we went. I'd just have to be extra careful.

"Are we going hunting?"

"No. I mean, I thought I'd show you things. There's a lot to see."

"Deer crab?"

"Oh, sure. And birds and insects and kats—all sorts of things. Listen. Hear that?"

"Pii, pii," he repeated.

"Exactly. That's a turnstone lizard."

"More lizards! I can't remember so many lizards."

I spotted it near a stump. "I know, it's hard. There's lots and lots of kinds. Shh. See it? It's black and white and brown with big stripes."

I knelt and helped him spot it.

"Wow. It's a jewel lizard," he said.

"Not quite. You wouldn't want it in your garden. It digs things up. Do you see what's next to it? That dead bush? It's getting closer and closer . . ."

The bush, of course, was a stick-feather bird. It suddenly grabbed the lizard, bashed its head against the stump, and began to tear off legs to swallow. Roland jumped to his feet.

"Animals hide in the woods," he said. "Eagles sometimes. Mommy says the woods are dangerous. That's why I can't go there alone."

Mommy says—of course she does.

"We make sure the eagles stay away," I said. "There are things to watch out for, but mostly the things that hide want to avoid us, not get us." Mostly. I didn't want him scared, so I'd have to find something non-scary fast. "Let's keep going."

He seemed relieved to get away from the bird. We walked a little, then I had an idea. "Can you think of other things that hide?"

"Hide?" He looked around.

"How about kats?" I suggested. "Why is their fur green?"

"Um, they're green so they can pretend they're grass lizards. A whole lot of them." He laughed. A joke, apparently. So I laughed too.

Then I saw a good example.

"How about that, there on the tree trunk? That's lizard poop for sure, right?"

"No, Daddy. It's not." He had me figured out.

"Right." I reached out and nudged it. It flew away.

He shrieked with delight. "A poop bug!"

"A blue firefly, actually."

"That's a firefly? They're so pretty. Everybody likes to watch them."

"Their light is pretty. But when they land, they look like poop so that birds and lizards don't eat them. Most people don't know that. They just look at the lights that fly around at night and don't find out about what's making the light. But now you know." Our eyes met, sharing a secret.

Just above us on the tree, I realized, there was a spider close enough to reach out and touch my shoulder.

"Let's keep going and see what else we can find."

"What if kat poop is really little bugs? I mean, little bugs that looked like kat poop?"

"You really like kats, don't you?" The city kept a colony of pet kats. "What do you like about them?"

He began to tell me about the dance he and the other children were learning with the kats, and demonstrated the steps. I tried to pay attention, but I kept thinking about the spiders.

Far too many of them. They usually lived in the mountains just below the tree line, rarely in our woods. Maybe they had had a population explosion. Maybe the weather, cool and dry for springtime, made them feel comfortable lower down. Maybe our colony attracted them. Or maybe something was pushing them down, like predators or hunger.

I spotted something Roland needed to know about, and I hoped it wouldn't scare him. I'd try to make it sound good.

"I'll show you something else that's not what it seems like. See those flowers? Those are irises. See how they sparkle? Very pretty. But don't touch them. They have tiny pieces of glass on them, and they'll cut you. Do you know why? Because they like blood. It's good fertilizer. Now don't be scared. Just know what they are and don't touch."

"They're very sparkly."

"Yes, they are." Not far away, a spider sat in a tree over a patch of moss that was really a kat, flattened to the ground, hiding in plain sight. I took a step to lead Roland away before the spider figured it out, but the boy wouldn't move.

"They're like jewel lizards," he said. "The flowers look like red lizards and yellow lizards."

"You're right. I never noticed that, but they do look just like lizards."

"Maybe the flowers catch things that think they're going to catch lizards."

"I bet that's it. Pretty smart to see that." Why hadn't I before? I complain that people don't look, and I don't look myself sometimes.

"They can't catch me," Roland said, "because I'm smarter than they are!"

"Exactly. Let's go. You know, when we have our hunters' meeting, you should come and tell us about that, about the flowers. We're always trying to figure things out. Well, that's something that you figured out about irises."

"Me? I can talk at the hunters' meeting? Really, Daddy?"

"Yes, you can. The discoverer gets the honors." I'd watch him talk and feel proud of my boy.

We were desperate to know more about the spiders. Their venom could kill a kat or other fair-sized animal. No one knew what it could do to a human and no one volunteered to find out. They never attacked us, either, though if you got too close to a nest, they'd gibber and wave their legs and snap their jaws to drive you away. They'd steal, too. Fishing crews had to watch out. They moved too fast for us to catch them and dodged arrows like it was a game. In fact, they had figured out the range of our arrows and knew to stay just beyond it.

We often met and talked about spiders, everyone together: hunters, farmers, fishers, even the kitchen crew, because our kitchen garbage might attract them so it couldn't be dumped just anywhere. We never could dump it anywhere, actually, but spiders had people scared. Tiffany, for example, Roland's mother, who for one brief time made herself seem like the perfect woman for me—but that's another story—was preaching extermination. I worried that if we started a fight, the spiders might keep it going. As the lead hunter, I needed to offer a plan of my own.

Honestly, I didn't know enough about spiders to know what to do.

"What's that?" Roland said, grabbing my leg and hiding behind it. Something was crashing through the underbrush toward us. I knew right away.

"Over there?" It was moving fast and barking loud.

"It's big, Daddy."

I picked him up. "No, it actually isn't, and it won't hurt us. It's just birds, a lot of them. Bluebirds. See?" He hung on tight but leaned to get a better look. "Bluebirds. Hear them bark? There's lots of barks, so you know it's not one big animal, it's a lot of little animals. They like to run around and make a lot of noise so they can scare up things to eat. All in a line, zig-zag. Look, they're stopping. Maybe they found something. Let's see what."

I walked toward them slowly. "Usually they let you get close. When you get too close, they tell you." I was almost five steps away when the alpha bird turned, barked at me and glared. I took a step back. It went back to eating.

"That's as close as we can get. They don't want trouble, so they warn you. They don't attack if they don't have to. What do you think they're eating?"

He leaned out bravely. I leaned with him. The bird turned and barked, casually, just a reminder. I knew what they were eating from the way they were arranged around it, but I waited for Roland.

"It's purple! Is it a slug?"

"Yes, they like to eat slugs. That's why you should never hurt a bluebird reef. We want them to live around us, so we respect their homes."

Slugs. Chunks of mobile slime that dissolve flesh. If there was something to exterminate, those would be it. But we could never get them all.

Where there's one, there's more. I heard a sudden hum too close to the left . . . something moved fast. I stepped back. It was a spider wrestling a slug, brown legs wrapped around a purple glob. A brief squirm, then the fight was over. The spider picked it up with four legs and hurried away on the other four, not as fast or graceful as usual but gibbering in a way that I swear sounded proud.

So they caught slugs, and were happy to do it. Efficient, too. News to me, and worth knowing. Just a few animals could do that. Maybe a chemical protected them, or extra-tough skin. It would be more than handy to have another slug-eating animal around. Especially if they turned out to be no more scary than bluebirds. But would Tiffany believe that?

Roland was still watching the birds. Good. The spider fighting the slug might have scared him, and his mother wanted him scared of the forest. I did not. Yet another difference between her and me. She liked safe things, and I liked living things.

Every night I dreamed of the forest, and every day I woke eager to go there. Not everyone did, of course. They liked making things with their hands or coaxing crops to grow. They were satisfied, and who could blame them? But the forest—you're there, but you don't make it and you can't coax it. It's not even an it. It's a you, I mean, the forest is alive and does things, reacts, watches, even attacks. Full of tricks and beauty. I hoped I'd showed some of that to Roland. But he was getting fidgety in my arms.

"Time to go home?"

"Okay, Daddy."

Something in his voice troubled me, and I tried to figure it out as I headed down a trail that led out of the woods. He seemed unhappy. With me? With the forest? Was he bored? Or worse, scared? Good thing I hadn't pointed out the spiders. Who knows what Tiffany had told him?

We kept talking on our way out. He asked "What's that?" "What's that?" about trees, lizard hoots, but more like a game than curiosity. A couple of times I saw him looking in one direction while he asked about something the other way. Young children had short attention spans. We probably had been there too long.

I set him down when we reached the fields, and he pointed at a lentil tree, its purple leaves contrasting with the greening fields around it.

"Mommy says you have to grow them far apart so if one gets scorpions, they doesn't get all the trees," he said.

I knew that, but didn't want to disappoint him. "Is that why? So there's a tree here, and there, and way over there."

"And you have to prune them. Every spring."

"Carefully, I bet."

"Very carefully. And you can't plant snow vines next to each other. They fight."

"Like this?" I raised my fists.

"No. With roots and, um, with just their roots. It's very challenging to maintain an orchard."

Those were Tiffany's words exactly, right down to her intonation. Of course, she spent more time with the boy, so she had a bigger influence, and maybe he'd grow up to tend orchards or crops instead of hunt in the forest. Perfectly acceptable.

The city rose across the fields, surrounded by a brick wall. Two hundred people. After four generations, we finally had enough to eat, even a surplus. We had domesticated several plants and animals, and were still learning about others. Every year we discovered new surprises about the planet. And every kind of work was needed. Maybe Roland would become a carpenter, a medic, or a cook. All perfectly respectable.

"You know," he said, "we don't hide. I wonder what animals think? They see us and we don't care if they do." He sounded like a little adult. Who was he copying now? "They think we aren't scared. If we're not scared of them, should they be scared of us?"

"That's a good question."

"That's a good question," he repeated.

Well, maybe I had helped him see that the world could be bigger than you are, and that was okay. Even if you didn't understand everything in it.

"We have to take care of our trees," Roland said, sounding like himself again. "If they're really happy, maybe they can dance." He looked up. "Are trees happy in the forest?"

"I think so. That's where they live. Did you like the forest?"

He spent a long moment thinking. "Yes. I saw lots of things." He looked up with a sly smile. "Daddy, you didn't see. There were spiders everywhere, and they were looking at us."

Story Copyrights

IAN DOUGLAS's
MONUMENTAL SAGA
OF INTERGALACTIC WAR
THE INHERITANCE TRILOGY

STAR STRIKE: BOOK ONE
978-0-06-123858-1

Planet by planet, galaxy by galaxy, the inhabited universe has fallen to the alien Xul. Now only one obstacle stands between them and total domination: the warriors of a resilient human race the world-devourers nearly annihilated centuries ago.

GALACTIC CORPS: BOOK TWO
978-0-06-123862-8

In the year 2886, intelligence has located the gargantuan hidden homeworld of humankind's dedicated foe, the brutal Xul. The time has come for the courageous men and women of the 1st Marine Interstellar Expeditionary Force to strike the killing blow.

SEMPER HUMAN: BOOK THREE
978-0-06-116090-5

True terror looms at the edges of known reality. Humankind's eternal enemy, the Xul, approach wielding a weapon monstrous beyond imagining. If the Star Marines fail to eliminate their relentless xenophobic foe once and for all, the Great Annihilator will obliterate every last trace of human existence.